A ROGU...
OF ROMA...

Mary Balogh, bestselling Regency writer and award winner, is the talented author of wonderful historical romances, including *Beyond the Sunrise, Deceived, Tangled,* and *Longing.*

Edith Layton is known for her highly acclaimed romances featuring strong heroes who simply sizzle with sexuality. A winner of many prizes for her writing, she recently earned a Reviewers' Choice Award for Best Short Story.

Melinda McRae, a rising romance star, is the immensely talented winner of the 1991 Reviewers' Choice Award for Best New Regency author and the 1992 Waldenbooks Award for Bestselling Regency. You won't want to miss her very first historical romance for Topaz, *Prince of Thieves.*

Anita Mills, *Romantic Times'* Best New Regency author in 1987, now creates glittering, sensual historicals like her recent Topaz titles *Falling Stars, Secret Nights,* and her latest, *Comanche Moon.*

Mary Jo Putney soared onto the bestseller lists with romances featuring smashing heroes like Reggie in the now classic *The Rake and the Reformer.* Her recent Topaz romances include *Thunder and Roses, Petals in the Storm,* and *Dancing on the Wind.*

ANNOUNCING THE

TOPAZ FREQUENT READERS CLUB
COMMEMORATING TOPAZ'S
1 YEAR ANNIVERSARY!

THE MORE YOU BUY, THE MORE YOU GET

Redeem coupons found here and in the back of all new Topaz titles for FREE Topaz gifts:

Send in:

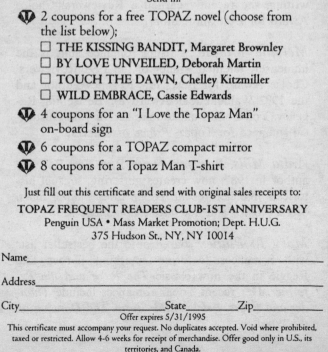 2 coupons for a free TOPAZ novel (choose from the list below);

☐ THE KISSING BANDIT, Margaret Brownley

☐ BY LOVE UNVEILED, Deborah Martin

☐ TOUCH THE DAWN, Chelley Kitzmiller

☐ WILD EMBRACE, Cassie Edwards

4 coupons for an "I Love the Topaz Man" on-board sign

6 coupons for a TOPAZ compact mirror

8 coupons for a Topaz Man T-shirt

Just fill out this certificate and send with original sales receipts to:

TOPAZ FREQUENT READERS CLUB-1ST ANNIVERSARY
Penguin USA • Mass Market Promotion; Dept. H.U.G.
375 Hudson St., NY, NY 10014

Name_____

Address_____

City_____State_____Zip_____

Offer expires 5/31/1995

This certificate must accompany your request. No duplicates accepted. Void where prohibited, taxed or restricted. Allow 4-6 weeks for receipt of merchandise. Offer good only in U.S., its territories, and Canada.

Dashing and Dangerous

More Rakes and Rogues

Mary Balogh

•

Edith Layton

•

Melinda McRae

•

Anita Mills

•

Mary Jo Putney

A SIGNET BOOK

SIGNET
Published by the Penguin Group
Penguin Books USA Inc., 375 Hudson Street,
New York, New York 10014, U.S.A.
Penguin Books Ltd, 27 Wrights Lane,
London W8 5TZ, England
Penguin Books Australia Ltd, Ringwood,
Victoria, Australia
Penguin Books Canada Ltd, 10 Alcorn Avenue,
Toronto, Ontario, Canada M4V 3B2
Penguin Books (N.Z.) Ltd, 182–190 Wairau Road,
Auckland 10, New Zealand

Penguin Books Ltd, Registered Offices:
Harmondsworth, Middlesex, England

First published by Signet, an imprint of Dutton Signet,
a division of Penguin Books USA Inc.

First Printing, June, 1995
10 9 8 7 6 5 4 3 2 1

"Precious Rogue," copyright © Mary Balogh, 1995
"Sweet Revenge," copyright © Melinda McRae, 1995
"Buried Treasure," copyright © Edith Felber, 1995
"The Devil's Spawn," copyright © Mary Jo Putney, 1995
"A Good Woman," copyright © Anita Mills, 1995
All rights reserved

Cover art by Pino Daeni

 REGISTERED TRADEMARK—MARCA REGISTRADA

Printed in the United States of America

Without limiting the rights under copyright reserved above, no part of this
publication may be reproduced, stored in or introduced into a retrieval sys-
tem, or transmitted, in any form, or by any means (electronic, mechanical,
photocopying, recording, or otherwise), without the prior written permission
of both the copyright owner and the above publisher of this book.

BOOKS ARE AVAILABLE AT QUANTITY DISCOUNTS WHEN USED TO PROMOTE
PRODUCTS OR SERVICES. FOR INFORMATION PLEASE WRITE TO PREMIUM MAR-
KETING DIVISION, PENGUIN BOOKS USA INC., 375 HUDSON STREET, NEW YORK,
NEW YORK 10014.

If you purchased this book without a cover you should be aware that this
book is stolen property. It was reported as "unsold and destroyed" to the
publisher and neither the author nor the publisher has received any payment
for this "stripped book."

Contents

Precious Rogue

❦

by Mary Balogh

Holly House, Summer 1818

She had so little time to herself. It seemed unfair that her peaceful solitude should be shattered after a scant fifteen minutes. Nobody ever came to the lily pond, since it was a full ten-minute walk from the house and inaccessible by carriage because of the trees. She had come to think of it as her own special hideaway—whenever she could get away by herself, that was. That was not very often.

She was high up in the old, gnarled oak tree that she had appropriated as her own, sitting comfortably on a sturdy branch, her back braced safely against the trunk. She had not brought a book with her as she usually did. She had learned by now that she would not read it anyway. When she was at the lily pond, surrounded by the beauties of nature and filled by its peace, she liked nothing better than to gaze about her and allow all her senses to come alive. And sometimes she merely set her head back and gazed upward at branches and leaves and sky and went into a daydream.

There was so little chance to daydream. Night dreams were not nearly as pleasant, since one could not control them—or even remember them half the time. She daydreamed about—oh, about many foolish things. About being beautiful and charming and witty, about having pretty clothes and somewhere special to wear them, about having friends and beaux, about loving and being loved, about having a home and a husband and children. All foolish things. She always reminded herself as she climbed nimbly downward back to the ground and reality that she was well blessed, that it was downright sinful to be discontented, that there were thousands of women far less fortunate than she—and that was an understatement.

But today she had only just begun to relax. She was still enjoying the sight of the pond with its large lily pads almost hiding the water and of the trees surrounding it and of the blue sky above. She was still enjoying the smell of summer greenery and the sound of silence—oh, blessed silence. Though the world about her was anything but soundless, of course. There were birds singing and insects whirring and chirping. But they were natural sounds, sounds to which she did not have to respond.

And then an alien sound. A man's voice.

"Ah," he said, "a lily pond. How charming. I do believe Mother Nature threw it down here this very minute in a desperate attempt to rival your beauty and distract me. She has failed miserably."

A trilling, female laugh. "What absurd things you say," the woman said. "As if I could rival the beauties of nature."

There was a pause as the two of them came into sight beneath the old oak tree and stopped beside the lily pond. Mr. Bancroft and Mrs. Delaney—two of the guests from the house. The house was full of guests, Nancy having just completed her first Season in London but not having quite accomplished the purpose of that Season. Oh, it was true that she had found her future husband. Everything was settled except for one minor detail. The gentleman had not yet proposed.

It was a mere formality, of course. The two of them had a clear understanding. Mr. Bancroft was young, unmarried, heir to a barony, and thoroughly eligible in every possible way. He had paid court to Nancy quite persistently through the spring, dancing with her at a number of balls, accompanying her to the theater one evening, driving her in Hyde Park one afternoon, and generally hovering in her vicinity as much as good manners would allow. And he had accepted her invitation to spend a few weeks at Holly House.

Two facts about him particularly recommended him to Nancy and her mama—or perhaps three, if one took into account the indisputable fact that he was excessively handsome and elegant. Nancy sighed over the fact that she was about to net one of London's most notorious rakes. All the female world loved him, and half the female world—or so the rumor went— had had its heart broken by him. It was a singular triumph for Miss Nancy Peabody to be the one to get him to the altar. Not that she had him there yet, of course. But she would before the summer was out. He had made his intentions quite clear.

The rather strange fact that recommended him to Mrs. Peabody was that he was poor—as a church mouse, if gossip had the right of it. Mr. Peabody, on the other hand, was enormously wealthy and had only his daughter on whom to lavish his riches. It might have been expected that the Peabodys would wish to ally their daughter with wealth, but far more important to Mrs. Peabody was to see Nancy move up the social scale. As Mrs. Bancroft she would be a baroness-in-waiting, so to speak. And until that day when Mr. Bancroft would inherit his uncle's fortune as well as his title, he would have to rely upon the generosity of his father-in-law to keep him in funds. He would be a husband kept firmly to heel.

It all seemed wonderfully perfect to Mrs. Peabody.

And now he was down below the oak tree telling Mrs. Delaney that nature could not rival her beauty. What a ridiculous untruth, the young lady in the tree thought. Mrs. Delaney was too fat—though she had to admit that it was the type of fatness that some men might find appealing. Mr. Delaney was not one of the guests at the house, though apparently he was not deceased.

And Mrs. Delaney had fished for further compliments. Mr. Bancroft did not disappoint her.

"In you, ma'am," he said, "the beauties of nature have combined with breeding and taste to produce dazzling perfection. How can I appreciate the scene around me when you are here with me? I do protest that you make your surroundings appear quite insipid."

The young lady in the tree held her nose.

Mrs. Delaney tittered. "I do not believe a word of it," she said. "You flatter me, sir. I wonder why." She reached out a lace-gloved hand and rested her fingertips upon his sleeve.

Mr. Bancroft possessed himself of the artfully offered hand and raised it to his lips. "Flattery?" he murmured. "You have not looked in your glass recently, ma'am, if you believe that. I have had eyes for no one else since arriving here three days ago. And I have had sighs for no one else."

"Now, that is a bouncer, sir," she said, allowing him

to return her hand to his lips for a second kiss. "Everyone knows that you have come here to court Nancy Peabody. She is a remarkably pretty girl, it must be admitted."

"Girl," he said. "Ah, yes, *girl*, ma'am. You are in the right of it there. A pretty girl can please the eye. It takes a beautiful woman to stir all the senses. A mature woman of your years. A woman who has passed the age of twenty."

It appeared to the young lady in the tree that Mrs. Delaney had passed her twentieth birthday long since, but it was a clever way of paying a compliment, she supposed.

"Sir," Mrs. Delaney asked, "are you flirting with me?"

The girl in the tree held her nose again.

"Flirting, ma'am?" His voice was like a velvet caress. "I do protest. Flirters have no serious intentions. Mine could not be more serious."

"Indeed?" The lady's voice too had become hushed and throaty. "Do you intend to tumble me on the ground, sir, when I am wearing my favorite muslin?"

The watcher stopped holding her nose. She felt sudden alarm.

"Ah, no," he said. "Such charms should be tasted and feasted upon in the privacy of a locked room, ma'am. And worshiped. They should be worshiped on a soft bed."

The lady withdrew her hand from his and tapped him lightly on the arm with it. "I have heard it said that you have some skill in—worshiping," she said. "Perhaps it would be amusing to discover the truth of the matter for myself."

"I am, ma'am," he said, making her an elegant bow,

"your humble slave. When? I pray you will not tease me by keeping me waiting."

"It would please me excessively to tease you," Mrs. Delaney said with her trilling laugh, "but I really do not believe I could bear to tease myself, sir. The door of my bedchamber will be unlocked tonight if the fact is of any interest to you."

"I shall burn with unrequited passion and adoration until then," he said, and he bent his dark head and set his lips to the lady's for a brief moment.

"It promises well," she said. "Alas that only half the afternoon has passed. But we should return to the house for tea, sir. Separately, I do believe. I would not have it said that I dally with handsome strangers in the absence of my husband." She laughed merrily.

He bowed to her. "Far be it from me to sully the brightness of your reputation, ma'am," he said. "I shall remain here for a while and discover whether the beauties of nature will be more apparent in the absence of your greater loveliness."

"How absurd you are," she said, turning from him to walk back to the house in virtuous solitude. "And what a flattering tongue you have been blessed with."

The young lady who had been an unwilling witness to this tender love scene was partly amused and partly shocked—and wondered how long the gentleman intended staying at the lily pond admiring the beauties of nature. He sat down on the grassy bank and draped his arms over his raised knees.

Mr. Bancroft probably needed the rest and the solitude as much as she did. He was a busy gentleman. She had been passing his room quite early this morning, bringing Mrs. Peabody a second cup of chocolate, which by rights her maid should have been doing, when the door had opened and Flossie, one of the chambermaids, had stepped out looking rosy and bright-eyed and slightly disheveled. Behind her as she closed the door there had been the merest glimpse of Mr. Bancroft in his shirtsleeves. It had not taken a great deal of imagination to guess that at the very least the two of them had been exchanging kisses.

At the very least!

And now he had made an assignation to spend the night, or at least a part of it, in Mrs. Delaney's bed, tasting and feasting and worshiping. It was really quite scandalous. When Nancy confided to anyone who was prepared to listen, evident pride in her voice, that her intended husband was a rake, she was making no empty boast.

And then an insect landed on the young lady's bare arm, and she slapped at it without thinking. The slap sounded rather like the cracking of a pistol to her own ears. She held her breath and directed her eyes downward without moving her head.

He had obviously heard it. He turned his head first to one side and then to the other before shrugging slightly and resuming his contemplation of the lily pond.

It amused him to break hearts. Oh, no, that was not strictly true. He supposed it might be mildly distressing to cause real suffering, real from-the-heart suffering. He always instinctively avoided any entanglement in which it seemed likely that the lady's heart might be seriously engaged.

It would be more accurate to say, perhaps, that it amused him to deflate expectations. Many of his acquaintances avoided eligible females as they would avoid the plague, terrified that they would somehow be caught in parson's mousetrap no matter how warily they stepped. Not he. He liked to live dangerously. He liked to see how close he could come to a declaration without ever actually making it or feeling that honor compelled him to do so.

He enjoyed watching young ladies and their mamas setting about entrapping him, believing that their subtleties went quite undetected by him. He liked watching them tread carefully at first and then become quite visibly triumphant as they preened themselves before less fortunate mortals. He was never quite sure what the full attraction of his person was, since he always pleaded poverty into those ears whose accompanying mouths were most sure to spread the word. A baron's title was not exactly equivalent to a dukedom, after all, especially when it was a mere future expectation. His uncle was not yet sixty and was the epitome of health and heartiness. And one could never be quite certain that his uncle would not suddenly take it into his head to marry again and start producing sons annually.

But he knew that he was considered a catch. Perhaps his reputation and his elusiveness was the attraction. Just as men felt compelled to pursue women with reputations for unassailable virtue, even if they were not wondrously beautiful, he supposed that women might feel a similar challenge when presented with a rake.

And so after paying casual court to the rather pretty and definitely wealthy Miss Nancy Peabody for much of the Season, he had accepted the invitation to spend a few weeks at Holly House, even though his friends had made great sport of both the invitation and his decision to accept it, pulling gargoyle faces and making slashing gestures across their throats and pronouncing him a sure goner. They all clamored loudly and with marvelous wit for invitations to his wedding, and one of them volunteered to be godfather to his first child nine months after that event.

The pretty and wealthy and conceited Miss Peabody amused him, as did her gracious and pompous mama and her silent father, who appeared to be a nonentity in the Peabody household.

This visit, after all, afforded him a few weeks of relaxation in the country with congenial company and prospects enough with which to satisfy his sexual appetites. He might have made do with the buxom and eager maid who had made herself very available to him both yesterday morning and this morning, hinting of her willingness even before he had thought to sound it out. But Flossie was of that lusty breed of females who invited him with raised petticoats and parted legs to the main event without any preamble and then bounced and bucked with unabashed enthusiasm while he delivered. Just as if they ran a race. He doubted if it had lasted longer than two or three minutes either yesterday or today. And then she had been up and straightening her clothes and pocketing his sovereign and going on her way to continue with what she had been busy at, almost as if there had been no interruption at all.

He needed more. He would get more—considerably more—from Mrs. Delaney, whose reputation was quite as colorful as his own, though he had never yet had her himself. Tonight he would, and he would feast on her as he had promised, slowly and thoroughly, and several times more than once. He had no doubt that he could expect little sleep of the coming night, but sleep was always worth giving up in a good cause.

He would have her for perhaps a week and then be overcome with an onslaught of conscience over her married state before sounding out one of the two or three other prospects that the guest list had presented to his experienced intuition. Two for certain. The third probable.

Oh, yes, it would be an amusing few weeks. Not the least amusement would be that derived from looking into the faces of Miss and Mrs. Peabody on the day he took his leave of them, his leg still quite, quite free of a shackle. It was perhaps unkind of him to look forward to the moment. Undoubtedly it was. But then, what did kindness have to do with anything?

It was as he was thinking along these rather uncharitable lines, enjoying the quietness of his surroundings and the rare interlude of solitude and relaxation, that he heard the sound. He could not identify it, but it was unmistakably a human sound. A glance to either side showed him that no one was coming through the trees toward the lily pond, but the edge of his vision caught the lightness of some fabric up in the old oak tree close by. It was a dress. Worn by a woman or a girl. Someone who had just been entertained to the events leading up to an assignation. He was very tempted to punish her by sitting where he was for an hour or more. But he was too curious. He had not looked directly at her. He did not know who she was.

"Are you not getting cramped up there?" he asked after five minutes, not looking up. "Would you not like to come down?"

He expected confusion, stuttered apologies, a scrambled descent. A cool voice answered him without hesitation.

"No, thank you," it said. "I feel safer where I am."

"Do you indeed?" he said. It was the voice of a young woman. A light, pretty voice—a cultured voice. "Are you afraid I will pounce on you and ravish you here on the ground?"

"I imagine," she said, "that you expended enough energy in that direction this morning with Flossie. And I would expect you would wish to conserve energy for tonight with Mrs. Delaney. But I would rather be safe than sorry."

He felt a gust of very genuine amusement. The voice was very matter-of-fact, neither frightened nor accusing. He was reluctant to look up. He was very afraid that the person would not live up to the voice.

"Ravishment is not in my line even when my energy is neither expended nor being conserved," he said. "You are quite safe from me. You may descend without a qualm. And it might more accurately be said that Flossie seduced me than that I seduced her. Mrs. Delaney, as you must have witnessed, was quite as eager as I to acquire a bedfellow for the night."

"I thought," she said, "that you were going to worship her."

He chuckled and looked up. She was tucked snugly between the massive trunk of the tree and a sturdy branch, her knees drawn up, her arms clasped about them. She was dressed quite unfashionably in drab gray. Her light brown hair was pinned back in a knot at the neck without any nonsense of curls to soften its severity. Her face was thin and rather pale and quite unpretty. Except for the large gray eyes, which looked unblinkingly down into his.

"Little bird," he said, "you have a sharp tongue. Who are you?" She looked like a governess, except that there were no children at the house. He got to his feet and strolled to the foot of the tree.

"Patricia Mangan," she said. "It was a foolish question, was it not? You are none the wiser and must either ask another question or walk away."

"I'll ask the question," he said, feeling wonderfully diverted. "Who is Patricia Mangan? Apart from a little bird who likes to eavesdrop on private conversations, that is."

"Oh, yes," she said. "I rushed from the house to this spot an hour ago just so that I might listen to all the private conversations that go on below. It must be the busiest spot in all England, sir. But I must express my gratitude to you for insisting upon a private room and a soft bed for your feasting and worshiping."

He grinned at her. "Would you have been thoroughly embarrassed if I had been less cautious and less patient?" he asked and was rewarded by the sight of Miss Patricia Mangan blushing rosily. He grinned again. "Or perhaps envious?"

"I cannot tell you," she said, having abandoned the momentary weakness of the blush, "how unspeakably thrilled I would be to be told that the beauty of nature quite paled beside my own. Your sincerity would bring me tumbling out of the tree to comply with your every demand."

"Ah," he said, "but I would never say such a thing to you, Miss Mangan. It would be patently untrue."

"I believe," she said, "I would prefer the quite ungentlemanly setdown, sir, to the ridiculous flattery to which I was just the unwilling witness. At least the setdown was honest."

He chuckled. "A woman immune to flattery," he said. "Almost challenging. Who are you, Patricia Mangan? You still have not told me."

"You have seen me a dozen times," she said. "Well, half a dozen, at least. I am the shadow to be seen frequently behind the shoulder of Mrs. Peabody. It is my function in life, sir, to be a shadow. It can be vastly amusing. I hear and see all sorts of things because people do not realize I have eyes and ears. Indeed, people do not even realize I exist. I am Mrs. Peabody's niece, only daughter of her brother, the Reverend Samuel Mangan, who committed the unpardonable sin of dying without a penny to his name. My aunt rescued me from destitution, sir."

"And took you to her bosom as if you were her own daughter," he said. Was she speaking the truth? Had he seen her before? Was she frequently in Mrs. Peabody's shadow, at her constant beck and call? He had not noticed her.

"Yes," she said. "Or so she tells me several times each day—whenever I do something to displease her."

"Dear me," he said. "Are you really so disagreeable and so disobedient, Miss Mangan?"

"Oh, more so," she said. "I pretend to be obliging just so that I will not be turned off and have to beg my bread in the streets. You ought not to be dallying with either Flossie or Mrs. Delaney, you know. You are to marry Nancy—or so she and Mrs. Peabody say."

"Am I?" he said. "But I am not married to her yet, little bird. Perhaps I am sowing my wild oats before settling to a sober and blameless married life. Or perhaps I am an incurable rake and will continue with my

Mary Balogh

wicked ways until my life is at an end. And perhaps it is none of your business."

"Nothing ever is," she said. "But I would remind you, sir, that you are the one who chose to talk to me. I was quite content to sit in silence and watch the clouds scud by. That is why I came here, you know."

"You escaped?" he asked. "You flew the nest?"

"Perhaps Mrs. Peabody went into the village with some of the lady guests," she said. "Perhaps I had finished the tasks she had left me and had an hour or so to myself. And perhaps now I will be late back at the house and will be scolded. And perhaps it is none of your business."

"Touché!" he said. "Come down from there, Miss Mangan. We will walk back to the house together."

"So that I may be seen in your company and be thought to be setting my cap at you?" she said. "I would be scolded for a week without a pause for breath, sir. I can escort myself back to the house, I thank you."

"Come down!" he commanded. He had the notion that she was a small female and wanted to confirm the impression. He did not like small females, being rather on the tall side himself. He liked tall, generously endowed women.

"Oh, yes sir, right away, sir, if you are going to use that tone of voice on me," she said. She came down the tree with sure, agile movements, as if it was something she was quite accustomed to. She had trim ankles encased in white stockings, he could not help but see. Not that he had been even trying to avert his gaze. "You had better stand well back if you do not wish to be bowled over. I have to jump from the bottom branch."

20

"Allow me," he said, making her his most elegant bow and then reaching up and lifting her down before she had a chance to tell him if she would allow him or not.

His hands almost met about her waist. She was as light as the proverbial feather. When he set her down, the top of her head reached perhaps to his chin. Not the width of one hair higher. She was slender almost to the point of thinness.

Those large eyes of hers looked up into his. "Certainly," she said. "Yes, do please help me down, sir. I may slip and sprain an ankle if left to myself. But now that you have done so, you may remove your hands from my waist whenever you wish."

From sheer principle he took his time about doing so. "Tell me," he said, "do you have to use a knife with your meals, or is your tongue sharp enough without?"

"I could almost pity Nancy," she said. "You are not really a gentleman, are you?"

"I have been severely provoked," he said. He offered her his arm, which she took after a moment's hesitation, and began to lead her slowly through the trees in the direction of the house. "You could always save poor Miss Peabody by warning her about my, ah, expenditures of energy this morning and tonight."

"Ah, but she already knows you are a rake," she said. "It is your greatest attraction in her eyes. Well, almost the greatest."

The greatest being that he could elevate her to the rank of baroness at some distant time, he supposed.

"Of course," she added, "she will expect you to be a reformed rake once you are married."

"Ugh!" he said.

"Reformed rakes are said to be the best, most constant of husbands," she said.

"Best as meaning most experienced?" he asked. He was enjoying himself more than he had since leaving behind his male cronies in London. "Constant as meaning most constantly able to please in— You are steeling yourself not to blush again, are you not, Miss Mangan?"

"And you are thoroughly enjoying trying to make me do so, sir," she said. "I would have you remember, if you will, that I am the daughter of a parson."

"Why are you so different from your cousin?" he asked. "Why are you dressed so differently? Why were you not with her in London for the Season? *Were* you there?"

"I was in London," she said.

"But were not brought out with her?" he said. "Why are you not mingling with your aunt's guests now?"

"I live in greater luxury here than I knew at the parsonage," she said. "All my needs are seen to. Mrs. Peabody is to find me a suitable husband."

"Ah," he said. "That must be a delightful prospect."

"Yes," she said firmly, "it is."

The trees were thinning. He was not sure he wanted to be seen with her any more than she wished to be seen with him. He stopped, took her hand from his arm, and raised it to his lips.

"My dear little bird," he said, "we must not be seen consorting in clandestine manner like this. With the greatest reluctance I must part from you. Your beauty makes the sunshine seem dim, you know."

"Oh." She fluttered her eyelashes. "I was dreadfully afraid you would not have noticed, sir. I shall go this way. You may go that. So much for my lovely solitary hour." She sighed and turned to hurry across the grass toward a door at the side of the house.

He watched her go before strolling off in the direction of the terrace at the front of the house. Her step was light, her stride rather long. He could almost picture her with a basket over her arm, delivering food and clothing to the poor in her father's parish.

What a very amusing and refreshing little creature, he thought. There appeared to be no artifice in her at all. He felt no sexual stirring for her, but he stood and watched her nonetheless, a half smile on his lips. He rather believed he liked her. Liking was something he rarely felt, or thought of feeling, for a woman.

It was very true what she had always thought about the relative merits of dreams and daydreams. Dreams could not be controlled, and they were not always pleasant. Sometimes they were quite the opposite.

She woke up in the middle of the night aching with grief, and she realized that she had actually been crying in her sleep. Her cheeks were wet, she found when she touched them, and her nose felt in dire need of a good blowing. She felt beneath her pillow for a handkerchief, blew hard until she could breathe more comfortably, and tried to remember what had made her so miserable. That was the trouble with dreams. They were often hard to remember even when they had aroused such a real and deep emotion.

Mama's death, perhaps, and Papa's following it a scant year later? The contrasts between her life then and her life now? The almost total absence of love from her life now when it had used to be so filled with it? No. She turned back the sheet neatly to her waist and crossed her hands over her stomach. No, she would despise herself if she ever allowed self-pity to rule her. It was such a negative, such an unproductive emotion. She had long ago done all her crying and tucked her memories away into the past. That was the past; this was the present. Perhaps the future would be different again. That was life. In her twenty-two years she had learned that life was unpredictable and that all one could do was live it one day at a time, always refusing to give up hope when times were bad, always consciously enjoying the moment when times were good.

Except that these days there were so few good times. It was a thought not to be dwelled upon. It was too bad that dreams could not be controlled, that one must wake up in the middle of the night bawling like a baby and not even knowing exactly why one wept.

He would be in Mrs. Delaney's room now, she imagined, her thoughts flitting elsewhere, either sleeping the sleep of the justly exhausted in her arms or else doing with her what would make him exhausted. Was that what had grieved her and then awoken her—the fact that he was not doing either of those things in her bed?

What a strange, shocking thought! And yet her breasts felt uncomfortably taut, and when she reached up one hand she could feel that the nipple she touched was hard against the cotton of her nightgown. And there was an aching throbbing down between her legs.

"Oh, dear God," she whispered into the darkness. It was a prayer. She followed the introduction with confused apologies for sin and pleas for forgiveness. And then she apologized for her insincerity and promised to enter the Presence again when she was truly sorry and could truly expect forgiveness.

"What must you think of me?" she asked God.

God held his peace.

For the first time in a long while she had stopped being a shadow. Just for a few minutes. He had talked to her and looked at her and laughed at her and insulted her and kissed her hand and mocked her with that silly compliment about the sunshine and called her his little bird. And what had she done? She had talked back and matched wits with him and scolded him and set her arm through his and—oh, yes, she might as well admit the ultimate humiliation.

She had gone and tumbled headlong in love with him.

Stupid woman. Idiotic woman. Imbecile.

She had despised Nancy for wanting him when she knew that he was a dreadful, unprincipled rake. Yet now she was being as bad as Nancy. Horrid, ghastly thought. He was here at the house to court Nancy. He would be married to her before the end of the summer in all probability. And yet he had tumbled Flossie yesterday morning—Patricia was not so naive as really to believe that he had merely kissed the girl. And tonight he was feasting upon the almost fat and definitely voluptuous Mrs. Delaney—a married lady. And beneath the roof of his future father-in-law's house.

Was there ever such an unprincipled rogue?

Yet she was besotted with him because he had asked who she was and then demanded further details. Because he had a handsome face and compelling dark gray eyes and a manly muscular figure and elegant costly clothes. And because she had felt his lips and his breath against the back of her hand. Because for a few minutes she had come out of the shadows and had been dazzled by the sunshine. She made the sun-

shine look dim, he had said, deliberately teasing her
with the lavishly untrue compliment, knowing that she
would have some answer to amuse him.

Idiot. Imbecile. Fool. She set her mind to thinking
of a few other names to call herself. And she fished
the damp handkerchief from beneath her pillow again.
She was going to need it when she had finally scolded
her snivelings to a halt.

She hated him. He could have played the gentleman
and pretended not to have seen her up the tree. He
could have gone away and left her to enjoy the pattern
the branches made against the sky. But oh, no, he had
had to talk to her and make her fall in love with him.

Oh, she hated him. She hoped that he was not finding Mrs. Delaney enjoyable after all. She quite fer-
vently hoped it.

He was finding Mrs. Delaney something of a disappointment. Oh, she was quite as voluptuous without
her clothes as with them, and she was quite as skilled
as she was reputed to be and quite as eager to give
whatever pleasure he demanded and in whatever manner and at whatever pace he chose. If she had been
able to keep her mouth shut, he might have found
himself thoroughly contented to bed only her for the
remainder of his stay at Holly House and to forget
about the other three prospects he had in mind.

But the lady liked to talk. While he undressed her
and she undressed him. While they were engaged in
foreplay. While he had her mounted. And after they
were finished. He never minded a certain amount of
eroticism whispered into his ear or even shouted out
to him at the most crucial moments of a sexual en-

counter. It could be marvelously arousing. He liked to do it himself.

What he did not particularly enjoy—what he did not enjoy at all, in fact—was having the events of the previous day mulled over when his body was clamoring to shut down the workings of his mind or to have gossip repeated and commented upon while he labored to make the lady as mindless as he. He did not expect love from her—heaven forbid!—but he did expect a little respect for his famed prowess as a lover. The woman came to lusty climax each time he mounted her body, and it seemed genuine enough, but he never knew quite where it came from. It was almost as if, like Flossie and her ilk, she needed only the last couple of minutes for her own pleasure but was quite willing to grant him all the extra minutes provided he would allow her to make free with his ears while she waited for the good part.

During the second night and perhaps the seventh or eighth encounter all told, he loved her almost languidly in his tiredness and actually opened up his ears to hear what she was saying. She was planning the rest of their summer—*their* summer. He was to go to Brighton, where Mr. Delaney was a minor player in Prinny's court. They would have to be moderately discreet, but Mr. Delaney would not make any great fuss anyway. Mr. Delaney, it seemed, had a greater love for clothes and gossip than he had for any exertions of the body. In the autumn they would go to Bath, where Mrs. Delaney had an aged aunt. It was unclear where Mr. Delaney would be, but regardless the affair was to flourish in Bath until the winter drew them back to London. Mr. Bancroft, Mrs. Delaney knew, owned a very superior love nest there where they could meet once or twice a week. Or perhaps more often—she nipped his earlobe with her sharp teeth as an inducement to him to make it three or four times a week.

He finished what he was doing to her, having the good manners to allow her to shout out her own completion first, disengaged himself from her, reluctantly shook off the need to try to doze for a while, and promptly decided it was time for his crisis of conscience.

"It is a dream utopia, love," he said, regret in his voice. "It cannot be done. Your husband—"

Mrs. Delaney cozied up to him in such a way that if he had not already had her seven or eight times during the past one and three-quarter nights, his temperature might have soared. As matters were, it stayed exactly where it was.

"It weighs heavily on my conscience to have usurped another man's rights," he lied after she had protested. "You are too beautiful for your own good, my dear, and I am too weak for mine. But we must not continue. Let it end here, and let me be able to remember that for two all too brief nights I knew heaven on earth."

The lady, he thought as he tiptoed to his own room in some relief several minutes later, did not know the rules of the game for all her reputed experience. He wondered in some alarm if after all she was smitten with him. Surely she did not put up this much fuss every time a lover shed her. Or was she more accustomed to doing the shedding?

It did not matter. He was free of her. He would give himself tomorrow night in which to recuperate and then see what he could accomplish with Lady

Myron, widow. She was a quiet lady, tall and nicely shaped, older than he at a guess, and unknown to him before this week. He had no tangible reason to believe that she was not a perfectly virtuous woman apart from certain looks she was throwing his way. More than once—he was certainly not imagining them. Come-hither looks if he had ever seen any. Well, he would try coming hither and see what came of it.

In the meantime he felt as if he had at least a week of sleep to catch up on and only a few hours in which to do it, unless he slept until noon, as some of the ladies were in the habit of doing.

But the annoying thing was, he discovered over the coming hour as he lay in his own bed, at first flat on his back, and then curled on his right side and then stretched on his left and then spread-eagled on his stomach, that sleep just would not come. He was beyond the point of exhaustion. That damned woman was inexhaustible. She was always ready to settle for a good gossip when his body was screeching for sleep. Of course, she never expended her energy as recklessly as he did. She must have learned that from experience. Now whenever he seemed in some danger of nodding off, he found that he was bracing himself for her next sally into conversation—even though she was a few rooms away.

Damn the woman. Damn all women. They would be the death of him. Sometimes he wondered if all the pleasure to be derived from them was worth the effort. And he must be exhausted to the point of death if he was starting to feel that way, he thought, kicking off the bedclothes and levering himself off the bed to go and stand naked at his window. Dawn was graying the landscape already. He ran the fingers of one hand through his hair and blew out air from puffed cheeks.

Maybe it was just that he was getting old. Twenty-nine on his next birthday, though it was still more than eight months away. Almost thirty. Time to be settling down. He could almost hear his mother saying the words in her sweet and quiet voice. He grimaced and wondered if he should stagger back to bed or get dressed and go for a vigorous ride.

And then he leaned forward to peer downward. A shadow flitted out from below him and darted across the lawn leading to the trees and the lily pond. A shadow that looked as if it was clad in a gray cloak and hood. A shadow that looked female. And small.

He found himself grinning. She had not lied. He must have seen her at least half a dozen times before he had caught sight of her up in the old oak tree. Almost wherever Mrs. Peabody went in the house, her little gray shadow went with her. The little shadow was made to carry and fetch—stools and shawls and embroidery and vinaigrettes and a dozen and one other things. She did it all with a quiet grace and downcast eyes. And it was true—incredibly true—that no one else seemed aware of her existence. Just as one could stand in the large hall of a grand house, he supposed, and think oneself alone when all the time there were perhaps a dozen silent footmen lining the walls, waiting to open doors or run errands.

In the day and a half since he had become aware of her, he had not once—not once!—been able to catch her eye. But knowing that she had eyes and ears and intelligence and a sense of humor and a quick wit, he had set about amusing her by being lavish in his attentions to Mrs. Peabody and untiring in his flattery of Miss Peabody.

She had brightened that day and a half for him. She was not at all pretty, especially since he could get no glimpse of her eyes, and she was far too small and had a figure that was trim but not in any way luscious. Her clothes were abominable, and the best that could be said of her hair was that it shone and looked clean and healthy. And yet it amused him to know that he was one of the few people at Holly House who was even aware of her existence. And to know that she was hearing every lying, flattering word he uttered and was silently scolding him.

And now she was off to her retreat again, fleeing the nest before her day of drudgery was to start. Poor girl. He felt an unaccustomed wave of compassion for her. He was not famed as a compassionate man.

He looked back at his rumpled bed with some distaste. If he lay down again, he would not sleep, he knew, especially now that daylight was beginning to replace darkness. And there was nothing worse than lying in bed, tired and unable to sleep. Much better to get dressed and stroll down to the lily pond to tease a certain little bird. He remembered her sighing and lamenting the lost hour of solitude—*lovely* solitude, she had called it. But he shrugged his shoulders.

He was not famed as a considerate man, either.

He walked through to his dressing room and lit a candle.

Sometimes she walked in the early morning down to the crescent-shaped lake. It was always deserted and lovely at that time of day. But there was something just a little too artificial about it. It had been constructed and landscaped to be lovely and it was, but it was a man-made loveliness. Sometimes she took the longer walk back to the hill behind the house so that she could see the surrounding countryside. She liked to do that particularly if there was likely to be some trailing mist in the lowland to add drama to the scene. But almost always, at whatever time of day she was able to get away by herself, she went to the lily pond. It was secluded and rather neglected. It was hers.

There had been no dew last night. She tested the grass with one hand, brushing it hard back and forth. Her hand remained dry. She sat down on the bank, drew her knees up, wrapped her cloak more closely about her for warmth, and clasped her legs with her arms.

It was the time of day she loved most—early dawn, even before the sun rose. She was not quite sure why she liked it, since it was a gray time of day. Perhaps it was the knowledge that there was a whole new day ahead. Perhaps it was the hope that the sun would rise to a cloudless sky and that the whole day would be correspondingly bright. Perhaps it was just that she knew this early in the day that there were still several hours to go before her aunt would summon her and begin the constant demand for service. Not that that in itself was something to be dreaded—Patricia had always led a busy life and did not enjoy endless idleness. But she could never please. There was always irritability in her aunt's voice when it was directed at her. If she set the second cup of chocolate of the morning on the left side of the bed, she should have set it at the right. And if she set it at the right, then it should have been placed at the left. It never failed. And the rest of the day always proceeded accordingly.

Patricia sighed and rested one cheek on her up-drawn knees. She had had that dream again last night, whatever it was. She had woken up again with wet eyes and aching heart. She would be glad when all the guests were gone. Though of course then there would probably be a wedding to prepare and the certain knowledge that soon Nancy and he ...

She closed her eyes. No, she would not think of him. How very amused he would be if he knew ... And how irate her aunt would be. And how contemptuous Nancy would be.

He was quite shameless in his flattery of both her aunt and Nancy. It amazed her that they both seemed to lap it all up as a cat would cream. Could they not see that the man was all artifice, that he never spoke a true word? And had they not seen the complacent looks of Mrs. Delaney yesterday? The fact that she had spent a very satisfactory night in bed with Mr. Bancroft seemed to be written large over her whole person. And had they not noted the looks Lady Myron and Mr. Bancroft were exchanging? They were lascivious looks, to say the least.

Was he spending half a night in each lady's bed? And devouring Flossie for breakfast? Patricia hoped that he would drop dead of exhaustion. Oh, yes, she really did. Men with such low morals ought not to be allowed to live on to enjoy them. And any woman who allowed herself to fall into his clutches was quite as bad as he and quite as deserving of a bad end.

Oh, dear.

And then she heard the unmistakable sounds of someone approaching. She tensed though she did not move. No one ever came here. Not at this time of day especially. She did not want to be disturbed. She had so little time to herself. Perhaps it was one of the gardeners come to cut the grass around the pond. Perhaps he would go away again when he saw her. She was not one of the great personages of the house, but then she was not a servant, either.

The footsteps stopped. "Ah," a voice said. "Little birds who fly down from their branches are in danger of being devoured, you know. Big bad wolves—or more probably sleek stealthy cats—are likely to creep up on them unawares and pounce on them."

Her heart performed a painful somersault, and she wished she had gone to the lake or to the hill—anywhere but the lily pond. "If I were you," she said, not moving, "I would not apply for the position of big bad wolf or sleek stealthy cat. You would starve. I believe that on your way here you stepped on every twig that was available to step upon and brushed against every branch that could be brushed against."

"Did I?" He chuckled. "But you did not fly up to the safety of your branch, little bird?"

Her head was turned away from him, but she could hear that he was seating himself on the grass beside her.

"So that you might order me down and lift me to the ground again?" she said. "No, thank you, sir. When a pleasure has been tasted once, it quite loses its savor."

"What an alarming thought," he said. "What are you doing up and out so early?"

"Seeking a solitary hour at the lily pond," she said. "*Vainly* seeking, that is. And you, sir? Has Mrs. Delaney tired of being worshiped? Or is it Lady Myron?

And has not Flossie yet appeared to perform any of her morning duties?"

"I see that your tongue and a whetstone have been no strangers to each other's company during the past two days," he said. "Would you not agree that despite my nocturnal adventures I have been behaving with faultless gallantry to my intended and her mother? Come, you must admit that."

"Where I was brought up," she said, "we were taught that it is a sin to lie. I do not know where a hot enough corner of hell will be found for you when you die, sir."

"I prefer not to dwell upon the prospect at the moment, thank you," he said. "But come, Miss Mangan, would this not be a dreadful world and would not gallantry die an ignominious death if we all spoke the truth without fail?"

She smiled, but he could not see her expression since her face was still turned away from him.

"Well, that at least has silenced you," he said. "Just picture it, my little bird. 'Madam, you are plain and totally lacking in any shape that might be called feminine. Silks and muslins appear lusterless when hung on your person. Looking at you is a pain only intensified when you open your mouth and speak. Madam, would you dance with me?' or 'Madam, would you care to shed your clothes and jump into bed with me? You appear to have been formed expressly for the purpose of satisfying my lust.' Would I gain myself a place in heaven and a golden harp to play upon if I spoke thus honestly to a lady?"

"Your lack of tact would doubtless make it impossible for you to indulge in any other sin," she said. "No woman would allow you within a five-mile radius of

her. You might well find yourself living a spotless existence, sir."

"Ugh!" he said.

She could resist no longer. She still wished herself
a million miles away, but he was close by. She could
tell that by his voice. He was sitting very close to her.
She turned her head to rest the other cheek on her
knees, and gazed at him. He was wearing a dark cloak.
He was bareheaded. He was sprawled on the grass
beside her, propped on one elbow. And his eyes were
laughing at her. She remembered then what it was
that had caused her great stupidity in the first place.
It had happened when he had smiled and laughed at
her. Nobody ever smiled at her these days.

"Little bird," he said, "your eyes are too big for
your face."

"Am I to thank you for your honesty?" she asked.

"If you wish." He grinned. "The thought has just
struck me. Did you have a tryst here? Is there some
burly and impatient swain hiding in the bushes waiting
for me to make myself scarce?"

"There are probably half a dozen of them," she
said. "But no matter. They will all come back tomorrow. It is my eyes, you see. They slay men by the
dozens."

"Mrs. Peabody is choosing you a husband," he said.
"Is he chosen yet, little bird?"

She thought she detected mockery in his voice.
"Yes," she said. "He is a tenant farmer. A *prosperous*
farmer," she added, emphasizing the adjective.

"Is he?" He plucked a blade of grass and set it
between his teeth. "And ruddy and rotund and sixty
years of age?"

"He is handsome and slender and only two years my senior," she said.

He smiled slowly at her. "And how old is that?" he asked. "Twenty-three? Twenty-four? And already a prosperous tenant farmer? He is an industrious man, or a fortunate one."

"His father died young," she said, "and left him everything."

"Ah." He chuckled. "I have heard that even the coolest corner of hell is a mite uncomfortable, little bird."

"You will never know, will you?" she said. "You are going to turn virtuous and spend your time on useful accomplishments, like practicing the harp."

He chuckled again and stretched out on the ground, one arm behind his head. With the other hand he reached out to touch her arm and ran it down to her elbow and then down to her wrist, which he encircled so that he could draw her arm away from her knees and down to the ground. He clasped her hand firmly and closed his eyes.

"I am weary," he said. "And don't tell me that you know the cause, little bird, and that I deserve to be. One day, when you are married to your young and virile tenant farmer—your *prosperous* farmer—you will discover that the cause of the weariness can be worth every sleepless moment. Talk to me. Tell me about your life at the parsonage. At a guess I would say you were happy there. Were you?"

"Yes," she said. "Yes."

He opened his eyes and turned his head to look up at her. "Tell me about it, then," he said. "Tell me about all the sinners you led back into the fold. I am sure there were many of them. You would have scolded them with your sharp tongue and made them stubborn, and then you would have gazed at them with those too-large sorrowful eyes and melted away all their resistance. Is that how you did it?"

"Yes," she said. "Every Sunday morning before service all of Papa's parishioners had to file past me outside the church and gaze into my eyes for thirty seconds each. The church was always full of weeping penitents afterward."

He chuckled and squeezed her hand. "Tell me," he said. "Who was Patricia Mangan before she came here?"

She was the much adored only child of parents who had both been in their forties when they were blessed with her, as they had always put it. They had been married for almost twenty years before she came along. Her father had always likened himself and her mother to the biblical Abraham and Sarah. She had played a great deal, both alone with her imagination and with the other village children, and had gone to school with them to be taught by her father, the schoolmaster. But there had been work too—household chores set her by her mother, parish chores set her by her father. She had never been idle.

She had never really thought about her happiness until everything came crashing to an end. She had not been conscious at the time that she was living through an idyll. It had seemed to her a normal, plodding, unexciting type of existence if she ever thought of it. She rarely did. She had just lived it.

And then when she was seventeen Patrick had been killed in Spain.

"Who was Patrick?"

She had been hardly aware that she was talking

aloud, that she had an audience. Patrick was the younger son of a gentleman who lived in a small manor outside the village. He had gone to the wars as a young ensign and been killed in his first battle. Patrick had been her childhood sweetheart, the boy she had loved. They were going to be married when he came home, a great hero. In her naivété she had not really considered the strong possibility of his dying.

But she had learned a swift and thorough lesson about death. Her mother had died less than a year later of a fever, and her father of a chill a year after that. At one moment it had seemed that she had everything—everything to bring her contentment and a continuation of the world as she knew it. And at the next it had seemed that she had nothing. Though that was not true, of course. She must not complain. Her father had had a sister who had done very well for herself by marrying Mr. Peabody, a prosperous gentleman. Patricia had been offered a home with them.

"Little bird," Mr. Bancroft said, first squeezing her hand again and then lifting it to his lips. "I am sorry. Life often seems a very unfair business, does it not?"

"Not to me," she said untruthfully. "Many women who are left destitute are forced to sell themselves, sir. I have not been brought that low."

"And there is always your future with your lusty farmer to look forward to," he said. "Tell me about your future. What will constitute a happy life to you?"

A husband and a home. A gentle and a kindly man. A good friend and companion. She did not care about good looks or social prominence or unusual physical strength or intelligence. Just an ordinary, honest, constant man.

"A rake would not do you, then?" he asked.

No, certainly not a rake. Someone she could depend upon. And a home of her own. It would not have to be very large or very grand or even very lavishly furnished. Just so that it was her own with a garden for her flowers and vegetables, and perhaps a few chickens. Oh, and dogs and cats. And children of her own. More than one of it was possible. Loneliness could be hard on children even when there were loving parents and plenty of village children to play with. Children should have brothers and sisters if it was at all possible. And she wanted to hold babies in her arms. Her own babies.

Nothing else really. She did not crave wild adventure or excitement in her life. Only contentment. She would wish too that her husband would live long, that he would outlive her—and that she would not lose any of her children in infancy, as so many women did.

It was not a very ambitious dream. But it was as far beyond her as the sun and stars. She was not speaking aloud now. It was an impossible dream. Her aunt would never let her go. She was too useful. And she had no dowry. And no beauty. Perhaps if she went away and tried to find employment . . . But as what? A governess? A housekeeper? A lady's companion? She was a lady's companion already. None of those types of employment, even if she could find any without any experience or recommendations, would find her a husband.

If only Patrick had not dreamed of the glory of being a soldier. But that was long in the past. He had become a soldier and he had gone to war and he had been killed. There was no point in indulging in if-onlys.

Mr. Bancroft was sleeping, she realized suddenly. His hold on her hand had loosened, and his breathing was deep and even. His head was turned toward her.

He was so very beautiful. She let her eyes roam over his perfect features, over his thick, dark hair. Patrick had been blond. The folds of his cloak hid the shape of his body, but she knew that he was both slender and muscular, that a broad chest tapered to narrow waist and hips. One of his legs, encased in pantaloons and Hessian boot, was raised at the knee and free of his cloak. She could see his thigh muscles through the tight fabric. For all his attention to women, which had led her to imagine that he must spend most of his life in bed, he must work hard at keeping himself fit.

He was so very beautiful. She could feel the warmth of his hand about hers and told herself with great deliberateness that she would always remember this moment. He was a dreadful and shameless rake, and she must be thankful that her lack of beauty and charm and fortune had led him into treating her like this, like a younger cousin, perhaps, when he might have been trying to seduce her. She had had these quiet minutes with him and would be able to treasure them in memory for the rest of her life.

She was glad she had no beauty with which to tempt him. She was glad he had never tried to make love to her. She bit her lip and tried to believe her own very deliberate thoughts.

It was full daylight. The sun was probably springing over the eastern horizon, though she could not see it here among the trees. She must go back to the house and prepare herself for the day. She was tempted to sit here until he awoke. Perhaps it would be hours later. But she did not have hours to spare. Besides, she did not want to talk with him anymore. She did not believe she would be able to keep up any of their usual banter. She felt a little like crying.

She wanted to kiss him. She wanted to lean down and touch her lips to his forehead or one of his cheeks. Or perhaps even his own lips. But she might wake him. She would die of humiliation if he awoke while her lips were touched to his.

So she merely raised his hand slowly and dipped her head to meet it and set her cheek to the back of it. And she turned her head and brushed her lips against the back of his wrist. Then she set his hand down carefully on the grass, got quietly to her feet, gazed down at him for a few moments longer, and walked softly away into the trees—far more softly than he had approached a half hour or so earlier.

He was not sleeping. He merely did not want to continue his conversation with her. He did not want to have to walk back to the house with her.

She had let him into her world, a very ordinary world, but one so alien to him that he did not know how to respond to her. Life had been cruel to her— viciously cruel. And her dreams, though humble ones, were quite, quite beyond her grasp, he knew. He did not for one moment believe in the young and hand- some and prosperous tenant farmer or in the ruddy, rotund, elderly one, either. She was too valuable to Mrs. Peabody. Mrs. Peabody was the type of woman who needed someone more than a personal maid to fetch and carry for her, and someone who was always there on whom to vent her spleen. Someone who could not answer back.

Patricia Mangan would never hold any of those babies in her arms. It was such a humble ambition for a woman to have. She did not crave silks and jewels and fashionable beaux—only a kindly, constant husband and a small and cozy home and some babies of her own.

It was not pity he felt. He did not believe it was pity. His little bird was too sensible and too courageous a woman to be pitied. It was rage he felt. A rage against Mrs. Peabody, perhaps. A rage against God, certainly. Though he was not sure that God could be blamed for what people did to one another when they had been given the infinitely precious gift of free will.

He wanted to draw her down into his arms, to hold her against him, to warm her soul against his body. But to what end? He knew of only one thing to do with a woman's body when it was against his own. He knew nothing about giving comfort. And she did not need comfort anyway. She did not seem to pity herself, or if she did, it was something she fought in the quiet of her own heart.

He felt humbled by her.

He could not talk to her. And so he conveniently fell asleep and waited for her to go away. It was his answer to anything troubling in his life—close his eyes and wait for it to go away.

She did go away eventually—after lifting his hand to her cheek and kissing the back of his wrist.

God! Oh, Lord God!

He did not know what she meant by it. A mere tender affection because he had listened to her—and fallen asleep while she spoke? Or—or something else?

Hell and a thousand million damnations!

*   *   *

The guests had been at Holly House for two weeks and were to stay for another week. Patricia did not like their being there even though there was one distinct advantage to her in that Mrs. Peabody was frequently engaged in outings with them and left her with more than usual freedom. But she did not like their being there nevertheless.

She did not like *his* being there. She wanted him to go away. She wanted to be free of him. Since the morning at the lily pond she had been alone with him only once, for a mere few seconds and they had exchanged only seven words, four of his and three of hers. But she wanted him gone anyway. His presence in the house and frequently in the same room as she occupied with her aunt weighed heavily on her spirits.

The only time they met face to face, or almost face to face, was one morning when she was hurrying along the upstairs hallway with Mrs. Peabody's second cup of chocolate and he came out of his room just ahead of her. He closed the door and waited for her to draw level with him.

"Good morning, little bird," he said quietly.

"Good morning, sir." She did not raise her eyes and she hurried on past him. But she was upset for the rest of the day.

Mrs. Delaney was annoyed with him. Patricia could tell that from the way the lady flirted so ferociously with all the other gentlemen who made up the party— including even Mr. Peabody. Lady Myron was Mr. Bancroft's current favorite and probable bedfellow. The lascivious looks they had been exchanging more than a week ago had become considerably hotter. And when the lady was passing him one day in a doorway, Patricia saw that she leaned deliberately forward and slid her bosom across his chest—as if the doorway was no more than six inches wide. His eyes had smoked down at her.

It amazed Patricia that no one else noticed such things. Perhaps one observed more easily when one lived the life of a shadow. Everyone else was perhaps too busy living. And everyone else seemed to assume that a betrothal announcement would be made before the final week drew to an end.

They could not be blamed for thinking so, Patricia thought, and undoubtedly they were right. He was markedly attentive to Nancy, leading her in to meals, standing behind her to turn the pages of her music when she played the pianoforte, walking out with her, strolling on the terrace with her after dinner before the evening entertainment began, dancing with her if that was the order of the evening, partnering her in cards or charades. He smiled at her and talked with her and devoured her with his eyes and made it appear that he was smitten to the very heart.

Most of them could not be blamed for not knowing that he had spent his nights with Mrs. Delaney at the start and was now spending them with Lady Myron and was also exchanging interested and assessing glances with Mrs. Hunter and had tumbled Flossie on at least one occasion.

Why should they know or suspect when a very obvious courtship was developing before their eyes and when Mrs. Peabody and Nancy were so very openly in expectation of an event to be celebrated before they sent their guests on their way?

Patricia was usually excluded from the social events that took place beyond the confines of the house. But she was informed that she was to accompany Mrs.

Peabody on the picnic out to the hill one afternoon. She could make herself useful for a change, she was told, instead of being idle and indolent. She was going to have to revise her lazy ways after the guests had gone home. There was going to be dear Nancy's wedding to prepare for, after all. And perhaps she did not realize that her keep was costing Mr. Peabody a pretty penny. It was time she did something to earn it.

And so Patricia found herself on a warm and only slightly breezy summer afternoon seated in the open barouche beside Mrs. Peabody, Nancy and Nancy's young friend, Susan Ware, opposite them, Mr. Bancroft, riding like the other gentlemen, close to the other side of the conveyance, heaping gallantries on the ladies—on the three ladies, that was. Patricia was merely the shadow of one of them.

That morning at the lily pond had had results. Talking about her past and putting into words her dreams—as she had done to no one before, or not since Patrick's departure for Spain, anyway—had set her to thinking. And realizing what an abject creature she had become. What a victim. Could she really be quite this helpless? Was it possible that her aunt really owned her for the rest of her life, just as if she were a slave? Was it so impossible to try to shape a life of her own?

The new parson at home, the one who had taken over from Papa, had been a friend of his. Patricia had met him once or twice before her father's death. She had heard since in the letters she sometimes received from the Misses Jones that he did not like teaching at the village school, that he considered it to be outside the limits of his responsibilities. He did it only because there was no alternative.

What if she presented him with an alternative? Patricia had been thinking it over during the past week. What if she offered to teach at the school? She did not know how she would be paid and she did not know where she would live, unless it was in that rundown cottage that no one had wanted to live in for the past ten years or so because the former owner had hanged himself inside and his ghost was said to linger there. But what if something could be worked out?

She had written to the parson, and she was waiting hopefully and anxiously for an answer. If only . . . Oh, if only something could be worked out. She would not need a fortune, only enough with which to clothe herself and feed herself and keep herself warm.

"Girl!" She could tell from Mrs. Peabody's sharp tone that it was not the first time she had spoken. "My parasol."

Mrs. Peabody's parasol was at her side, at the side farthest from her niece. Patricia had to lean across her to reach it. She handed it to her aunt.

"And it is to shade my complexion as it is?" Mrs. Peabody said. "Lazy girl."

Patricia raised the parasol and handed it to her aunt.

"Really, Patricia," Nancy said, "you can be remarkably dense. Oh, Susan, do look at the darling bonnet Lady Myron is wearing. I am positively *green* with envy."

"My dear Miss Peabody," Mr. Bancroft said, leaning down from his horse's back and setting one hand on the door of the barouche, "the bonnet would be wasted on you. The beholder would look into your face and not notice the beauty of the hat at all. You see, it is only now that I deliberately look that I realize how exquisitely lovely is the one you are wearing."

"Oh, such things you say, Mr. Bancroft," Mrs. Peabody said and laughed heartily.

Miss Peabody blushed and twirled her parasol and looked triumphantly about her to see who had heard the compliment.

Patricia would have held her nose if she could have done so without being observed. She did not look up at the gentleman, though she had the feeling sometimes that he indulged in such extravagant flattery partly for her amusement. She wondered if he would continue to say such things to Nancy once he was married to her.

Blankets had been spread on the grass at the foot of the hill. Mrs. Peabody had seated herself in the middle of one of them, Patricia slightly behind her, while most of the guests amused themselves in slightly more energetic ways until tea was served.

Most of them climbed the hill in order to gaze admiringly at the prospect Mrs. Peabody had promised them from the top, though she did not go up herself to display it to them. Mr. Bancroft led the way, Nancy on one arm, Susan on the other. A great deal of trilling laughter wafted down the hill after them. And then some of them strolled about the base of the hill while others walked the half mile to the east to look at the Greek folly that Mr. Peabody's father had had built years ago in the form of a temple. Still others wandered to the west to lose themselves among the trees that hid from view the river winding its way down in the direction of the crescent-shaped lake.

Mr. Bancroft went with the last group, though Nancy, who had elected herself leader of the expedition to the folly, appeared somewhat chagrined. He walked with Lady Myron and two other couples.

Patricia sat on the blanket the whole while, opening and closing her aunt's fan in concert with the passing clouds, fanning her aunt's face when the sun shone for too long, arranging a shawl about her shoulders when a cloud took forever to pass over, carrying messages to the footmen who brought the food, first to wait awhile and then to hurry along instead of standing idle for all to see.

And then when the footmen were busy setting out the food, which had been prepared in such variety and such abundance that it surely would have fed the five thousand with more than a dozen baskets of crumbs to spare, Mrs. Peabody decided that the wine should have been served first. Everybody would be thirsty from the heat and their exertions.

"Go and help, girl," she said impatiently to Patricia. "Make yourself useful. Go lift the wine basket from the wagon and take it over to Gregory. Instruct him to open the bottles immediately."

Patricia went to make herself useful. But the wine must match the food in quantity, she thought as she tried to lift the heavy basket down from the wagon. It must weigh a ton. And it was an awkward size. She wormed her hands beneath its outer edges and slid it to the edge of the wagon.

"Here, I'll take that," a hearty voice said from behind her. "It is almost as big as you are, little lady, and probably twice as heavy."

Patricia turned her head gratefully to see Mr. Ware, Susan's father, hurrying toward her, smiling jovially.

"Thank you," she said, standing back as his hands replaced hers beneath the basket. But the basket was teetering on the edge, and she withdrew her hands a moment too soon. Mr. Ware roared out a dismayed warning, Patricia's hands flew to her mouth, and the basket came crashing to earth, bursting open and spilling its contents as it did so.

Perhaps one bottle alone would not have smashed since the wagon board was not particularly high off the ground and the ground itself was carpeted with grass. But bottles and glasses tumbled against each other and smashed with a glorious crashing and flying of glass and spilling of wine.

Everyone's attention was drawn—it was such a magnificent disaster. Mr. Ware first swore and then apologized—but whether for his language or his clumsiness was not apparent—and then started to look sheepish. Patricia kept her hands pressed to her mouth for a few moments and then started to assure the gentleman that it was not his fault, that she had withdrawn her hands too soon.

And then Mrs. Peabody was there.

If it was really possible for anyone to turn purple in the face, Patricia thought, then her aunt had just done so, and her bosom seemed to have swelled to twice its normal buxom size. If Patricia's own mind had been working coolly, she would have realized perhaps that her aunt for once in her life had forgotten her surroundings and her audience and the impression she was about to make on them. But it was not a cool moment.

"Imbecile!" Mrs. Peabody shrieked at her niece. "You clumsy oaf! Is this the gratitude I receive for opening my home to you when my brother left you without a farthing to your name, and for clothing you and feeding you and treating you like my own daughter?"

"Oh, I say, ma'am," Mr. Ware said with an embarrassed cough, "I am afraid the fault was mine."

Everyone else was still and silent, as if posing for a painted tableau. They had all returned from their various walks.

"I saw it all," Mrs. Peabody said. "It is good of you to be so much the gentleman, sir, but you need not protect the lazy slut."

"Aunt!" Patricia's voice was hushed and shocked. There was a faint buzzing in her head.

"Silence!" Mrs. Peabody's palm cracked across one of Patricia's cheeks, and she turned away. "Now, what is to be done about this? Gregory, back to the house immediately for more wine."

The lady seemed suddenly to remember who she was and where she was. She smiled graciously about her and set about soothing her guests and tempting them with all the edible delights spread out before them and assuring them that the wine would be brought and served in no time at all.

"Oh, I say," Mr. Ware said ineffectually to Mrs. Peabody's regal back. "Oh, I say." He looked helplessly and apologetically at Patricia.

But Patricia was stunned, hardly even aware yet of the stinging of her cheek. She had been called a slut and she had had her face slapped—in public. Everyone had been watching and listening. Everyone!

She turned suddenly and began to run. She did not know where she was going or what she was going to do when she arrived there. She knew only that she had to get away, that she had to hide. Instinct took her in the direction of the trees. But even when she was among them, panic did not leave her. She turned north, away from the house, and ran recklessly among closely packed trees and hanging branches, heedless of slashing twigs and threatening roots. She could hear someone sobbing and did not even realize that it was herself.

And then she remembered the other folly, the little ruined tower down by the river, with the circular stone seat inside. She could collapse onto that. She could hide there for a while. For longer than a while. Forever. She could never go back to the house.

She had stopped running. She approached the folly from behind with quiet, weary steps and rounded the circular wall to the opening and the seat.

Mr. Bancroft was sitting on it, a lady with him. Patricia could not even see who she was until he raised his head, startled, from kissing her. Mrs. Hunter. Her dress was off her shoulder on the left side and down to her waist. He had his hand cupped about her naked breast.

Panic hit again. Patricia went fleeing away with a moan, crashing through trees once more until her breath gave out and a stitch in her side had her clutching it. Her cheek was hot and throbbing. She set her forehead against the trunk of a tree and closed her eyes. When the pain in her side had dulled, she wrapped her arms about the tree and sagged against it.

He was getting bored. Three weeks was too long a time to spend at one country home in company with the same twenty or so people. He would be thoroughly glad when the remaining week was at an end and he could get back to normal life.

And what was normal life? He would follow the

fashionable crowd to Brighton for a month or two, he supposed. There was always plenty happening there, plenty of congenial male company and wild wagers with which to fill his days, plenty of bored and beddable females to add excitement to his nights.

And then where? A duty visit to his mother and his uncle? Yes, he supposed so. He loved his mother dearly. It was just that her reproachful glances and accusing silences made him uncomfortable at times. She always gave the impression that she was waiting patiently for the day when he would have finally sowed the last of his wild oats and that she was perhaps giving up hope that he would ever be finished with them.

And then where? Bath? London?

He was getting bored, he thought in some alarm. Bored not just with the present reality but with the general condition of his life.

He had been conducting a heated affair with Lady Myron for more than a week. She was everything he could possibly ask for. She had a body that could arouse him at a glance, and she made that body and all the sexual skills she had acquired over the years fully available for his pleasure all night and every night. She had an energy to match his own and was eager to learn new skills from him and to teach him those few he had never before encountered. She made no demands beyond the moment.

But he was bored. And puzzled. After a week he was tired of such a desirable lover? Why? He could not think of anything wrong with her beyond the fact that they had nothing in common except a zestful enjoyment of a good tumble between the sheets. Her conversation—on the few occasions when they talked—was all of horses and hounds and hunting. He had no particular interest in such country pursuits. But that could not matter, surely. A woman's body and her sexual prowess were all that mattered—and Lady Myron passed muster on both counts.

But he found himself eyeing Mrs. Hunter appreciatively during the days and wondering how she compensated herself for the fact that Mr. Hunter, not present at the Holly House gathering, was a septuagenarian, and by all accounts a frail one at that. He began to suspect that somehow she did it and that she would be only too willing to do so with him before the party broke up.

And so she maneuvered it and he maneuvered it that they spend some time alone together on the afternoon of the picnic, both Lady Myron and Mr. Crawford, Mrs. Hunter's escort, having been shed somewhere along the way. And they discovered the convenience of the little folly by the river and sat inside it by mutual but unspoken consent.

The lady did not waste time on conversation or other preliminaries, he was delighted to find. She turned her face to his and kissed him. And when he had fully accepted the invitation and got his arms about her, she reached up a hand and drew down her dress to expose one breast many minutes before he would have got around to doing it for himself.

He was, he realized with pleased certainty, about to feast upon the full delights of the woman in the middle of the afternoon on a hard stone bench. And he was being given the distinct impression that she was ravenous.

Interesting!

It was at that moment and just as he had got his

hand on the woman's breast and was listening to her throaty murmur of appreciation that he knew some-one else was there. Lady Myron, he thought as he lifted his head, and he had a momentary vision of the two woman going for each other's hair with clawed fingernails—or else both going for *his* hair.

But it was Patricia Mangan. She stood there only for a moment before she moaned and disappeared, but he had the instant impression of a torn dress and a bonnetless head with hair pulled loose from its con-fining pins, and of a wild, unhappy face, one side of it red and swollen.

"Good Lord!" he said, relinquishing his hold on Mrs. Hunter's breast and jumping to his feet. He could hear the loud crashings of a panicked retreat.

"It is just that strange drab little creature who hangs about Mrs. Peabody," Mrs. Hunter said crossly. "She must be playing truant. It would have served her right if she had seen more. She will not dare return. Come!"

When he turned his head to look down at her, she was smiling invitingly up at him from beneath lowered eyelids and pushing down the other side of her dress.

Strangely, he thought afterward, he did not hesitate, even though the feast was being laid out before his eyes and was ready for instant devouring.

"Something has happened to her," he said. "I had better go and find her. Can you make your own way back to the picnic site?"

"What?" The lady sounded incredulous and looked magnificent bared to the waist.

"I shall see you back there," he said and strode away. And another strange thing, he thought later, was that his mind did not linger on the abandoned feast for even a single moment.

He could think only of the fact that his little bird seemed to have broken a wing and that he had to find her. Fortunately, she was doing nothing to hide the sounds of her progress through the dense forest of trees.

Gray was a drab color, but it was a light gray and a light fabric. It was just as visible against the trunk of a tree as it had been up in the branches of the old oak tree at the lily pond. He paused for a moment, looking at her. And then he moved up behind her and set his hands lightly on her shoulders.

She did not react for a moment. She must have heard him coming, he decided. He had been a little afraid of startling her. And then she turned, her head down, and burrowed it against the folds of his neck-cloth while her arms came about his waist and clung as if only by doing so could she save herself from falling.

"Little bird?" he murmured and was answered with a storm of weeping.

Weeping women had always embarrassed him. He never knew quite what to do with them. He closed his arms tightly about her, lowered his mouth into her hair, and murmured mindless nonsense to her. He might have been holding a child, he thought, except that she was not a child. She was warm, slender, soft woman.

"What happened?" he asked her when she had fallen silent at last.

"Nothing," she said, her voice muffled against his chest.

"Ah," he said. "My neckcloth has been ruined for nothing. My valet will be thrilled."

"Give him my apologies," she mumbled. Her teeth were chattering, he could hear.

He leaned back from her a little and lifted her chin with one hand, though she tried ineffectually to push it away. Her eyes and cheeks—and nose—were wet. Her face was red and blotched all over from crying and a uniform red on one side. Most of her hair was down and hanging in tangles about her face and over her shoulders. She looked wretchedly unpretty. And inexplicably and startlingly beautiful to his searching eyes.

He drew a handkerchief from his pocket, dried her face and her eyes with it, and handed it to her. "Blow," he said.

She drew away from him and blew. And bit her lower lip as he took the handkerchief away from her again and stuffed it back in his pocket.

"Tell me what the nothing consisted of," he said.

"I smashed all the wine bottles and glasses," she said.

"Over someone's head?" he asked. "How spectacular! I am sorry in my heart that I missed the show. Tell me what happened."

She told him.

"And found yourself in massive disgrace with Her Majesty, I suppose," he said.

"Yes." She was regaining her composure as he watched.

"What happened to the one side of your face?" he asked, feeling fury gather like a ball in his stomach. He knew with utter certainty what had happened.

Her face trembled almost out of control again. "She struck me," she said. "She called me a slut."

Pistols at dawn. How he itched to be able to challenge the woman to meet him. Right smack between the eyes. That was where he would place the bullet. He would let her shoot first and then make her stand there in frozen terror waiting for him to discharge his own pistol. And he would.

He reached out to set an arm about her slim shoulders and drew her against him again. She did not resist. She was shivering.

"I will avenge that for you, little bird," he said. "My honor on it. Do you believe I have any honor?"

She did not answer his question. "I suppose I overreacted," she said. "It was my fault, after all. It is just that I have never been struck in my life. And the face seems a particularly insulting place to be hit. And in public."

She pulled back from him and smiled at him.

"It does not matter," she said. I will not be staying here long. I am going to teach in a village school. My home village. I will be among people I know. And I think I will enjoy teaching children. I shall be going soon."

"What has happened to the young, handsome, virile, prosperous farmer?" he asked. "Has he withdrawn his offer?"

She hesitated for only a moment. "I do not love him," she said firmly. "I do not believe it is right to marry without love, do you? What a foolish question. You do not believe in love. But for me it is not right. So my future is all settled. My *happy* future."

"Is it?" he asked her. "You have been granted the employment?"

"I am just waiting to hear from the parson," she said. "It is a mere formality. He is bound to say yes. He was a friend of Papa's."

Ah. Another impossible dream. Another humble, impossible dream. He smiled at her, picturing her for no fathomable reason seated in a rocking chair, her head bent to the baby suckling contentedly at her breast. The dark-haired baby.

She was fully recovered. "I am all right," she said. "You had better return to Mrs. Hunter. I am sure she did not enjoy being abandoned at such an interesting moment. She will, I do not doubt, be growing cold. In more ways than one, sir."

He smiled slowly at her.

"You are going to come to a bad end, you know," she said. "What if I had been Lady Myron? Or Mrs. Delaney? Or Flossie? Or Nancy?"

He could feel amusement bubbling out of him.

"You think it is funny," she scolded. "It is not. Someone is going to get hurt. With any luck it will be only you with a broken head."

"That's my little bird," he said appreciatively. "Tongue sharpened at both edges and pointed at the tip. Take my arm. I am going to take you back to the house."

"Mrs. Hunter—" she began.

"—may go hang for all I care," he said. "I am taking you back home. It can be either on my arm or slung over my shoulder. The choice is yours."

"Well, if you put it in that gentlemanly way," she said, "I shall make my free choice. Your arm, I think."

"Now," he said, guiding her around overhanging branches, "let me regale you with my life history, shall I? You told me yours early one morning a week or so ago. I shall return the favor if you think you can bear it."

And so he did what he had never done with any woman before. He let her into his life.

He did not even fully realize he had done it until he thought about it later, standing at the window of his room in unaccustomed solitude, waiting for everyone else to return from the picnic. He talked without stopping, knowing that despite her spirited efforts to pull herself together, she was in reality very close to collapse and still to a certain extent in shock. She leaned against him as they walked in a manner that would have been provocative in any other woman or under any other circumstances. But he knew that she leaned because her legs were unsteady and her head dizzy.

And so he talked to her and knew that despite her distress she listened. She even asked him some questions about his mother and about his two married sisters and their children, his nieces and nephews.

He took her up to her room when they reached the house after instructing a footman in the hall to have a hot drink and some laudanum sent up to Miss Mangan.

"You will throw them into consternation in the kitchen," she said. "I do not have maid service."

Fury knifed into him again. "Well, then," he said, having taken her to her room and into her room, despite her look of surprised inquiry, "I will perform one service of a maid for you myself. Hand me a brush. Your hair looks rather like a bush after a severe wind storm."

"What gallantry," she said, but her eyes looked wary.

"Sit down," he instructed her, gesturing her to the stool before a dressing table mirror. He drew out the remaining pins from her hair and began to brush it, teasing the brush through the tangles at first. He kept brushing even when her hair was smooth. He could remember doing the same for his mother numerous times as a boy. She had suffered from bad headaches and had always claimed that it was soothing to have someone draw a brush through her hair.

Patricia Mangan had beautiful hair, he noticed. Thick and wavy and shining and waist-length and actually more blond than brown. The style she normally wore it in was doubtless her aunt's idea. Though perhaps at the parsonage too she had been advised to tame its wantonness.

The hot tea and the laudanum were a long time coming. Flossie gawked when she came flouncing in with them. She left with considerably more respect in her step and with a shiny half sovereign in her pocket.

"I really do not need the laudanum," Patricia said, rising from the stool and turning to him a face that was blushing charmingly.

"But you will take it," he said. "And you will lock your door after I have left and rest. You will refuse to be roused for the rest of the day. Will that give you time enough to recover?"

She nodded.

"I shall take my leave of you, then, little bird," he said.

It was something he did by instinct, without the medium of thought. Something he might have done to a sister who had been hurt and whom he had comforted. He cupped her face with his hands, pushing his fingers into the silkiness of her hair, and lowered his head to touch his lips to hers.

Except that with a sister he would have raised his

head after the merest touch, not lingered there, feeling the trembling of her lips beneath his own.

Except that a sister would not have looked at him afterward with huge unblinking eyes.

Except that with a sister he would not have stood outside her closed door a few moments later, gulping air, waiting for his knees to reform themselves beneath him so that they might assist his legs in getting him to his own room.

A stupid thing to have done, he told himself. Remarkably stupid.

Life for the next week was not as bad as it might have been. Patricia guessed that her aunt was embarrassed by the memory of her outburst at the picnic—it would doubtless appear ungenteel to her. And so she said nothing to her niece about it. Patricia was left alone to sleep for the rest of that day, and in the days to come she became her aunt's quiet shadow once more.

No one else paid her any attention with the exception perhaps of Mr. Ware, who went out of his way to avoid her. Not even Mr. Bancroft took any notice of her, for which fact she was profoundly thankful. She was very much afraid for the first day or two that he might make a public scene, demanding that her aunt apologize to her or something horribly mortifying like that.

On the contrary. He appeared to redouble his attentions to Nancy and Mrs. Peabody, sending them into a positive flutter of expectation. If he was still carrying on with Lady Myron or Mrs. Hunter or Mrs. Delaney, there were no outward signs of it during the days following the picnic. He seemed to have put all else aside in order to concentrate on bringing his courtship to happy fruition.

Patricia refused to allow herself to mourn. He had been kind to her. Yes, amazingly for such a man, he had been. And when he had taken her face in his hands and kissed her lips—no man had done that since Patrick had smacked heartily at them the night before he left to join his regiment—he had been giving comfort as if to a child or a younger sister.

Oh, yes, she had no illusions. And so there was no point at all in allowing herself to become heartsick. That she loved him was her own foolishness. It was something she would not fight, because she knew it was something she would keep with her for a long time to come, and his kiss was something she could relive perhaps for the rest of her days. But she would not allow it to upset the quiet equilibrium of her days.

Something else did that. She had a reply from the parson at home. He wished he had known sooner of her interest in teaching the schoolchildren. He had recommended the hiring of a teacher just two months ago, and one had begun her duties just last month. He remembered Miss Mangan with fondness and wished her happiness and God's blessings on her future.

Oh, yes, it upset her. She had counted upon this new idea of hers so much. She had dreamed of the escape it would bring her and the independence and sense of worth and self-respect. But she would not give up. Now that she had thought seriously of taking employment, she was not going to crawl back into her shell. She would try again—somehow. Perhaps her uncle would help her. He was quiet and totally dominated by his wife, but he was a sensible and a kindly man, she believed. Perhaps he would know how she might come by employment. She would ask him after the guests had gone home.

And then there was the other upset, the one she had thought herself fully prepared for. The betrothal. Nancy to Mr. Bancroft.

Patricia was in the drawing room after dinner two evenings before the party was to end, though she had not been at dinner. There was no space for her at the dining room table while their guests were with them, she had been told three weeks ago. But she had a function in the drawing room. She was seated behind the tea tray, pouring tea.

When the gentlemen joined the ladies after their port, Mr. Bancroft made his way immediately to Nancy's side and proceeded with the customary gallantries. Patricia, as usual, insisted upon feeling only amused at what she heard. And then, when Mrs. Peabody had joined them and when somehow he had gathered about them almost all the ladies—Patricia had the strange impression that he had maneuvered it so, though she did not know how he had done it—he took Nancy's hand in his, raised it to his lips, and gazed with warm intensity into her eyes as he spoke.

"I have asked for and been granted a private interview with your father tomorrow morning, Miss Peabody," he said. "I doubt I shall have a wink of sleep tonight, such is the anxiety of my heart. It is my fondest hope that by this time tomorrow I will be the happiest of men."

Nancy knew just how to behave. She blushed very prettily, lowered her eyes, opened her fan and fluttered it before her heated face, and answered in a voice that was little more than a whisper—but since everyone was hushed, it carried to the farthest corner of the room.

"I do not know what can be so important that you

must speak to Papa in private, sir," she said. She allowed herself a peep upward. "But you deserve to be happy, I am sure."

He was returning her hand to his lips when Patricia decided she could be of no further use behind the tea tray. Everyone had been served with a first cup, but someone else must pour the second. With the present steadiness of her hands—or lack thereof—she would doubtless fill the saucers as well as the cups. She slipped quietly from the room.

And lay fully clothed on top of her bedcovers for long hours into the night, staring upward at the canopy, a pillow clasped in her arms.

He had coldly plotted his revenge. No, perhaps not quite coldly. It had never been his way to hurt anyone more than that person deserved to be hurt, though he had never pretended to be either a considerate or a compassionate man. His first idea would have brought too great a humiliation to someone whom he had intended only to embarrass. His desire was to punish the mother, not the daughter.

Until the daughter gave him good cause to be added to his black list, that was.

No one at the dinner table the evening after the picnic mentioned the incident that had happened there. He guessed that the memory of it was an embarrassment to all of them. Indeed, conversation seemed somewhat strained and over-hearty. Calling even a servant a slut in public and slapping her face hard enough to cause swelling was not considered genteel behavior among members of the *ton*.

He took Nancy Peabody for a stroll out on the terrace after dinner, as he often did.

"Did you hear what happened after you were forced to return to the house with a nosebleed, sir?" she asked him.

"Did I miss something?" he asked. "Beyond a precious hour of your company, that is?"

"Oh, that." She tittered. "I am sure you must have seen more than enough of me in the past few weeks, sir."

He returned the expected answer.

And then she proceeded to tell him about the breaking of the wine bottles. His little bird, it seemed, had been sent to lift down the wine basket from the wagon. It must have weighed as much as she did. And she had dropped it after summoning Mr. Ware and demanding that he carry it for her—and then had tried to put the blame on him. Poor Mr. Ware, like the gentleman he was, had been quite prepared to accept responsibility.

"And then when Mama tried to reprimand her gently and smooth over the situation," Miss Peabody said to his interested ears, "she was impertinent and Mama was forced to be quite sharp with her and send her back to the house. Poor Mama. It quite spoiled her afternoon. And mine too, sir, you may be sure. You would not believe all Mama and I have done for Patricia. Mama has been a second mother to her, and I have been a sister to her despite the fact that her own mama was nothing more than the daughter of a curate who was hardly even a gentleman. But she has returned nothing for all our kindness except sullenness and sometimes open impertinence. Mama is a veritable saint for putting up with her."

"And you too, Miss Peabody," he said, patting the arm that was resting on his. "There are not many young ladies who would watch another taken to the bosom of their mama without losing the sweetness of their disposition as a result."

"Oh, well." She tittered. "It is not in my nature to feel jealousy, sir. And one must be charitable to indigent relatives."

He led the conversation into more congenial channels, and they talked about her for the remaining ten minutes of their stroll on the terrace.

He gave her a second chance. Two days later, they all went to church in the morning. He took Nancy up to ride beside him in his curricle. They drove the mile home from church in a slow cavalcade, his curricle behind the barouche that carried Mr. and Mrs. Peabody, Patricia, and Mrs. Delaney.

"I see," he said, "that your cousin has been forgiven and taken back to your mother's bosom."

Patricia Mangan had been granted the honor of carrying Mrs. Peabody's parasol and her prayer book.

"Oh, yes," Nancy said, tossing her head so that the feather on her bonnet nodded appealingly. "Mama is too forgiving by half."

"And you are not?" he asked, looking at her with raised eyebrows.

She perceived her mistake immediately. "Oh, yes." She laughed. "To my shame I must confess to an excess of sensibility, sir. I am even more tender-hearted than Mama—or so Papa always tells me. But she ought not to have been forgiven, you see. By her carelessness she smashed a dozen bottles of Papa's best wine and twenty of the finest crystal glasses. And she did not even apologize or shed a single tear. She has never shown any gratitude at all for all we have done for her. I hate ingratitude more than almost any other vice, sir."

"It is disturbing to know that some of our acts of charity go unobserved and unappreciated by those whose sole function in life should be to make us feel good about ourselves," he murmured soothingly.

"Yes." She looked dubious, as if she had not quite grasped his meaning. "I believe she should have been turned off, sir."

"Even though she has nothing else to go to?" he said.

"Well, that is her problem, is it not?" she said.

"Even if she was to end up on the open road with nowhere to go?" he said. "Or in the nearest town with nothing to do and nothing to sell except . . . Well, what I was about to say is not for such delicate ears as yours. And of course, you would not really turn her off, would you? You were merely telling me what you would do if you did not have such a tender heart."

She sighed. "You are right, sir," she said. "Papa says he does not know how I will manage servants of my own when I find it impossible even to think of disciplining them when they break things or do not do things as they ought to be done."

Mr. Bancroft turned the conversation again. But he had heard what he needed to hear and what he had fully expected to hear. He had given her two chances and she had squandered both.

He plotted his revenge quite coldly. All his attention was concentrated upon it for the remaining days of his stay at Holly House. He lost interest in all else. He terminated his affair with Lady Myron with one pretty speech and neglected to develop the affair with Mrs. Hunter that had had such an extremely promising beginning. His nights were spent alone. He did not sleep a great deal more than he had done during the first two weeks of his stay—though he doubtless expended a great deal less energy—but at least he was alone. He tended to spend many hours of each night lying on his back with his hands clasped beneath his head, thinking. And reliving a certain kiss, which had been easily the least lascivious he had ever given, even as a green boy.

His plot approached its culmination two nights before the guests were to leave Holly House. After the ladies had left the dinner table and after the gentlemen had drunk their port and risen and stretched and decided that the moment of rejoining the ladies could be postponed no longer, he spoke quietly to Mr. Peabody, asking if he might have a private word with that gentleman the next morning on a matter of some importance.

And then he proceeded to the drawing room to tell Miss Nancy Peabody about his hopes and anxieties, though with the skill of long practice he succeeded in gathering about him almost all the ladies before he began to speak and soon enough all the gentlemen were listening too.

It had been well done, he thought in self-congratulation as the evening proceeded. And tomorrow would come the denouement. There was only one part of it that he was unsure about—totally unsure.

And so he had a largely sleepless night again.

He had noticed her slipping from the drawing room, unseen and unlamented by everyone. No, not by everyone. And even Mrs. Peabody missed her when guests had talked up the thirst for second cups of tea and there was no little shadow seated behind the tray to pour them.

Well, tomorrow, he thought with grim satisfaction, his hands clasped behind his head. Ah, yes, tomorrow. But his heart thumped with unaccustomed nervousness when he thought about part of tomorrow.

All the ladies were gathered in the salon by late morning. All of them without exception. Even Mrs. Delaney, Lady Myron, and Mrs. Hunter were there, and even those ladies who usually slept until noon and then spent another hour or two in their dressing rooms with their maids.

The air positively pulsed with excited expectation. Mr. Bancroft had been closeted in the library with Mr. Peabody since shortly after breakfast. Nancy and Mrs. Peabody had explained to everybody who had been unfortunate enough not to witness it for themselves—though in fact there was no such person, except Patricia—that before leaving the breakfast room Mr. Bancroft had bowed over Nancy's hand again and lifted it to his lips again and gazed at her with adoring eyes—the adjective was supplied by Mrs. Peabody, Nancy being too modest to use it herself—and murmured to her that he had one hour of excruciating anxiety to live through before putting the question to *some lady*—he had emphasized the words, not naming her—the answer to which would determine the happiness or misery of the whole of the rest of his life.

Nancy was becomingly flushed. Her eyes shone. She looked about her with slightly elevated nose as if she pitied all the other lesser mortals who were not about to receive an offer from Mr. Bancroft. She was dressed in her very best muslin, though it was still only morning, and her hair was a glorious and intricate mass of carefully constructed ringlets and curls.

She looked, Susan declared, faint envy in her voice, like a princess.

They all waited for the moment when the door would open and someone—surely the butler himself and not a mere footman—would summon Nancy to the library to receive the addresses of her beau.

Patricia sat quietly on her chair just behind Mrs. Peabody's, thinking determinedly about her own planned talk with her uncle during the afternoon if in all the excitement she could get him alone. She was going to ask him if he knew how she would go about applying for employment as a governess or schoolteacher.

And then the door handle was heard to turn and all the ladies fell instantly silent and turned toward the door, awaiting the summons. Nancy sprang to her feet, her hands clasped to her bosom. Mrs. Peabody smiled graciously about at her gathered guests.

It was neither a footman nor the butler who opened the door and stood in the doorway for a moment, looking impossibly handsome and elegant, before proceeding inside the room. It was Mr. Bancroft himself. Nancy's lips parted and she leaned a little toward him. Mrs. Peabody clasped her own hands to her bosom.

"Ma'am," Mr. Bancroft said, proceeding across the carpet toward Mrs. Peabody, smiling at her, and then turning his gaze on Nancy, "my meeting with Mr. Peabody has been brought to a successful and happy conclusion. It seems that at least some of the anxieties that kept me awake and pacing last night have been laid to rest."

Mrs. Peabody sighed. "Of course, my dear sir," she said. "Mr. Peabody has never been a difficult man with whom to deal. He would certainly not find it difficult to deal with a future baron."

But his eyes were upon Nancy, devouring her. "Miss Peabody," he said, "may I be permitted to compliment you on your appearance this morning? Your taste in dress is, as always, exquisite. But as always the loveliness of your person quite outshines the finest muslin."

"Oh, sir." Nancy's eyes were directed quite firmly on the floor.

"And so." Mrs. Peabody's voice had become hearty. "You will be wishing to step into another room or perhaps outside—"

"Outside, with your permission, ma'am," Mr. Bancroft said with a bow. "It is a lovely day for a lovely lady and for what I hope will be a lovely conversation."

"And you have a lovely way with words, sir," Mrs. Peabody said regally. "You will wish to step outside, then, with my—"

"Yes, ma'am," he said, smiling his most dazzling and charming smile. "With your niece, if you please."

Mrs. Peabody's mouth hung open inelegantly. Nancy did a fair imitation of a statue. So did all the other ladies. Patricia's head snapped up and all the blood drained out of it at the same moment. Mr. Bancroft continued to smile at his hostess.

"With my—?" she asked faintly.

"With your *niece*, ma'am," he said, transferring his gaze and his smile to Patricia. "With Miss Mangan. I have your husband's permission."

"With—Patricia?" Mrs. Peabody stared at him in disbelief.

"Thank you, ma'am," he said, bowing to her once

more and stretching out a hand toward Patricia. "Miss Mangan, will you honor me with your company for a stroll outside?"

She merely stared at him, quite as dumbfounded as everyone else until his eyes warmed and one eyelid closed in a slow half wink. And she understood in a flash. She understood what he had done and was doing and why.

The—oh, the *precious rogue*!

She got to her feet and, when he stepped close enough, placed her hand in his. Her own was icy, she realized when she felt the warmth of his.

"Thank you, sir," she said, allowing him to place her hand on his sleeve and lead her from the room, in which a pin might have been heard crashing to the carpet.

It was, Patricia decided, quite the most delicious moment of her life.

It had worked beautifully. He had feared that perhaps she would not be in the salon with the other ladies, that perhaps she would have to be sent for. That would have spoiled the drama of the moment a little. But she had been there and everything had proceeded according to plan, almost as if he had written the script and all the players had learned their lines and actions to perfection.

And here she was, tripping along at his side, the top of her head reaching barely to his chin. His little bird, who had kept him awake for a weekful of nights, though not in the usual way.

"To the lily pond?" he suggested when they were outside the house and down the marble steps. "It seems the appropriate place to go, does it not?"

"To the lily pond." She smiled up at him, tying his

stomach in unfamiliar knots. No one had told him that when she smiled she was pretty even by objective standards. Not that he could really see her by objective standards any longer.

He had expected her to be quiet, serious, wary. Puzzled. Reluctant to come with him. But she was still tripping along.

"Well, little bird," he said, "did you like it? Was it appropriate?" He did not expect her to understand his meaning. He thought he would have to explain.

"It was quite the most fiendish scheme I have ever been a witness to," she said. "It was cruel in the extreme. You will certainly fry for this one, sir. They are going to have to construct a particularly fiery corner for you in hell. I *loved* it."

He chuckled. "Did you?" he said. "I expected that after I had confessed all to you, you would lash out at me with both sharp edges of your tongue. Have I pleased you, Patricia?"

She darted a startled look up at him. "Yes," she said. "Thank you. Doubtless my life here will be made a misery once I have returned to the house and once you have gone on your way tomorrow, but it will be worth every moment. Perhaps I am cruel too, because undoubtedly Nancy will suffer dreadful mortification, but I cannot help feeling spiteful and glad. And I will not have to suffer for long. Soon I will be leaving here to teach."

"Will you?" They were among the trees already, and he was parting branches for her so that her face and arms would not be grazed. "You have heard from the parson who has your father's living?"

He watched her hesitate and then smile. "Someone else has that appointment already," she said. "But it will be better to go somewhere new anyway. My uncle is going to help me find something. It will not take long, I think. I am looking forward to it."

They were at the lily pond, and he gestured for her to sit down before seating himself close beside her.

"Are you?" he said. "I am disappointed."

She turned her head to look at him.

"It was common knowledge why I went to talk to your uncle this morning," he said.

She smiled with bright mischief. "What did you talk to him about?" she asked. "You certainly deceived everyone quite spectacularly."

"I went to talk about a marriage contract," he said.

"Oh." Her smile faded. "I see. I misunderstood. You are merely teasing her, then. Punishing her for a little while. You will ask her later today or tomorrow. Well . . . Well, it is good enough. It still felt good."

"Little bird." He took one of her hands in his and held it tightly. His heart was thumping like a hammer. This was the part he had been unsure about. He was still unsure. "It was you I talked to your uncle about. It is you I intended—and have intended for all of the past week—to ask to marry me."

She stared into his eyes, her own huge. Was she trying to drown him? She was succeeding.

"Will you?" he asked. "I can think of every reason in the world why you would say no, but I must ask anyway. Will you marry me, Patricia?"

"Why?" He saw her lips form the word though he heard no sound.

"Because I love you, little bird," he said. "Because you flew down into my heart from the branch up there that first afternoon I saw you, and have lodged in my heart ever since. Because you have wrecked the life

with which I have been quite contented for the past
ten years and have got me to thinking of constancy
and a permanent home and a garden and cats and
dogs. And babies, my love. And you, darling."

"You feel you owe it to me," she said. "You think
this is the best way to spite them. And you feel sorry
for me. You don't need—"

He dipped his head and kissed her. And brought
one hand behind her head to hold it steady while he
did it more thoroughly, parting his lips over hers, lick-
ing them and teasing his tongue through to the flesh
within.

"And you are a rake," she said.

"Guilty," he said. "But past tense, not present or
future, my love. I don't know how I can be sure of
that, and I certainly don't know how I can convince
you that I am. But I know it is true. I know it *here*,
darling." He held his free hand over his heart. "I will
be a model husband, as reformed rakes are reputed
to be, I believe. Or so someone once told me."

He kissed her again. And coaxed her backward to
the ground so that he could do so without having to
hold her head steady. Her arms came about him as
he slid his tongue past her teeth into her mouth.

"I have not a farthing to my name," she said, twisting her face away from his after a heady couple of
minutes. "You have to marry money because you have
squandered your own fortune."

"Tut," he said. "Where did you hear such a mali-
cious rumor, little bird? It is one I put about myself
quite deliberately at regular intervals in order to dis-
courage fortune-seeking mamas. On this occasion it
seemed to work the other way, I must admit. I believe
your aunt expected to have more power over a poor

man than she would have had over one who was independently wealthy."

"You are not poor?" she whispered.

"Not at all," he said. "Gambling has never been one of my vices, my love, though almost everything else you might name has. Will you marry me now that you know I am almost indecently wealthy?"

"But I am not," she said.

He kissed her again—her mouth, her eyes, her temples, her chin, her throat. He touched her breasts through the cotton of her dress and found them small but firm and well shaped. Perfect for his babies—and for his own delight.

"I cannot," she said, pushing first his hands away and then his face. "I do not know—"

"I will teach you," he said. "It will be my joy to teach you, Patricia. Little bird, I have not slept in a week, fearful that you would say no, knowing that I am unworthy of you, knowing that I have nothing to offer you but security and a fortune and my love. I am not going to let you say no. I was going to be very noble and honorable about it, but I have changed my mind. I am going to use all my expertise on you here, or as much of it as becomes necessary until you are mindless enough to say yes. Say yes now so that I will not have to live with guilt afterward. Why are you laughing?"

Gloriously, wonderfully, she was laughing up at him. Giggling up at him, her arms about his neck.

"You lifted me down from that tree without waiting for my permission to do so," she said. "And you took me home from the picnic last week with only the choice of whether I would go on your arm or over your shoulder. Why change things now? Why wait for my acceptance? You might as well marry me and be done with it."

He was sure of her suddenly. All anxiety fled, leaving not a trace behind. He grinned down at her. "Parsons can be sticky customers, though, little bird," he said. "They wait to hear the bride say yes and will not proceed with the marriage service until she has done so. Unreasonable of them, I always say, but that is the reality. Are you going to say yes when he asks?"

Her eyes were huge again. "Are you quite, quite sure, sir—Mr. Bancroft?" she asked.

"Josh," he said. "It is my name, you know. Joshua. My father was rather fond of the Bible. My sisters are Miriam and Hagar."

"Joshua," she whispered.

"Or darling for short," he said, grinning at her again. "As with Patricia. Little bird for short. Will you marry me?"

"If you are quite, quite sure," she said.

"I am quite, quite sure," he said against her lips. "Will you?"

"Yes," she whispered. "Joshua. Darling."

"And three words more, if you please, little bird," he said, closing his eyes and brushing his lips lightly over hers. "I have said them to you already."

"You precious rogue," she said out loud.

He threw back his head and shouted with laughter. "Well," he said, looking appreciatively down at her, "you have asked for it now. I am going to have to live up to your expectations, am I not?"

"Yes, please, Joshua," she said.

"Starting now?" He smiled tenderly at her.

"If you please, sir," she said.

"Starting now, then," he said, lowering his head.

Sweet Revenge

❦

by Melinda McRae

1

Yorkshire, England, 1822

David North, the ninth Viscount Denby, leaned back against the cushions of his elegant traveling coach, a self-satisfied smile on his face. He had waited so long, never dreaming he would have the chance to carry out the revenge he'd yearned for. But fate had intervened in his favor—fate, and a particularly tricky fence in Yorkshire.

Jonathan Ridgefield had been dead two years now, and his lovely lady had finally emerged from her mourning to take up her life again.

And David would have his revenge on her at last.

Fifteen years had not dimmed his pain and anger. The wound she'd inflicted was still as deep as it had been on that cold December day long ago, when he'd come home from Spain and found Chloe wed to his cousin. David had been reported missing, was presumed dead, but in his mind, if Chloe loved him, she would have waited until she knew for certain.

Instead of the warm homecoming he'd anticipated, David found only pain and torment. He hadn't exchanged more than a few words with either his cousin or Chloe over the intervening years.

79

But the time for revenge was here at last. Chloe was a widow now, and David would make certain that she'd rue the day that she'd chosen the wrong cousin.

The trees cast long shadows across the lawn by the time the coach pulled up in front of the red brick Elizabethan house belonging to his brother-in-law, Baron Tavistone. David jumped from the coach and dashed up the stairs, leaving the footmen and his valet to struggle with the luggage. Surprise was critical to his plan. If his sister suspected why he was here, even the birthday present he'd bought wouldn't mollify her.

As he'd hoped, Georgiana was resting in her rooms before dinner. Tossing his hat and gloves to a waiting footman, David continued up the stairs to his sister's room. Halting at the door, he made certain Georgie's gift was still in his pocket. A woman would overlook any number of sins for a piece of fine jewelry.

He rapped softly on the door and entered at her invitation.

"Happy birthday, sis."

Georgiana, Lady Tavistone, stared at him, mouth agape. "David! Whatever are you doing here?"

David shut the door behind him. "I've come to celebrate your birthday, why else?" He looked at her with narrowed eyes. "Are you really certain you are eight-and-twenty? You barely look half that to me."

"Oh, David." Georgiana launched herself at him so quickly he barely had time to open his arms to her. "I would have sent you an invitation, but I didn't think you'd come." She stepped back and gave him a reproachful look. "You didn't go home for Christmas, after all. Or come for my birthday last year. Or the year before that."

David laughed. "We will be here for days if you

plan to list all my sins. I know I've been a miserable brother, and you can have my head later. But first let me give you this." He reached into his pocket and handed her a small box. She eagerly tore off the lid, then squealed with delight.

"Diamonds! Oh, David, you didn't!"

He shook his head ruefully. "I'm afraid I did."

"Harry will be positively green." She clapped a hand to her mouth. "But you can't! I told everyone not to bring any presents."

"Then I'll just have to take them back." He grabbed for the box, but she jerked it away.

"Don't be silly." She took out the diamond earrings and fastened them to her ears, darting to the dressing table to admire their reflection in the mirror.

David stepped up behind her. "I thought these would make up for my shortcomings as a brother."

"You beast." She looked at him with a knowing expression. "Now tell me, why are you really here?"

He sat in one of her overstuffed chairs, stretching out his long legs before him. "Frankly, Georgie, I was bored."

She laughed. "And you think you won't be here? You, the man who said Harry was so dull he could make the dead yawn?"

David smiled sheepishly. "I was cross at the time."

"If you're bored, you must have given that raven-haired dancer her congé. I warn you, don't you dare try your flirtations on Mrs. Mitchell's daughters. They're much too young for you."

"I didn't come here to flirt. I only thought it was time that I should show a little more familial devotion."

She wagged a finger at him. "You're up to something, I know it. I'll figure it out eventually." She spotted the clock on the dresser table. "Goodness! We both need to dress for dinner. You are going to spoil all my numbers at the table. Why *didn't* you tell me you were coming?"

David grinned. "And ruin the surprise? I can eat in my room if you wish."

"No, no, you will eat with us. But you will have to suffer with the room up the half stairs—it's the only one unoccupied."

"I shall endure the insult."

She stood on tiptoes and kissed his cheek. "I am so glad you are here, David."

"Me, too."

She pushed him toward the door. "Now, go. We can talk more later."

"As bossy as always," he said, but smiled.

"David?"

Turning, he saw the apprehension in her eyes.

"Chloe's here."

He did not try to mask his grin of pleasure. "Chloe is here? How delightful. I thought she was still in mourning."

"I convinced her that it had gone on long enough. Please do be nice to her, David. She needs to smile again."

"I'll do what I can to cheer her up."

He sauntered down the hall toward his room.

That had gone better than he expected. Georgiana was suspicious, but for all the wrong reasons. She'd begged him to do exactly what he came here for. He'd be more than willing to accommodate her request.

Sisters could be downright useful at times.

* * *

Chloe Ridgefield sat patiently while Georgie's dresser patted the last curl of the new coiffure into place.

"Doesn't that look nice, ma'am?"

She examined the reflection in the mirror, startled by her unfamiliar appearance. Those cascading curls made her look elegant, sophisticated—not at all like she felt.

"Do you think it is too . . . fashionable?"

"Nothing wrong with being fashionable," Hutchins sniffed.

Except it is wasted on me, Chloe thought. She smiled with a pleasure she did not feel. "Thank you, Hutchins, it is lovely. Georgie herself will not even recognize me."

Hutchins curtsied and departed.

Hastily, Chloe took another peek at herself in the mirror. Perhaps it was an omen, this unexpected gesture of support from Georgiana. In the last few months, Chloe had been plagued with a growing sense of restlessness, the feeling that her life was about to change for the better.

Not that she could complain about her situation. Jonathan's family had been more than kind to her after his death—too kind, in fact. Chloe knew she was an awkward presence in the house, a reminder of the beloved son and brother who was gone. If only there had been a child, a son of their own. Then she would have a role to play as mother of the heir. But now she was merely "poor Chloe," another family obligation to deal with.

She almost wished they were cruel to her, so she could justify leaving. Yet the mere mention of her desire for a home of her own was met with hurt and reproachful glances. She'd be "poor Chloe" until they carried her out of the house to her final rest.

At least Georgie had not forgotten her. Although

it was dismal to think that these cozy gatherings were all she had to look forward to.

Yet as she descended the stairs after the dinner bell sounded, Chloe could not shake the overwhelming sensation that something momentous was about to happen.

Harry, Lord Tavistone, greeted her in the hall. "My, don't we look fetching tonight." He gave her a broad wink. "Georgie will be green with envy."

Chloe laughed lightly. "As it was Georgie who insisted Hutchins do my hair, I don't think it will come as a great surprise." She took his arm as he led her into the drawing room.

Harry came to a sudden halt in the doorway. "Good God!"

"What?"

"Denby's here! I don't believe it."

Chloe was glad she still had hold of Harry's arm, because for a sickening moment she thought her knees would collapse beneath her. *David was here.*

David. In childhood they had been inseparable: she, David, and his cousin, Jonathan. Then she and David fell in love. Knowing her parents would not favor a match with a rebellious second son, David went to Spain to win fame and glory. Instead, he lost his life, or so she thought. Inconsolable with grief, Chloe offered no resistance when her father suggested she marry Jonathan. She wed him in a dim haze, clinging to him as her one remaining tie with David.

Then David returned—alive. Her whole world collapsed and nothing was ever the same again. David behaved as if she and Jonathan did not exist.

Now they were both here to celebrate Georgie's

birthday—a situation fraught with peril. She hoped, for Georgie's sake, that he would be civil to her.

"Why should David's presence be such a surprise?" she asked Harry, amazed at the calmness in her voice. "It is Georgie's birthday—and he is her brother."

Harry laughed. "Denby is the last person on earth to bow to family obligation. I better find out why he's come."

Chloe held his arm firmly as they crossed the floor. Dread and longing warred within her. She wanted to talk with him, wanted to smile and joke and act as if they were still friends. Yet she feared what he would say to her—if he even deigned to speak with her. She could not forget his last, bitter words to her.

For a moment her step faltered and Chloe tried to pull away from Harry, but it was too late. He called out in greeting, and David glanced their way, his dark eyes widening in surprise as he caught sight of her. Brushing past the other guests, he came toward them with hurried steps, a surprised smile on his face.

He halted before her. "Hello, Chloe."

She nodded politely. "David."

He took her hand and brought it to his lips. "I was delighted when Georgie said you would be here."

Chloe stood mutely, uncertain what to say. Once, talking with David had been easy. But that had been long ago. The man who stood before her was more stranger than friend. A stranger who had every reason to be angry with her.

Harry finally broke the uneasy silence. "Your being here is a surprise, Denby. Georgie didn't say a word."

David grinned lightly. "That's because Georgie didn't know I was coming. A birthday surprise."

Chuckling, Harry slapped his brother-in-law on the

back. "Trust you to come up with the ultimate present. Georgie's no doubt pleased as punch."

Chloe watched the two men, noting the striking contrast between Georgie's placid husband and David's barely suppressed energy. He was tall, lean, and still indescribably handsome, very much like the youth she'd known so well. Yet there was no ignoring the hardness of his gaze, the cynical twist of his lips. Even if Georgie had not kept her informed of all the scandalous gossip, Chloe would have known David had changed.

With a parting remark, Harry darted away. Chloe toyed with the fastening of her glove. Was David as tense as she? She tried to think of something to say, to ease the awkwardness.

"You are looking well."

David laughed. "You mean my dissolute lifestyle has not yet ravaged my body."

She smothered a smile. "I doubt you are responsible for half the exploits to your credit."

"Dear Chloe, always rising to my defense. You are such a *good* friend." He squeezed her fingers and his expression softened. "I wish I could have been there, Chloe. For the funeral. I know I wrote, but it seemed so inadequate—and so late."

"You were out of the country. I understood."

"Chloe!" Georgiana's voice rang out as she approached. "You look marvelous. I knew that hairstyle would be lovely on you." She turned to her brother. "Don't you agree?"

He nodded. "Indeed. Like my dear sister, Chloe seems to grow lovelier with each passing year."

Georgiana slapped his arm playfully with her fan.

"Isn't he a beast? I think he came here just to remind me I've added another year."

David bowed gallantly. "You will still look lovely at five-and-sixty."

Georgiana made a moue of distaste. "God forbid that I live so long." She turned about as the butler announced dinner. "David, will you partner Chloe? I intended Harry to take her in, but she deserves a more dashing escort."

He smiled warmly. "It would be a pleasure." He held out his arm to Chloe.

A strange sense of calm descended upon her as she walked beside him. These few moments had gone well. David seemed more than amiable. Was it possible he had forgiven her? Could they heal the rupture between them?

Thank goodness Georgie had invited her here.

After seating Chloe, David took his own chair and leaned toward her, his mouth only inches from her ear. "I am relived to be back in Georgie's good graces. I upset all her plans by arriving unannounced."

"A justifiable complaint on her part."

"Ah, but she was mollified by the present I brought her." He nodded toward the gems glittering in his sister's ears. "Not even Georgie can resist a new pair of eardrops."

Chloe laughed lightly. "You always were very good at atoning for your mistakes. I remember the time you broke the arm off my doll, and presented me with your rock collection as compensation."

He looked sheepish. "The practice stayed with me, I'm afraid. Except now my offerings are more expensive."

After taking a sip of wine, David shot her a sidelong glance. "How is your father-in-law?"

A shadow crossed Chloe's face. "The earl declines daily. I fear he will not last much longer."

David felt little emotion at the news; he barely knew his uncle. It was Jonathan's death that had mattered. Chloe would never be a countess now. But the dashing of her ambitions wasn't enough for David. He wouldn't be satisfied until he claimed his full revenge.

It would not be long now. . . .

He played the attentive escort throughout dinner, virtually ignoring the lady on his other side. Social niceties rarely concerned him. And as an *old* friend of Chloe's his rudeness could almost be excused.

She was even more lovely than he remembered. It had been four—no, closer to five—years since he'd seen her last. Only a slightly crinkling about the corners of her sparkling blue eyes gave a hint to the passing of time. Her hair was just as he remembered it, a froth of golden honey, thick and silky.

Despite Georgie's enthusiasm, David didn't like the way Chloe'd fixed her hair. Her elegant bearing demanded simplicity, not those fussy curls. But perhaps he only thought so because in his mind's eye, she was still frozen in time at the age of seventeen, with her hair unpinned and a bewitching smile on her face.

A *treacherous* smile, he corrected himself. The smile of a woman who professed to love one man, then wed another.

Well, he would have the last laugh.

He'd never dreamed it would be this easy. First Georgie insisted that he look after Chloe; now Chloe acted as if she was genuinely glad to see him. That was the real triumph—he'd feared he would have to spend a great deal of effort regaining her confidence. Chloe's willingness to think the best of everyone was a big point in his favor.

She'd never guess his attentive interest had an ulterior purpose until it was too late. He'd be more than happy to encourage the resumption of their "friendship," waiting patiently until the moment came when he could trample it underfoot.

Just as she had done all those years ago.

He turned to Chloe and smiled warmly. "More wine?" She nodded and he signaled the footman, then glanced down the table at his sister.

"Georgie, I see you still set an impressive table," he commented. "I vow I have not eaten half so well in years."

"If you stayed in England, dear brother, you would probably eat better. Lord knows what strange things they offer as food in some of the places you've been."

His eyes brightened mischievously. "Shall I tell you?"

Georgie gave a mock shudder. "Please don't."

Turning to Chloe, he winked. "Curiosity will eventually get the best of her—mark my words."

"I should like to hear of your travels," Chloe said shyly.

David grinned. "I'd like to tell you about them—when we find ourselves in a more comfortable setting."

Following dessert, the ladies excused themselves and retreated to the drawing room. As they walked across the hall, Georgie took Chloe's arm in hers.

"You and David seemed to get along well at dinner."

Chloe smiled wistfully. "He didn't pull my hair or call me brat once."

"I hope he's outgrown that stage by now. Tell me what he said."

"Oh, nothing significant." Chloe stopped suddenly and looked at her friend. "Do you think he's changed so terribly much, Georgie? One minute he seems like the David of old, but at other times . . . there's a coldness to him that was never there before."

"Better that than his deplorable wild streak. Do you remember when he was sent down from Cambridge? Oh, how Papa went on and on about that . . . It's a miracle David left for the army or I think they would have come to blows."

"I am glad to see him." And to her surprise, she was. There was an awkwardness between them still, but Chloe sensed it would fade in time. Would she then have the old David back at last?

She truly had not realized how much she missed him until this moment.

"Yes," Georgie was saying. "You three were quite the trio—David, Jonathan, and Chloe."

"You were there too," Chloe reminded her.

Georgie laughed. "Oh, I was no more than a very detested hanger-on. You three were the friends. How I envied you all."

"Now the tables are turned," said Chloe with a shaky laugh. "Do you think this time David will follow us about, begging to join in on our fun?"

Georgie shot her a disbelieving glance, and they both broke into laughter.

Pleased by his early success, David made no pretense of disguising his interest in Chloe. The moment the men entered the drawing room, he was at her side. It was time to continue his campaign.

"The moon is out and the air is warm. Would you like to take a stroll?"

Chloe smiled at him. "I should indeed. Let me get my shawl."

She met him in the hall and they went out into the garden, walking between the neatly trimmed boxwood hedges edging the flower beds.

"There is nothing better than a warm summer night in England." He leaned against the gate, arms folded across his chest. "I always forget how much I miss this old island until I return home."

"Nights like this remind me of our midnight fishing expeditions," she said. "I don't think we ever caught anything, but it was such fun."

"Or the time we went rowing on the lake—"

"And nearly drowned me," she added.

"That was Jonathan's fault. When he stood up, you—" David halted suddenly. One didn't seduce a woman by talking about her dead husband. "I'm sorry, Chloe. I didn't mean to mention Jonathan."

She took his arm. "It is all right, David. I'd rather you did talk about him. I don't know why people think one doesn't wish to speak of the dead."

"I don't want to cause you pain."

"I miss him terribly," she said, as they ambled down the path. "But it has been two years since he died. Life must go on." Chloe squeezed his arm. "I am glad you are here, David."

He sighed. "After the way we parted ... It was pride that kept me away. You had Jonathan, after all; neither of you needed me."

She halted suddenly, facing him. "We would have welcomed you, David. You didn't need to stay away."

"It would not have been the same, though, would

it? Perhaps I didn't want to admit that we had all grown up."

Chloe smiled. "Now here we are, almost in our dotage."

"Me perhaps, but not you." He halted and twined a curl of her hair around his finger. "You are still the same lovely girl I remember."

"David, I—"

He put a finger to her lips. "Hush. There is no need to dwell on the past. It is gone—and forgotten. Let us be friends again."

"I should like that," Chloe said.

"Good." He patted her hand and they resumed their stroll.

He'd come here without having the exact form of his revenge planned. He'd only known he was going to do his very best to hurt Chloe. And now, seeing her vulnerability, he knew exactly how he would do it. It would be an even more pleasurable experience than he dared hope.

Bedding Chloe Ridgefield might turn out to be the most satisfying sexual experience of his life. Each moan of pleasure he elicited from her would only heighten his victory.

Chloe was going to be very, very sorry that she had married his cousin.

2

Chloe awoke to bright sunlight streaming through her window, but even a pouring rain could not have dampened her mood this morning.

She and David could talk again. All evening she'd held her breath, fearing that their fragile truce would disintegrate. But he himself had put the past to rest, saying it no longer mattered, that they could be friends again.

For a moment all the intervening days washed away, and it was the summer of her sixteenth birthday. Chloe had been expected to act like a young lady, but that didn't keep her from joining the cousins in their adventures. She'd been quite the hoyden.

Until David had kissed her one day in the folly behind the high-walled garden. In that short instant she realized what she should have already known— that she loved him. Not like the brother he'd almost been, but as a man. The realization stunned her. And he was almost as shocked as she.

And they both knew, for the first time in their lives, that Jonathan was not to be a part of this. Without discussing it, they excluded him from their secret. The entire courtship was a matter of shared glances, shy smiles, knowing winks—and stolen kisses.

Not until David was ready to return to school did they dare to put a name to what had happened. They were in love, deeply, irrevocably, forever. They would be married when David could provide for her—as a younger son he must make his own way.

Yet she did not expect him to choose the army, which only meant further separation. But over her and his family's objections, David bought a commission and prepared to leave for Spain. Chloe pleaded to go with him, but they both knew her parents would not countenance a marriage. With luck and a few promotions, David might be able to care for a wife before too long.

Then, six months later, came the news he was missing and believed dead. Chloe was prostrate with grief.

Only Jonathan brought her any comfort; only with Jonathan could she bear to talk about David. And then, pressured by her parents to make a good match, and grateful for his kindness and understanding, she agreed to marry him. Even then, she knew she didn't love him, couldn't love him the way she'd loved David. It was her greatest guilt that even when she married Jonathan, even when she lay next to him on their wedding night, it was David she thought about, David she longed for.

Then came that horrifying Christmas day when David stormed into the hall, a ghost come alive, demanding to know why she hadn't waited for him. And there was nothing she could say because she knew he was right. She had betrayed him, betrayed their love. She should have known he wasn't dead, known that he would never leave her like that. She had failed him, had been weak when she should have been strong.

David was angry and bitter, as he had every right to be. He returned to Spain, his daring exploits duly reported in the papers. For four long years Chloe dreaded the arrival of the mail, fearing news of his death. Even after she finally reconciled herself to her life with Jonathan, there was a part of her that rejoiced when she learned that Colonel the Honorable David North marched into Paris with the victorious allies.

And by the time David's father and brother were killed in a sailing accident, and he unexpectedly inherited the title, she only faintly recalled his accusing words: "If only you'd waited."

David stood at the window, one arm braced against the frame, gazing out onto the rear lawn.

His dreams had been troubled. Seeing Chloe again had brought memories flooding back with frightening clarity. How he'd adored her, loved her, trusted her. He'd been such a fool ever to trust the words of a woman. But now it was his turn for revenge. She would feel the sharp sting of rejection at last.

Georgie'd planned a picnic lunch down by the lake. David could spend the day at Chloe's side without having to lift a finger in effort. It was almost as if Georgie was actively working to help his cause.

He'd play the "old friend" for one more day, although he thought he'd successfully allayed Chloe's apprehensions last night. By tomorrow, he'd become the attentive lover, and she would fall into his hands like a ripe plum. He'd noted all the favorable signs— she was lonely, vulnerable, receptive to attention.

Chloe Richardson would be in his bed before the week was out. And then he would have his revenge.

Georgie's "picnic" resembled a casual meal only in that the guests ate while sitting on the ground. Otherwise, they could have been dining in the house. The food was served on fine china, hovering footmen filled and refilled their wineglasses, and nary an insect dared to intrude.

Sitting beside Chloe, David glanced ruefully at his heaping plate of food. "Trust Georgie to hold such a formal picnic." He held up his fork. "This is the good silver, for God's sake."

"You would rather we ate with our fingers?" Chloe asked, her tone teasing.

"It wouldn't be the first time I'd done that."

"In Egypt?"

"And other places."

"What exotic land do you plan to visit next?"

"I think I shall stay home for a while. I find the scenery in England can be equally exotic—and pleasing." He flashed her an admiring glance, delighted by the blush that rose to her cheeks.

Chloe toyed with her food. "Georgie and Harry are going to Italy in the fall. They have asked me to come along."

"Have you never been?" he asked, knowing full well that she hadn't. He knew every detail about Chloe's last fifteen years.

She sighed. "Jonathan was content to remain at home."

"Then, by all means, go. I think you will enjoy it." A footman came by, and David grabbed a pastry from the tray, setting it on Chloe's plate. "Have another blackberry tart. As I recall, they were always your favorite. Remember the time we ate that entire pot of jam?"

Chloe laughed uneasily. "You remember the oddest things."

"I remember *everything* about you, Chloe," he said, pitching his voice low and husky. She looked away again, but he took her hand. "How roses are your favorite flower, and blue your favorite color."

"You make it sound as if I have not changed at all."

"You are prettier." His eyes took on an appreciative gleam. "And shapelier."

"And you have become an accomplished flirt."

He grinned. "Years of practice." Propping himself on one elbow, David eyed her longingly as she ate her tart. He wanted to reach out and wipe the smudge of blackberry from the corner of her mouth, then kiss those sweetly shaped lips.

He felt a spurt of anger at his lack of restraint; he should not move so hastily. He was going to be in full control of this seduction. He was not a green school-boy, to be lured back into her clutches again.

She seemed convinced of his sincerity, with no trace of last night's wariness. How easily women were duped! A few sweet words, an ardent caress or two, and she would be climbing into his bed.

He could hardly wait. Revenge was a powerful aphrodisiac.

Jumping to his feet, David held out his hand to her. "Let's walk down to the bridge." He would make love to her under the very noses of the other guests. Georgie would think he was merely following her wishes by entertaining Chloe.

He felt a twinge of guilt as he thought what Georgie would say when this was all over. He might never be welcome here again. But he'd gone through most of his adult life caring little for what his family thought; he wasn't going to start worrying about them now.

Dutifully carrying her parasol, he walked beside Chloe at a sedate pace. He stifled a grin. In their younger days they both would have dashed across the lawn at a breakneck pace. But Chloe was no longer the young girl of his memories. She may not have grown taller, but she certainly had a woman's shape.

Still, there was an aura of almost childlike innocence about her—or was it only his own guilty thoughts, knowing what he planned?

He frowned at his observations. Chloe might present the picture of innocent, but he knew otherwise.

When they reached the Palladian bridge, David pulled a crust of bread from his pocket and handed it to Chloe. "For the swans," he said with a quick grin. She'd always liked to feed the water birds.

The radiant expression on her face told him that she still did. "You remembered! Goodness, I have not done this in ages."

"High time you did, then."

He leaned on the railing, watching her carefully as she tore off hunks of bread and tossed them into the water. Soon a noisy collection of birds, mostly ducks but with one or two swans, collected beside the bridge, demanding to be fed. His plan was going well.

He had no trouble remembering Chloe's favorite foods, her favorite pastimes. And he intended to use every memory to his advantage, until she was firmly convinced of his attention.

"Oh, dear, that is the last of it." Chloe smiled ruefully. "They will be angry with me now."

"They are spoiled rotten." David took her arm, leading her across the bridge. "You saw how quickly they came. Georgie's brats probably feed them ten times a day."

"They are not brats," Chloe said defensively. "They are the sweetest, most well-mannered children on earth."

He grinned. "Paragons of virtue, in fact. But brats nonetheless." He tapped a finger on her nose. "I remember when you were classified in that group."

She looked at him questioningly. "Was I really such a brat? Did you and Jonathan mind me that much?"

David stopped and took her hands in his. "I called you brat long after I wanted to call you something else."

Seeing the surprise in her eyes, he smiled to himself, then dropped her hands again. "I see Georgie waving to us. She probably thinks I have monopolized your time long enough." Tucking her arm in his again, he led her back to the picnic site.

As they retraced their steps, Chloe shivered, despite the warm afternoon. The look in David's eyes had sent a frisson of remembrance up her spine, reminding her of the day they'd first kissed. There had been that same soft expression in his dark brown eyes.

And with the memory came an even more startling thought—did he still feel the same way about her as he had all those summers ago?

She shook her head. That had been fifteen years ago. They were young and in the throes of love for the first time. A man like David, who had seen the death and destruction of war, visited far-off lands, and collected mistresses the way other men collected snuff-boxes was not going to caught up in the memories of a childhood romance. It was her fanciful imagination, nothing more.

Besides, at their bitter parting, he'd assured her that he no longer cared for her. His pleasantness now was merely the joy of meeting old friends again.

That was more than she dared hope for. Even if she wished it could be more.

Georgie greeted them with a cheerful wave as they approached. "Harry thinks we ought to take advantage of the nice weather and go on an expedition to the ruins." Georgie fanned herself. "I think it is too warm to do anything more strenuous than sit."

"Shall I row you about the lake?" David suggested. "If I get up enough speed, you might even feel a breeze."

"David, you are an angel. Harry, go ahead and take

the others to visit the ruins. I shall stay here and allow David to soothe my spirits."

David almost extended his invitation to Chloe, then stopped himself. He didn't want to appear too eager. He would let her think about the things he'd said for a while.

Pulling off his boots, he picked up Georgie and deposited her on the seat of the boat, then climbed in at the other end. Fitting the oars in the locks, he rowed them away from shore.

"Chloe looks positively beaming today," Georgie observed. "I think it has done her a world of good to come here. She's been shut up in that house ever since Jonathan died."

"Chloe knows her own mind. If she was not out in society before, it was because she didn't want to be."

Georgie's eyes narrowed. "I hope you are not using your usual tricks on her. Remember, David, she is the widow of your cousin, not one of your flirts."

"Chloe knows me too well to be swayed by my pretty words," he said ruefully. "The disadvantages of having grown up beside her, I'm afraid."

"Good. You have such a nasty habit of leaving a trail of broken hearts in your wake. I don't want that sort of thing going on under my roof."

He placed a hand across his chest. "How can you say such a thing? I am merely the victim of unrealistic expectations. Women these days . . . you say one word to them and they anticipate a proposal."

"Hardly a reasonable expectation with regards to you, in truth." She leaned back and examined him carefully. "It is time you thought about marrying, David. You're the only one left, you know. You need a son."

"A *legitimate* son."

She sat up. "Don't tell me you have a dozen bastards scattered about the countryside!"

He laughed. "None that I am aware of, anyway. But you forget, I'm not the last. There is Great-Uncle Fordham."

"That sanctimonious prig? Some viscount he would make."

"If the Duke of Devonshire shows no inclination to marry, why should I? We can both live in paradisiacal bachelordom for the rest of our lives."

"Somehow, I think you must have had a reversal in love in your younger days," she mused. "I see no other reason why you are so averse to the matrimonial state."

"It's only because I could never find a woman as complacent as you, Georgie. All the others think to reform me. You, at least, know that's impossible."

"Not impossible," she said. "Merely not worth the effort. A rakehell brother is of no consequence to me."

"Exactly. And if I could find a lady who agreed with you, I'd marry her in an instant."

Her eyes danced with anticipation. "You wait, David North. I'll be on the lookout for just such a woman. And when I find her . . ."

He grinned. "I'll be out of the country."

3

In the morning, David eagerly volunteered to accompany Chloe while she painted. It gave him the perfect opportunity to further his seduction.

"I'm glad you aren't fond of wood carving," David said as he set Chloe's easel on the ground with a thump. They had walked to the knoll on the far side of the lake. "I don't think I could have carried a log this far."

She laughed. "You were the one who insisted on bringing the easel. I'm used to painting without it."

"But how could I put such a obstacle in the face of the premier watercolorist in the neighborhood? Art must be served."

"I'm nothing more than an amateur." Chloe began to unpack her paints and brushes.

"Liar." David grinned. "I've seen your work."

Quickly, he set up the small easel and spread out the rug. "Do you need help with anything more?"

Chloe shook her head. "You can be off, if you like. I don't expect you to stay here all afternoon."

David looked unhappy. "That is the whole reason I came—so I could spend the afternoon with you."

"You actually want to sit here for hours and watch me paint?"

"No, I only want to sit here and watch you."

Chloe blushed. To cover her discomfort, she drew out her paper and set it on the easel. "I thought I would do a picture of the park for Georgie. As a birthday present."

"She would like that," David agreed. He stretched out on the rug, leaning on one elbow, watching her.

His deep scrutiny made her nervous. Not because she minded it when others watched her paint—Jonathan had often done so. No, it was only that she was too aware that it was David who watched her—and watched her with an intensity she found unnerving and exciting.

She felt like a giddy schoolgirl again, full of blushes and awkward silences. At first, she'd dismissed David's flirtatious remarks as part of his mischievous nature. Now, she wondered if there was more to them than she'd thought. He'd given up other pursuits to accompany her, and she could not think of a thing to say to him other than inane remarks about the weather.

What did one say to the man one had once loved?

She looked straight ahead and tried to concentrate on the vista spread out below her. Georgie's house was nestled among the trees, with the green lawn stretching off to the placid lake on the right. It was a beautiful setting. And a simple one that would not tax her modest skills. Georgie would be pleased.

Then why couldn't she paint it?

Because her mind was too preoccupied with the man who lay beside her. Preoccupied with what he thought of her, what he felt for her, what he wanted from her.

"Is something wrong?" David asked.

She smiled ruefully. "I neglected to tell you I am a very *slow* painter. Sometimes I will look at the scene for an hour before I even wet my brush."

He tucked his arms behind his head and looked up at the cloudless blue sky. "We have the entire afternoon," he said. "Look your fill."

Chloe surveyed the landscape again. The problem was, she didn't really want to paint. She wanted to talk with David. She knew what he had done over the last fifteen years, but she wanted to know what he thought about it. Wanted to know in what ways he had changed—and if there was anything left of the young man she'd once adored.

"Tell me about the places you've seen. What country is your favorite?"

"Spain," he said without hesitation.

She glanced at him with surprise. "I would have thought that would be your least favorite."

"I learned a great deal there."

Chloe clenched her brush, then took a deep breath before the words tumbled out. "We are all so glad you came through unscathed, after that first scare. I don't think you know how hard it was on everyone—even your father. I prayed daily for your safe return."

His lips curved into a smile. "Did you? Perhaps that was what brought me through, then. Thank you, Chloe."

She laughed nervously. "It seems so silly, to be finally telling you this so many years later. We should have held a grand welcome home party for you. But you never really came home."

"Perhaps because I found it too painful," he said softly.

Chloe shut her eyes. She did not have to ask him why. She had come between him and his cousin, broken apart the friendship of their youth. Jonathan and David, who had once been thought inseparable, had barely spoken more than a dozen words after David came home from the war. All because of her.

"Can you ever forgive me?" she whispered.

"Forgive you?" David took her hand in his. "There is nothing to forgive, Chloe."

"I never should have married Jonathan," she said, her voice choking. "I caused both of you so much pain."

"It doesn't matter anymore, Chloe. That was a very long time ago."

She glanced at him and saw the tender expression in his brown eyes as he brought her hand to his lips. "Jonathan is dead now. And I am very, very much alive."

For an instant, the intensity of his gaze sent a shiver of apprehension up her spine. But then the look was gone, replaced by the warm, encouraging expression she'd seen before.

He squeezed her hand. "Paint, Chloe. I'll tell you all about my travels."

With silent appreciation, David eyed the wispy tendrils of dark blond hair that danced about Chloe's neck whenever she moved. She was a damnably attractive woman. He fought the urge to reach out and stroke her nape.

He wondered, if he pressed the issue, whether he could take her here on the hillside, this very afternoon. He'd seen the mix of guilt and desire in her eyes, and knew this seduction was going to be laughably easy. Yet he wanted to drag out the process longer, tempting her until she begged for his touch. Then, and only then, would he bed her. For in order for his revenge to be effective, Chloe had to want him as desperately as she thought he wanted her.

Truthfully, he wouldn't have to feign interest in her. It took only a casual glance to make it obvious that Chloe Ridgefield was no longer a seventeen-year-old girl. She was a mature, experienced woman now, with a body that bespoke the changes. Taking her to bed would be a pleasure.

He wondered about the sexual relationship between her and Jonathan. Had he treated her like a dutiful wife, keeping passion and sensuality at bay during their marriage? David hoped so. He would take great delight in showing Chloe what a skilled *lover* was like, showing her what she'd given up when she'd married his cousin. Smiling broadly, David envisioned the cries of delight he'd draw from her.

Only her despair after she'd realized that he'd duped her would be more satisfying.

He could hardly wait.

For two hours he regaled Chloe with tales of his travels abroad, glossing over the deprivations and hardships while focusing instead on the adventures and amusements. He reveled in her interested attention, appreciated her eager questions. He'd almost forgotten that Chloe was as smart as she was beautiful.

It was a pity Jonathan had never taken her to the continent. David thought Chloe was one of the few women who would actually value the experience. With her artist's eye, she would enjoy the varied scenery, would delight in the art and architecture of other cultures. Chloe wouldn't constantly pine for the placid English countryside, like his less adventuresome countrymen.

Of course, he would not be the one to take her, but he almost hoped she would go with Georgie in the fall. Then he shook his head. After he was done with her, he didn't care what Chloe Ridgefield did with herself.

Suddenly tired of talking, he fell silent and in the warm afternoon he drifted to sleep.

Something tickled his nose. Drowsily, David swiped his hand across his face, but the sensation continued. Opening his eyes, he saw Chloe bending over him, paintbrush in hand, a mischievous smile on her face.

David grinned at her. "Don't tell me you've painted

my nose blue? Is this my punishment for falling
asleep?"

"We will blame it on the fresh air," said Chloe, a
teasing tone to her voice. "Or perhaps the strain of
carrying my easel so far."

"That must be it," he agreed, sitting up suddenly,
until his eyes were on a level with hers.

Funny, he had forgotten just how enticing a mouth
Chloe had. The rosy color of her lips owed nothing
to cosmetics and virtually begged to be kissed. He was
tempted, until he remembered his plan. David waited
until he was certain Chloe noticed the focus of his
attention, then he abruptly stood and stretched.

Pulling his watch from his pocket, he pretended to
be dismayed at the passage of time. "Georgie will
think I have kidnapped you. Are you ready to
return?"

He saw a faint wistfulness cross her face before she
nodded. While she packed up her painting supplies,
he folded the easel.

"At least the trip back is downhill," he joked, heft-
ing the lightweight stand.

"Next time we shall employ a pack mule," Chloe
said.

His eyes met hers. "Next time ..." He injected a
tone of longing in his voice. "I look forward to carrying your easel wherever you go."

Upon returning to the house, he left Chloe with
Georgie and Mrs. Mitchell and sought out Harry for
a game of billiards.

David still could not believe how smoothly his plan
was working. He had just the right thing planned for
tonight—moonlight and the memory of old times

would provide the perfect atmosphere for rekindling passion.

By tomorrow night he firmly intended to have Chloe begging at his door.

Biding his time through dinner, David played the gracious guest. He'd made his preparations earlier; all was in readiness. Now he must wait for the evening to end and for Chloe to retire. While he conversed with the others, he watched her with the intensity of a predator stalking his prey.

He did not for a moment think she would refuse to come with him tonight. After all, wasn't she the one who'd first suggested it? She'd be delighted at the idea. And while they relived one childhood pastime, David would remind her of another.

At last the guests began drifting away to bed. The moment Chloe said her good night to Georgie, David snapped to alertness. Timing was key—he didn't want Chloe falling asleep before he could get to her.

He waited five minutes, then made his own escape. Hastening to his room, he changed from his evening clothes and dashed out onto the lawn. Heaving a sigh of relief at seeing a light in Chloe's chamber, he pulled a handful of pebbles from his pocket and began pitching them at her window. He hoped they hit with enough noise to attract her attention.

After ten or more hits, he grinned with delight when she came to the window and peered out. He tossed another pebble and she opened the window.

"David! What are you doing?"

"I'm going fishing. Come and join me."

"Fishing?" She laughed. "David, you rascal. I can't go fishing at this hour of the night."

"Why not? You used to."

She looked pensive for a moment, then she smiled. "You are the devil, David North. I'll be down in a few minutes."

He waited impatiently by the kitchen door, with the fishing poles, lantern, and a packet of worms. Fishing was the last thing on his mind, but Chloe didn't need to know that.

Breathless, her eyes dancing with excitement, Chloe slipped out the door.

"I can't believe I'm doing this," she said as they struck out across the lawn. "I feel like a child again."

"I wouldn't mistake you for one," David said. "You look too much the woman now."

She ducked her head modestly and they continued down to the lake in silence.

"Harry assured me there were fish," David said when they reached the bridge. "Do you wish me to bait your hook, or would you like to choose your own worm?"

Chloe grimaced. "I *have* grown older, for the thought of touching one of those things appalls me. Please, do the honors."

David baited her hook, handed her the pole, and she tossed the line into the water. He readied his own pole, then stood beside her.

Chloe jiggled her line. "I suppose you've taught Georgie's children all the fine points of fishing."

"I haven't been here often enough to do so." He sighed deeply. "It is a regret I have—that I don't have a son to teach all my tricks."

"You could remedy that situation."

"Ah, but then I'd need a wife," he said lightly. He edged closer. "What of you? You must be saddened at the thought that you and Jonathan never had children."

"Some things are not meant to be."

He put a comforting arm around her shoulder. "I'm sure you make a marvelous aunt."

"It's not quite the same, though, is it?" she asked sadly.

He set his pole against the railing and held out his hand. "I really don't feel much like fishing. Would you like to walk?"

Chloe nodded and they stepped off the bridge onto the moon-drenched lawn. David squeezed her fingers tightly.

"It has been very different coming back to England this time. Before, I could hardly wait to be gone again. But this time . . . I feel a real longing to stay."

"Will you take up residence at Linwood?"

He frowned. "I will have to eventually, won't I?"

"It is a lovely home."

"And far too full of memories."

She stopped and laid a hand on his arm. "Let the good ones outshine the others, David. I would like to see you happy."

"I am. Now." He ran his fingers across her cheek. "Happier than I have been in a long, long time." Then he bent and brushed her lips with his.

He wrapped his other arm around her waist, pulling her close, crushing her against his chest as his mouth explored hers.

Sweet, she tasted so sweet. Memory blended with the present, confusing him momentarily, making him forget for an instant just why he held her, why he kissed her. A deep stab of desire shot through him.

Chloe. He was holding her, kissing her, and it felt so wonderful.

Revenge. The word jolted his brain. He was here to hurt her, the way she had hurt him.

With slow deliberation, he teased her lips apart with his tongue, entering her mouth, tasting her, tempting her. Stroking his hand up and down her back, he groaned with unfeigned need as he pulled her closer, suddenly wishing they were inside the house, with a warm, inviting bed only inches away. Damn subtlety, damn his careful plans. He wanted to sink himself into her soft, warm flesh this instant.

"Oh, Chloe," he moaned against her lips. "I have missed you so."

Wrapping her arms about his waist, she returned his kisses with an enthusiasm that surprised him. Tearing his mouth from hers, he pulled her head against his chest, dropping soft kisses on her hair.

"I never dreamed I would hold you again like this," he whispered, his hands roving over her back.

"If only we could go back—"

"Hush," he said. "Let's not talk about the past. We cannot change what happened. Think instead of the future." He tucked her head under his chin as he willed his body back under control. "Starting with today. Georgie will have my head if I keep you up too late—you are going to town with her in the morning, remember?"

"I would rather stay here with you," she said dreamily.

"So would I." It was not a lie. Standing here together, with her clasped in his arms, it would be so easy to forget, so easy to pretend ...

But fifteen years of pain couldn't be exorcised with just a few kisses.

He drew back and tilted her chin with his finger, kissing her gently. "There is endless time before us, Chloe. We need not be greedy tonight."

Taking her hand, he led her back to the bridge, where they retrieved the fishing poles. Slowly, hand in hand, they returned to the house.

Georgie bubbled with excitement as she and Chloe drove to the village after breakfast. "So tell me, Chloe, what have you learned about David? He is practically living in your pocket. I knew he would enjoy seeing you again."

Chloe smiled at her friend's attempt to draw her out. She would tell Georgie a few things—but not everything. "He talks about staying in England for a while."

"What, he hasn't planned a trip to the jungles of South America or the deserts of Africa? Don't tell me his penchant for exotic places is fading at last."

"He talked about going to Linwood. It is hard to believe that the house sits empty now."

"That's what I try to tell him—if he doesn't want it, at least rent it out. But you know how willful David can be when he puts his mind to it. He still barely acknowledges that he's the viscount."

"He seems to have made little concession to the fact," Chloe admitted.

Georgie leaned closer. "He hasn't even set foot in the Lords. And I suspect he deliberately left the country in order to avoid the coronation."

"He seems . . . discontented, in a way."

"David? I don't see why. He does whatever he wishes,

whenever he wishes. In that respect he has not changed in the least. He indulges himself far too much."

"Maybe to make up for the fact that he wasn't indulged when he was younger."

Georgie snorted. "David's always managed to have his way in everything. Father acted so shocked when he ran off and joined the army, but we all know David was soldier mad. He only used being sent down from school as an excuse to do what he'd wanted to all along."

Chloe bit her lip. David had gambled recklessly to earn the money to buy his commission—the commission that was going to bring him fame and glory—or at least an income that would allow them to marry. She must accept part of the blame for his expulsion from Cambridge.

If only she'd been older then ... They could have married, she could have followed him to Spain, and none of the rest would ever have happened.

"Chloe?" Georgie eyed her with concern. "Is something wrong?"

She smiled gaily. "I was only thinking of something David said last night—about forgetting the past and thinking of the future."

Georgie nodded. "An excellent idea. Advice you should take to heart. It is high time you took up your life again."

"David thinks I should go to Italy with you."

"Wonderful! I think he should come with us as well." She grinned. "After all, Harry and I would be proper chaperones."

Chloe knew she blushed, but she couldn't help herself. If Georgie only knew how desperately in need of chaperonage she was! She could hardly believe the ardency of those kisses she'd shared with David by the lake, but it had felt so right, so enticing to be in his arms. As if she belonged there. As if she was meant to be there.

As if all that had happened in the past fifteen years was only a detour on the paths their lives were meant to take. That now, finally, they could be together.

By the time David climbed from his bed, Chloe and Georgie had departed for town. They would be there for most of the day, he guessed. Nothing could hurry Georgie when she went shopping.

He didn't mind. He had waited fifteen years. He could wait a few more hours. Until tonight. When he would insinuate himself into Chloe Ridgefield's bed, and into her body.

Then tomorrow his revenge could begin.

Surprisingly, Georgie conducted her business in town with a minimum of fuss, and she and Chloe came back at the house earlier than he expected.

"The others went out walking," David informed them. "If we hurry, we can catch them."

Georgie sank into a chair. "I can think of a long list of things I would rather do than run after Harry. Besides, that sky looks threatening."

"Chloe?"

"Let me get my bonnet."

The moment Chloe left, Georgie eyed David with growing suspicion. "You are spending a great deal of time with Chloe."

He looked back at her with wide-eyed innocence. "Isn't that what you asked me to do?"

"Yes, but . . ."

"Has Chloe complained? Am I boring her?"

"Oh, nothing like that. In fact, she was decidedly close-mouthed about the whole situation. That makes me suspicious."

David laughed. "You never change, Georgie. Always concerned about everyone else's business."

"It comes from all those years of being excluded by you three," she said dryly. "Whenever one of you wouldn't talk, I knew you were up to something."

"If I have nothing to tell, and Chloe has nothing to tell, I guess you will have to keep wondering," David said. He headed for the door, then turned. "Be sure that if there is anything you need to know, I will tell you."

"David!"

He shut the door behind him and waited in the hall for Chloe, greeting her with a warm smile when she came down the stairs. She looked particularly fetching in that bonnet.

She looked doubtfully at the sky when they stepped out onto the rear lawn. "I fear Georgie was right—it does look like it might rain."

"Not for a while," David said confidently. "We have ample time to take a walk. Although maybe we shouldn't try to catch the others—do you mind?" He put her hand on his arm.

"Mind if we are alone again?"

He patted her hand. "I missed you today. That's why I didn't go with the others—I wanted to be here when you came back."

"David, I—"

"How long are you planning to stay here?"

"Georgie wants me to stay all month, but I should return home next week."

He darted a searching glance at her. "And what will

you return to, Chloe? I'm sure the situation there cannot be comfortable."

"The family means well. In fact, they are too considerate at times."

"I've been thinking—perhaps it is time I reopened Linwood. You would come, wouldn't you, if I did?"

Chloe smiled. "I would love to visit."

"Don't say a word to Georgie—if she found out my plans, I'd find her on the doorstep the next day, ready to take charge."

"Remember, Harry's taking her abroad this fall. You can present her with the fait accompli when she returns."

"A good idea." He stepped around a rock in the path. "Except if you go with them, how can I consult you during the process?"

"You don't need my help. It is your house, after all."

He shook his head ruefully. "It is ironic, since I never thought to live there again. Perhaps that is why I delayed so long; I am not accustomed to the idea that it is mine."

"Life has a way of taking strange twists and turns."

"Yes, it certainly does." He looked pensive for a moment before continuing. "Did you and Georgie enjoy yourselves this morning?"

"Shopping with Georgie is always an adventure."

David laughed. "That's not what Harry calls it. 'Disaster' is the term he uses."

"Well ... I suppose London has too many shops, even for Georgie. But we managed quite admirably in town."

"And did you buy anything?"

"A few trinkets for my nieces and nephew. Nothing of consequence."

He squeezed her arm. "I knew you would be a doting aunt."

"It is not difficult. They are sweet children."

David frowned and held out his hand. "Was that a drop of rain I felt?"

Chloe looked about apprehensively. "Perhaps we should go back."

He looked up, puzzled. "I don't feel anything now; I must have imagined it. Unless you are cold. I don't want you to become chilled."

"I'm fine."

They had not walked much farther when the skies opened and the deluge poured down.

David grabbed Chloe's hand and pointed at the trees. "The summer house is over there—it's closer than running back." Pulling her along, they raced to the shelter.

"Goodness," she said when they reached the building. "I did not think so much rain could fall so quickly."

"A summer shower. Intense but short-lived. We will have to wait it out." He rubbed his hands together as he examined the small room. Carpeting, several chairs, and a sofa gave the room a cozy appearance. "At least we shall be comfortable while we wait."

He stepped toward Chloe and reached for the ribbons of her bonnet. "I don't think you need that in here." He removed it and tossed it on one of the chairs. "Are you certain you are not cold? You can wear my coat."

She took off her shawl and spread it over the back

of a chair. "This is a bit damp, but the rest of me is dry."

"Good." He took her hand and drew her over to the sofa. "I guess we will just have to amuse ourselves somehow until the rain lets up."

"What do you suggest?" she asked with a saucy lilt to her voice.

He'd planned to wait until this evening, but the present opportunity was too good to resist. He bent his head and kissed her softly. "Perhaps we could start where we left off last night." Drawing her into his arms, he kissed her until they were both breathless.

Abruptly, he released her and sank onto the sofa, pulling her onto his lap so his mouth was level with hers. With calculated deliberation he kissed her again, urging her lips to part, teasing her with his tongue. While one hand caressed the back of her neck, the other sought the fastenings of her pelisse, undoing the hooks with skillful speed. Then his fingers stroked over the swell of her breast.

David felt her start and he froze. But when her arms wrapped around his neck and her tongue sought out his own, he knew it was desire and not fear provoking her reaction. He touched her breast again, his thumb seeking and caressing the hardened nub of her nipple through her dress. She shifted on his lap, increasing the ache in his groin and the pounding of his blood.

"Oh, Chloe," he whispered against her ear. "You cannot know how many times I dreamed of holding you like this. Tell me I'm not dreaming, tell me this is real."

"It's real, David."

He was not lying. Images of Chloe in his arms had taunted him for years. First, in the biting cold and freezing heat of Spain, when thoughts of her were often the only thing that kept him alive. After he had discovered her marriage to Jonathan, the images didn't change, only his reaction to them. He wanted her cowed and weeping, begging for his forgiveness. As he bedded every one of the uncounted women over the years, he invariably thought of Chloe. No one had been able to drive her from his mind.

But now he would achieve his release.

He slid from beneath her and laid her down, sinking to his knees on the carpeted floor. Burying a hand in her hair, he drew her mouth to his while his other hand caressed her breasts. Vengeful desire heated his blood, throbbed in his loins. He would show her, would show her what—

A loud shout and a giggling laugh caused him to jerk away and sit back on his heels. Chloe scrambled to a sitting position as they both heard the sound of approaching voices.

"Good God, it's Harry and the others." David jumped to his feet and snatched Chloe's shawl from the chair, flinging it about her shoulders while she fumbled with the hooks of her pelisse.

Damnation. David's frustration was tempered only by the knowledge that had Harry arrived five minutes later, the situation would have been much more awkward.

"Thank goodness, at last." Mrs. Mitchell and her daughters burst into the room, skidding to a halt at the sight of David and Chloe.

David stepped forward. "My dear ladies, you've found your refuge." He turned as Harry and Mitchell entered. "Caught in the storm, eh?"

"Blasted rain," said Harry. He peered at David. "Looks like you escaped the worst of it."

"Pure luck. We were nearly here when the rain started." He looked back to the ladies and made a courtly bow. "You'll catch your death if you have to wait here long. I'll go back to the house and bring the carriage."

"I'll come too," Harry said. "Can't get much wetter than I already am."

Flashing Chloe a rueful smile, David gallantly dashed out into the rain.

4

Chloe could not restrain her eagerness as she dressed for dinner. She wanted to see David again. It did not matter if they were surrounded by the others. Being in the same room with him was enough—for now.

A delicious shiver ran up her spine as she recalled their embraces in the summer house. She had no doubts now what David thought of her, what he felt for her. And her own feelings, the ones she had fought against for so long, were freed again.

Was this what she'd unknowingly anticipated these last months? The chance to start over with David, to live and love again? A few short days ago she would not have believed it possible. Now ... she felt the hurt and sorrow of the last fifteen years melt away.

Few people ever had a second chance at love. She and David were so very lucky. And she knew that Jonathan, of all people, would agree.

She sensed David's gaze on her the moment she

stepped into the drawing room. Chloe had taken particular care with her toilette tonight—begging Georgie for the loan of Hutchins—and she knew she was in her best looks.

He walked up and took her hand, bringing it to his lips. "You look lovely tonight, Chloe."

His eyes were bright with desire, and Chloe suddenly wished that the meal was over, the evening at an end. Then the butler announced dinner.

She sat next to David, as she had every other night. They chatted in an unexceptional manner. Not one word betrayed the boiling impatience that lay beneath their polite exchanges. But Chloe knew that things were different, knew that she and David were now far more than old friends who had met again. They were almost . . . lovers.

Lovers. If Harry and the others had not sought shelter from the storm, she and David would have been lovers by now. The thought sent a thrill of anticipation through her. In her heart, David had always been the lover she wanted, the one she dreamed of. Yet she still found it difficult to believe that she and David were finally to be together. She half wondered if this was all a dream.

If so, she did not want to wake up.

Dinner dragged on for what seemed like hours, and the time in the drawing room passed with excruciating slowness. Chloe toyed with the idea of pleading a headache and retiring early, but then she would have Georgie hovering about her, trying to make certain she felt better. This was one night when she did not want Georgie, or anyone else, around.

Except David.

Chloe remained in the drawing room until quite

late, laughing politely at Harry's jokes, stealing shy glances at David when she thought no one was looking, all the while watching the hands on the clock creep silently around. She restrained her eagerness until Georgie rose to retire, then followed her up the stairs.

Time, however, did not pass more quickly once she reached the sanctuary of her room. Chloe anxiously paced the floor. Would David come to her? And what type of welcome did he expect if he did? If she remained dressed, it would be obvious she expected him. Yet if she didn't change, would he think that she wished to preserve propriety between them, despite the way she'd melted in his arms earlier?

But if he found her in her night rail, would he think worse of her? Would he think she was accustomed to entertaining men in her bedchamber?

It was much more natural for her to prepare for bed, Chloe decided, as she pulled the pins from her hair. That way, if he didn't come tonight, she wouldn't feel so foolish.

If he didn't come, she would die.

After the ladies retired, David remained in the drawing room with Harry, nursing his brandy. He had no doubt Chloe was waiting for him upstairs, but he was in no hurry. An impatient lady was an eager lady.

At last he stretched, bade good night to his host, and made his way upstairs to his room. Stripping off his coat, David laid it across the bed, then removed his waistcoat and cravat. There was no need to pretend; Chloe knew why he was coming to her. After kicking off his shoes, he picked up a candle and opened his door.

Standing silently, David listened for any noise in the corridor, but all was quiet. In stocking feet, he padded quietly down the carpeted floor until he reached the door at the far end. Without hesitation, he turned the latch and stepped inside, quickly shutting the door behind him.

Chloe was standing at the window, gazing out into the dark night, but she whirled about when he entered. She was dressed for bed, in a froth of white and lace, with her hair curling about her shoulders. An unexpected jolt of desire took his breath away.

Covering his surprise, David set his candle on the table, then turned back to lock the door.

"I have no intention of being interrupted again," he said before he crossed the room and drew her into his arms.

Chloe wrapped her arms about his neck. "I hoped you would come."

He smiled. "Wild horses could not have kept me away." He kissed her tenderly. His blood was already racing, as remembered sensations from the afternoon mingled with the anticipation of what was to come. He felt as excited as a green schoolboy and took a deep breath to settle himself. He wanted to make sure this was a night she remembered for a long, long time. He wanted Chloe to be haunted by him, as she haunted him.

He undid her wrapper, parting it to reveal the thin night rail beneath. His hand moved lower, cupping her breast, gently squeezing it. She moaned against his mouth. Her responsiveness sent heat surging through him. "I am going to die from wanting you."

In answer, she pulled his head down until their lips

were only a fraction of an inch apart. "I want you too, David."

He smiled again. "Then I suggest we find a comfortable place to continue this discussion." Scooping her up in his arms, he carried her to the bed and gently set her down atop the counterpane. With trembling fingers he pulled off her wrapper, and reached for the tie at the neck of her gown.

"David."

He halted, seeing the shyness in her eyes.

"The candles . . ."

With a quick laugh, David snuffed out the candles—except for the one at the bedside table. He was damned if he was going to do this in the dark. He wanted to watch Chloe's every move, her every reaction. And he wanted her to see him as well.

"One candle." He reached for her again. "I want to see you, Chloe. To know that it is you in my arms at last."

He stretched out beside her on the bed, reaching again for the opening at the front of her gown. He would teach her a thing or two before the night was out, branding her body with his, leaving her with a deep longing that would never be satisfied.

Slowly, carefully, he pulled the night rail over her shoulders, freeing her arms from the sleeves. Then he eased the cloth down over her breasts, baring them to his view.

He sucked in his breath. "You are so beautiful, Chloe," he whispered before he bent his head to suckle at her breast.

David chuckled at her gasp of surprise. He lifted his head and looked at her. "You like that?" Lowering his mouth to her other breast, he alternated between the two, drawing the hard nub between his teeth, gently nipping while his hand kneaded the soft flesh.

He nearly jumped off the bed when she slipped her hands under his shirt, her fingers tracing erotic patterns across his skin. Frantically, he tugged at his shirt, pulling it over his head and flinging it away. Chloe's hands were everywhere, stroking, caressing him. Confusing him as well.

Brushing his fingers over her silken skin, David willed himself to relax, but it was difficult. Chloe's soft moans tortured his control. He nuzzled again at her breasts as he pushed at her gown, bringing it down over her hips, tangling in her legs until she was free and naked before him. He rose to his knees to look at her.

"God, Chloe, I have wanted this for so long."

She smiled at him, a smile that was a delicious mixture of embarrassment and shyness. Had she never been naked before her husband?

He kissed her again, his tongue darting into her mouth while his hand swept across her abdomen, brushing against her soft curls. His fingers sought lower, probing, looking for the slickened wetness that he knew he'd find. He almost cried out in triumph when he touched her damp heat, but smothered her surprised gasp instead.

Slowly, carefully, he stroked her, feeling her open beneath his fingers, soft and yielding. A jolt of triumph rushed through him when she arched against his hand. She wanted this. She wanted him.

His victory was almost complete.

In a swift motion he pulled away, stripping off his pantaloons and stockings. He bent and kissed the inside of her knee, pressing airy kisses along her thigh until his mouth hovered over the soft triangle of hair. Briefly, he touched his tongue to her.

"David!"

He grinned. She *had* been a sheltered bride. "Trust me, Chloe," he said, slipping his hands under her and lifting her to his mouth.

Chloe was shocked, embarrassed by his intimate kisses. Yet she could no more tell him to stop than she could tell herself not to breathe. Her fingers clutched his hair while her body moved wantonly beneath him. Fire filled her, fire that burned hotter and hotter until she thought she would ignite. An explosion racked her with a white-hot heat as she moaned out his name.

Color flooded her face and Chloe fought the urge to hide behind her hands, the pillow, anything, everything. Then David looked at her, grinning at her pleasure, and her guilt fled before the look of raw desire on his face.

"Ah, Chloe," he whispered, kissing her. "I can't wait any longer."

He settled himself between her legs, pressing against her yielding flesh, slowly, inexorably taking possession of her. Her fingers danced along his spine, urging him forward, willing him to press into the very heart of her. She wanted him to possess her, to be possessed by him, David, the man she had always wanted, always needed. Always loved.

Her mouth sought his, their lips meeting in frantic kisses, wet and moist like the other place where they bodies joined. Her body moved without urging, arching against him, striving to bring him closer, deeper, as fifteen years of suppressed wanting burst forth.

"David, oh, David," she moaned, clutching him

closer as he thrust into her body. Her breath caught and quickened, disbelieving, as the fire flooded through her again, spiraling her higher and higher until she burst against him as he exploded inside her.

They lay in a tumble of arms and legs and sheets, their labored breathing sounding loudly in her ears. She cradled him against her chest, stroking his hair, hardly daring to believe that he was really there with her. Tears sprang to her eyes at the realization that he was.

He raised his head. "You're crying."

She brushed her eyes. "Just silly female sentimentality."

He wiped a tear from her cheek and rolled on his back, pulling Chloe with him.

"I never stopped loving you, David," she whispered. "When we thought you were dead . . . I wanted to die myself. If it hadn't been for Jonathan . . . He kept me alive."

David winced. For one brief moment, lost in the warmth of her body, he'd forgotten. Now her words brought it all back.

"I should be grateful," he said, although he wasn't. A true friend wouldn't have married her after such a short time. And a woman who loved him wouldn't have married another, either. They'd both betrayed him.

But he had the last laugh now. He'd finally possessed Chloe in the most intimate manner, made love to her with a passion he knew her husband never had. Now she had a taste of what she had missed, and before the night was out, he intended to emblazon that knowledge into every part of her body.

So when he told her what he really felt, her regret would be all the worse.

So she would spend the next fifteen years of her life aching for what she couldn't have.

He stroked her hair, twining a lock about his finger. Her breasts pressed against his chest, her thigh lay between his own, and he was aware of every point of contact between their bodies. Too aware. Already, his body responded to her nearness.

He nuzzled her neck. "You're driving me mad with wanting, Chloe. I cannot get enough of you."

She ran a finger down his chest and sent a flash of heat racing through him.

"You're tempting fate," he said warningly, capturing her hand.

Chloe laughed lightly. "And what dastardly fate will befall me if I persist?"

He pulled her up so her face was even with hers. "This," he said, plunging his tongue into her mouth.

Faint streaks of dawn lit the sky when David at last slipped from her bed, dressing quickly. He unlocked the door, then paused, looking back at the bed. Chloe's sleeping shape was barely discernable in the dark.

Had it been enough? Would she remember this night for the rest of her life—first with hope, then with despair as the realization of his indifference washed over her?

He prayed so. Because he didn't dare spend another night with her. It would be too easy to forget, too easy to lose himself in her enveloping softness and let the years of hate and pain slip away. He deserved more than that, deserved the revenge he'd so carefully plotted.

By tonight, Chloe Ridgefield would know exactly

what he thought of her. Would know that all his sweet words were just that—words. Would know that as far as he was concerned, her body could have been anyone's, that she was indistinguishable from all the other ladies over the years. That she'd been no more than a convenient subject for his physical release.

Except this time her face had not risen up to haunt him, for it was there before him, beneath him, and above him. He knew precisely with whom he sported. And that knowledge had brought him a pleasure far beyond a mere physical release.

When she awoke, Chloe was horrified to discover how late she had slept. It was long past noon. But David had not allowed her to sleep during the night . . . Blushing hotly, she climbed from bed and rang for the maid, then crawled under the covers again.

Her body ached, but with a soreness that spoke of pleasure rather than pain. She colored again at the remembrance of some of the things he had done—the things *she* had done. David had shown her passion and pleasure she'd never dreamed of, even after all her years of marriage.

She could not wait to be with him again.

After bathing and dressing, Chloe went downstairs. She hoped David would not be with Georgie—one look at the two of them together and his sister would know what had happened. To her relief, Georgie was alone in the morning room.

Georgie eyed her with a speculative glance. "My, we look in spirits today. Dare I ask the cause?"

Chloe shrugged casually. "I certainly had plenty of sleep."

"One would think you'd danced until dawn," Georgie observed.

Chloe struggled not to laugh. She would have to share that observation with David—dancing indeed! "I suppose everyone else has gone about their business."

"Yes, they have left us here again. Harry and the men rode off somewhere, and Mrs. Mitchell took the girls to the village. You and I can have a nice cozy chat."

"I thought we talked ourselves out yesterday," Chloe said.

Georgie laughed. "You cannot fool me. Something has happened since yesterday, I can tell it from your eyes. Is it David? What has he been up to?"

"Reminding me of all the horrid things I did as a child," Chloe said with a laugh. "I have to look in the glass periodically to make certain I'm not twelve again."

"I don't think David sees you as a child. I've noticed the way he looks at you."

"Oh?"

Georgie nodded. "He can barely take his eyes off you."

Chloe blushed.

"I think there is more going on than you are telling me," said Georgie, pouting. "But why should my friend, or my brother, tell *me* anything? I'm such an inconsequential person."

"I think—" Chloe began, then stopped.

Georgie leaned forward eagerly. "Yes?"

The voices of Mrs. Mitchell and her daughters sounded in the hall.

Forcing brightness into her voice, Chloe turned to

Georgie. "Shall we see if they would like to take a walk down to the lake? The breeze will feel refreshing."

Georgie accepted the idea with resignation.

The walk to the lake was a mistake, however, for the bright sun gave Chloe a throbbing headache. When they returned to the house, she went to her room and lay down, a cold cloth across her forehead. She was still exhausted from last night, and a nap would do her good.

She slept, and by the time the first dinner bell rang, she felt better. After dressing hurriedly, she danced down the stairs. She hadn't spoken with David all day, and the very thought of seeing him again gave a spring to her step. Her only fear was that she would turn a revealing shade of red if he dared to look at her as he had last night.

Late as she was, David was even later, for he wasn't in the drawing room. Chloe was not concerned until she saw Georgie's worried expression.

"What is wrong?" Chloe asked.

"My brother. He and Harry went to look at Winston's hunters, then stopped at the inn for some ale. Foolishly, Harry left David there and he still hasn't come back."

"I'm sure nothing is wrong."

"So am I," Georgie snapped. "He's only being his usual thoughtless self. I'm not going to wait dinner just for him."

Chloe smothered a smile. If David was as tired as she, he'd probably fallen asleep. She could not wait to tease him about it.

Harry appeared at her side. "I am to take you in to dinner."

"Is this your penalty for losing David?" Chloe asked him teasingly.

He smiled. "You are angry with me too, I suppose. He's a grown man! I can't order him around for the convenience of you ladies."

Chloe patted his arm. "I don't expect you to."

Harry glanced at his wife. "If only Georgie was more understanding . . ."

The guests were partway through the first course when David sauntered into the dining room, still dressed in his buckskins.

He grinned widely. "Am I late?"

Georgie gave a disgusted snort. "Late, and not dressed for dinner."

He pulled out his chair and sat down. "I'm sure no one will mind." He leaned toward Chloe as the footman offered him soup and gave her a broad wink. "Will you, Chloe?"

Chloe tried to cover her distress with a bright smile. It was not the crumpled shirt that bothered her, or the messily tied cravat. After all, he hadn't changed his clothes all day.

But the smell of cheap perfume that clung to him was quite another thing. There was no doubt how David had spent his afternoon—and what type of person he spent it with.

David—dallying with a barmaid, or worse, only hours after he'd left her bed. Chloe felt as if she'd been slapped.

She prayed that there was some reasonable explanation. One that would make her laugh when she discovered the truth, and how far afield her suspicions had strayed. David would soothe her foolish fears.

Yet as she forced herself to take a bite of food, he

didn't say a word to her, but concentrated entirely on his dinner. Not until the bread of mutton was served did he pause, look up, and catch Georgie's eye.

"I will be leaving in the morning," he announced.

"Pray tell, why?" his sister asked.

"Georgie, Georgie, you can't expect me to spend my entire summer in Yorkshire. I've celebrated your birthday well enough."

"Thought you wanted to look at those hunters," Harry murmured.

David waved a dismissive hand. "Not now. If I still want them in the fall, I'll be back. As entertaining as my stay has been, I do have other obligations." He raised his wineglass in mock salute. "Be cheered that you kept me here this long."

Chloe spent the remainder of dinner in a daze, barely aware of the conversation around her. All she could think about was David's words—"I will be leaving in the morning." Announcing it at the dinner table in the most casual manner, as if it had no meaning for her—or him.

Something had happened, she was certain of it. She desperately needed to talk with him, in private, to discover what it was.

Chloe deliberately kept away from Georgie when they went into the drawing room; she did not want to get drawn into a discussion about David's sudden change of plans. What could she say? That the news was as much a surprise to her as anyone?

She wanted to slip away quietly and seek the solace of her room, but that would draw Georgie's attention. Instead, Chloe pasted a false smile on her face and spent a miserable thirty minutes chatting with Mrs. Mitchell, while waiting for the men to arrive.

Yet it wasn't a surprise when they entered the drawing room—without David. Chloe stiffened her spine and continued talking with Mrs. Mitchell about the best way to control birds in the kitchen garden.

At last Chloe could endure no more and she excused herself, claiming her headache had returned. She went up the stairs with slow deliberation, hoping she would find David in his room. He owed her an explanation.

Rapping lightly on his door, she received no answer. Cautiously, she pushed it open. David lay stretched out on his bed, reading.

"Hello, Chloe," he said when he saw her, not bothering to rise.

"David, what is wrong?"

"Wrong? What makes you think something is wrong?"

She bit her lip. "After last night I thought . . . Why are you leaving?"

He shrugged. "I've accomplished what I came here to do."

Chloe swallowed hard, wondering why he was being so hurtful. "I would like you to stay."

David shut his book with a snap. "And you probably expect me to immediately change my mind at those words. Give it up, Chloe. We had a rather nice evening together, but that's all it was. An evening."

She stared at him, too stunned and hurt even to speak.

He shook his head. "Chloe, you needn't put on such a shocked expression. You were a married lady, after all. You know how these things work."

"No, I don't," she said in a choked voice. "Tell me."

"You mean you were faithful to Jonathan all through your marriage?" He stared at her with an expression of incredulity. "Good Lord, I didn't think there were *any* virtuous wives left in England. How quaint."

Chloe's stomach clenched and for a moment she feared she might be sick. "You mean last night meant nothing to you?"

He smiled blandly. "I wouldn't say that—it meant a great deal to me. I've always wondered what you would be like in bed, and now I know."

"But I thought . . . that is, you said . . ."

David's eyes grew cold. "You thought there was more to it—that I might be enamored of you again? I'm not such a fool as to fall for that trap twice, Chloe."

"The way you talked about Linwood . . ."

"Yes, you would like to come to Linwood, wouldn't you? Now that it needs a mistress."

In one swift movement he rolled off the bed and stood before her, clamping his hand about her wrist. "But you threw away any chance of that when you married Jonathan. Did you think I was going to 'forget' your little lapse, Chloe? Forget that you married him instead of me?"

Chloe stared at him, wondering how she could have been so terribly mistaken. He was still angry with her—furious, even. She knew now that his attentions over the last days had been a deliberate, calculated effort, so he could humiliate her.

How could the man she loved have changed so much?

"You're not the same David I knew." Chloe blinked

back tears. "*He* would never have done something like this."

"You've only yourself to blame for the change, Chloe." He laughed harshly. "I should be grateful, actually, for you managed to strip me of all my youthful, romantic illusions before I made a bigger fool of myself. God, to think what an innocent I was."

"I never meant to hurt you."

His eyes flashed angrily. "Well, damn it, Chloe, you did. And if I've caused you even a fraction of that pain, I'm glad."

Chloe shut her eyes. David *didn't* care for her. All his words had been a carefully plotted plan to fool her, to have her admit that she still cared, so he could show her that he didn't. And oh, it had worked so very well.

"Now, my dear, if you don't mind, I wish to get an early start in the morning. After all the sleep I lost last night, I need my rest." He ran his fingers over her cheek. "Don't worry, Chloe, I never talk about my conquests. Your little lapse from propriety is safe with me."

She pulled her hand free and fled through the door.

Georgie was going to have his head over this, he knew—he really would have to leave first thing in the morning to avoid her wrath. But his mission had been accomplished—he'd lured Chloe Ridgefield into thinking he cared for her. The devastation on her face when he told her otherwise was all the confirmation he needed.

He smiled. Making use of that barmaid at the inn this afternoon had been an inspired piece of genius. Apart from the shirt he'd sacrificed to her abominable perfume, it had been an effortless hoax on his part. Well worth the cost of the shirt.

He didn't want to think about how he'd had no interest in actually bedding the chit. After all, he rarely dallied with barmaids. But it had been more than that; memories of his night with Chloe had dampened his enthusiasm as effectively as a bucket of cold water.

She was still the only woman he wanted, the only woman who sparked his desire.

But she didn't know that and he certainly wasn't going to tell her. She thought he'd jumped from her arms into another's—just as she had all those years ago. From the stricken look on her face, that knowledge didn't sit well with her.

Yet strangely, he felt no sense of triumph, no thrill of victory. David felt nothing beyond a dull weariness.

Tomorrow, after a decent night's sleep, he would feel better. Tomorrow, he would have time to savor his victory.

5

Chloe put on her brightest face when she went down to breakfast in the morning. She didn't want anyone, particularly Georgie, to know how miserable a night she'd spent.

It had been a night of recriminations and regret. Regret at her own stupidity, regret at her naivete in thinking that she and David could go back to the way things had been between them. David, at least, had had the sense to know that one could not recapture what had been lost. And she had lost David forever the moment she married Jonathan. David had every right to hate her.

Yet she could not blame him for what had happened here—that was her fault. She'd allowed herself to be seduced by his sweet words, cajoled by his winning smile. Because she wanted so badly to believe, she'd deceived herself into thinking that he cared for her again.

Chloe laughed bitterly. Oh, he cared, all right. Cared enough to carry out his well thought-out plan for revenge. She should be flattered he'd expended such effort.

It was only a mark of how badly she'd hurt him, how deeply he'd suffered. Now, perhaps, he could go on with his life and forget her.

Unfortunately, it would not be so easy for her.

Chloe was the one who'd thought that night of passion and discovery meant more than it had. Foolish, stupid Chloe. Yet while she regretted her stupidity, she did not feel shame for what she had done, what she'd allowed David to do. She had wanted him as badly as she thought he wanted her; he had not forced himself into her bed and into her body. She'd invited him willingly. And if that wasn't exactly proper behavior for a lady, well, at least she could be grateful that her fall from grace had been in private.

One night of pleasure, a few days of happiness, and now she was tossed again into a pit of despair deeper than any she had known—except for the painful months when she had thought him dead.

Perhaps it might have been better for all of them if he had been. . . .

Horrified at the thought, she buried her face in her hands. No matter what David had done to her, how he had lied to her, she could not wish him dead. It was her fault, after all, that he hated her so. If she'd been stronger, if she'd been able to resist the pleading of her parents and Jonathan, she would have been waiting when David came home. But because of her weakness, she'd agreed to marry Jonathan, and broken David's heart.

She thought she'd learned to live with her failing—and David had accepted it as well. But now she knew he hadn't forgiven her, and she was not so sure she could forgive herself, either. David still carried the pain that she had inflicted.

But the same fierce determination that enabled her to survive the painful discovery that David had not died in Spain would carry her through now. Georgie might be suspicious, but Chloe would never let her know just how badly she hurt.

Georgie was at the breakfast table, and Chloe put on a warm smile, ready to begin the charade.

"My brother is the biggest beast imaginable," Georgie said, taking a sip of her tea. "Do you know he up and left this morning, before I was even awake?"

Chloe carefully buttered her toast, highly aware of Georgie's close scrutiny. "That's David—he likes to come and go as he pleases."

"I thought you'd be disappointed to see him leave. You two spent so much time together."

"It was nice to talk with him again. And he promised to invite everyone down to Linwood—"

"David's going to Linwood?"

Chloe winced inwardly at her mistake. David hadn't wanted Georgie to know. "He talked about it."

Georgie clapped her hands. "How marvelous. I cannot wait to have Christmas there this year. Italy in the fall and Christmas at Linwood. It will be a wonderful end to the year. You will come as well, of course."

"Christmas is a long time away," Chloe said. "We can talk about it later. You may decide after the trip to Italy that you never want to see me again."

Georgie laughed. "More likely, I will never want to see Harry again."

Chloe refilled her tea cup. "I should like you to say that in front of him."

Georgie grinned. "He is a dear, I admit. But if we are going to spend two months together traveling, I don't think I would mind a few days apart either. Perhaps you and I should visit Brighton. That would be refreshing."

"You do have other guests," Chloe reminded her.

"Oh, dear, I do, don't I?" Georgie looked guilty. "Well, perhaps after they are gone. I do not think they will stay much longer."

"I cannot stay much longer either. If I am to go to Italy, I must make arrangements."

"What arrangements are there to make? Pack your bags and go." Then Georgie's eyes widened. "You do not mean to say that you will have to ask permission from Jonathan's family? I never heard of anything so ridiculous."

"Of course not. But they will want to know my plans, all the same. And I need to purchase so many things. If I don't start now, I will never be ready in time."

Georgie sighed. "First David, then you. Next thing you know, everyone will be gone and I shall be all alone."

"If you become lonely, you can visit me at Thornby.

Now, what are we to do today? I feel like I've been a neglectful guest with David here."

"Let's go for a drive."

As she went to get her pelisse, Chloe breathed a deep sigh of relief. She had survived that ordeal without arousing Georgie's suspicions. Now she only needed to make it through the rest of her visit. Chloe wished she could leave immediately, but the connection between her departure and David's would be too obvious. She would have to endure several more days of forced gaiety, and hope that she could keep up her cheerful facade around Georgie.

But once Chloe left, she wouldn't have to pretend anymore.

Conflicting emotions waged within David as his carriage neared Linwood. He'd been to the house more than once since the death of his father and brother, but never with the intention of staying. His visits had always been short, and hurried.

Now he determined to remain longer. To try to feel at home here again. If the ghosts from the past would let him.

And if not, he would be off again to some exotic foreign spot, where he could forget again, for a while.

Rather than bothering with the formality of the front entrance, David directed the coachman to drive to the stable block. He didn't feel like playing the viscount today. All he wanted to do was have a bath and a brandy. He was tired from the long drive and two sleepless nights spent in indifferent inns.

Tired of reliving that last encounter with Chloe, seeing the pain in her face when he told her he didn't care, that it had all been a deliberate attempt to seduce her.

Climbing from the coach, David left his valet to deal with the luggage and stalked to the house. He was not going to let Chloe chase him out of Linwood, or England, again. It was his house now and by God, he was going to live here.

The housekeeper uttered a surprised shriek when he stepped into the hall.

"My lord! What are you doing here?"

"I wonder that myself, Mrs. Jenkins," he said wryly. "But I think, for a time, that I'm home."

She threw up her hands in dismay. "And just like you to arrive without any warning. The rooms are all closed off, there's precious little food in the pantry, and my best maid's out visiting her sick mother."

David smiled. "It will be all right. I don't wish to cause any problems. As long as I can have a bath, a cold supper will do fine."

"That's all you're likely to get," she said with a sniff.

"I should turn off the lot of you," he said with a mock fierceness that fooled neither of them. It was difficult to command respect among a staff that still remembered his youthful antics.

"Upstairs you go," Mrs. Jenkins said. "That man of yours may have to help with the water, seeing as we're shorthanded. I'll take off the covers in the drawing room, and the dining—"

"Just the study," David said. "I can eat there, and I don't need to sit in that barn of a drawing room all to myself. You can see to the other rooms in the days to come."

Her expression brightened. "You're going to open the house again?"

"Perhaps." If he could bring himself to stay.

* * *

By the time he'd finished his bath and slipped into the fresh clothes laid out by his valet, David felt infinitely better. Linwood wasn't such a bad spot. It was time he acknowledged the fact that his father and brother were gone, and like it or not, he was the viscount now. He might as well accept the inevitable and establish himself here. There was a lot to be said for the comforts of English life.

In the study, as he relaxed with a glass of brandy while waiting for his supper, his mood improved even more. He'd never hated Linwood, only hated the memories of Chloe that it evoked. But he told himself he'd exorcised that demon from his brain at Georgie's, and now he could enjoy his home again.

Yet if that were true, why did he need to keep telling himself that? He should feel elated, overjoyed at being free from the past, but images of Chloe kept crowding into his brain, disturbing his peace.

Chloe laughing on the hillside behind Georgie's house. Chloe moaning with delight as he pleasured her body.

Chloe with tears brimming in her eyes when he told her that it had only been a casual encounter, a meaningless bit of pleasure.

She'd had no right to look at him like that. . . . He'd only done to her what she'd done to him. But the thought brought him little comfort. Revenge had not yet brought him the peace he sought.

It was because he was at Linwood. He'd spent so little time here recently that he hadn't had the chance to develop an adult perspective about the estate. As he took up his responsibilities as viscount, his youthful recollections would fade.

Yet he felt strangely pensive throughout the evening, and as he climbed into bed after too much brandy. He wasn't ready to sleep in the chamber reserved for the viscount—that was challenging his father's image too much, even for David. He settled instead for the familiar comfort of his old room.

But as he lay staring at the ceiling, listening to the tall clock in the hall chime the second hour, he realized that coming home was not going to be as simple as he thought.

Just as purging his soul of Chloe was not going to be simple.

He had been too optimistic, too confident. Now he feared that one night with Chloe Ridgefield was not going to be enough to overcome fifteen years of pain.

How many nights would it take? Ten? Twenty? A hundred? Or would her face and form haunt him forever? What did he have to do to free himself from her hold?

Was there anything he *could* do?

He tossed and turned throughout the night, and when the first shafts of dawn lit the sky, he was up and dressed. Determined to confront his memories, he walked toward the folly at the far end of the garden. The place where he'd kissed Chloe for the first time.

The moment he stepped inside, he knew it had been a mistake to come back to Linwood. There were too many memories here, memories made all the more vivid after seeing Chloe. His scheme for revenge had gone perfectly, but it hadn't been enough. It hadn't driven Chloe's image from his mind. If anything, the visions were only stronger.

The silky thickness of her hair, the soft smoothness

of her skin . . . the burning heat as he thrust into her body.

And he realized, with a sad finality, that he would never be free of her, because he'd been lying to himself all these years. It wasn't hate that surged through his mind at the thought of Chloe; what he felt for her was love. A love that was bruised and battered by the years and his attempts to run from it, but a love that was still there.

He should have recognized it instantly—the joy he felt at seeing her again, the happiness he experienced in her presence. The fact that all thoughts of hurt and revenge fled from his brain whenever he held her, kissed her, should have told him something. But he was too blinded by his own stubborness and stupidity to understand.

Crossing the folly, David peered at the window. There, etched in the glass of the lower pane, were the intertwined initials: D and C.

The sign of their love, scratched in the glass on the morning he'd left for the army. It had been just after dawn, and Chloe had slipped from her house to meet with him one last time.

He held her tightly and his resolve nearly failed. He loved her so much; how could he leave her? But he had to if they were ever to marry. So with his knife they took turns etching the glass, as a symbol of what was to be.

What still might have been if he hadn't deluded himself so.

With an agonized cry, David sank to his knees. He didn't want to love her. He wanted to hate her for believing him dead, for marrying Jonathan. Wanted to punish her for the shock and pain he'd felt when he'd come home and found her lost to him. He'd spend the last fifteen years running from the truth, as if by denying it, it would hurt less. Yet despite his efforts, he still loved her as deeply as he had on that cold morning long ago.

And now the knowledge only hurt more. Because he could have made it all right again, and instead he'd thrown it all away.

Chloe. What had he done to Chloe? He'd used her, humiliated her, then taunted her with his words. And he'd done it deliberately, with cool, calculated effort. David remembered the stricken expression in those deep blue eyes. He'd wanted to hurt her, and he had. She would never forgive him.

He would never forgive himself.

David did not know how long he sat there, steeped in misery. Half an hour? An hour? At last, some sound startled him and he returned to an awareness of his surroundings, the morning coolness of the folly, the hardness of the stone floor. The pain in his heart.

He had to see Chloe, had to tell her how wrong he had been. Tell her that he'd been a victim of madness, born of his pain, and that he begged her to understand, even if she couldn't forgive.

He must tell her how he felt. Because he'd lied to her, pretending that he didn't love her. She needed to know just how much he cared, how tormented he'd been without her. It wouldn't excuse what he'd done, but it would explain it. If he told her the why, he might be able to find some way to live with himself. Some way to sleep at night again.

Dashing back to the house, he raced to his room and frantically rang for his valet. David hastily dressed for riding. He didn't want to bother with the carriage on this journey. When the startled valet appeared, David ordered him to pack a change of clothing and see that his horse was saddled.

Hastening to the study, he scribbled a quick note to the factor, told a startled Mrs. Jenkins that he was leaving, then took off at a run for the stables. But halfway there he halted and turned back to the house. In his room, he went to the chest beneath the window, lifting the lid and digging through the contents—souvenirs from far-flung locales, his officer's sword, his military dress uniform. At the bottom he found the small silk bag he'd brought back from Spain all those years ago and stuffed it into his pocket, then raced out of the house again.

Yorkshire was a good two-day's ride away. He didn't have any time to waste.

Georgie let out a small cry of surprise when David marched into the drawing room, dirty, disheveled, and exhausted.

"Goodness, why are you here? Is something wrong?"

"I need to talk with Chloe."

She eyed him curiously. "I'm afraid you missed her. She's gone back to Thornby. She wanted to have plenty of time to prepare for the trip to Italy."

"Damn!" He turned to the door. "I'll talk with you later."

"David! You come back here. Where are you going? You can't just come and go like this."

"I have to talk to Chloe."

"You look such a fright I doubt she would even want to see you. Sit down and compose yourself. I'll ring for tea."

David opened his mouth to protest, then shut it. Georgie was right. He needed to rest. He hadn't had more than a few hours of sleep in days, and he felt miserable. Ten or fifteen minutes spent with his sister was not going to make much difference if he had to chase Chloe all the way back to Norfolk.

Georgie practically pulled him into a chair. "Now tell me what is going on."

David looked at her, and sighed. "I've made the stupidest mistake of my entire life."

Her eyes brightened. "And it has to do with Chloe? I knew it!"

He glared at her. "What did you know?"

"I suspected something was amiss when you left so suddenly. It was obvious Chloe was unhappy—though she emphatically denied it. That's what convinced me. No one bothers to deny what isn't true."

David stared at her, then shook his head at her feminine logic. "I will be lucky if Chloe ever speaks to me again."

"What did you do?"

He swallowed nervously. "Pretended I didn't love her."

"Love!" Georgie squealed. "You and Chloe? I knew it! I could tell from the moment you arrived that something was going on." She grabbed his hand. "Oh, David, I am so excited. Chloe is too full of spirit to remain a widow. You are such old friends; everyone will approve."

A grimace crossed his face. "You don't know the half of it, Georgie. Chloe and I were engaged when I went into the army."

"What? No one ever told me that. Did Papa know?"

"It was a private matter between us," he said stiffly. "Then, when I was reported dead ... she married Jonathan."

Georgie's eyes grew wide with dawning horror. "And when you came back ... oh, David, how terrible. The three of you must have been miserable."

David stared at her for a moment, at first with puzzlement and then with growing awareness. He shook his head at his stupidity. "You know, until this moment I never really thought about how they must have felt. I was too wrapped up in my own misery. I felt so betrayed ... by both of them."

"That's why you traveled so much."

He nodded. "I couldn't bear to see them together."

Georgie gave his hand a comforting pat. "But Chloe is free to marry you now."

"Chloe despises me."

"What did you do?"

David jumped to his feet and prowled the room. "I acted like a fool," he said at last. "I told myself that I was still angry with her. I wanted to punish her, wanted her to experience the same pain I had."

"So you told her you didn't love her. That should not be too difficult to rectify. Chloe's a sensible woman."

"Worse. I made her think that I cared, then told her I did not."

"Hmm." Georgie frowned.

He knelt before her, grabbing her hands. "What am I going to do, Georgie? I hurt Chloe badly. She will never trust me again."

"You could let time do its work. Wait until we return from Italy. She might be more amenable then."

"I can't wait that long."

"Then tell her the truth. Tell her that you are the most stubborn, pigheaded man in the world and would cut off your own nose just to spite your face. That's what you've done, after all."

David had the honesty to look chagrined. "Why is it that love and hate feel so similar, Georgie? I've been telling myself for fifteen years that one was the other."

"Because they are two sides of the same coin. You were just too stupid to notice the difference."

He grinned. "I am glad I have you to keep me in my place, Georgie."

The tea tray arrived. Georgie insisted that he stay and drink with her, even though he was afire with impatience to be gone. At last, after draining his cup and cramming several biscuits into his pocket, he took his leave, promising to write as soon as he spoke to Chloe.

"And if you botch this, brother, *I* may never speak to you again either," she called after him as he hastened to the door.

It was late in the afternoon of the following day when he reached Thornby. He dreaded the thought of having to make polite conversation with his aunt and his cousin when all he wanted to do was try to explain his boorish behavior to Chloe. But he would walk over hot coals if it helped him convince Chloe of his sincerity.

His aunt, miraculously, was away from home, but Stephen Ridgefield eagerly greeted his older cousin.

"David! Good to see you. What brings you to Norfolk? I didn't even know you were back in the country."

David smiled politely "I grew tired of wandering and came home to celebrate Georgie's birthday. That's why I'm here—to speak with Chloe. She forgot something at my sister's, and I've brought it to her."

Stephen sent the footman to find Chloe, then clapped David on the back. "Come into the study and have a brandy. You look like you need it. Sisters can be the devil, can't they?"

David nodded.

Stephen had just handed him the brandy when the footman returned and mumbled a few words to his master.

"Chloe's maid says she is resting." He gestured toward a chair. "Make yourself comfortable."

Reluctantly, David sat down. Stephen chatted eagerly about Thornby and the latest agricultural improvements he'd implemented while David listened with growing impatience. He wanted to see Chloe. At last he looked pointedly at his host. "Would you ask if Chloe is ready to see me yet?"

Stephen sent the footman again and turned back to David. "Surely, you can stay the night. Father's ill, as you know, but I am sure he would enjoy seeing you."

"I am not certain—"

"If you need to be on your way, I can deliver the package to Chloe. I think the excitement of such a long visit was too much for her—she's been a bit peaked since she returned."

The footman returned and whispered to Stephen. His brow rose and he looked at David with a speculative glance.

"Chloe says that she is not receiving today."

David slammed his glass down on the table and bounded to the door. "Is she in her room?"

"Yes, but . . . I say, Denby, you can't go up to her. She isn't feeling well."

"Don't I know it," David said under his breath, ignoring his cousin. He raced up the stairs, Stephen and the footman trailing behind him. "Where's her room?"

"At the end of the hall, but—"

David stopped and spun around. "This is a private matter between Chloe and myself. You will wait downstairs."

Stephen looked at him, then nodded and retreated.

Stopping outside Chloe's door, David rapped lightly on the panel. Receiving no answer, he reached for the latch, but the door was locked. He knocked louder.

"Chloe, I know you're in there. Open the door."

"I have nothing to say to you," she retorted.

"Open this door right now or I'll knock it down." To emphasize the threat, he aimed a strong kick at the lower panel. The door still remained closed, so he gave it another kick, causing it to shudder with the force of the blow.

He heard the click of a key in the lock and the door opened a fraction.

"I have to talk with you, Chloe."

"Oh? I thought you said all you needed to at Georgie's. Or don't you feel that you humiliated me enough?" Chloe stepped back and flung the door open. "Come in. Insult me further. Tell me what a wicked woman I am."

David stopped and sucked in his breath at the sight of her. She was dressed plainly, in a simple frock, with her hair down and curling about her shoulders, but she looked exquisitely beautiful—and unhappy. There were dark shadows under her eyes, and her expression was weary.

He took a step into the room. "I didn't come here to insult you, Chloe. I came here to apologize."

Her laugh was tinged with bitterness. "Isn't that just like you, David? Thinking a few mumbled words of apology will make up for everything? That might have worked when I was a child, but not anymore. Now get out."

He took another step into the room and shut the door behind him. She leaped forward, but before she could reach it he spun the key in the lock and pocketed it.

"Neither of us is leaving until we have said all there is to say."

"That should not take long. I have nothing to say to you."

"Well, I have a great deal to say to you." He looked at the chair. "Would you mind if I sat down?"

"Yes."

He swallowed nervously. "I went to Linwood after I left Georgie's." Watching her warily, he leaned against the dresser. "It has changed very little. I even slept in my old room."

David frowned. "I haven't had a decent night's sleep in ages, Chloe. Three days ago, I was up at dawn, trying to find peace in the park. Instead, I found myself in the folly." He took a step toward her. "Do you know what I found there? Our initials, still etched into the glass."

She eyed him coldly. "Did you break the pane? I would have."

He shook his head. "I will treasure that glass forever, for it made me remember how I felt about you that day. The same way I've felt ever since."

She stared at him, her face marble-like in its stillness.

"I thought I hated you all those years, Chloe. I did such a good job of convincing myself that I really believed it. But I didn't hate you. If I wasn't such a stubborn fool, I would have realized it the first moment I laid eyes on you again at Georgie's. I still loved you."

She turned away. "You speak very prettily. But you talked that way at Georgie's too."

"Only part of what I said there was a lie," he said quietly. "What I said to you that night, when I told you I didn't care. I wanted to hurt you, Chloe. I wanted you to feel a part of the pain I felt when I came back and found you'd married Jonathan."

David took a step toward her. "Do you know how I felt? To survive months of pain and agony, only to discover that the woman I loved had given up and married someone else?" He grabbed her shoulders and his fingers tightened. "Do you know how that felt?"

Chloe's eyes flashed angrily. "Do you think it was easy for me? In the same moment I discovered that you weren't dead—and that we could not be together . . ."

"If you'd waited. . . ."

Chloe lay her hand against his cheek. "David, I am so very, very sorry. I know I was weak, know I did wrong. But I had to live with my mistake too. I tried to be a good wife to Jonathan, but I still loved you. I only pray that I hid it well enough. He deserved so much better."

His hands dropped to his sides. "Chloe, I have been a stupid fool. I convinced myself I hated you because I couldn't bear the thought of living without you." He clasped her hand in his. "I still can't. Tell me we can start over. Let me court you, woo you, convince you that I do love you."

Chloe didn't reply and her silence frightened him. "Chloe, I know I've given you little cause to trust me. But you must. I swear on that pane of glass at Linwood that I'll never do anything to hurt you again."

She blinked back tears. "I want to believe you, David."

"I know I've lived a ramshackle life, but that will change. I only traveled so I would not have to risk seeing you with Jonathan. I don't need to run away anymore. I'm ready to live at Linwood—if you will be my wife."

"Oh, David." She wrapped her arms about his waist and buried her face in his shirtfront.

With his right hand David dug in his pocket and pulled out the small bag. "I brought this back from Spain, for you." He pulled out the chased silver ring and slipped it on her finger. "I hope it will do for a betrothal ring, until I can get you something more elegant."

Chloe twisted the ring on her finger. "This is the only one I shall ever want." She reached up and pulled his mouth down on hers.

"And we shall go traveling for our honeymoon."

She wrinkled her nose. "I don't think I wish to go to Egypt."

"I was thinking more of Italy."

Chloe's eyes danced. "Georgie will be angry. I am supposed to go with her."

"Somehow, I think Georgie will understand." He gathered her into his arms and kissed her until they were breathless.

A loud pounding sounded on the door. "Denby? Chloe? What's going on in there?"

Chloe was too busy returning David's kisses to respond.

"Chloe?" Stephen's voice sounded concerned.

"Go away, Stephen," Chloe said.

"I demand that you tell me what is going on!"

"I'm proposing to your sister-in-law," David shouted back. "Go away."

"What?"

At Stephen's startled exclamation, David and Chloe both laughed.

They were wed in indecent haste, two weeks later by license, and the tenth Viscount Denby, the Honorable Jonathan Ridgefield North, made his appearance a scant eight months later.

Buried Treasure

❦

by Edith Layton

June, 1699
Glen Cove, Long Island, New York

The path of moonlight on the water shone silver as pieces of eight. The water in the Sound was dead calm. The night was still, except for the men's harsh breathing and the scuffed sounds of their footsteps as they struggled through the sand to the land beyond. Their dirks, swords, and pistols were snugged secure in their belts, and although their bright earrings swayed to their steps, they were silent as bells without clappers. Even the parrot that rode a shoulder of one of the men was still as a jade statue. No other ship except the one that had brought them could be seen in the waters beneath that luminous moon tonight. But still, no one spoke until they let down the heavy chest they had staggered under—and that only when they were under a sheltering tree at the edge of the beach they'd come upon.

"Gawd! Weighs a ton," one man sighed as he finally straightened his aching back. "Mebbe two. We should of had more men with us. Me back's broke entirely."

"Aye, Master Quickwit," another scoffed, "so there'd be more to share with?"

"Ye mean fer the cap'n to worry about," the first man said with a sneer.

"Oh, I don't think so," a bulky man said as he stepped from the shadows to stand over the chest. "I don't worry about any of you. Should I?"

The silence was profound. Then the first man spoke up again with a great deal of false gusto. "Nah. I never meant that, Cap'n. Trust me wi' your life, ye can."

"No," the captain said quietly, "I believe it is you who trust me with your lives, isn't it? Of course," he went on as the silence deepened, "you all have been at this business longer than I. I might not have it right. But I believe that I am the one with the power to leave you all here to guard the chest for me for eternity, if I so chose. Am I not?"

"No need to talk like that, Cap'n," another man said, shifting his boots as he spoke. "No need a'tall. Sure, you're cap'n, and we do as you says, we do. Jewel here, 'e's just gibbering in 'is beard, is all."

"Jewel," another of the men said with humor in his voice, "complains like other fellers sneeze, Cap'n. Were he not kickin', we'd wonder were he breathin'."

"You lookin' fer trouble from me?" Jewel asked the man menacingly, his hand flashing to the dagger he had thrust into the sash belted across his wide middle. Then he crouched and spread his bandy legs apart and glowered at a muted sound he heard coming from a man leaning against the tree. "And you. You laughin'? Mockin' me, Dancer, eh?"

"Relax, Jewel," one of the men said, "it were only a jest."

"Were it?" Jewel asked, his small eyes narrowing more. "Or were it that he wants somethin' of me?"

"When I want anything from you, you'll know it, I promise," the man he'd called Dancer said. "But don't wait on it. I wouldn't want ice from you in Hell."

"*I* want only that you fellows plant that chest for me, and plant it deep," the captain said. "And now. Of course, if you don't wish to . . ."

The men fell silent and picked up the shovels they'd brought with them. They began to dig.

The captain strolled behind the lean man called Dancer. "I'd advise you to keep your laughter to yourself, lad," the captain said softly, "do you wish to end this journey all of a piece, that is."

Dancer shrugged, and then got to digging with the rest of them.

When the hole was deep enough, they lowered the chest in. Then they stood in a ragged ring and looked down with satisfaction. They were a colorful company, even in the moonlight that bleached them all to the colors of sand. They wore long frockcoats, flowing shirts, and had wide sashes over their ragged trousers. Their soft boots were cuffed high on their legs, and they wore their hats or kerchiefs low over their tanned foreheads. Their hair was too long for any fashion but their own. Some had eyepatches, most had scars, and all were tanned the color of teak. Their captain was dressed as a prosperous man of business, the only concession to his livelihood the many rings that glittered on his fingers.

The captain paced off the site, back to the beach and the rowboat they'd come in. Then he paced back again, muttering to himself and nodding. He was memorizing the number of steps he'd taken, and in what direction, when he heard the men begin to argue again.

It was done before he got back to them, though he hurried.

He saw only the flash of steel. The man he'd called

Dancer stood with his hand on his heart, staring at Jewel in astonishment. Then he turned and looked at the captain.

"I—I didn't even have my knife in hand!" he said in amazement, looking at his blood, black as midnight in the moonlight, as it poured between his fingers. Then he fell.

The men stood still, in shock.

"He were only jesting!" one of the pirates said, looking at Dancer and the dark pool spreading beneath him in the darker shadows as he lay before them.

"One time too many," Jewel said. He was still crouched for the kill, and his small eyes scanned the others. "Who's next? C'mon," he said, waggling the fingers of his left hand, his knife glinting in the bright moonlight in his right one. "Who wants to argue wi' me? Eh? I had a grievance, din't I? I done what I had to. He goaded me, he vexed me sore. But I waited. A man can't fight 'board ship. I knows the rules of the Brotherhood. But he can on land. On land is where we are. C'mon, who wants to take issue wi' me?"

"What 'e says, 'tis so," muttered one pirate, eyeing the still form on the ground before them.

"So it is," the captain said on a sigh, looking down at Dancer.

"But 'tis a hard thing. He had no warning, did he?" another said.

"Was I s'posed to send him a letter, eh?" Jewel asked. Looking around and seeing their averted eyes, he grinned at last, showing all his yellow teeth to the night. "Well, well," he said jauntily, sheathing his dagger in his sash again. He sauntered around the fallen man, and prodded him with one foot. "No more jests,

Dancer, eh? Be tellin' them to the Devil now, I s'pect. Eh? Be *wishful* I'd give you ice now, I s'pect, eh?" He laughed and kicked the body.

"Leave him be!" the captain said harshly.

It was an odd thing for a pirate captain to say, because most wouldn't have minded if Jewel had torn the fellow's guts and gizzards out and made a necklace of them on the spot. But Kidd was new to the sea, and every man jack of them knew it. He was also on the run for his life, and in no position to lose them now, and every man jackal of them knew that too.

"O' course, o' course," Jewel said generously. "Leave him be, right here, and forever. Let's bury him wi' it. On it. Many's the cap'n who leaves a body to guard his treasure, Cap'n. Ye said it yerself, and I seen it done. Trust the captains to get a body to work for them forever, eh, lads?"

He laughed uproariously. But the others didn't. The lad had been a handsome one and no mistake, and no few of them knew that was really why he'd grow no older than the night now. They'd heard him reject Jewel's offer of friendship when he'd first appeared among them—and after too. But work was work, and theirs was a hard life. They looked at the captain.

"No time for anything else," he admitted. "Let it be done."

The rowboat left the island as quietly as it had come. Nothing stirred in the sea but the oars as they bit deep and surfaced again, as the little boat sped to join the great ship waiting for them near the horizon. Some of them gazed back at the rapidly diminishing sight of the island where they'd left the treasure, and the dead man who would guard it for eternity now.

But a light breeze had picked up, and the island was a welter of shadows. They were too far, in any case, even to see the spot where they'd buried their treasure. Or the hand that clawed up from out of the sand there. And then shot up in the air, wavering frantically—almost as though it was waving farewell to them.

There had been sand in his eyes and his ears. He'd opened his mouth to scream and could not. It had to have been a nightmare. No man could live so. No men could let another die so. He remembered trying to scream; he remembered the panic that set him clawing and scuttling and writhing to find air to fill his lungs. He had, somehow he had. But then he had no breath left to scream. He'd only strength enough to squirm and twist and pant until he'd freed himself from his grave. Or so, at least, he must have done. Because he wasn't dead now. The pain made him wish he were. But when he closed his eyes and sought sleep, he remembered the nightmare and came awake again. This, he thought, remembering a sermon he'd once heard when he'd been young, must be neither death nor life, Heaven nor Hell. Dark and painful, and wracked with equal parts remorse and horror: he must be in Limbo.

But were there voices in Limbo?

"Poor fellow," one voice said, "poor lad."

"But he's a pirate, Father. Just see how he's dressed!"

"We can't know that."

"We saw the ship sail off."

"He could have been a captive on that ship," a gentle woman's voice argued.

Dancer tried to open his eyes. It had been a long while since he'd heard a woman's voice.

"And he could have been a cutthroat."

Dancer froze. He was aware enough to understand they were talking about him, and hard experience had taught him to be still when that happened.

"But someone tried to cut his throat, poor fellow," another woman's voice said, "or at least, his heart out. And he's so young. Have some charity. He might be your age, Jeffrey."

"He might be a killer," the voice said stubbornly.

"Softly, softly, lad. He might be dead by morning," another voice said with sorrow. " 'Tis a wonder he got so far as it is. They must have dumped him off the ship, and the tide did the rest. Because the men found him half in the water, and more than half dead too, poor soul."

He struggled to open his eyes, to tell them he'd be damned if he'd die, in more ways than one. Someone put a cool hand on his forehead. It comforted him. They didn't do that in Limbo, he thought.

"Poor fellow," the gentle voice said, "sleep, sleep."

He didn't want to, he wanted to see who spoke such sweetness.

"There, he's resting easy."

No! he tried to cry. And heard the voice fade as he fainted.

When he opened his eyes again, it was morning—on this earth, he thought with relief. But it might as well have been another one because he'd never woken to such comfort in all his life. Not even in the best bordellos in Hispaniola. There were no gilded chairs and feathery palms. He lay on plain cotton sheeting, not satin. But he stared around the room and felt the peace and plain comfort of it soothe him.

The bed he lay in was huge, with posts at the foot and head. It was intricately carved and polished to a high sheen, and he could see it was made of solid mahogany. If there was anything his life at sea had taught him, it was the appreciation of good wood. The fittings in the room were also stoutly made, the chests and chairs fashioned of thick oak. White curtains shaded the sunlight that flowed in through the big windows, but let in enough to show the varied colors on his coverlet, and all the bright hues of the rag carpet that covered the wide-planked floor. It smelled clean. It was quiet. He was alone. It was, he thought, as he watched a slight breeze make the curtains belly out like clipper sails, a sort of heaven, after all.

The door opened and he quickly closed his eyes. It was better that a man knew what he was opening them to before he did. Both his life at sea and the one he'd led before he'd ever set sail had taught him that.

She opened the door and peered in. He lay still as one of the carved figures on his headboard, she thought. In fact, he lay so still that she caught her breath and hurried to his bedside to put a hand on his forehead. He was warm, but it wasn't the hectic heat of fever anymore. It was a healthy warmth; he glowed with the banked fires of life. He rested easily at last. And so she gazed her fill at him for the first time without fear of looking her last at him.

She lived in a place where men went to sea to earn their livelihoods and protect their families. But still she'd never seen his like before. He seemed a creature of the sea, not just a man from it. His chest was covered with bandaging and he wore one of her father's nightshirts, but still it was clear he was lean and well made, with wide shoulders and a strong young neck. His skin was dark against the white sheets, the total tropical brown of a man who had lived outdoors beneath alien suns. His overlong crop of shaggy hair was wheat at its roots, and there were strands of purest gold and platinum where the sun had bleached it. His face was young, but even in repose it was not a boy's. He had high, sharp cheekbones, a sharp, straight wedge of a nose, and far too much jaw for true handsomeness. But that strong chin was graced with a cleft. And his face, with its light stubble of golden beard grown since he'd been put in the bed, fascinated her more than any handsome man's ever had.

She was used to rescuing the creatures from the waters that surrounded her island. It was a wild coast, where northeast storms and the rag ends of tropical tempests that strayed up from the south often signaled the change of seasons. She'd weathered many storms in her short life and nursed many wild seaborne creatures before freeing them to ride the tide again. But he, she thought with a shiver, was as alien and exotic as any bird that had ever been blown off course and brought in to their safe harbor.

He'd been in bed nearly a week. Her mother had tended him most of the time, with her father doing the more intimate duties for him. But she'd watched over him every day since the morning they'd brought him in too, and had never seen him conscious. Now he was still inert and silent before her. He lay in the second-best bedroom, with the early morning sunshine shining in on its familiar trappings, and a soft morning breeze puffed at the curtains. Nothing could be more familiar, safer, homier. And yet she found herself hesitating to come close enough to him to straighten his sheet. It was foolish, she scolded herself, to feel so wary around him. He was completely at her mercy.

Until he opened his eyes. She gasped.

He knew why. It had happened before.

"Hello," he said, his low voice rusty from lack of use. "Do I live? Are you real? Am I?"

"Oh," she said, her color rising, because his voice was only that of a man's, and a tired, weak one too. "Yes, you're certainly alive," she said briskly, to cover her embarrassment at her fear of him. "How do you feel?"

"But are you real?" he asked, so he could see the charming color climb in her cheeks again. He'd known women whose cheeks were the tints of wild rose, sunny sienna, and all the hues of scarlet from hibiscus to poppy. But he couldn't remember when he'd last seen a lass blush. Or seen a maid's pale complexion turn pink and not stay that way until the color was removed with soap, or water, or tears.

She was young and pretty although she was plainly dressed and wore no paint at all, and that too was a novelty to him. He was used to women whose colors screamed their sex from half a tavern away. He was used to more spectacular ones too, but she was indeed a pretty woman. Slender and shapely, her hair was smooth and straight and seal brown, and her eyes hazel and sheltered by long lacy lashes. She had a small, straight nose and warm pink lips. He noticed there were freckles on the bridge of that little nose. The sight of them filled him with a queer tenderness that tempered his lust. But not for long.

The modest green-striped cotton gown she wore didn't flatter her. But it couldn't conceal the lovely shape of her high breasts and small waist. He only glanced away from that entrancing sight when he realized she was backing tiny steps away from him. It was wise of her, but it would never do. He hurt, and had no more energy than a flea. But he breathed. And he'd endured worse. Still, he sensed he'd be a long time healing. He'd no intention of spending all that time in bed alone.

"Oh!" he gasped, putting his hand to his heart as though he was stricken, and lay back and closed his eyes again.

She stepped back to him quickly. He saw, through half-closed eyes, that she was alarmed. Better, he thought with an inward smile as she came closer. She bent toward him. He scented flowers.

"Mother!" she cried.

Damnation, he thought on a resigned sigh. He'd overplayed his hand. But it was a poor one anyhow, he reminded himself ruefully. He didn't know what he could have been thinking of—well, he did, but it was folly. Having been so close to death made him want to prove he was alive, and he knew no better way than with a lass. But his chest *did* hurt, and he didn't know who she was or where he was. It was no time to be thinking of lasses, pretty little ones who blushed or not. It wasn't like him either. He was a man who always used his head. It must have been the injury, he thought. Thinking of that, and how narrowly he'd escaped being buried alive, he grew solemn.

So he looked gray under his tan, and grim, when the older woman who must be her mother came hurrying into the room.

"What's amiss? Has he taken a turn for the worse?

I thought he was on his way to healing," the older woman said as she bustled to his bedside.

"He was—he woke. He spoke," the girl said in confusion, "but then he gasped and closed his eyes again."

"Don't fret yourself on my account," he said weakly, struggling to rise and catching his breath sharply as he failed. This time he wasn't shamming. He looked up at the women. "It's only that I tried to move and discovered myself unable. I'm not used to being an invalid. I . . . ah . . ." He paused and saw how the older woman was looking at him. The younger kept her eyes averted this time. A faint resigned smile was etched around his hard mouth, "Don't worry, mistress. It takes some folks like that. I'm used to it. Besides, I only see myself when I'm shaving, and only in a dim mirror at that. The sailors on that accursed ship that stranded me sometimes called me 'Shark'. I see you can see their point."

"Fiddle," the older woman said briskly, "they're lovely eyes, silver as Spanish coins."

But "shark" was exactly right, Hannah thought, looking at him again. She'd never seen a live shark that close, of course. But they too must have such eyes when they coursed the seas in search of prey: eyes the color of their skins, bright and silver, glinting with danger and knowledge men didn't possess. The stranger's were tilted and shining, beautiful and odd, and terrifying. And so attractive that she avoided them now.

"Spanish coin?" he asked with a hint of weary humor. "False as that? Is that what you think of me, mistress?"

"I think you're a fine rogue," Hannah's mother said,

"to jest and flirt like a cavalier when you've a dagger wound deep as my hand in your chest. And just waked to find yourself in a strange place too. Well, we've passed a week trying to get you to the point of realizing that. So let me introduce ourselves. You're in the house of Jedidiah Jenkins, of Glen Cove. I'm his wife, Rachel, mistress of this home. And this is my daughter, Hannah. And you, sir?"

He answered, but he was obviously still confused, she thought. Because he stammered, and had to catch himself and think before he even got his own name right.

"I give you thanks for all your efforts, Mistress Jenkins. I am Danc— Dans— Dan Silver," he said.

"Before I tell you the way of it, I've an odd question to put to you," he said.

The wounded man sat propped up on pillows in his high bed. The morning sun showed him pallid beneath his tan and yet he seemed restless, though they knew he hadn't even the strength to sit up by himself yet.

The four members of the Jenkins family filled his sunny room.

Mistress Rachel sat in a chair by his bed, her tall, broad, genial husband Jedidiah, beside her, puffing on his pipe. Lanky young Jeffrey, whose face showed he was hovering between suspicion and fascination as much as he was between boyhood and adulthood, lounged in the doorway—too interested to leave, too embarrassed about his interest to come all the way into the room. And the lovely Hannah sat by the window wreathed in morning sunlight.

They'd come into his room to hear his story. They were his rescuers, they deserved a tale about his plight. He'd make it a fair one for them. Whatever he was or had been, he knew the value of a fair trade. But first he needed some answers. They were folk who lived by the sea. Before he told them anything, he had to know what they knew of it.

"They say when a man faces the worst there is, sometimes kind nature hides it from him if he survives," he began. "I woke with a pain in my chest, to find I'd escaped death. But how did you find me?"

"Some boys were putting out for lobsters. They found you on the beach, half in the water and half out, and with half your blood gone, or so it seemed. It was the cold water kept the rest in you. So it often happens," Jedidiah said wisely, "salt and the cold seal it in.

"Many's the hook I've set in my own hand, and many's the time I've healed the wound that way," Jedidiah mused. "I was a fisherman before I quit the sea to do my trading from a desk. But it's done me well. I've the biggest house hereabouts. That's why they brought you to us. You were so mazed with pain you were actually trying to crawl out to sea instead of the shore. You may thank Providence the tide was coming in, and you were too weak to fight it. You were taken from the sea covered with sand and blood, and brought straight to us. We can't tell you more than that—and the fact that a privateer was seen sailing out of the sound the night before."

Dan Silver nodded his shaggy head. "It's a wonder, then, that you took me in," he said. "Weren't you afraid you'd taken in a pirate?" he asked flippantly. But he watched them closely.

"Even had we, we had little to fear," Jedidiah said,

"seeing as how you near to death you were. But are you telling us now that you are of that persuasion?"

"Why, were I, I'd be a fool to tell you, wouldn't I?" his guest said with a bitter smile. "But they're not so cruel to those of their number as they were to me. Still, I can't ask you to take my word for what I am, friends, since you don't know me. I owe you my story. What I am, I shall tell you now. And leave it to you to believe what you will."

His odd silver eyes filled with a faraway look.

"As to how I came here—you know almost as much as I do," he said on a long sigh. "As for my life before that? I'm a common seafaring man, and have been since I was a lad. I was born in England and stayed there only until I was old enough to get my feet wet. I've seen seven and twenty summers, and in that time I've traveled six of the seven seas. There's many an entertaining tale I could tell you. But not today. That tale begins when I set sail last year from London town."

They nodded. He had the accent, and there was no sense denying it.

"I hired on a fine merchantman bound for the Caribe Indies to trade in spice and fine cloth," he went on. "Alas. We never got so far. Not a month out, we were hailed by cutthroats. We tried to outrun them—"

"Ah, there's folly," Jedidiah said on a puff of fragrant tobacco.

"Just so," Dan sighed. "For they took it much amiss, I can tell you. I'll not go into details," he said with a significant glance toward Hannah, "but I tell you, they were not pretty, not at all. They did board us. I survived, to be sure. As did most able-bodied men—who were not officers. That's their way, you see.

I'm by nature a survivor. It occurred to me that were I a good sailor, I could sail on with them until I could win my way to freedom. I *am* a good sailor, though they didn't want me as such. But I can stroke an oar as well as any living man. So I did. It was hard work, but a man may work hard for many masters. While I was prisoner they didn't seek new booty, so my conscience didn't hurt so much as my body."

He chuckled as they did. But then his long face grew harsh shadows, his eyes grew a flat silvery sheen like water before a storm, and his voice roughened. "Ah, but not a month past, I overheard a conversation below decks. Then I knew I had to escape while I still could. They were going to Madagascar to sell all their ill-got gains, you see . . . including me."

Hannah gasped, but her mother and father only nodded.

"The beys, they do say, buy men of Christian flesh as slaves," Dan explained.

"This is so," Jedidiah said on a sigh.

"Aye," Dan went on, "and once a man is sold into bondage there, he never sees freedom this side of Heaven again. Since I wasn't at all sure I could gain admittance there, I tried to escape."

He waited while the women hid their grins and the men were done laughing. But then Jedidiah looked at him shrewdly.

"But the ship that was sighted in the sound the night before we found you was the *Antonio*. That's Captain Kidd's. He's no corsair. He's a New York merchantman known from Manhattan Island to Oyster Bay."

"Merchantman turned pirate," Jeffrey spoke up from the doorway.

"Aye, more's the pity," his father said. "But even so, the beys get their Christian slaves from the Barbary Coast, not Long Island Sound, lad."

"True," Dan said quickly, "but a privateer will take on any sort of merchandise if there's a profit in it. And a man on the run lightens his cargo where he can and when he can. All I know is that when I heard I was bound for Algiers, I knew I had to try to escape if an opportunity presented, whether it was a false rumor or no. No, I reasoned that even if I died in the attempt, it would be better than living with the Turks with a collar around my neck and hot coals on my feet—that much I knew. Kidd's wanted for piracy in London and is all a pother to escape with his name *and* his treasures."

"So it *was* Kidd's vessel you were on," Jedidiah said.

Dan sat up straight. The effort made him wince, and his face grew ashen beneath his tan.

"My illness has loosened my wits along with my tongue," he said quickly. "I owe my life to you good people, I'll not risk yours. There are things it's better not to know. So I'll only say I was discovered trying to escape. I remember fighting. I felt a knife thrust, and then a long fall to water. After that I remember nothing until I woke in this bed. More than that— I cannot say. Forgive me. Or turn me out. But that is all."

He sat back with the air of a man who has just thrown the dice and waits to see how they fall.

"Aye, toss you out, and we'll have the bother of burying you," Jedidiah said.

His wife shot him an angry look, but before she could say what she'd opened her mouth to do, her husband went on. "No, the only thing worth burying here is fish heads. Keep your secret, Master Silver. There's little we can do with it anyway, were you pirate or not. Kidd's sought wherever he goes, and it's not Long Island fisher folk will take the prize money for him. But they say he's burying his treasure from here to Gardiner's Island so that it won't fall into the hands of the English. I don't suppose you know ought of that, do you?"

"Of course I do," Dan said, grinning. "Pirate captains always tell their prisoners the why and where of it. Sometimes they give them maps to their treasure as well. It helps to pass the long evenings between the dancing and pipe music, don't you know."

When they were done laughing at him, he said more seriously, "But I wish he had. Seriously, my friends, I am only a poor seafaring man, with no more worth in life than the wages due me at the end of a voyage. My voyage has ended beforetime. I have nothing but my thanks for you. How can I repay you?"

"Get well," Jedidiah said as he rose to his feet. "We ask nothing else."

"Done!" said Dan so fiercely he started coughing.

"Not quite," Jedidiah said with a wry smile.

"Are you sure we're wise to keep him here?" Rachel Jenkins asked her husband when they were alone. "We know nothing of him, after all. And we do have a daughter."

"What, then? Throw him out? And our daughter is a clever girl," her husband answered comfortably.

They sat in their bedroom and talked as they always did when they prepared for bed. It was their only true quiet time together, when she was too tired to knit or mend and he, too weary to whittle or tinker with his fishing gear or rifle any longer.

"Yes, she's clever but mortal, I remind you, Mr. Jenkins. He looks a lusty lad," she said as she brushed out her hair.

"Lusty but not likely. The fellow was near death the other day."

"But don't you wonder why?" she asked, putting down her brush.

"What's eating at you, my dear?" he asked, marking his place in the Bible with one finger as he gazed at her. "Out with it."

"You know me too well, Mr. Jenkins," she admitted with a sigh. "Here it is, then. There was a privateer in the sound the other night. He came off it and doesn't deny it. I know he told a good story, but he may be a pirate. That is what he may have been."

"Yes. Maybe so. But so have many of our friends and neighbors been. Or do you think old Bellamy got all his gold from catching cod? Or Mr. Wickham his money to start his dry-goods store from picking winkles? No, no. We live off the sea in many ways, and there's many a man of our acquaintance who's gone a'pirating. And do we blame them for it? No, we look away and pretend they were common sailors or whalers. But no honest tar can come up with the sort of money that so many of our leading citizens have. You know it well, Mrs. Jenkins. The sea is a hard master, worse for those lads who take the king's coin. Worse still for them who didn't mean to. You know how it is when a captain needs a full roster by the next tide. Then a crew is kidnapped—'impressed'—well, call it what they may, it's the same thing. The men they need are carried off from the streets to the ship, and all in the name of the king's navy. Men—and boys—sent to sea for years when all they want is to stay at home with their loved ones. Sometimes it's not much better for those who sign on with pirate masters thinking it will be a fine, free life and finding it little better than slavery. And not at the hands of the beys, neither."

He sighed. "For some, being on a privateer means being free. But the wise ones chart a course to the land soon as they are able. I don't hold with pirates. Some are the scum of the earth. But some are men looking for freedom, and some just lads gone wrong looking for the light. There's too many boys who think it's a life filled with adventure too. We thank God on bended knee each night our Jeff hasn't felt Jolly Roger's lure, don't we?"

She sighed. "You're right on all counts, Mr. Jenkins. But what about our Hannah?"

"Why, what about her? It's not as though the fellow is in any condition to do any damage in this house."

"That's not the sort of damage I was thinking about," she said as she lay her brush down. "I've never seen a prettier fellow."

"Pretty?" her husband asked in astonishment. "The fellow's about as pretty as a shark."

"You men don't understand," she complained as she tugged on her lace nightcap.

"Oh, but we do and better than you think, Mrs. Jenkins," he said on a chuckle, coming up behind her to lift the lacy thing off her head so he could run his hands through her hair. He smiled down at her. "Far better than you think."

It was much later, as she curled against his side in their big feather bed, that she spoke again. "It's not what the lad might do that I fear," she fretted. "It's what a lad like that might make a girl do."

"Not our Hannah," he muttered sleepily.

"Well, I suppose not," she said doubtfully before she closed her eyes to sleep. "She is a very sensible girl, to be sure.

". . . and," she reassured herself a half hour later before she finally allowed herself to sleep, "it's not as though she's alone in the house with him, is it?"

Hannah paused at the door to his room and frowned at the sound of laughter. It didn't sound the least bit funny to her. Because she recognized whose it was. Molly's laughter was girlish, and Sal's was muffled because she always covered her mouth with one hand. But both maidservants were supposed to be working—not laughing. Molly was supposed to be in the kitchen getting dinner ready. Sal was only supposed to be making the bed up around him. Whatever they should have been doing, neither was supposed to be smothering giggles.

It stopped when she walked into the room.

"Oh!" Sal said, her hand flying to her mouth in mid-giggle. "S'cuse me, I'm sure, Miss Hannah, I was only just going."

"So I see," Hannah said. "But what were you only just doing?"

"Ah, helpin' poor Moll here with the linens," Sal said, and dropped a quick curtsy before she fled the room.

"I were just finishing," Molly protested as she scurried out after Sal.

Hannah turned to see the patient.

Her father had said that even if he was a pirate,

he'd be no harm to anyone until he could move out of his bed. Her mother agreed, but she had looked a little worried. Now Hannah knew why. Maybe men couldn't see the danger in the fellow. But he had only to look at a girl for her to know exactly how dangerous he was. Especially propped up in bed, looking so tan and fit and comfortable. Hannah had grown up in a community where half the men worked the sea, and a man's bare chest was as common a sight as a storm cloud to her. But she'd never seen his like before.

He should have looked like an invalid, with that great white bandage wrapped around his chest. But he lay back against his pillows, his nightshirt open, and all a girl saw was the tanned skin where the bandage wasn't. Skin and the taut muscle beneath that moved when he shifted his position and smiled at her. And then all a girl saw was the white of his teeth against the tan of his face and the creases the smile made in his lean cheeks. And that only because she was trying so hard to avoid looking at the knowing smile growing in those amazing eyes. He looked about as helpless as a sting ray.

Hannah had a youthful father, a younger brother, four uncles, and three male cousins. She had beaux all over the island and one in Manhattan too. She never lacked for a dancing partner at a party, and her parents were always warning her to be careful in her choice of a husband because a husband was forever. She didn't need their warnings. She loved flattery and attention, and got it in plenty, but she often wondered how much flattery a married woman got. No fellow so far had tempted her very much. In truth, now that she was one and twenty, she'd started worrying about that, wondering if there was some fault in her. All her friends were wed, or engaged to be. But she couldn't get up much enthusiasm for any lad. It seemed that every man she knew was someone she had known forever.

This man was an unknown, and so was the fluttery feeling in her stomach when he smiled his dangerous smile at her.

"How are you this morning?" she asked abruptly.

"Better ... now," he said, on a grin.

She ignored the insinuation and came to his bedside. But there was nothing for her to do for him. His sheets were crisp and clean, his bandage snowy, there was a carafe of water and a tumbler by his bed, and an untouched bowl of fruit besides.

"Is there anything I can do for you?" she asked anyway, moving the bowl of fruit an inch so as to have something to do. And to avoid seeing speculation in those knowing eyes that followed her every step.

His smile was so bright it bordered on bold. But just as she was about to walk from the room, he said seriously, "Aye. There be. There is a thing, if you would, Mistress Hannah.

"I've been here three days that I know of, and a week, they tell me, before that. I've no complaint about my treatment," he said earnestly. "Truly. How could I? Your family kindly saved me from the sea and nursed and fed me too. I'm a lucky fellow indeed, and well I know it. Were I to live to a hundred I couldn't thank you enough. But there is a favor.... It's not that I'm ungrateful, mind. But I'm unused to biding in one room, all pent up. One room that doesn't move, at that. So, could you bide with me a while, mistress, and tell me about the day? I have a window, to be sure. But your mother is afraid I'll take a chill, so it's sealed as tight as a mermaid's purse. And lying here as I must, I can't see out it. Might you tell me something of the weather and the tides too? Or news from the town, or country? I feel quite out of it, you see."

"But Molly and Sal were just here . . ." she said and stopped, blushing, remembering how one look at her face had chased the pair of them back to their chores.

"And fine lasses they are too," he said enthusiastically. "But more interested in giggles than conversation. And who else is there to talk with? Your mother has her duties cut out for her, as does your father. Your brother, I fear, does not trust me entirely. Not that I blame him," he said quickly, "coming to you from the sea like a bit of driftwood as I did, why should he? But I mean no harm—'deed, I couldn't do any did I mean any," he chuckled. His handsome face grew grave again. "I hoped you, Mistress Hannah, might have time for a chat. I must truly be getting better, because an invalid doesn't care about the world around him—and the truth is that I'm restless as a crab on a hot deck."

It was a reasonable request. For all he looked magnificent in his nest of white linen, he also looked sorely out of place. He was too vital a man for the room itself. But he didn't look threatening. Only ill at ease. There wasn't a trace of anything piratical in his face now. Instead, he looked so humble that her fear of him was replaced by concern for his feelings.

"No one's brought you a newspaper?" she asked. "But that's no problem. Father gets the paper once a week. I'm sure he'll share it with you."

"Thank you," he said after a moment of silence, "but that would never do. I chose the sea too young, you see. I can read the stars and the clouds, the wind and the tides. But I can't read a paper of any kind. I'm sorry," he said, and he seemed to be, "but there it is. But if you ..." He gazed at her and it seemed his tan face grew a little ruddier, "that is to say," he said quickly, "might *you* consider reading it to me? I dislike to ask, but it's a thing I'd hardly ask of your father," he added with a crooked smile.

"Why, but I'd be pleased to," she said, trying to hide the fact that she was shocked. He spoke like an educated fellow—and every man she knew, fisherman or merchant, could read. Not bondsmen or hired hands, of course. But even the poorest fellows in town went to school until they learned that, at least.

"Or maybe even show me the way of reading the letters, so I could do it for myself and not be such a bother to you," he said carefully. "I haven't the art of it, but maybe that's because I was never really shown the way of it. I can try, if you would care to try me ... I understand if you cannot," he said quickly, looking away, smoothing the patchwork quilt at his chest with one big tanned hand. "Forgive me my presuming, mistress."

"Well, but I wouldn't understand if I could not!" she said angrily, because she was vexed with herself for her confusion. "I'd be glad to, Mr. Silver. And I'll start as soon as you feel able."

"Mistress Hannah, behold me able," he said. "I sorely need to exercise something, if only my poor brain. Ah, but only if you call me Dan. Because it would be a hard thing, I think, for you to say, 'Look again! That's a *A* not a *Z* Mr. Silver, you blockhead!'"

"Very well, but then I must be Hannah too. Because Mistress Hannah makes me feel like a schoolteacher. And mine was a caution, and two years younger than Moses too!"

"Very well, Hannah," he said, so softly she colored up and ducked her head.

"I'll just get a primer. I still have mine. And a slate, with some pencils, I think. Yes. Paper and ink wouldn't be a good idea if we are going to work while you are abed. And we can," she said with sudden inspiration, her eyes gleaming. "I'll get a board, we can lay it across the bed. Oh, this will work wonderfully."

He smiled at her enthusiasm. And his smile remained, although it was different, as he watched her trim figure as she left the room.

"You're doing wonderfully well," Hannah said an hour later. She sat back and looked at him suspiciously. "Are you sure you're not teasing me? I could swear you know your letters."

"Don't jeopardize your soul, Hannah," he said with a laugh, lying back against his pillow again. "I know the shape of them, and the name of some, to be sure. but I never stayed long enough to know all that they can do. It hinders a man to be ignorant. This is a wonderful opportunity for me, I could almost thank the villain who laid me low."

"Can you remember more about that now?" Hannah asked eagerly.

"They say the mind heals itself by covering over such pain until it can be dealt with, so it must be with me. I can't remember more than I woke with. It seems—sometimes, in the night, that I dream of it. Because I awake in terror. I will tell you that. But I remember nothing when I do. Just as well, I think. But here, no need to mourn me. As you can see, I thrive now. And I know my alphabet, and in the correct order too, do I not?"

"But I don't understand, you speak so well," she said, brushing aside his question. Because he did, she thought, he spoke like a man of learning.

" 'Deed, I hope so. I've an ear. It's so with many men who have no letters, Hannah. We learn to read faces and voices as other men read books, and we do it well—perhaps because we have nothing else in our minds," he laughed. But then he grew serious. "Early on, I learned that a man is marked by his speech as surely as by his clothing. A man who speaks well does well. So I copied the men who owned the ships, not those who sailed them. I was a poor lad, Hannah. I intend to be a richer man someday. I'll do anything I must to be that," he said, and he said it like a vow. "So thank you. This is a rare opportunity. There's not too many teachers sailing the seas. And none half so lovely on land either, I daresay."

His compliment would ordinarily have turned her pink. But she was thinking too deeply to be self-conscious. "Did you never think of quitting the sea?" she asked.

"Oh. Yes. Many times. But I don't know the land as I do the sea. And only a fool jumps in with two feet without knowing where he's going. But now? Well. I am learning—many things. And perhaps now I've more of a reason to look to the shore," he said gently.

They were close. She'd set a board over the coverlets on his knees and established a makeshift desk there. But she had bent from her chair to see what he'd written, and so their faces were very close now. She heard the hesitation in his deep voice at the last. When she looked up, startled, she could see that his

odd silver eyes were fixed on her face, and there was
a look in them she couldn't look away from. Although
she should, she thought with an odd sense of panic.
Oh, heavens, she should.

Her face went pink, then pale, except for her lips,
he thought. They remained pink, though they parted
in surprise. They looked soft and plush and were so
close. Close as his hand, as he reached to her. He
touched her cheek with the tips of his fingers and felt
how soft her skin was, and heard her next indrawn
breath. And leaned forward to claim her lips, because
he knew to the second when they would part farther
for him. But so, it seemed, did she.

Because she gasped and moved back at the last second. He would have fallen on his nose if he hadn't
been watching for her slightest movement. As it was,
he couldn't control the slight gasp of pain he felt as
he overbalanced and met nothing but air.

"Oh! Are you hurt?" she cried, ashamed of what
she'd expected. The man was an invalid, in her care.
She rued her wild imagination as much as her unruly
thoughts. He'd looked at her so intently she thought
he'd moved close—but he couldn't have meant to kiss
her. The poor man must think her mad. She swept the
improvised desk from his lap, and pushed him back
against his pillows. "Should I call Mother?" she asked
in dismay.

His eyes were closed against the knowledge of his
folly, not the pain. He'd moved too fast for his pur-
poses, not his healing body. But he knew how to make
the best of the worst. He'd spent his life trying to
do that.

"No," he groaned, "it was only a spasm. There,"
he said, opening his eyes, " 'tis passed."

But her hands were already undoing his shirt as she anxiously examined his bandages. They were still snowy. Her eyes went to his, and then slewed away in embarrassment. Away—to the side. She looked at his cheek and then his ear, and stared. Because she saw the hole in his earlobe. It looked like it had been pierced for an earring. And though many a seafaring man had tattoos, and many more bore the teakwood tan his skin did, only a pirate wore jewelry in his ear.

She was afraid of more than his kiss now, he saw.

"Yes," he said quickly, "I see you see it. One of their little jests. They did it one night when there was little other sport offered. With a hot needle, and a bottle of rum—for them, not me—and many a rude quip beside. I can only hope time heals it. I bear enough damage on this poor old hide of mine."

He gave a shaky laugh and shrugged. But he also turned slightly as he did, so that the opened shirt fell from his shoulder and she could see part of his back. She gasped, as he knew she would. Only then did he straighten and begin to button his shirt with carefully trembling hands. "Sorry," he muttered, "I'd have spared you that."

Her hands covered his, but they were shaking too. "Did they do that too?" she demanded, furious at seeing the obscenity of the many long, white, welted scars that streaked across that smooth, tanned back.

"It doesn't bear speaking of," he said.

It didn't. He'd earned them from many masters. Until he'd learned that a lad with wits was best off pretending he had none if he was a lad aboard ship with no name except for his own to save him from the lash. They'd served their purpose, and fixed his goals. They served him again now. Because she'd for-gotten his ear by looking at his back.

"No more lessons today," she said shakily.

He nodded in agreement. There would be time enough for them tomorrow. Those she'd teach him, as well as those he was determined to teach her.

He tried to come to dinner the next night.

"I'm tired of being such a deadweight," he argued. "Bad enough I came to you in such a state. But now I can feel my energy returning. I don't want to lie like a stump and be waited upon. I can't think of a worse burden than a guest who cannot dine at table with you," he protested.

He wavered where he stood at the foot of his bed. But he stood tall. He wore his host's castoffs. And though he was an invalid and Jedidiah was a tall man, his broad chest strained at the buttons of the old broadcloth shirt. Jedidiah noted that strong chest and the bandages still wrapped around it. Then he saw his guest's strained face. He nodded. And had to bite his lip as he watched the big man walk, slowly and stiffly and with obviously stifled pain. But though everyone in the family held their breath, their guest made it unharmed to the big, warm kitchen where they ate their daily meals.

He sat with care, and folded his napkin and laid it in his lap. His big, tanned hand shook as he lifted his soup spoon. The serving maid held her breath, Han-nah held her tongue. Rachel Jenkins and her husband winced, and even their son grew still in the face of such obvious courage. They watched him look down at his plate, and wondered if he'd collapse in his soup bowl.

Jedidiah rose from the head of the table. But not to propose a toast.

"You'll dine in bed, lad, until you can do a jig," he commanded.

His guest looked downhearted, but he was forced to take his host's arm again when he staggered back to his room.

But as soon as he was alone in it, with the door closed behind him, he straightened. And grinning, danced a little jig around his bed. It winded him and left him aching, so that he was pale and winded when the maid came with his dinner tray. He accepted it humbly, but he was delighted. Because pain was such an old companion of his he didn't pay attention to it unless it stole his thoughts. This was merely hurting, and so endurable.

Everything was as he needed it to be. He needed only time. And solitude. And the complete trust of these good people who sheltered him.

"Would you like me to write a letter for you?" Hannah asked idly a few mornings later as she gathered up her teaching tools. "Oh, I know you're getting better and better at it," she added quickly. "But I could do it for you in no time, and it would get out faster that way. There must be someone who would like to know you're all right."

Maybe one or two, he thought, but they couldn't read. There were definitely some others who would sleep better knowing the opposite. But it was better for him if neither friend nor foe knew how or where he was at the moment. But that wasn't a thing he wanted her to know.

She held her breath as he withheld his answer. She

had never let herself think it, but now she had to: a wife would want to know where he was.

"No," he said, and she let out her breath, "I doubt there's a soul who'd care. Truth is, I've wandered this far from home because there was no home to wander from." It was the truth, but his smile was twisted because truth wasn't something he was used to telling women. But truth to tell, he realized with some shock, he couldn't remember discussing much with any of the women he'd met before—apart from the price and quality of the services they provided, of course. Still, this lovely creature was as pretty to look at as she was easy to talk with. Since he couldn't do much more than look yet, talking was pleasurable. And it would make what would come after even more interesting, he decided.

"My family died of a contagion, it took half our street," he went on. "All my brothers and most of my mates too. It was odd I took the fever so lightly since I was the youngest, and always running after them all with my nose running, or so they always jested. Aye," he added in a colder voice, "it was odd—so odd that no one would take me in after. It's why I first signed on at sea. A captain who needs a crew is not too particular. Nor does he care so much about a lad's history as he does his future."

"How old were you?" she asked.

"Ten," he said with a shrug.

She clucked her tongue angrily, her expression thunderous.

"No, no," he said, holding up one hand, "don't blame them. I don't. Everyone has their superstitions. Sailors feel that way about albatrosses, you know. It's an ill-omened creature—as is any fish that's white when it's supposed to be silver, black, or blue. If a seaman happens to catch one, it gets thrown back with a curse, no matter if it's big enough for ten men's dinners. And the heartiest tar will shake in his boots if he sees St. Elmo's fire flickering in the masts. It does, you know, on some strange nights—it shivers up and down the masts like a web of lightning before it fades away. But if you touch it, it's cool and damp," he said with wonder. "Ah, but the sea's a strange place and no mistake. A man could sail it ten years times ten and never know the half of it."

"Oh," she said, bending her head and paying too much attention to the spine of a book she was holding, "so I suppose you can't wait to return to it?"

"Oh," he said softly, "I suppose it could wait awhile. It's not going anywhere, is it?"

She looked up at him with a radiant smile. He smiled back at her, and reached out a hand to touch a silken strand of her hair lightly with the tips of his fingers. She blushed.

He shook his head. Fish in a barrel, he thought with wonder. A pretty, shapely, sweet little fish swimming round and round in a barrel. Just waiting to be put on his plate. He was as amazed as delighted. He'd never met anyone, male or female, who was so unprotected. Because take away her father and mother, slip her out from under her mother's watchful eyes—just winkle her out of her family's snug little house, and she'd be helpless as a clam out of a shell. And as tasty. It would have made him uneasy if it didn't excite him so much.

She lowered her eyes. Her heart was beating fast. He smoothed the strand of hair between his fingers, and she could swear she felt it to her toes. It was as if the surface of her hair suddenly had as much sensitivity as her scalp. She'd actually forgotten to be afraid of the look in his eyes until he touched her, and now she didn't know how she could raise her eyes to his startling, knowing ones again.

"I can't imagine not having a family. I've never even been alone," she confessed, "except when I've gone off berrying in the wood—that sort of thing."

"A woman shouldn't be left alone, not ever, there are too many dangers," he said, and meant it.

"But I don't know," she said slowly, raising her eyes, forgetting her fear of him in the need to explain herself to him. "I think sometimes that a person can't think so deeply when they're with people. Why, you know, I think that's why famous artists and poets and such are always men. Because people leave them alone if they want to be alone. Everyone worries so much about women, and there's always so much for her to do for other people, that she never gets a chance to listen to herself thinking for very long."

"I don't know if being alone is any great thing," he mused. "Some nights, when you're all alone at the top of a mast, with nothing above you but stars and nothing below but the watery deep, a man gets to feeling like he's nothing, nothing at all. Oh, he can put pictures in the stars, and make believe he knows everything going on beneath him in the sea. But alone like that, rocking in the darkness high above the deck and far below the moon, knowing how trifling a thing even the biggest ship really is—only wood on water, after all—it's no pleasant thing to think about. Then with only the wind in the sails to hear, because the water's too far beneath and there's no shore for it to lap at, he gets to feeling like he's the only one of his kind in the world, and that it makes no difference if he is. If he's not a poet or an artist, then what's he to do with all that emptiness?"

He was startled by what he said. It wasn't like him to share such thoughts. But when he looked at her there was no mockery in her eyes. There was no answer in them either. Only deep sympathy. That was such a peculiar thing for him to see that he refused to think about it. Instead he saw how fascinated she was by him and thought of how near she was to being netted by him. She was already caught. It was only a matter of being reeled in. His words were the lure, his smile the hook. And his touch . . .? He closed his hand in her hair. And catching her by that silken strand, he slowly drew her face near to his.

He kissed her—lightly, briefly, as a brother might. "Thank you for caring," he said in a deep, sad voice. And waited to see what she would do now. Because he was in no hurry. A hasty man went hungry. He would never reel in his line until he was sure his hook was well sunk. And he know full well that this was neither the time nor the place to enjoy his catch. But he wanted to see how well he'd judged his skill.

She didn't know what to say or do. But because she was a woman she didn't have to do anything, because they'd been alone a whole fifteen minutes and so now she heard her mother's voice in the hall. She backed away. His hand left her hair, but his eyes never wavered from her lips.

"It's nothing," she said, flustered.

But he smiled, content. Because he knew it wasn't.

"How is the patient doing?" Rachel Jenkins asked, looking from her daughter's flushed face to her guests's quiet smile.

"Fine," they both said at once.

And that was exactly what bothered her.

"I've wonderful news!" Hannah said as she came into his room. "Father says it's time for you to leave!"

His head swung around from the window, and his eyes glinted more brightly than the sunlight he'd been staring into. He looked dangerous in that moment. But she'd learned to disregard such looks. He'd been nothing but gentle and charming. It was only that his size and startling looks made her feel weak and frightened sometimes. She had learned to deal with it. The only trouble was that in the past week she'd learned it was impossible for her not to deal with.

She couldn't stay away from his room for very long anymore. He was the most exciting thing that had happened to her in her short life. He treated her parents with respect, her brother with amused patience, and Molly and Sal had nothing to complain of from him—except, Hannah thought with smug delight, for the fact that they'd nothing to complain of from him. He joshed with them, but never flirted. The only woman he ever treated like a woman was herself.

Those few of her girlfriends who were not married envied her fascinating guest. Those who were wed looked at her knowingly, until she blushed. Because she'd little conversation anymore, except about him. And she refused to let them come goggle at him.

"The man is an invalid, not a traveling medicine show!" she told them at church the first Sunday after he'd come to them.

"Oh, Lord, send me a tall, strong, broad-shouldered blond invalid," her old friend Rebekah had sighed, and they'd all laughed. But Hannah had hurried home after services to see if he needed anything.

All he needed, he told her with his quirked half smile when he saw her, was to see her again.

He altered everything. She'd been merely content before. Now every day was filled with anticipation. She woke in the morning rejoicing because she knew that when she finished her chores she could give him his lessons. And she went to sleep at night pondering the lessons he'd taught her. She taught him his letters, and he was learning amazingly fast. But so was she. Because when his lessons were done, it was time for hers. She'd discovered that if she asked prettily enough, he'd sit back and spin her stories about some of the places he'd been and some of the astonishing things he'd done. He had a way with a tale. In fact, his deep, smooth voice gave her chills even when he wasn't describing strange lands and people. She was very glad that Jeffrey, who had distrusted him so much at first, had now got into the habit of slouching into the room to listen to him too. Otherwise she feared she'd make a fool of herself because of the way he enthralled her.

"Of course," he said now as he rose to his feet, "I'll be ready to go in a moment. It's not as if I have to pack," he added on a strange laugh. "I'd just like to say good-bye to your parents and then I'll be on my way."

"What? Oh no, no, no," she said on a trill of laughter. "Not 'go' as in 'go'! Go as in 'go out and sit in the sun for a while.' Goodness! None of us think you're ready to leave. It's just that we thought you might like to get some fresh air and move about in the garden for a while. And get your tan touched up a bit," she said mischievously, "because you've faded to the color of tobacco, and when you first came you were pure teak!"

He relaxed, his eyes glinting with laughter now. "Teak, with a nice green finish, I think. It's very good of you, I'd like that very much, thank you."

They strolled in the garden. He walked without hesitation, but his stride wasn't as long as his long, muscular legs were capable of. That might be because he was walking in step with her, his sun-streaked head bent as he talked with her.

Rachel Jenkins saw them from her kitchen window and frowned.

"Jeffrey?" she said.

He rose from his luncheon and tugged on his coat. He looked over her head and stared out the window.

"They're walking. He's likely telling her a tale or two. I wish I could hear them," he said enviously. "But Father wants me at the office, to listen and learn. Old Tate is selling off his winter acres and we're high bid, we hope."

"I thought now that school's out you'd be with them every minute," his mother said fretfully. "We agreed to never leave them alone too long. But I have to go to Amy Fletcher's house. We're doing up that quilt for her wedding come September."

"Well, but I can't," he said. "Though I wish I were with them. It's true I didn't care for him being here at first. But he's a good fellow and he tells a rare tale."

His mother clucked her tongue.

"You still think he's a rascal?" Jeffrey asked curiously.

"I can't say what sort of a man he is," she answered,

her face troubled, "but I know he is a man. And an attractive one."

"So he is," her son answered on a shrug. "But what can he do in the garden in plain sunlight?"

If Jeffrey didn't know, she certainly wasn't going to tell him. But she decided it was high time his father taught him about more than mortgages and crops. Still, it was noontime, and on Long Island, and the fellow had recently had a knife pulled out of his chest. But next week, Rachel vowed, there'd be no more strolling in the garden. If he was well, it would be time to set the fellow to some task to keep his mind— and his eyes—off her daughter. Her dratted picky daughter who had never looked at a man as she did at him, until her mother had almost given up hope because all her girlfriends were getting wed before her. But, Rachel thought with more pleasure, if he was as good a man as he appeared to be, and he was to become a man with a promising trade, why then . . . Mistress Rachel smiled as she bustled from her kitchen, full of dreams, to do her chores.

Hannah strolled on with her fabulous invalid. She looked up at him and saw how the light kindled his hair and gave color to his high cheekbones. His eyes were clear as the summer sky, or the sea itself. In fact, the day flattered him so much she could hardly believe that only a few weeks past they'd feared he might not live through the night.

"You're a way from the shore here," he remarked.

"Not such a long way," she said. "No place around here is. But we are far enough so that even the worst storm tides can't touch Mother's garden. That's why they built our home here. She refuses to grow pumpkins for King Neptune, she says."

She laughed up at him. The sunlight spun rainbows in her long, smooth brown hair because she'd taken off her bonnet and was holding it by its strings. That would win her a new freckle or two, he thought, and then thought of how he'd like to taste the few he saw sprinkled like cinnamon on the bridge of that saucy nose. He had known far more beautiful females, but none like her. Because she was a good girl, protected and cherished, and from a fine family. Pretty little creature, he thought with affection. Better still, she was bright and clever, and free with him now that she knew him. But not free enough.

He'd never been so close to a woman he wanted without having her, and it was as strange as it was exciting to him. He considered the frustration was well worth it. It gave him something to think about when he wasn't planning his revenge, and escape, and success. Because he never doubted he'd have all three—and her—before he was gone from here.

The house was at the end of the lane, and beyond that there was a path that led, she said, to the sea.

"But you're not ready for that yet. Not today," she said. "Father said a turn around the garden for a start. And that's all we shall do."

"Hannah!" he complained, stopping in his tracks as she turned back toward the house. "Am I a garden snail, to walk the length of a leaf and then back down again? Or a yard dog, to be kept on a tether? Oh, it would be a cruel, cruel thing to keep me from the sight of the sea when I can smell it clear and hear its roar."

"What a fib! That you cannot," she laughed. "It's a long walk down the path, and up a hill and down another before you can even see the sound. And Father said 'the garden' clear."

"But the sea is God's garden," he protested. "Do you want me pining away? There are crabs—little blue ones with scarlet claws—that thrive on Carribean shores. If you take one a mile from its home it will die, do you pack it in seaweed, keep it in a bucket, or sluice it down with water from the sea—it makes no difference. Away from the pull of the tide where it was born, within a day it will die."

"But you, sir," she said with a grin for his foolishness, "are not a little blue crab."

"No, but I am a big blue fellow. Ah—please, just another step or two, out the gate and down the road, so that I can feel free even if I am kept imprisoned in a magic garden by a cruel jailer."

It was so silly, he so big and bold, calling her a cruel jailer, when it was clear she couldn't prevent him from anything he set his mind to. She giggled and followed as he opened the gate and led her down the path to where he wanted her. To the bend in the road where it was bordered by trees and bushes and wild grape, so that no one from the village or the house could see them.

Once there, in the dappled shade, he stopped, put his hands on his slim hips, and took a long, deep breath.

"Are you all right?" she asked at once. "Oh, see what you made me do? Now you've overdone."

"Nay, the trouble is that I haven't done enough," he said as he caught up her two hands in his. "That's been my trouble, gentle jailer, for many days now," he said, smiling down at her.

But it wasn't quite a smile. And he wasn't exactly

joking. She was trying to decide just what it was when he gave her hands a little tug, and she found herself drawn up close against him. She was just trying to decide whether she was embarrassed or thrilled by the feel of his long, hard body next to her own when he bowed his head and kissed her. And then she couldn't decide anything, because all she could do was feel.

She'd been kissed before. But that was like a drowning woman thinking she'd been in the water before. Everything about him flooded her senses: his sun-warmed, hard body, his strength, the gentleness of his mouth, the sweetness of it, the intense pleasure a touch on her lips gave to her whole body.... She was lost in newfound pleasure until his tongue slipped between her lips. The shocking newness of that, the fright and then the thrill of it, made her stagger. And so he drew her closer so she wouldn't have to trouble herself with standing. Only breathing.

Sweet, he thought with growing pleasure, sweeter than he could remember a woman's kiss being. Her body was soft and lithe and giving in his arms. He stood in the shaded sunlight with the free wind at his back, and held a willing woman in his arms, and felt right and good again. If he could take her somewhere and be alone with her for an hour he would be entirely healed. But he was no boy, and no fool. And no matter the sweetness and temptation, he never forgot he was a lone man on a strange shore. A visitor in an alien place had no right forgetting where he was, whatever he was doing.

"Oh, Hannah," he said with regret as his mouth left hers. Because he knew her name would bring her back to her senses.

"Oh, my!" she said, and blinked. And stepped back.

She didn't know where to look. Her face was pink and her eyes wide, and she looked so altogether shocked he found it very hard not to pull her back into his arms again. Because he knew he could make her forget her name again. But it wasn't wise right now. The time wasn't ripe.

And so he could have blessed the bird, although a moment later he damned it.

He spotted it from the corner of his eye. It flew down from a hickory tree, coming down from out of the deep green recesses of it like a bright-feathered comet, and landed hard on his shoulder. He didn't flinch. The sound of its wings were as familiar to him as the weight of it as it settled on his shoulder. It rubbed its small, warm head against his chin, and crooned deep in its throat.

But Hannah stared, her hand to her mouth in utter surprise.

"Pitheth of eight!" it said in its high, cracked voice. "Pitheth of eight!"

Hannah's eyes widened in childlike pleasure.

Dan shrugged. But he knew it would take more than that to dislodge the bird.

"Ah, me corithone!" it cooed as it bobbed up and down, rubbing its green head against his cheek. "My heart'th delight!"

But Mistress Rachel wasn't delighted. And Master Jenkins was so downright suspicious he didn't try to hide it.

Hannah explained.

"Dan said it was on the ship he was thrown off. He remembers it. It obviously remembers him. He had a kindness for it. The other men would have let it starve," she said indignantly.

The parrot sat on Dan's shoulder and stared down at them, its small black eyes unwinking.

"I don't know why it's here," Dan said, and the parrot rode out a shrug. "I wouldn't have credited it—for it seemed to belong to the ship rather than any one man. But I confess I appreciated its company when I sat alone in the night, staring at the stars. And so I often shared my breakfast with it. Which was more than most of the other men did. That's the only reason I can think for its preference for me. It was a marked preference, I admit. Still, I never thought it would follow me. Do you think it came off the ship when it saw me hit the water?" he asked as he scratched the small green head with one long finger and the bird closed its eyes in what looked like ecstasy.

Hannah felt a warmth in the pit of her stomach and almost envied the bird.

"Well, they do say the creatures think like men. They live as long as we do," Jedidiah said as he watched the small creature as it snuggled closer to the big man, "and wed each other for life, it's said. So it's only natural they could form a fondness for a human. I've heard stranger things. Birds of the land often do leave ships of the sea when they approach a pleasant shore. There's fruit trees down the coast too, at Wilson's place. The smell of the peaches might have carried on the wind and tempted the little fellow."

The bird shuffled its feet on a broad shoulder. "Ah, me corithon!" it cried in its creaky voice. "Me corithon!"

"Or something else may have tempted it more," Jedidiah said.

"If so," Dan said with a little smile, "it's a hasty heart we have here. I'm not the first this bird has loved. I think it was trained to speak by a Spaniard. It's says 'my heart, my heart' in Spanish when it's happy."

"Pitheth of eight! Pitheth of eight!" the parrot croaked, bobbing up and down.

"And that," Dan said with less glee, "when it wants to make a fuss."

"Pitheth of eight, corithon. . . ." Hannah sounded it out, and then laughed. "It lisps!" she said with delighted discovery.

"Yes. Well, I said I think it was taught to speak by a Spaniard," Dan said.

"Aye. And 'pieces of eight' because it was a Spanish pirate that taught him, or maybe because he was stolen from a Spanish ship," Rachel said, watching him narrowly. "Because if they are loyal creatures, only death or theft could have separated it from its master."

"Yes. Likely," Dan agreed in the thoughtful silence that followed that.

They spoke about his future as well as his past in the dark of the night that night in their bed.

"No saying he was a pirate," Jedidiah said.

"No saying there's any harm even if he was," his wife agreed. "But he's up and about, and his eyes tell me what he's thinking about. And honest sailor or reformed pirate, he's no saint. Hannah's heart is in her eyes too—whenever she sees him. And to my mind, she sees him too much. We don't know where he's been, Mr. Jenkins. Nor where he's going."

"True," he said after a pause. "But at least, we can see that she doesn't go with him until we do."

"Good," she said with relief.

"And then we'll see what else we can do," he murmured before he turned on his side to sleep.

But his daughter couldn't sleep. Hannah lay in her bed, turning so often she tangled her sheets to ropes. Then she rose and paced, and looked out the window and saw nothing but the soft mists of a damp Long Island night. She thought she might as well abandon all attempts to sleep. She drew on a robe and decided to tiptoe down to the kitchens to find something to eat. Halfway there, upon the stair, she heard it.

At first she thought it was Dan's exotic green bird. It stayed in his room at night as by day, reluctant to go farther than his shoulder. But it was not the bird that spoke. This was a terrible sound, a smothered croak that came, however strange, from a human throat. And from his room.

She knew the halls of her father's house as well as her own heart, and ran to Dan's room quickly. She listened at the door and heard the sound clearer. He was muttering, "No, no, no," when he wasn't protesting something else wordlessly and with horror. She'd come into this room when he'd been helpless before, and so after only a second's hesitation she went in now.

He was alone. But he was clawing the air, straining, his eyes closed tight, his head thrown back against his pillows. He was bare to the waist, and his broad chest was damp with sweat. The parrot had flown to his bedstead, where it sat, agitated, flapping its wings, but silent.

"No, no, no," he muttered, turning his head, as he'd

done when he'd burned with the fever that had followed his injury. But when she put her hand lightly on his forehead she found his skin chill and damp.

"No, no, no," she echoed with sympathy so great it welled up in her throat and hurt. She leaned over him. She touched his arm, and he shivered. She held his clenched hand, and he startled. His eyes flew wide and he rose in one swift movement and caught her by the shoulders and pinned her down to the bed beside him.

"What?" he snarled. "Oh, Lord," he said, seeing her. He loosed her and fell back, dazed. "Is it real?" he groaned, still half asleep. "The sand around me: the more I dig, the more comes back. I'm digging my grave as I fight for the air. Oh, God, will I never get out!"

Before she could think of what to say to reassure him, he was upright beside her, his hand gentle on her cheek. "Did I hurt you?" he asked in his normal voice. "It was the dream again. Are you all right? Hannah, forgive me."

"I'm fine," she whispered. "But you? I heard you. I came to see."

"And see what you get for it," he groaned. "Lord, look at this! You're in my bed in the middle of the night! What will your parents say? Hannah, leave. Now. Go to your own bed. Never have I had to say a thing I meant less," he said with a shaky laugh, "but please—go. I'm fine now."

She rose and went to the door. She looked back.

"I'm sure," he said without her asking, "now, shoo!"

When she left and closed the door behind her, he fell back to his damp pillow, one arm across his eyes. He was a strong man, but he didn't know where he'd found the control to send her away. He'd woken from horror to find himself visited by a woman from the kind of dream that comes to men who have been at sea too long. Her hair had been loose, drifting in a perfumed, silken curtain to her waist. And her waist! She'd been soft and curved under his hand—all he needed. But all he needed was to be found with her in his bed.

He'd have her in his bed yet, but not now, and never where they could be found. But he would, he promised himself. The planning of it finally enabled him to relax. His pulse slowed, his breathing calmed, and, his desire banked, he lay back and waited for sleep. It was a long time coming because he feared it as much as he needed it. Because this wasn't the first night he'd clawed his way up out of sleep, covered with sweat and filled with stifled screams.

He didn't understand why. He should have rejoiced at his good fortune, and slept his usual deep and dreamless sleep. Because he had been lucky. They hadn't buried him deep. They couldn't have, because when he'd waked in pain in the damp dark, encased in sand, he'd immediately realized what they'd done. It was hideous, but it was a hideous profession, and he was lucky enough to know it. Another man might not have, and would have been doomed. As it was, he'd heard of such things, and so instead of wasting the last seconds of his life in confusion, he'd understood. His horror had given him the strength to scramble free. It had been a desperate struggle but not a long one. It had been easier because they'd obviously sat him upright on the chest—trust Jewel to have had the last laugh. But the last laugh would be his. That, he vowed. And finally, on that vow, he slept.

Hannah didn't. Not for a long while. She wasn't worried so much for him now as for herself. He was the most fascinating man she'd ever known, and every moment she spent with him fascinated her more. He looked like a bold corsair and spoke like an English gentleman. Yet he was humble as a boy because he didn't know his letters. But he learned so quickly, she almost believed he was teasing her by pretending to be illiterate. It wouldn't matter if he was. She was glad of any excuse to be with him. It was breathlessly exciting. Because although he was a perfect gentleman with her, the look in his wild eyes was as palpable as a touch—and the thought of his touch kept her tossing and turning in the night. But he never spoke of the future. And she hadn't the right—or the courage to ask him about it.

But her father did.

"You're mending," Jedidiah said, and puffed on his pipe before he spoke again. "We're pleased at your progress, to be sure. But it's that very progress that's the crux of the problem here," he said, staring down into his pipe so as to avoid his guest's brilliant eyes.

"As well it might be," Dan Silver said quietly. "An able-bodied man has no business battening on a family once he's on his feet again. I was meaning to talk to you about that myself, sir."

The two men sat in Jedidiah's parlor before a cheerful fire.

"I've been your guest for weeks now," Dan went on. "You gave me back my life. There's no way I can repay you. But I'd like to earn my way from now on, because I can. I think it would be more comfortable for everyone if I did."

Jedidiah didn't deny it. They both knew Hannah

had been given chores to do, been taken on visits and told to visit others so often she'd not been alone with their guest since the day the parrot had found him a week before. Other things had changed since then too. The invalid had been allowed out. He disappeared for long hours each day, accompanied only by the uncanny green bird. He was seen tramping the shoreline, looking out to sea. He was obviously restless. Hannah was as obviously impatient to see him again.

"Widow Clark, down in town, and the Remsons, who have the farm out by the pond," Jedidiah said, "both say they'll be happy to board you in exchange for work received. Remson's got a bad back, and the widow could use a strong back on her place. They'll provide good meals and a snug berth until you find your way and know what it is you want to do."

Jedidiah busied himself by puffing his pipe to life again. He hated asking the fellow what was none of his business. His daughter was his business, but he couldn't even ask the fellow's intentions, because the lad hadn't professed to have any. Hannah was the one who couldn't take her eyes off him. It wasn't like her, and that wasn't a thing Jedidiah liked.

"I'm sure they would," Dan said. "But I was wondering . . . Ah, it's no secret I'm troubled by dreams, Master Jenkins. I hope I've not disturbed anyone in the night. I can forget what happened to me, but I remember in my sleep each night. It's best, I think, that I live alone until I can tame the dreams. And better still if I could live alone until I know where I'm going." He looked down at his clasped hands and said thoughtfully, "I couldn't help noticing there's an abandoned shack in the woods, by the sea, down near the point. It's a room, nothing more, but I'm a lone man, nothing more. I thought I could fix it up, make it sound. I'd like to bide there. That way I could work for both the widow and the fellow with the bad back. I'd take my pay in food. I could get my feet back on the ground without being beholden to anyone, and have privacy at night until I'm fit to live among men again."

"Don't see why you can't," Jedidiah said thoughtfully. "It's been empty long enough. The fellow who owned the place came here to see if he liked the land well enough to farm it. He gave up a few years back.... Do you know? It might be the very thing. We could give you a bed and some provisions.... Might well be the very thing," he mused.

Because once the lad was out of the house, he thought, Hannah wouldn't have to watch him so close. And they wouldn't have to watch her so close either.

"Thank you, I'd like that," Dan said.

"And after that ...?" Jedidiah asked, using their easy companionship to prod a little more.

"After that?" Dan said with a smile. "Many things, I hope. I never tried farming, but I can learn. Now I've my letters, I can learn more. I'm a good sailor too, and a good sailor can be many things in a thriving port." He lifted his brilliant gaze and looked straight at his host. "But a man must have hopes for a future before he speaks of it—especially to the father of the one he may harbor some hope for. Doesn't he? Or should I say, can he?"

"We'll see," Jedidiah said, greatly pleased.

"I can't ask more," Dan said sincerely.

He smiled, thinking that was true enough. But he certainly could take more. And certainly would.

*   *   *

The house seemed empty when he'd gone. He worked for the widow and Wilt Remson, and Hannah heard nothing but good of him. Sometimes she'd see him in the fields. Sometimes she'd hear of how he paced the water's edge at sunset, skimming stones and staring at the path of the sun on the sound. She'd healed enough wild creatures to know how they pined until they could return to the air or the sea. The thought of him readying to leave wounded her in ways she'd never felt.

She missed his bright jests as much as the solemn moods he'd try to conceal when he saw she noticed them. She missed his outlandish stories and the sly grin he wore to let her know he was joking—as well as the hungry look he had when he thought she wasn't watching. Her parents kept her busy, but busy as she was, her mind was always with him. She thought of him alone in the night in the woods, with nothing but the green bird and his nightmares for company. A week had gone by since he'd left, and she hadn't exchanged a word with him. But it was as if he'd called to her.

She had a basket of food to deliver to his door, and she'd been told to do it after she dropped off some yard goods for Mrs. Haggerty, down the road. That would make her delivery take place after noon, while he was still out in the fields. But she managed to get into a long chat with Mrs. Haggerty. In fact, she seemed so fascinated by that good woman's troubles with her daughter-in-law that Mrs. Haggerty, giddy with the unexpected pleasure of having someone interested in her troubles, invited her to tea. And was delighted when she tarried long after.

Hannah left with an earache, a frozen smile, and a

vastly contented neighbor. And a guilty conscience. Because if she hadn't exactly deceived her mother, she knew very well that she'd wouldn't please her by appearing at Dan's door at dusk. But she thrilled herself.

He was genuinely surprised to see her. She was staggered by how wonderful it felt to see pleasure replace the surprise in his crystal, glowing eyes. Their brilliance illuminated his tanned face, and dried up all the conversation on her lips.

"I thought you were angry with me," he said.

"No, no," she managed to say, and tucked her chin down as though looking in her basket.

He put one finger beneath her chin and tilted her face up to his. "I haven't seen you in days," he said simply.

"Well, no, but you were working, and I was busy. . . ."

"And your parents, rightly, didn't want me near you," he said on a sigh, and turned from her. He put his hands in his pockets and looked out to sea.

The hut he lived in was on a cliff overlooking the sound. It was a calm evening, and there was nothing to be seen but gulls on the sunset-bronzed waters below. She saw him staring out over the sound, his face still, his wide shoulders silhouetted against the vast, empty waters. She wondered what he saw there, beside the beautiful view. And never knew that he saw neither sunsets or birds but only a road. The one that had taken him here, and the one that would take him away. He turned back to her.

"I'm a vagrant, a vagabond, a fellow snatched from the sea, and owed to it forever," he said with a sudden burst of candor. "And you're a girl from a good family." He shrugged. There was nothing else to say. But he watched her closely. He had his plans for her and doubted she'd elude them. But he was a fair man. She should know it in some way. If she chose to stay despite it, so be it. He had little conscience, and so it needed little appeasement.

"So, does that mean I can't deliver a basket of good bread and cheese to you?" she said saucily, taking refuge in a jest.

But he wouldn't have it. He cupped her face in two hands and gazed at her steadily. The bright, burning look in his eyes held her as surely as his hands did. He nodded, satisfied with what he saw. And then he kissed her.

She was entirely lost. His mouth was hot and intoxicating, his hands were hard and soft on her body. She leaned in to him, too shy to put her hands on him, too pleasured to make him stop touching her. She never wanted his kiss to end. It almost didn't. But he never became so lost in the incredible sweetness of her mouth that he didn't remember he had no right to it. He released her.

"Fly away home, little ladybird," he said in a hoarse voice. "It's dusk, you shouldn't be out alone in the dark."

"But you are with me," she said.

"So I am. Wouldn't your father be pleased?" he said bitterly.

"Why shouldn't he be?" she asked, dazed with pleasure, terrified at her boldness, terrified lest he never be so bold with her again.

"Why, indeed? I have no family, no occupation, and nothing but my back and two hands to recommend me. Wouldn't any father be pleased with me being escort to his dear daughter in the dark?"

"Father doesn't judge a man for his past. Only his future," she said.

"Truly?" he asked. "And if that was to be with you?"

Her eyes grew wide. A faint tinge of wild rose appeared in her cheeks. "He wouldn't mind," she said faintly.

"Would you?" he asked and chuckled deep in his throat when she could only shake her head.

Their next kiss lasted until he knew he wouldn't be able to contain himself much longer. Then he stepped away.

"Come, I'll walk you home," he said. He took her hand and kissed it before he put it in his, and walked her down the long path to her house.

He had to remind her to give him the basket when they parted at her gate. "Best you say nothing until I can say more," he told her soberly. "When I've a future and a date, that is to say. Please. I should be the one to have that pleasure. All right?"

She nodded. He took another long kiss from her, and then pushed her gently toward her house. " 'Til then," he said, and waved. When she looked back, he was gone again, into the shadows of evening.

He strolled back in the dark, pleased with himself. It wasn't as if he'd promised her anything but a word about his future, and a date. If she'd take him on that word, he'd take her. Even though the future he saw lay across the water, and the date when he'd stay with any one woman was one he couldn't count to—and he never had any trouble with his numbers.

He wanted her badly. The women he'd known had

been hard and tart. She was sweet and yielding. He rose in the night from his nightmares, but also sometimes in a different form of excitation, with the taste of her still on his lips and the vision of her long dark hair and smiling lips still imprinted on his sleep-blinded eyes. Beyond her physical attractions, she was kindhearted and good, and he'd had little enough of that in his life.

Born in poverty, he'd run to the sea to find his fortune. He'd found pain at the hands of many masters instead. He'd decided to come ashore forever when he'd gotten drunk that night in Liverpool. And woke to find himself aboard a new vessel, laboring for the king—and the king didn't care if he lived or died any more than any man ever had. He'd worked out his years before the mast, and then signed on with the only men the king's navy feared. Now he breathed deeply of the ferns and bracken on the path around him. The earth smelled sweeter than the sea, but the sea was his home. He'd be gone from this place as soon as events warranted. But before he left, he'd have her. He'd had small pleasure in his life, he thought. He deserved some now.

He'd leave her with the memory of pleasure, the knowledge that not all men were safe, and the wisdom to expect nothing more than what one could get for oneself. That wasn't a bad legacy. Because it was, after all, all he had.

He reached his doorstep and the green bird fluttered down to his shoulder.

"Thweetheart, thweetheart," it muttered.

He laughed and stroked its silky head. "A bird to love me, eh? Ah, well, why not? You screamed me out of my sleep in the sand, love. Yours was the voice that woke me to life. So I'm yours forever, then, is that it? Faith! You're possessive as any lass, aren't you? I'll bet you're ten times more faithful. Wait, I'll share a biscuit with you," he promised.

He shook off the bird, put two hands on his lean hips and stretched the work-weary muscles in his long frame. He'd eat and then sleep, and then rise to work in other men's fields until he found a way to return to his own. He yawned and stretched again. But then he froze, his hands still in the air, and stared out at the moonlight on the water. He had the eyes of a shark, they said. But his vision was that of a seabird. He lowered his arms slowly. He saw a tiny shape, a spot, a blotch, an absence of moonlight far out on the horizon. But he knew what it was. They were back.

His heart, the heart that a dirk had missed by an inch, picked up a new, heavy beat. They were back. That meant he had a chance to get the other things he wanted badly: a way to leave. And revenge.

But he would have to move quickly.

She paced the moon-shadowed path and looked back over her shoulder every so often in fear. Because every snapped twig and fallen leaf sounded like a footfall. There were no strangers here, except the one she was stealing off to see. And no wild animals except for fox and deer, raccoons and possum, who were more afraid of Hannah than she could ever be of them. But if her parents should rise and find her not in her room, where she was supposed to be ... But why should they? They hadn't checked her bed since she'd been a little girl afraid of ghosties and terrors in the night. Now she feared nothing so much as not seeing him again.

He'd brought her back her basket at dawn, before he set off for work. Before he'd left, after he'd thanked her parents, he whispered to her.

"Come to me tonight, at eleven bells. Alone. Tell no one. I can say no more now. Only as you love me: come, love."

It had been hard to think, to talk and walk normally all day, just thinking of his voice as he'd said "love." Because he had sounded in need and forlorn. And though she'd never had a secret from her parents of any higher order than a smuggled toad in her bedroom, tonight she slipped through the wood to his house on the cliff without a backward look, except in fear of discovery.

"You're here!" he said, and took her in his arms, and closed the door behind them.

The little hut smelled of fresh-hewn wood, green pine, and the sea. It was swept clean and kept painfully neat. But that didn't surprise her. Many kinds of men were good sailors, but a good sailor was always a tidy man. There wasn't much room in the shack that he'd repaired, but every piece in it was stowed where it belonged. There was a bed with her mother's old patched coverlet over it, a chair, and a table. His coat hung on a nail on the wall. All his other gear was in an old sailor's bag near his bed. The one window that faced the sea was open. The other was shuttered. One lamp was lit.

She drew back from his kiss. "What is it?" she asked, her eyes searching his face in the dim shadows. "What's the matter?"

"Did you tell anyone?" he asked urgently.

She shook her head in denial until her cloak's hood fell back from her hair. He pushed the hood back farther and gazed down at her. His hand went to the buttons at her throat. She gazed at him with wide, fearful eyes.

"Dan," she said again, "what is it?"

"I missed you," he said.

"What?" She blinked. "You made me sneak away, you made me crazy all the day, and only because you . . . missed me?"

"There's no 'only' about it," he said. "I didn't think I could get through another long night without you. How many nights can a man go without sleep? I almost fell into the thresher today. The sun sets, and seals my doom. I wait out the night until the morning, and then waste the day dreaming of you—and hoping for a glimpse of you. I can't bear it, love."

"But tonight is Friday. We'll see each other in church S-sunday," she said, stammering because he'd slipped her cloak off, and his hand was still at her nape, toying with the buttons of her dress now.

"In church," he echoed, "and shall I get to harmonize with you? What joy. Hannah, I need you closer than that. I'll swear you know that, love."

"Ah, me corithon, me corithon," the parrot piped.

Its harsh tones were ridiculous in light of what Dan had just said. Hannah laughed too loud. She was distracted, but relieved the strange mood had been broken.

But it hadn't been. Because without taking his eyes from her, Dan opened the door with one hand and the parrot flew out into the night.

"I need you, love," he said, and closed the door against the night.

His lips met hers, and then moved to her cheek, to her neck, as he loosened one button after the other, and saluted each new bit of her skin that was revealed. She shivered in his arms, and drew in the fresh, spicy scent of him, and held hard to his wide shoulders. He caressed her breast, and as she drew in her breath in shock, he took the rest of it away with his warm, searching mouth. The buttons opened, and he began to slide her dress away from her shoulders.

"Dan," she murmured in as much fear as delight, "we mustn't, you mustn't."

But she kept kissing him and burrowing into his arms. Because no man had ever done her an injury, and she couldn't believe the one she loved most would do anything that wasn't right. He would stop when the time came. She knew that as well as she knew she didn't really want him to.

He stopped, and she was lost. He looked down at her soberly.

"No. I must, you must. We must," he said. "You know that."

"But you said . . ."

"I said I'd tell you when the time was right. It is. You will be mine. And so why not tonight?"

She didn't know why not. They would be man and wife, wouldn't they? He'd declared himself. She knew no other man she wanted, and knew she'd want no other. Her parents weren't thrilled with him, but had allowed they might come to be if he got a regular job. She knew he would. He was no fool: there was no other way he could have asked for her, and he knew it. And above all these reasons, and beyond all reason, she knew he needed her now. As much as she needed him. They wouldn't wait on their wedding. She wouldn't make him wait now. She raised her lips to his.

He sighed against her mouth. She felt his lean, muscled body relax, and then coil into action again as he raised her in his arms and carried her the few steps to his narrow bed.

"Better," he whispered as he set her down in the fluffy coverlets. "Ah, better," he breathed as he settled beside her.

She turned to him without shame and with absolute trust. After all, she'd been waiting for him all her life, although never in her wildest dreams of love had she dreamed of a lover like him. Strong and gentle, wild and yet restrained, he was all she'd hoped for. His face was her mirror; she thought herself beautiful when she saw herself in his eyes, and was glad that she deserved him. Because she thought him so miraculously handsome she couldn't look her fill of him. She was thrilled by the sight of his powerful body as he took off the last of his clothing. But not so much as she was by the feel of his naked form against her own. She was staggered by the sensation but not afraid. How could she be? She had discovered the other half of herself at last.

He took his time with her. He had the time to do it in. The moon was rising. They wouldn't be here until long after midnight. She'd stay until then. And then he'd leave her. Forever.

He felt no guilt, he told himself. He'd won her fair and square as rigging. He'd chosen his words carefully, so she could never call him liar after either, even in her thoughts. "The time was right for him to have her. She would be his. And why not tonight? He *should* be the one to ask her father." So he should be—if he ever did.

Everything he'd said was true. If it wasn't what she

thought, that wasn't his fault. Neither was the fact that
all the world wasn't filled with simple island folk. He
would give her a night to remember in every way.
And maybe, he thought as he felt her body warm
beneath his questing hands, she wanted no more than
that. She'd have no more, at any rate. He was a pirate
and a rover, a man whose road lay over the water,
and tonight he visited her as the tide visited the shore.
He'd be gone by dawn's light. Better for her that way
too, he thought.

He'd had many women, and he'd left every one of
them. In that, she'd be no different from any of them.
Only better. Because her mouth was impossibly sweet
and her high, firm breasts even sweeter, and the damp
he eventually sought in her nether lips told him she
was ready for him, as every other woman's always
had. But she was different. She was Hannah, and he
couldn't forget it for a minute, though he tried.

It was Hannah's long, dark, fragrant hair that he
loosened to lay over his own shoulders now. It was
Hannah's innocent mouth he tutored to expertise. It
was Hannah who turned and twisted beneath his
tender, insistent ministrations. It was Hannah's small,
tentative hands that dared to touch him at last, drifting
down from his powerful shoulders to his lean flanks.
She shied away until he placed her hands on him again
and then retreated, only to touch him once more until
he groaned with the pleasure of it.

But still she was like no other he'd ever known. She
bore the scent of soap and flowers, not harsh perfume
and sweat. She muttered no curses, whispered no pro-
fanities, gave out no squeals women thought a man
liked to hear. She only breathed, "Ah, Dan. Oh,
Dan," again and again, until his heart nearly broke

because he so yearned to have her call him by his real name.

So he stopped her mouth with kisses and bent to her. And realized he'd never caused a woman pain with his entry before either, not even for the second he saw Hannah open her eyes in surprise. But what undid him entirely was the thought—while thought was still possible for him—that no other woman had ever looked at him with love as he made love to her.

And Hannah held on to his wide shoulders and received him the way the shore receives the incoming tide: because it was inevitable, and right. She took the cresting of the wave of his pleasure as he pounded against her. And rose to meet it and heard the broken tumble of his ecstatic cry even as she took his body deep within hers.

He held her close long after, and that too was a thing that had never happened before. Because he knew he'd done an extraordinary thing. Now too he knew what he would do, if he could. But it was too late.

"Sleep now," he crooned to her as he petted her long silky hair. "I'll wake you and get you to your bed long before the light."

But long before that, when he saw her breathing was deep and even, he stole from the bed. He dressed in the dark and picked up his bag. And at the last he left her the note he'd so painstakingly written the night before. He put it on his table, where she'd find it with his last gift to her. He regretted only that he couldn't kiss her one more time. And then he crept from the hut and strode out into the night.

Her eyes opened as the door closed. She could no more sleep after the amazing thing they'd done together than she could fly. But he'd wanted her to, and there was enormous pleasure in just lying next to his warm, breathing body, savoring their intimacy. And then terrible pain, watching him through downcast eyes, as he'd stolen away like a thief in the night.

The bent tree stood at the seam of the beach and the land. The tide had eaten away half the earth at its roots, yet it flourished in the peculiarly aggressive way of all things that dare to live at the edge of the sea. Tonight the moon was almost full and gave off a translucent light. The pirate ship on the horizon was like a black cutout pasted on the margins of a molten silver sea. The light was bright but not quite like daylight, so the men who stepped from out of the rowboat that beached itself on the shore could see clearly but not with depth and accuracy. It was as though they were looking underwater.

Their stocky leader strode onto the shore and paced to the tree. He stopped and pointed. The men with him bore shovels, but they hesitated. A squat fellow among them laughed.

"Don't want to disturb dear Dancer, do ye?" he chortled. "But why not? I be sure he'll be glad of the company. Maybe he's waitin' with a quip fer us. Aye, he'll be grinnin' some, to be sure. He be grinnin' more in a month or so, but we'll see teeth enough tonight, I don't doubt. Come, let's see how the climate's improved his complexion, shall we?" he asked, and set to digging with zest.

"Get to it," the captain said glumly. "Ignore the body and bring me the chest. I need it sooner than I thought. Jewel's right, damn his eyes. Dig."

The other men picked up their shovels and joined

in, but they were silent as the sea tonight. They dug for several minutes, but then, one by one, they stopped. Jewel dug on with increasing frenzy.

"They's naught here, Cap'n," one of the men said fearfully. "Nary a scrap."

"Aye, but moonlight's tricky," one of the men volunteered. "Want to pace her off again, Captain?"

"I know the tree. There's no other place it can be," the captain muttered, but he turned back to the sea and sighted the land again. He counted his paces and walked back, stopping in the same spot again. By now Jewel stood in the hole he was digging, and the only chest to be seen was his own, halfway above the sand.

"Leave off!" captain shouted. "There's nothing here! Someone's been here. It could have been any of you. I mind we made landfall thirty miles up coast from here not two weeks past. Some of you said you were restless and so were given leave to go ashore for a handful of days to raise some hell before we weighed anchor again. Now I wonder if anyone was raising something else ... any man who knows anything would be wise to speak up now."

"Captain," one of the men called, and in the eerie light his eyes were wide and wild, "t'aint our way! Mebbe it be one of the locals. This ain't a wild shore. Some lucky fisher lad could be setting on yer treasure now."

"Aye!" another pirate agreed. "Mebbe we could start askin' questions in this town. Ask some sharper, get some answers, get back yer chest double quick. Chick here, he looks nachural. Got no scars, nary a tattoo. Speaks regular too. Got fist like iron, though. We could send him, couldn't we?"

"Mebbe Jewel too," another called. "Seein' as to how he's so quick and sharp wi' a knife."

"Aye," the men murmured among themselves.

"He be here!" Jewel protested. "He has to be. I planted him, and I knows it. Tide's might of shifted, land moves by the sea. I'll shift a bit left, then right, I'll find him—"

"If it takes all eternity, right, Jewel?" a lazy, mocking voice called from out of the shadows. "But what if he finds you first, murderer?"

They froze in place. Even Jewel did. A lean, long shadow stepped out of the woods.

"Looking for me, Jewel? Or pretending to? Since whoever took the chest would have to shift its guardian too, so men would doubt it was ever there. But why bother? Here I am, hot from Hell for you."

Jewel stared. But then he put his hands on the rim of the hole he'd dug, and levered himself up and out of it. He squinted at the figure before him.

"I don't think yer come from Hell, Dancer. But I be glad to send ye there again," he said, crouching, his knife in his hand.

But the shadow held a knife too. And when it moved into a pool of moonlight, it was grinning. With Dancer's face. One of the pirates crossed himself, another blanched white as the moonlight. They all drew back, except for Jewel. And the captain.

"You're hard to kill, lad," the captain said with a smile in his voice. "I'm glad of it. You've brains, along with your brawn and courage. Much could be made of you, in trade or the high seas. I know merchants and pirates, but few who could be both. I've missed you sorely. But I miss my treasure too. I'm off to London sooner than I thought. Come, lead me to it."

"I was put in with it as caretaker, Captain, but I'm sorry. I abandoned the post. Well, not that sorry, actually." The shadowy showed a brighter grin. "Because I was saved somehow. I woke in a local man's bed. But I didn't wake for a week, and I'm not even sure I can help you dig for it now. Jewel's dirk was sharp but, like himself, slovenly. As now, he missed the mark. But it was close. So close as to bring me close to death's door and lying on my back for weeks wondering if it would open for me. So as to where the treasure is, I don't know."

"Aye, likely," Jewel snarled. "He woke in a strange bed and left a pirate's treasure to rot whilst he mended? Not he. He'd steal the coins off his dead father's eyes while he himself lay dyin', that one would."

"Possibly—if I'd ever known who he was," Dancer agreed. "But not this time. I couldn't. Your knife bit deep, Jewel, but as ever, not true."

"Try me now," Jewel said, beckoning with his free hand. "I'll settle the matter clear. Or are ye goin' to jest yer way out of it, so none will see ye got more quips than courage, eh? Dancer, the handsome lad who dances his way out o' tight spots—but not this time, I vow. Come, test 'gainst my blade, if ye dare, if ye be a man a'tall."

Dancer threw his bright dagger into his other hand and crouched. "Oh, Jewel, you don't know what I dare when I've an enemy who dares face me when he knows I'm ready for him! I've laid awake nights dreaming of this."

"Don't be a fool, lad!" the captain shouted. "Jewel's a killer. You have the shark's eyes, but he has the temperament. Settle it later with sword or pistol when your blood's not running so hot—or you'll spill it out again. You've courage, true. But you've been ill and he's a devil with his dirk."

"I don't fear him," Dancer called, never taking his eyes off Jewel. "I don't use my dirk so often because I don't hate my fellow man so much. But I can slip through the shadows like my namesake, Captain, and I've a taste for blood tonight."

"Aye, c'mon, c'mon," Jewel said, grinning and beckoning.

Dancer stepped forward. The men fell still, because the deadly dance had begun and there was nothing anyone could say that would influence the outcome.

But then there was a screech, a flapping, and a compact ball of feathers came flying out from the forest. It landed on Dancer's shoulder with such velocity, he staggered. But he recovered quickly, and held his knife out high in front of him.

"Don't try it, Jewel," he warned his opponent. "Don't even think it. One time you had at me unprepared. It will never happen again. I was startled merely. Let me rid myself of my friend and I'll be back for you."

"Thweetheart, thweetheart," the parrot cooed. But Dancer's grin was a thin line as he gave the bird his free hand to perch upon. Then he handed it to another pirate. "Take the green lad, Benson, and hold him tight. He might interfere, and I want no one on my side but the Devil himself now."

He stepped back in front of Jewel and nodded. "Have at me now, Jewel, or hold your peace forevermore."

"Not bloody likely," Jewel snarled.

They got in position again. And again there was a

wild cry from the surrounding forest. But this time it was a girl who came flying from the wood. Her long hair floated free behind her, her feet were bare, and she ran to Dancer's side.

"Don't, oh, Dan, don't," she cried, her hand on his arm.

"Oh, good God," he sighed. "Hannah, what are you thinking of?"

"Don't fight," she begged him. "You're not yourself yet. You lost so much blood—you've just healed. Let him say whatever he likes, just don't fight him."

He looked over her head at the men standing in a circle on the sand. Even the errant moonlight couldn't conceal their interested stares. She was young and lovely, and alone with them in the concealing night. But not quite alone, he realized, thinking quickly.

"This lady is going to be my wife," he said, putting his arm around her. "I claim her as my own. He who touches her, whatever happens to me, violates the law of the brotherhood." They nodded, every man among them, and he breathed easier. He turned to her.

"Hannah, I must," he said quietly. "It's a debt, and a challenge, my fate and our future, all in one. It's not a thing I can avoid. Nor would I wish to." Saying it, he knew it, and felt a surge of happiness, and then a new, odd, and curious peace settle upon him.

She gazed into his silver eyes for a long moment. The moonlight showed matching silver tears as they began to course down her cheeks. But she nodded and backed away, step by step, from him.

Dancer stepped toward Jewel, on the sand beneath the tree where he had been left for dead a month past. And Jewel grinned and greeted him with a swaggering bow before he resumed his deadly stance. They fought in silence, the only sounds their feet scuffing the sand, their breathing becoming harsher and louder as they danced. Because it was a dance. A thing of side steps and feints, leaps and pivots, approaches and retreats, but a dance to no music but their own rapidly beating hearts. It could be over in a second, and they all knew it. But until it was, it was a thing of shifting shadows and racing hearts—until one of them was stilled forever.

And then there was a grunt. And a gasp. And it was done.

Jewel stood smirking until he looked down at his lifeblood spouting from his chest, and he shuddered, like a harpooned whale in its final flurry. It was the last thing he did. He crumpled to the sand.

Dancer ran lightly toward him and knelt at his side. He plucked the knife from Jewel's lifeless hand gingerly, the way a man might cosh a dying bluefish, so as to avoid being bitten in its death throes. Then he swiftly thrust his hand into Jewel's coat. And sat back on his heels, grinning brighter than the waxing moon. He held something that glittered even more brightly in the palm of his bloody hand.

"Ah, Captain. Just as I thought. See? This is why he wanted me dead again so badly. Because a dead man is the best man to blame your own crime on. See. Just as I thought."

The captain came close and picked the glittering jewel from Dancer's palm. It was an ornate stone in a baroque setting, heavily crusted with gold, pendant in shape, and it shone in the night like a star.

"The Princessa's Diamond!" Kidd exclaimed. "From the chest."

"Aye. A gem that couldn't be easily sold because

it is so distinctive," Dancer said. "That's probably why he still had it on him. I couldn't have touched your chest, Captain. I was on my back in my sweet Hannah's father's bed. I admit, when I could rise from that bed I went looking—it was gone. Else," he said ruefully, "I wouldn't still be here. You know that."

The captain nodded and the men murmured among themselves. They all knew it was true. Jewel had been right about one thing. Dancer's odd eyes had always been fixed on treasure. The girl was a beauty, all right. But it was simple alchemy: mix Dancer with gold, and Dancer would vanish. The very fact that he was here this night was a sure sign he couldn't have known where the treasure had got to.

"But Jewel could get at it," Dancer went on, "and did. He wanted my heart on his knife to explain it. You're out a small fortune, Captain, unless you find where he's hidden it. But I bear him no grudge now. If he hadn't stolen your buried treasure, I wouldn't have stayed around to find mine."

He held out his arms to Hannah, and she rushed to him. He held her so tightly it was almost painful, but not so painful as his absence had been to her. He dropped his head and buried his face in her hair, and she could hear his heart as it shuddered steadily against hers.

"Well, then," Kidd sighed, "I'm fair diddled, aren't I? I'll set a search, but my hopes aren't high. I'm off to London soon, to plead my case. If you hear aught of my treasure, lad, send word to my wife in Manhattan. If not—ah, but there's more where that came from. I've hidey holes along this shore from here to Gardiner's Isle, and I mean to empty them this night. And then there's others on the Connecticut side. I don't suppose you're coming with me, are you, Dancer?"

"Thank you, but no, Captain," Dancer said, his face serious and still. "I valued gold above all else, until Jewel almost took me from this life. I've had time to think. I've my life before me now—and it's here."

"Well, then, start it with this," Kidd said, and flipped the pendant to him. Dancer caught it in one hand and closed his fist over it. "You might not be able to sell it, but your children can," Captain Kidd said. "Count it as my wedding gift. That—and the damned bird. Good luck."

"And to you," Dancer said, because there was nothing else to say. If the captain was going to face justice in England, he knew he'd never see him on this earth again, no matter the treasure Kidd unearthed for influence and bribes. England had sent Kidd to harry pirates, not to become one. He had, and Dancer was sure he would pay for it. Dancer came from England, and knew too well its revenge on those it deemed enemies of the crown. Kidd would pay his last crew handsomely. But it was a waste of his money, and their time. The money earned would never be spent on pleasure. Dancer pitied those who followed him to his fate. He also knew he'd nothing to fear from them. They'd trouble him no more than Jewel did now. England would see to that.

And the other pirates he'd served with would soon scatter across the seven seas and never seek him further either. Because they saw for themselves that his treasure consisted merely of one pendant they couldn't sell in their lifetime, one lisping parrot, and one lovely girl.

But it was more than enough for Dancer.

The pirates buried Jewel beneath the tree and went back to their rowboat. Dancer and Hannah watched them disappear over the water and fade into the night.

"So now you know," Dancer said seriously when they turned to each other again. "My name isn't Dan Silver. I said it was because I was afraid someone might hear it and know me. I am called Dancer. If you want me, you'll have to give me a first name as well as a new name. But do you want me now? Listen well before you tell me. I was a pirate. Don't deceive yourself about that. True, I was many things before I became a pirate, things that made me become one—perhaps. And it's also true that I'll never sail as a privateer again, at least not willingly. But there it is. Jewel took exception to something I said—or wouldn't do for him before." He shrugged. "However it happened, he hated me. He saw an opportunity and attacked me before I could defend myself or anyone could prevent him. Thinking I was dead, they buried me here with their ill-got treasure. I escaped my tomb—and that life. I came tonight to end it for good, one way or another, because I knew that did I not, it would always be waiting for me. It's over now.

"I can change what I will be, but not what I was. Do you want a pirate, love?"

"I want no other," she declared.

It was a long while before either said anything again, although they communicated to each other beautifully without words.

"We'll marry by this week's end, come what may," he said when he finally left her at her door. "Tell your parents tonight. I'll speak to your father in the morning. I'll find a trade, and build you a fine house someday, you'll see. But I want my name on you before my babe starts growing in you. First things first."

She smiled through glad tears, and clung to him long after their good-night kiss. Because it tasted like a greeting instead of a good-bye.

It was. He stepped lightly into the wood. But he ran when he remembered what he'd left in the shack. When he got there, he breathed a deep sigh of relief. As he'd hoped, she'd been too intent on following him to read his note or unwrap his gift. He burned the note and slipped the pile of golden coins he'd left for her into his pocket.

Then he pushed his bed until it was away from the wall. Then he knelt, and whistling under his breath, set to prying up the floorboards there.

He'd burned the chest plank by plank. And pitched the iron staves into the sea. That he'd accomplished the first night he'd crept out of the Jenkins' house. There might have been blood on the wood staves too then—his, from his reopened wound. And his blood as well on the handle of the shovel after he'd piled the sand back into the hole that had been his tomb and his treasure trove. But the shovel had been broken and given to the sea. Then he'd poured the coins into the pillow slip he'd brought with him, and dragged it into the wood. When he'd got his breath back, he'd hidden his trove beneath last autumn's leaves, behind a rock by an old oak, until he'd been fit enough to bring it here. He hadn't missed a thing.

But he had changed his plans. He'd meant to leave her some coins and sail away after he dealt with Jewel. And then steal back, months later, to retrieve his treasure. Then sail away again, for good this time. But he could no more leave her than his heart. He'd known it the moment he'd joined his body with hers. Or it might be, he thought, sitting back on his heels, that he'd known it the moment he'd seen her, no matter what yarns he'd told himself. Else why would he have taken such care to take the pendant to the meeting with Jewel so that he could plant it in his coat when he killed him, and then bring it out to show the world who had stolen it? Or have it on his own body when he died, if he had lost the fight, so they wouldn't have to suspect any of the locals of taking the treasure?

He'd been tempted, lured, landed, beached, and what of it? he asked himself now as he stirred his hand through his hoard of bright coins. He'd leave most of it here, and build a stout house over it. He'd live in that house, and year by year the pile would dwindle as he invested it wisely, so as to grow another, bigger one in a proper bank. Kidd had been a man of business and had amassed a fortune before he'd become a pirate. He was easily as clever as Kidd, if not more so. Because he knew when to leave the sea. And could do the same work on shore. Because a land pirate, as he'd learned from Kidd, could steal as much money in his own way, and not risk his hide either.

"Pitheth of eight! Pitheth of eight!" the parrot warbled as it flew in the door and landed on the bed.

"Yes, so you say," Dancer said as he buried his hoard again. "And more than that, lad."

Then he set to cleaning his shack and preparing himself for the dawn. When he would set in motion what was necessary to enable him to bring home his real treasure—and keep it by his side until he left the land, the sea, and the earth itself.

The Devil's Spawn

🍎

by Mary Jo Putney

Devonshire, 1819

"But what if he refuses?"

Dominick Chandler silenced her with a kiss, which was what happened whenever she tried to be practical. Roxanne Mayfield sighed and relaxed into his embrace for a moment before pushing away. Trying to sound stern, she said, "Papa is not going to be persuaded by kisses."

Gray eyes sparkling, he brushed an errant red curl from her cheek. "That's all right—I wouldn't want to kiss him anyhow."

Trying not to laugh, she said, "Dominick, please be serious, we haven't much time. It was hard to convince Miss Bartholemew to let me see you alone for even ten minutes, and that wouldn't have happened if she weren't half in love with you herself."

His expression turned grave. "It's true that I've been a bit wild in the past, but I've never done anything really dreadful. My birth is good, I have money of my own, and I'm reasonably eligible. Why would your father reject me? Here in the wilds of the West Country, there isn't a lot of competition for your hand."

She chuckled. "You mean he'll take your offer because I'm so hopelessly plain that otherwise he risks having me on his hands forever."

"Minx!" Dominick said appreciatively. "You know that's not what I meant. If you had had a Season in London, you would have had half the men in England at your feet. But then you might not have met me."

"A thought too terrible to contemplate." For the thousandth time she marveled that such a splendid man had fallen love with her. But he had; that she didn't doubt. Ever since they had met by chance while riding, there had been magic between them. Roxanne suspected that she was the only person who really knew the honest, caring heart that lay beneath his dashing exterior. When she had recognized that, she had started to believe his declarations of love.

His hands tightened on hers. "I'm no paragon, Roxanne, but I swear that I will never fail you."

"I believe you." She shivered. "But I'm afraid, Dominick. You don't know Papa. He . . . He's not always reasonable, and he is not going to like the fact that you and I have become acquainted without his knowledge."

"Since you spend all your time on the estate, how else could we have met?" Dominick said reasonably. "Granted, our courtship has been a bit irregular, but we've done nothing improper." He grinned. "I'm waiting for marriage before I do that."

She blushed and looked down, knowing how easily he could have seduced her if he had put his mind to it. She was lucky that he was honorable. But Papa was still not going to be pleased that she had a suitor. "If my father refuses your offer and forbids me to see you, what will we do?"

"Why, we'll run away and be married, my love."

Her eyes widened. "I couldn't do that. There would be the most dreadful scandal."

He arched his brows. "You wouldn't risk a scandal to become my wife?"

She bit her lip. What he was asking went against every principle of morality and propriety. To elope would be to carry a stigma for the rest of their lives. And yet ... Softly she said, "For that, I would dare anything."

His smile returned. "Then it's a bargain, my darling vixen. If your father refuses, we'll head for Gretna Green. Promise?"

Praying it would not come to that, she said, "I promise."

He gave her a last, lingering kiss, then turned to leave the drawing room so he could go to her father's study. As Roxanne watched him leave, a chill ran through her, a premonition that something would go horribly wrong.

Though her father was so absorbed in studying his bones and bits of pottery that he scarcely spoke to her, he did like having her around to order the household and write his letters. He hated change, and his first reaction would be to refuse any offer.

It wouldn't help that Dominick had a reputation for wildness and he was universally considered too handsome and charming for his own good. Yet Dominick was right; he was an entirely eligible suitor—something of a catch for quiet Roxanne Mayfield, if the truth be known. In time her father would come around. All they needed was patience, though that wouldn't be easy.

Her hands clenched. And if patience wasn't enough, well, there was always Gretna Green.

*   *   *

After entering the study, Dominick spent several minutes shifting uncomfortably from foot to foot before he cleared his throat and said, "Sir William?"

The baronet lifted his head and stared balefully at his visitor. "Who are you and what do you want?"

Sir William Mayfield was a renowned student of primitive civilizations, and Dominick had assumed he was an absentminded scholar. But as he looked into Mayfield's cold eyes, he suddenly understood Roxanne's trepidation. This was not going to be easy.

He thought of Roxanne's laughing spirit and warmth, her slim body and tantalizing red hair, and he cleared his throat again. "Sir William, my name is Dominick Chandler, and I would like your permission to pay my addresses to Miss Mayfield."

Pure shock washed over the baronet. Leaning back in his chair, he said, "Of the Wiltshire Chandlers?"

Thinking it a good sign that her father knew of his family, Dominick said, "Yes, sir. My father was Charles Chandler, and I am heir to my uncle, Viscount Chandler."

His pale eyes like ice, the baronet said without reflection, "So you wish to marry my daughter. You're what, twenty-one or twenty-two?"

"Twenty-one, sir."

"And Roxanne is eighteen." With startling suddenness Mayfield's calm manner gave way to rage. His face reddening, he snarled, "Do you seriously think I will allow my daughter to ruin her life by marrying a worthless, debt-ridden, dishonorable wastrel like you?"

Dominick stiffened, stunned by the virulence of the attack. Controlling his temper with effort, he said, "I'll admit that I've sometimes been intemperate, sir, but I'm not debt-ridden. I've inherited a competence from a great-aunt, and I'm about to take up an appointment with the East India Company. When my uncle dies, I'll inherit his title and a very pretty property. You won't have to worry about your daughter's future, sir."

Mayfield leaped to his feet. Though he was inches shorter than Dominick, his fury made him menacing. "There has never been a Chandler worth the powder to blow him to hell. You're a bad colt from a bad stable, boy, and I don't want you near Roxanne. Do you understand me? *I forbid you ever to see my daughter again!*"

Dominick felt the blood drain from his face. Thank God Roxanne had already agreed to elope with him. It was not the way he had wanted to start their marriage, but if an elopement was necessary . . .

Guessing his thoughts, Sir William growled, "Don't think that you can get around me, Chandler. I will discharge my daughter's worthless chaperone, and from this day forward she will not be allowed out of my house without two escorts—men, not simpering females who might be taken in by you. Every servant on this estate, every laborer, will be told to give the alarm if you appear. The gamekeepers will be instructed to shoot on sight. By God, I'll put mantraps around the property! Step in one of those and it will cut you in half. You'll never see her again, boy. Resign yourself to that fact."

Dominick had aroused exasperation in many, and occasionally anger, but never anything like this. Bewildered, he asked, "Is it me that you hate, or would you feel the same about any man who wanted to marry Roxanne?"

"Both. My daughter is mine, and she belongs here at Maybourne. But it's a special pleasure to deny you. I knew and hated your father. He was just as handsome, just as selfish, just as arrogant, as you." Mayfield hesitated, as if wondering how much to say, then continued, "He ruined the girl I loved. She killed herself after he betrayed her by marrying your mother, who was an heiress. I was never able to pay him back, and now he's beyond my reach, frying in hell. But the sins of the father are visited on future generations, and the good Lord has given me the opportunity to inflict a small measure of justice on you. I've waited many years for this moment."

A sick feeling twisted inside Dominick. His father had indeed been selfish and arrogant. He had abandoned his family for good when his son was seven, leaving behind nothing but a bad reputation that had tainted Dominick's life. Deeds that in most young men would be considered high spirits were considered proof of wickedness in Dominick. It seemed bitterly unfair that after doing so little for him in life, his father now had the power to cost him the girl he loved.

Hoping an appeal to reason might work, he said, "Is it fair that your revenge will cost your daughter her happiness?"

"Bah, happiness. For a woman, satisfaction lies in service. I need Roxanne here to run my household and see to my comfort. It will be a better life for her than having her heart broken by a rogue like you."

"You're wrong," Dominick retorted. "Roxanne and I love each other. We were born to be together, and you can't keep us apart. If we must wait three years until she is of age, we will. Since that is the case, you might as well consent now, and spare yourself alienation from your only child.''

'' 'Born to be together'—that's romantic rubbish.'' The baronet's eyes narrowed. ''Your mother is still alive, isn't she? Do you want her to know the full measure of your father's wickedness? She's frail, I understand. Such news might be injurious to her health.''

Dominick paled. ''You wouldn't be so cruel. She has suffered enough because of him.''

''To save my daughter I would do far worse.'' He paused, breathing heavily, before continuing with lethal menace, ''If you ever try to see Roxanne again, I swear by all that's holy that I'll tell your mother every loathsome detail of your father's crime.''

Dominick felt trapped in a nightmare. It had taken years for his mother to find a measure of peace after her husband's abandonment, and she had never regained her laughter. If she discovered that her marriage had been the cause of another girl's suicide, the shock might kill her. And Dominick would never forgive himself.

Voice shaking, he said, ''Very well, you win.'' He stopped as pain lanced through him. To give Roxanne up—never to see the wondrous warmth in her eyes, or to kiss her welcoming lips ... Never to introduce her to the mysteries of passion ...

Harshly, before he could turn around, he said, ''I swear that I won't try to see her again.''

''I want your word on that.'' Mayfield scribbled a few words on a piece of foolscap, then pushed it and a pen across the desk. ''Sign this pledge that you renounce her, and I promise that your mother will never learn what your father did."

The paper said: *I promise never to see Miss Roxanne Mayfield again.* Blindly Dominick lifted the quill, dipped it into the inkstand, and scrawled his signature across the bottom. It would have made more sense to slash his hand and sign in blood.

He turned and left before he broke.

While Dominick spoke with her father, Roxanne withdrew to her room and paced. The time dragged endlessly. The manor had gotten its name, Maybourne Towers, because it had a tower at each of the four corners. Her room was in the southwest tower. Though the circular shape was inconvenient, she had asked for the chamber when she was a child because it made her think of fairy tales and princesses. Yet though she had always loved it, now it seemed a prison.

Her perambulations took her to the west window. She glanced out over the park, catching her breath when she saw a black-haired man riding away. Merciful heaven, her father must have refused Dominick, or her beloved would not be leaving without seeing her.

He pulled his horse in and turned around to stare at the house. Though he was silhouetted against the light and she could not see his face, there was a kind of wildness in his movements. Roxanne waved frantically, but Dominick gave no sign of seeing her. The afternoon sunlight was reflecting off her windowpanes. She fumbled with the catch so that she could open the casement and call to him, but before she could unfasten it, he wheeled his horse and rode off furiously.

Driven by the greatest fear she had ever known, she

darted downstairs and went to her father's study. She took a deep breath, then went inside. "Papa?"

He looked up from his desk with a frown. "Yes?"

Clenching her courage, she said, "Did—did Mr. Chandler speak with you?"

"He did indeed. I'm deeply ashamed that you were so lost to decency as to engage in a clandestine relationship," her father said with icy fury. "Your precious suitor cost me half a year's income, but at least he's gone now, and good riddance."

The blood drained from her face. Refusing to believe the implication, she asked, "Wh—what do you mean?"

"He threatened to ruin you if I didn't give him money. He boasted of his power over you—how you believed everything he said. He wanted five thousand pounds to leave you alone, though he came down to a thousand quickly enough." Her father made a disgusted face. "It was worth that to get rid of him, but don't you dare believe the lies of another debt-ridden scoundrel. I can't afford a second affair like this."

She gasped, shocked to her core. "No, you're lying! Dominick didn't want money. He loves me!"

A contemptuous expression on his face, her father shoved a piece of paper across the table. "Oh? Read this."

She looked at the words scrawled on the page. *For a consideration of one thousand guineas, I promise never to see Miss Roxanne Mayfield again. Dominick Charles Chandler.*

Her vision darkened and she swayed on the verge of fainting. It couldn't be true. It *couldn't.*

Yet that was his signature—she recognized it from

the notes he had sent her. Charming, laughing letters, in which he had declared his love ...

Nausea swept through her. She had believed him. *She had been fool enough to believe him.*

In that instant her youth died. Setting the paper back on her father's desk, she said in a trembling voice, "It appears that I was mistaken in Mr. Chandler. I'm sorry for costing you so much, Papa." She swallowed hard. "It ... won't happen again."

"See that it doesn't." Her father rose and gave her an awkward pat on the shoulder. "You're a sensible girl. You'll see, this is all for the best. In Wiltshire, his father was called the Devil, and young Chandler was called the Devil's Spawn. You're better off without him."

She gave a brittle smile before leaving the room. No doubt her father was right—this was all for the best. But it was a pity that she hadn't died two hours earlier, when she had still believed in love.

Plymouth Harbor, 1829

After a nerve-racking climb up a wildly unstable rope ladder, Sir George Renfrew swung gratefully onto the deck of the *Lovely Lady*. To the nearest sailor he said, "I believe that Lord Chandler is expecting me."

"Right this way, sir."

Renfrew followed the sailor across the swaying deck, trying to remember when and where he had last seen his friend Dominick. It must have been five years ago, in Hong Kong. Or had it been in the Sandwich Islands? Somewhere exotic, at any rate, and that night they had gotten roaring drunk, making toasts to the good old days at King's College. He smiled reminiscently.

The sailor led him to a cabin door, then withdrew. Renfrew knocked and entered when a familiar voice called, "Come in."

Renfrew stepped into the lavishly furnished owner's cabin. "Dominick, old man, how—" His voice cut off abruptly.

In the center of the cabin stood a hulking savage, his face obscured by wild black hair and a riotous beard. He was almost naked, with a crude whale-tooth necklace swinging across his chest and only a loincloth to cover his modesty. Hard muscles rippled beneath his bronzed skin as he stalked across the cabin, a guttural sound vibrating deep in his throat and a stone-headed spear in his hand.

For a shocked moment Renfrew considered bolting. Reminding himself that he had faced Malay pirates in the South China Sea, he raised his cane and barked, "What have you done with Lord Chandler, you ugly savage?"

Amazingly, the brute began to laugh. "So I can deceive even you, George," he said in smooth, impeccably upper-class English. "That bodes well."

Renfrew gasped. "My God, is that you, Dominick?" He looked closer and saw the familiar gray eyes. With a sigh of relief he lowered his cane. "Dare I ask what you are up to this time?"

Dominick waved his friend to the padded bench built against one wall. "I've come a'wooing."

George snorted as he sat and accepted a glass of brandy. "You've been away too long. If you want to win a wife in England, all you'll need is your title and the fortune you made trading in the East. You'll have to beat women off with a club." In fact, he thought as he examined the other man's powerful body, even the title and fortune wouldn't be needed. Women had always become buttery and wide-eyed around his friend.

"I don't want any woman, but a particular one." Dominick settled into a chair and regarded his brandy glass, his manner utterly at odds with his appearances. "Remember the family I asked you to gather information about—the Mayfields?"

Renfrew thought back; it had been over a year since he had made his quiet investigation and sent the results halfway around the world to his friend. "Ah, yes, the eccentric baronet and his spinster daughter. I wondered why you were interested in them."

"Not *them.* Her," Dominick said succinctly.

"You want to court Miss Mayfield?" Renfrew said with surprise. "I've never met her myself, but by all reports she's a dry stick of a female. Hardly your type."

Dominick's eyes flashed. "Roxanne wasn't always a dry stick, I promise you."

More and more interesting. Beginning to understand, Renfrew remarked, "Sir William is some sort of authority on primitive cultures, isn't he?"

"Exactly." Dominick swirled the brandy in his goblet. "From your report, Miss Mayfield never leaves the estate except when in the company of her father. You also found that all letters go to Sir William, and he has long since discouraged her friends from calling." An edge of anger sounded in his voice. "She sounds very near to being a prisoner."

"I wouldn't say that," Renfrew objected. "She is merely a quiet woman who is devoted to her father."

"No," Dominick said flatly. "She's not really like that, but her father has given her no choice."

Obviously there was a story here, but it didn't look like Renfrew would hear it today. "What do you intend to do?"

His friend looked up. "Remember the strange case of Caraboo, about ten or eleven years ago?"

It took Renfrew a moment to place the reference. "As I recall, she was some kind of East Indian princess who had been kidnapped by pirates, then escaped near the coast of England and swam ashore, where she was taken in by a vicar and his wife. But she turned out to be a fraud, didn't she?"

"Correct. In fact, she was a poor Devonshire girl who spent time with the Gypsies, then married a sailor and picked up some Arabic and Malay from him. When he left her, she went off her head and started thinking she was a displaced Asiatic princess."

"An interesting tale, but what has that to do with you?"

Dominick grinned wickedly. "She became quite famous. Experts on primitive cultures came to study her and try to deduce her origins. People would have paid to see her, I imagine."

Renfrew's brows shot up. "You're hoping to lure Sir William Mayfield out to see you?"

"Exactly. From what you learned about the Mayfields, it would be almost impossible to communicate with Roxanne while she is at home, but Sir William would take her with him to investigate an interesting savage." Dryness entered his voice. "I gather that he needs her to take his notes and bring him tea."

"So you're going to walk into the middle of Plymouth dressed like that, and hope that Sir William and his daughter will come racing to meet you," Renfrew said with heavy sarcasm.

"Actually, I have a Polynesian canoe in the hold, and I'm going to paddle it onto a nearby beach." He chuckled. "Let people think that I sailed her all the way from the Pacific. That will bring my quarry in a hurry—Sir William was particularly interested in ancient navigators, I believe. He had a variety of theories, most of them wrong."

"You don't look like any Polynesian that I ever met. They don't usually run to beards, their features are shaped differently, and I certainly never saw one with gray eyes."

"How many Britons would know that? Besides, no one can prove that I didn't come from an island that hasn't been discovered yet. I'll give the experts a dash of Tahiti, a dollop of Sandwich Islands, perhaps a pinch of Samoa, and have them gibbering with confusion."

"Mm-m-m, it might work," Renfrew admitted, "though you'll freeze if you prance around in a loincloth in this climate."

"I'll wear my feather cloak if I feel cold," the other man said blithely. "It's most impressive."

Renfrew's eyes narrowed. " 'Fess up, Dominick. You didn't invite me here merely so I could admire your clever plan."

"Quite right." Dominick smiled wickedly. "There will be a stir when I'm discovered. Since you live in the area and have traveled widely, it would be quite reasonable for you to come see the wild man. I'll speak a garble of Polynesian languages, and you will profess to be able to understand some of what I say. With the distinguished Sir George Renfrew to certify my savage self, no one will doubt me." He stroked his wild black beard. "In fact, I shall become greatly attached to you and refuse to leave your side. You will become my keeper and protector."

Renfrew's jaw dropped. "Damnation, Dominick, I've turned respectable. Don't try to draw me into one of your mad starts. We're not at Cambridge anymore."

Dominick looked down his aquiline, un-Polynesian nose. "Not respectable. Stuffy. Hard to believe you're the same man who drove a herd of wild pigs through a Jamaican ball after the governor snubbed you."

"He deserved it." Renfrew tried vainly to repress a smile. "It was a most juvenile prank."

"But amusing." Dominick's face became serious. "This is very important to me, George. I will be eternally grateful if you help. You're the only man I can trust in such a scheme."

Suddenly uncomfortable, Renfrew stared down at his glass, swirling the brandy. He'd been in a bad spot once in Hong Kong, and Dominick had pulled him through it. His friend would not mention that. He didn't have to.

"Very well, I'll help if you wish," Renfrew said slowly. "But are you really sure about doing this? I gather that you fell in love with Miss Mayfield before you left England, but that was a long time ago. You're not the same person now. You may be setting yourself up for a crushing disappointment."

"Don't think I haven't considered that," Dominick said soberly. "It's true that we were both very young.

But there was something between us that was timeless."

Renfrew sighed. "Very well. Bring on the canoe!"

Sir William Mayfield folded his newspaper and laid it next to his breakfast plate. "The coddled eggs were overcooked, Roxanne, and the braised kidneys were dry."

She glanced up from buttering her toast. "I'm sorry, Papa. Shall I order more for you?"

"There isn't time today, but see that the cook does better tomorrow." He peered over his half spectacles. "Fetch your bonnet and notebook. We're going to see a primitive curiosity."

It was typical of him to overlook the fact that she had scarcely touched her breakfast, but it was easier to obey than to continue eating. She laid down her knife and got to her feet. "Very well, Papa. What sort of curiosity?"

"A savage who appears to have sailed here from the Pacific."

"Is that the fellow they're calling the Wild Man of the West Country?" she asked with interest. "I read about him yesterday in the Plymouth newspaper."

"You shouldn't waste your time reading such rubbish. However, that is the nickname that the vulgar have attached to the brute." He permitted himself a thin smile. "Admittedly there is a certain logic to it. He is certainly wild, and quite unlike any creature ever before seen in this part of the world."

It might have been rubbish, but the story had intrigued Roxanne. "They say he's six and a half feet tall, that he sailed here all the way from Polynesia, and there's only one man who can understand anything of his speech."

Sir William sniffed. "Sir George Renfrew. The fellow is only a jumped-up merchant, but he sees fit to submit articles to scholarly journals on the basis of having traveled in strange lands. True scholarship is done reflectively, at a distance, uninfluenced by raw feelings."

As her father did. When was the last time he had experienced life firsthand? Repressing the disrespectful thought with the skill of long practice, Roxanne said, "I'll get my bonnet."

Upstairs in her room, she glanced in the mirror. An errant lock had escaped from the bun at her nape, so she secured it with the ruthless jab of a hairpin. It wasn't easy to persuade her blazing red locks to behave, but she persevered.

She was adjusting a navy blue shawl over her gray, high-necked gown when her gaze went back to her reflection. Her hands faltered at the sight of the sober, colorless, impeccably ladylike image in the mirror. Suddenly, she was a stranger to herself. Where had the passionate, impetuous young Roxanne Mayfield gone? She was nearing thirty, and could not remember the last time she had laughed without restraint. Who was she to criticize her father for keeping life at a distance?

She drifted across the tower room. Though she tried never to think of Dominick Chandler, he still had the power to sometimes intrude into her mind. How many lives had he ruined in the years since he had destroyed hers? She gazed out through the west window. It was right there, by the beech tree, where she had last seen

him, the sun behind him, silhouetting his broad
shoulders. . . .

Her lips compressed into a harsh line and she
turned from the window. She had been fortunate that
he had displayed his wickedness to her father before
she could ruin herself.

A thousand times over the years she had told herself how fortunate she was.

Throat tight, she picked up a notebook and headed
for the stairs. Papa hated to be kept waiting.

It was a two-hour drive to Plymouth. As the carriage rattled to a halt in front of the Black Hart Inn,
Roxanne said hesitantly, "After we've seen the Wild
Man, can we drive down to Sutton Pool for a few
minutes? I like to look at the ships."

"Nonsense, Roxanne, that would be a complete
waste of time." Sir William climbed from the carriage
and gazed at the inn. "The savage is being kept here,
with Sir George Renfrew watching over him to make
sure that he causes no trouble." He gave a rusty laugh.
"Serve Sir George right if the brute murders him in
his bed."

Roxanne failed to see the humor in such a prospect,
but she could not suppress a tingle of anticipation as
she followed her father into the inn. This visit was the
greatest adventure she had experienced in years.

Inside, her father announced to the innkeeper, "I
am Sir William Mayfield. Take me to see the savage,
my good man."

The innkeeper gave a respectful bow. "Very good,
sir. He's in the assembly room. Several other gentlemen are observing him as well." He glanced at Rox-

anne doubtfully. "But I'm not sure the Wild Man is a decent sight for a young lady."

"Nonsense," Sir William said impatiently. "She's not a young lady, she's my daughter."

The innkeeper led them through the inn to a dim, high-ceilinged room where public dances and private banquets were held. Though the day was pleasant, a fire burned in the hearth, probably to give the savage the warmth he was accustomed to. Half a dozen men were clustered in the corner. In the center of the group, towering above them all, was a crested feather helmet.

Sir William marched confidently into the room. "Renfrew? I'm Mayfield."

A medium-sized man with blond hair and a pleasant face broke away from the group and came to meet the newcomer. "A pleasure to meet you, Sir William." His interested gaze went to Roxanne. "Is this Miss Mayfield?"

"Of course," her father said, not bothering with a formal introduction. "Have you made any progress in discovering where the savage comes from?"

Renfrew shrugged. "Somewhere in Polynesia is the best anyone can say. The fellow's language and customs don't accord precisely with any of the known island groups, though I can understand a little of his speech."

Her father ordered, "Roxanne, do a sketch of the savage's feathered helmet."

"His name is Chand-a-la," Renfrew said mildly.

Sir William shrugged. "A savage is a savage."

Roxanne bent over her notebook and did a quick sketch of the helmet. The man might not be six and a half feet tall, but from what she could see, he was well above average height. What had it been like to sail a canoe halfway around the world? How fascinating it would be if she could talk to Chand-a-la and learn about the wonderful things he had seen. And how strange and lonely he must find this northern land, so far from his sunny islands. She wondered if he would ever find his way home again

Suddenly the Wild Man broke from the knot of observers and strode toward her, a velvety feather cape swirling lushly around his shoulders. Roxanne gasped, her gaze riveted by the expanse of naked bronze skin. The patterning of black hair across his chest and midriff made him seem paradoxically even more naked.

No wonder the innkeeper had had doubts about admitting her; she had never seen so much bare male flesh in her life. His loincloth barely covered his—she groped frantically for a suitable word—his male parts.

Cheeks burning, she bent her head to her notebook and began to sketch the toothlike ornament that hung around Chand-a-la's neck. He stopped beside her, his large, bare feet entering her field of vision. As she stared at them with a ridiculous amount of interest, a baritone voice crooned, "Wahine," into her ear.

"That is the Sandwich Island word for *female*," Sir George remarked. "It appears to mean the same thing to Chand-a-la."

Dark fingers reached out and stroked the back of Roxanne's hand. "Nani."

"That might mean *pretty*," Renfrew said thoughtfully. "Or perhaps soft."

The Wild Man must be warmer than an Englishman, for his fingers seemed to scorch Roxanne. She edged backward, unwilling to lift her head and look into his face.

One of the onlookers murmured, "He's not so different from one of us. If I'd spent two or three years in a canoe without a woman, I'd certainly want to further my acquaintance with the first female who crossed my path." Someone hushed the fellow before he could say more.

Curiously Chand-a-la reached out, touching the brim of her bonnet. As if wanting to see her face, he said, "Wahine?"

"Behave yourself, you brute," Sir William said sternly. He raised his cane and shoved the tip into Chand-a-la's chest with bruising force, driving the savage backward. "Haven't you trained him to stay away from decent Christian women?"

Amusement in his voice, Renfrew said, "He's not easy to train, Sir William. But I'm sure he means no harm."

The Wild Man batted the cane away, saying in a voice of obvious disgust, "Malahini okole."

"Interesting," Renfrew said innocently. "In the Sandwich Islands those are the words for *stranger* and, er"—he glanced at Roxanne—"backside. I wonder what they mean to Chand-a-la."

"Obviously something different." Sir William frowned at the Wild Man. "Is the canoe here? I'd like to see it."

Before Renfrew could answer, Chand-a-la said, "Aole!"

Unfastening his feather cloak and tossing it aside, he went to the fireplace and pulled out two burning brands. He raised the torches above his head, then began swinging them in an intricate pattern that blazed through the dimness like wheels of fire. At the same time he started shouting, "Aie—yah! Okolema-luna—yah! Mahalo nui loa-yah!" and similar phrases.

Chand-a-la's chant might have been an ancient ritual, or it might have been nonsense syllables, but it filled the assembly room with a harsh, compelling rhythm unlike anything Roxanne had ever heard. While the scholarly observers began scribbling madly, she simply stared, mesmerized by the sight and sound of the Wild Man. He was magnificent, surrounded by fire, a being of primitive, masculine power. To see him was to be carried away to a world far different from prosaic England.

Her reverie was interrupted when her father snapped, "For heaven's sake, don't gawk, Roxanne. Take notes. Try to catch the words accurately so they can be translated when we know more about his language."

Reluctantly she bent her head, jotting a phrase, then taking a quick glance up before jotting another. Her cheeks colored again when she saw that Chand-a-la's loincloth was in danger of being dislodged by his energetic movements. Engrossed with his fire dance, he was splendidly unconcerned with propriety.

With a last booming "Aie-yah!" he hurled the burning torches into the fireplace, where they crashed in a shower of sparks. A collective sigh went through the watchers, as if acknowledging that they had been privileged to see a rare sight.

Even Sir William murmured, "Quite remarkable." His lips pursed as he noticed how bare the Wild Man was. "But the landlord was right—this isn't fitting for a female." He took Roxanne's arm and started to usher her from the room.

"But, Papa," she protested, strangely unwilling to

leave. "Surely you will need me for sketching and note taking."

"I shall manage," he said briskly. "Tell the landlord to find a maid to walk down to Sutton Pool with you. I expect that I shall be busy here for the rest of the day."

Chand-a-la was staring at her from the other side of the room. There was something about his posture that seemed familiar, but she could not place the memory.

With a sigh she turned to leave. Poor Wild Man, so far from home. She hoped the scholars treated him kindly.

Dominick stared at Roxanne's retreating figure, unable to believe that she was leaving so soon, before he had a chance to speak with her and reveal his identity. Damnation, he had never even looked into her face!

She seemed so small, her movements and dress subdued, as if she were a docile wren. He needed to get her away from this place and these people so he could find the real Roxanne again.

He gave a wordless bellow and bounded across the room. Sweeping her up in his arms, he darted into the hall. A chorus of shouts rose behind them, but the longed-for feel of her slim body emboldened him. This time he would not let her get away.

Roxanne gave a strangled squeak as powerful arms swooped her into the air. Merciful heaven, the Wild Man was carrying her off! For an instant she was paralyzed with shock.

She began to struggle. Her arms were pinned to her sides, but she kicked out with her feet, futilely, until she realized that she was exposing her limbs all the way to the knees. For decency's sake, she stopped thrashing. After all, he couldn't possible take her far, and she didn't sense that he intended to hurt her. He was simply curious.

As they whipped down the hallway, her gaze fixed on the small, delicately tinted shells that were woven into his beard. The effect was rather pretty. She had noticed that he didn't smell rank and primitive as she had expected. His scent was clean, with a hint of spiciness. Did savages bathe and use cologne the way civilized gentlemen did?

A customer was just entering the hall from the rear of the inn. As he gawked, open-mouthed, Chand-a-la shouldered past and burst through the door, bounding down the short flight of stone steps with a force that jarred Roxanne breathless.

The coach yard was deserted. Increasing his pace, the Wild Man bolted into the stables, his captive clutched against his chest. Roxanne was dazed, the familiar scents of hay and horses totally at odds with this bizarre abduction.

With a flourish Chand-a-la set her on her feet, snatched a bridle from a nail, and unlatched the door to a stall. Then he guided her into the stall ahead of him so she could not escape. The bay gelding inside shifted nervously as the Wild Man deftly removed its halter, then slipped the bridle on.

Though Roxanne knew he could not understand, she said urgently, "Please, Chand-a-la, don't do this. There's nowhere to hide, and they might hurt you when they catch you." She placed a pleading hand on his arm. "Come outside with me now."

He glanced down at her hand, and she felt the muscles in his forearm tense. It was an odd moment that ended when shouts arose outside the stables.

He raised his hand and fumbled at her throat. She gasped and tried to retreat, stopping when she backed into the wall. Surely he couldn't be trying to molest her right here in the stable, when rescuers were just a few feet away, she thought wildly. But what did she know about how a savage's mind worked?

With a quick yank he untied her bonnet, tugged it off, and flung it aside. Then he brushed her head with a gesture that was oddly like a caress. Her hair loosened and fell in thick waves around her shoulders. His black beard shivered—was that a smile behind the shrubbery?—and he said something. Though it was hard to make out his words because of the shouting outside, it sounded like, "Don't fear, *wahine.*" But that couldn't be, since he didn't speak English.

Timidly she looked into his face for the first time. He was so tall and the stall was so shadowy that it was hard to see his features clearly. She did discover that his eyes were surprisingly light-colored, not black as she expected.

The door to the stable opened with a squeal of rusty hinges. Swiftly Chand-a-la lifted Roxanne onto the horse's bare back, setting her astride so that her skirts crumpled indecently around her knees. Then he swung up behind her. Controlling the horse effortlessly, he rode outside, one hand on the reins and his other arm locked around Roxanne's waist as he brushed past the stable boy who had opened the door.

A dozen men were in the yard, several heading purposefully toward the stables while the others milled about in confusion. For a suspended moment everyone stared at the sight of Chand-a-la and his captive. Sir

William was in the midst of the group. Looking more irritated than alarmed, he barked, "There they are." He began striding forward. "Unhand my daughter, you ignorant aborigine."

An onlooker said with surprise, "Miss Mayfield's hair is quite splendid."

Another man said admiringly, "For a savage, that fellow has a dashed good seat."

Ignoring the comments, Chand-a-la set the horse into a trot, heading for the arch that led to the street. A man cried, "Quick, kill the brute before he escapes!"

A portly gentleman who carried a fowling piece raised it and aimed at the Wild Man and his captive. As he pulled the trigger, Sir George swung his arm, knocking the barrel skyward as it discharged with a boom. "For God's sake, man!" Renfrew roared. "You mustn't kill Miss Mayfield while trying to save her!"

As acrid smoke filled the yard, the Wild Man put his heels to the horse and they broke into a gallop, whipping under the arch and into the street. Turning the horse to the left, Chand-a-la began galloping toward the outskirts of town as if the hounds of hell were pursuing them.

Roxanne clung to the gelding's mane helplessly as they swerved around drays and shrieking pedestrians. The wind whipped her hair free so that it lashed across her captor's chest. It was terrifying to ride without the security of a saddle. If it hadn't been for the firmness of Chand-a-la's grip, she would have been pitched to the ground. She caught glimpses of white, shocked faces as they roared down the street. Dodging a woman carrying a child, the horse clipped a basket and rosy apples spilled out.

Dizzily Roxanne watched the fruit roll across the cobbles, then raised her head to see a pony cart loaded with hay blocking the street crosswise ahead of them. She gave a muffled shriek, sure a lethal accident was imminent.

Instead of swerving or pulling up, Chand-a-la set the gelding into a suicidal jump. Even though she was convinced they were doomed, Roxanne automatically tightened her legs around the horse and held still so as not to throw the beast off balance.

They soared into the air, the Wild Man's body pressing against hers, keeping their weight centered over their mount's forequarters. A clump of hay tumbled to the street, dislodged by a hoof, but they landed safely. The Wild Man laughed with sheer delight.

Wherever he came from, they had to have horses, for he rode superbly. Roxanne turned her head and looked over her shoulder into his hirsute face. His eyes were gray, like those of ...

She went rigid with disbelief. No, it wasn't possible. *It wasn't possible!*

Chand-a-la. Chandler. The wretch! The bloody-minded, faithless wretch!

The man who had broken her heart had returned. And when they got to wherever they were going, she thought grimly, she was going to wring his neck.

The sooner they got off the road, the better; Dominick couldn't have been more conspicuous if he had been painted scarlet. He kept the horse at a canter, hoping that he would remember the twists and turns that led to the cottage. During the days he had stayed there, he had come and gone by night and been heavily cloaked to conceal his wild appearance.

Luckily the cottage wasn't far, and it was approached by a sunken lane so no one was likely to see them during the last stretch. He was grateful that Roxanne seemed unafraid. A lesser female would be having strong hysterics.

He knew he should identify himself, but once they started talking, the explanations would be lengthy and possibly acrimonious. He preferred to remain silent a little longer. During a hard decade of traveling in the world's wild places, he had yearned for this moment a thousand times, and now he wanted to savor the wonder of her presence.

The cottage was set in the center of an apple orchard. It was the height of spring blooming, and the bewitching scent of blossoms hung heavy in the air as he pulled the gelding to a halt and dismounted.

When he lifted his arms to help Roxanne down, she came readily enough, sliding from the horse's back to land a foot away from Dominick. She really was a little bit of a thing, the top of her gloriously red head scarcely reaching his chin.

For a long moment they stared at each other. With ten thousand things to say, all he could manage was to ask softly, "Do you recognize me, Roxanne?"

"Of course I do," she said impatiently. "Have you lost your mind, Dominick Chandler?"

He laughed buoyantly. "I should have known that I couldn't fool you. I'm glad—you might have been frightened otherwise, and I certainly didn't want that."

"I find your solicitude unconvincing." Her eyes narrowed. "Having ruined my life ten years ago, it appears that you have come back to ruin my reputation as well."

He sighed as he thought of all the complications

ahead. "I didn't plan it this way, but I thought that masquerading as a savage might help me get close enough to you to talk. I couldn't bear it when I saw you leaving, so I acted on impulse."

"I can see that you haven't matured any since I last saw you," she said acerbically. Taking the gelding's reins, she led it to a stump, climbed up, and tried to mount, but the stump wasn't high enough. After failing twice—and showing a delicious amount of leg in the process—she said, "Help me up. If I return to town quickly, it might be possible to salvage my reputation."

"Is that all you're concerned about—your reputation?" He caught the gelding's reins. "I didn't go to this effort merely for the pleasure of running off with you for half an hour. We must talk, Roxanne."

"That's *Miss Mayfield* to you." Standing on the stump put her eyes on a level with his. "There's only one thing I want to do with you, and it isn't talk."

Of course; he should have had the sense to kiss her right away. They could find each more quickly in an embrace than by speaking. He moved forward, eager to take her into his arms.

She hauled back her right arm and slapped him across the cheek with all her strength.

His whiskers buffered some of the force of the blow, but he still rocked back on his heels. Eyes watering, he said, "You're angry over what happened."

It was her turn to look incredulous. "*Angry.* That doesn't begin to describe how I feel." For an instant her lip trembled. "The words don't exist, Lord Chandler."

"You know that my uncle died two years ago," he said with interest.

She looked away. "I noticed his obituary in the newspaper. Believe me, I was not following your inglorious career."

But she *had* noticed, and remembered. "Come inside and I'll make a pot of tea," he suggested. "I imagine that we could both use some."

"*I* could use some tea. What *you* need is a shave and some decent clothing."

She tried to rake him with a scathing glance, but her gaze faltered somewhere around his chest. He found her bashfulness enchanting. Taking the gelding's reins, he said, "I'll rub this fellow down if you'll start a fire and put the kettle on. I should be finished by the time it's boiling."

Not budging from her stump, she said, "Do thieves always take such good care of the horses they steal?"

He stroked the gelding's sweaty neck. "I didn't steal Thunder—he belongs to my friend George. He's a fine fellow. I wouldn't have cared to try jumping that cart with a strange mount."

She hopped from the ground into the lush, ankle-high grass. "You thought of everything, I see. Does the cottage belong to George as well?"

"As a matter of fact, it does." He led the gelding into the shed that leaned against the cottage. As he tethered it, he continued, "This is a remote corner of his estate. I stayed here for several days while we worked out the details of my plan. In fact, my baggage is still here."

She sniffed. "I'm surprised that you were able to convince a grown man to participate in something so childish."

Dominick grinned. "It took a few minutes, but once George agreed to help, he had even more fun than I did. What a stuffy lot those scholars were! It was amusing to lead them on.''

Roxanne's hands knotted into fists, and she fought the temptation to hit him again. This was all just a game to Dominick; he was no more serious now than he had been ten years ago. All of her pain, all of her agonized, sleepless nights, had been wasted. She was a thousand times a fool. Spinning on her heel, she marched toward the sunken lane.

In two quick steps he was beside her, halting her progress with a hand on her elbow. "Where are you going?"

"That's a foolish question," she snapped. "Back to Plymouth. If I can't ride, I'll walk. It can't be more than four or five miles."

"No," he said flatly. His grip tightened on her elbow. "You are staying here until I've had a chance to say my piece."

Faint sun-baked lines bracketed his eyes. He looked older, harder, and far more menacing than when she had known him before. For the first time she felt uneasy.

Well, she had changed, too. She was no longer the adoring, malleable female who had agreed with everything her sweetheart said. Jerking her arm free, she said, "You dare to hold me prisoner?"

He scooped her up again and carried her toward the cottage. "Having kidnapped you in front of an innful of witnesses, I can hardly be in worse trouble than I am already."

This time there were no potential rescuers in the next room, and she fought for her freedom in dead earnest. He grunted when she drove her elbow into his belly, then jerked his head back when she clawed at his eyes. Her fingertips raked down his cheek, leaving red marks in the flesh above his beard. "Stop that, you little hellcat!"

She redoubled her efforts and for a moment she thought he was going to release her. Instead, he changed his grip, locking her arms by her sides. To her fury, he seemed more amused than upset. "It's good to know that my darling vixen hasn't been obliterated entirely," he said in a dulcet tone.

She caught her breath, unnerved to hear his old, loving nickname. Ceasing her struggle, she said in a voice that could have chipped ice, "I am not your vixen, darling or otherwise."

He turned sideways and ducked his head as he carried her into the cottage. It was a simple place, but clean. The whitewashed walls, rag rug, and well-worn wooden furniture had a certain homely charm.

He set her down again. "You can either walk into the bedroom, or I can carry you. What is your preference?"

She gasped, truly shocked. "So the purpose of your masquerade is rape?"

He looked startled. Then, as he realized how she had interpreted his words, he flushed scarlet. "Surely you can't think that I would ever force you.'"

Her eyes narrowed. "Raping my body would be a mere bagatelle compared to what you did to my heart."

The blood drained from his face, leaving him pale beneath his tanned skin. "I'm truly sorry for what happened, Roxanne, but I had no choice."

She retorted, "One always has a choice, and the ones you have made do you no credit."

"Perhaps you're right," he said quietly. "But I did the best I knew how."

The pain in his eyes caught her off guard. This was the private, vulnerable Dominick with whom she had fallen in love. She vowed silently that she would not let him cozen her again, but she felt sudden sympathy for Eve, beguiled by the serpent in the Garden of Eden.

Trying to conceal her weakness, she said, "If you're not interested in rape, why do you want me in the bedroom?"

"So I can lock you in while I rub down the horse," he said with exasperation. "I want to insure that you're here when I'm done, and the bedroom windows are too high and small for you to escape." He surveyed her. "Though now that I think about it, you might be little enough to get out that way. It will have to be the pantry—it's the only other door that can be locked from the outside."

Wordlessly she stalked to a door that opened from the kitchen end of the room. Seeing that it was the pantry, she stepped inside and slammed the door shut behind her. As he latched it, she scanned her surroundings, glad that a high, narrow window let in light. The shelves were empty except for a few basic supplies and utensils.

A flash of reflected light caught her eye, and she saw that a small round mirror hung on one wall. She glanced in, and caught her breath. Earlier in the day she had looked at her image and felt old and dull. The reflection that met her gaze now was entirely different, with snapping eyes and blazing hair rioting around her shoulders. She looked . . . wanton.

The image was even more disturbing than the ear-

lier one. She turned away and yanked her hair back
into its usual knot. She had enough hairpins left to
secure it, though only just. As the minutes stretched
on, she wrapped her arms around herself, feeling the
spring chill now that she was no longer in the sun.

Why on earth had Dominick abducted her? Certainly not for love, since he had never loved her. And
in spite of the way he had hurt her before, it was hard
to believe that he was simply being cruel, if for no
other reason than that the effort involved was so great.
The whole mad affair must be a product of his warped
sense of humor.

Presumably he would release her soon, but nothing
could prevent the story from spreading all over the
British Isles. For the rest of her life she would be
known as the spinster who was abducted by the savage. People would speculate in hushed, excited voices
about what the Wild Man had done to her.

Would it be better or worse if it became known that
"Chand-a-la" was an Englishman? Either way, her father would be furious at the notoriety, and he would
blame her for it. She shuddered at the thought.

It was taking him a long time to groom that horse.
Her hands clenched as a horrible new thought struck
her. Surely he hadn't become so angry that he would
abandon her in this isolated cottage! He might be a
wretch, but he wasn't a monster. Yet how much did
she know about him? Nothing, really.

She found herself wondering how long it would take
to starve. No, she would die of thirst first.

The pantry was just large enough for her to pace.

After what seemed like an eternity, the door swung
open. Roxanne bolted out, her relief boiling into

anger. She was about to start snapping when she saw Dominick and her words died in her throat.

The Wild Man was gone. He had taken her at her word and shaved off the disreputable beard, trimmed his hair, and donned the impeccably tailored garments of an English gentleman. He must also have bathed and washed off some of the stain that had darkened his skin, for his complexion had lightened to a less conspicuous shade. No wonder she had been in the pantry so long.

Dominick made a deep, heavily ironic bow. "Is this satisfactory, Miss Mayfield?"

As a savage, he had irritated her. Now, as a gentleman, he terrified her. She had always known that his birth was higher than hers, but it had been easy to forget that when he had laughed and teased and coaxed her into loving him. Now he was the epitome of the arrogant, high-bred aristocrat.

Her jaw set stubbornly. She might feel drab and provincial, but she didn't have to admit it. "A great improvement, Lord Chandler." She sailed by him, head high, then settled in a Windsor chair and smoothed her skirts over her knees. "I believe you said something about tea."

The corner of his mouth quirked up, and he no longer seemed as intimidating. "As you command, Miss Mayfield."

With a flourish he produced an already prepared tray where a fat brown teapot steamed gently. Setting it on the table beside her, he said, "I believe this has steeped long enough. Will you pour, Miss Mayfield?"

She gave a prim little nod. "Very good, my lord." Like the pot, the cups were simple cottage earthenware, but she poured the tea as if the service was porcelain. "There is no milk, but would you like sugar?"

"No, thank you, Miss Mayfield." Dominick took the chair opposite hers. He guessed that the excessive formality was appealing to Roxanne's sense of humor, for there was a glint of amusement in her eyes as she handed him a cup. That was a good sign. What a pity that she had ruthlessly pulled back her hair again. Ah, well, what went up could come down again.

He took several sips, then set the cup down. Now that the atmosphere was calmer, it was time to talk. "I gather that you never received the letter I sent you after . . . that day."

She gave him a quick, startled glance, then looked down at her cup again. "I received no letter." Her voice trembled. "Though I can't imagine what you might have said that could have mitigated what you did."

Dominick was unsurprised to learn that her father had intercepted the letter. No doubt his servants feared the man more than Dominick's bribes could overcome. "It was not a brilliant example of epistolary art," he admitted. "As I recall, I said that I loved you, apologized abjectly for the fact that I had to leave, and promised that someday we would be together. Which is why I am here."

"So romantic," she said mockingly. "But words are cheap. What mattered were your actions."

His jaw tightened. It was time to stop protecting Sir William. "I don't suppose your father ever told you how he blackmailed me into giving you up."

"*He* blackmailed *you!*" She slammed her teacup into the saucer. "Surely your memory is faulty, Lord Chandler."

"Every word he said is engraved on my liver," he retorted. "Sir William said that my father, Charles, had seduced and abandoned the woman your father loved, and that she killed herself as a result. Your father wanted revenge, and he took it on me by swearing that he would tell the tale to my mother, who was in fragile health." Dominick's jaw worked. "Believe me, it was the most difficult decision of my life. But as much as I loved you, I couldn't pursue my own pleasure when doing so would cost my mother her peace of mind, and possibly her life. If I had done that, I would not have been worthy of your love."

Roxanne stared at him. "A touching story. It might have convinced me, if I hadn't seen with my own eyes the paper you signed."

It took him a moment to remember. "That's right, your father wanted my renunciation in writing. I was so numb that I did as he asked, though I didn't see the point. The paper was only as good as my word." He smiled humorlessly. "Which is to say, not good at all, since I did not feel bound by a promise extracted by force. What kept me away from you was concern for my mother. When I learned of her death, I returned to England, and here I am."

"Don't lie to me!" she cried, her face twisted with anguish. "You didn't give me up because you were a good son, but because my father paid you a thousand guineas to go away."

He stared at her, staggered. "That's utter rubbish. There was never any mention of money. If Sir William had tried to buy me off, I would have laughed in his face."

Her hands locked together in her lap, white-knuckled. "I tell you, I saw the paper. Your signature was unmistakable."

Dominick tried to remember back to what he had signed. When he did, he swore. "Damnation, your father must have added something. He wrote a sentence in the middle of a sheet of foolscap, saying that I promised never to see Miss Roxanne Mayfield again. I scribbled my name below. He could easily have added more."

Roxanne's face went white, leaving a pale, ghostly dusting of freckles on her high cheekbones. "No," she whispered. "*No*." She buried her face in her hands.

His heart ached for her. He wanted to take her in his arms, but guessed that she would not welcome his sympathy.

At length she raised her head and said huskily, "It's your word against his. I don't know what to believe. Perhaps it no longer matters what the truth is."

"The truth always matters," he said sharply.

She shook her head. "Perhaps my father did alter the paper you signed. Probably he believed that he was saving me from a disastrous marriage, and very likely he was right. We thought we were in love with each other, but we were children—what we felt was not love but the hot blood of youth. We both would have regretted our rashness."

"No!" Realizing that he had shouted, Dominick moderated his tone. "Yes, we were young, but the love was real. No doubt we would have had ups and downs as all wedded couples do, but I would never have regretted our marriage, and I would have done my damnedest to insure that you didn't."

She gave him a wistful smile. "You really are a romantic. But can you honestly deny that you've enjoyed your decade of adventuring? You must have done things, gone places, that would have been impossible with a wife and family."

"You're right that I traveled wide and far, and there was much I enjoyed," he admitted. "But I went because I needed to occupy myself to numb the pain of losing you."

Her brows arched delicately. "Are you going to claim that you spent ten years without touching another woman?"

He hesitated, sensing that he must be ruthlessly honest if he was to win her belief. "There were women sometimes. I am not a saint, and the years were long. But I never loved another woman, and there was never a day when I didn't think of you."

"You weren't thinking of me, but an idealized vision of me," she said softly. "Give it up, Dominick. Reality can never match a dream."

She looked so somber, so unlike the Roxanne of his memory, that he almost surrendered. Perhaps she was right and he had been cherishing an illusion.

Then he remembered how she had been earlier, with her hair tumbled and her eyes fiery. She had been alive then, as he guessed that she had not been for ten years. That passionate wench was his Roxanne, and by God, he wasn't going to let her go for a second time.

He stood, looming over her. "If we give up without trying, Sir William has won, and I will not permit that."

She sighed. "This isn't a contest between you and my father. Perhaps you're right, perhaps we would have made a success of marriage in spite of our youth. We will never know, for that time has past. I am not

that girl, and you are not that young man." She got
to her feet. "It's time for me to go."

His eyes narrowed. "The only place you're going is
Gretna Green."

She stared at him. "Don't be silly, Lord Chandler.
You don't want to marry me, and I don't want to
marry you. Don't try to hold on to the past from sheer
stubbornness."

"Don't tell me what I want and feel!" He caught
her gaze with his. "We are going to marry, and we
can sort out the wisdom of it afterward."

After a moment of appalled silence, she began to
laugh. "Dominick, you're absurd. Marriage is for life.
It isn't like going into a shop, then leaving if you decide that the stock is not to your taste."

"This stock is very much to my taste." His slow
gaze went over her from head to toes. She felt naked,
embarrassed, and . . . aroused.

Suddenly alarmed, she said, "This particular lot of
merchandise is not for sale. Take care, Dominick. Remember that this is England and try to avoid felonious
crimes in the future."

She moved toward the door. He stepped around
her, reaching the door first, then turned and leaned
against the dark oak planks, his arms folded across his
chest. "You're not going anywhere but Gretna
Green." He frowned as he considered. "Though there
is really no reason to go so far. You're no longer
underage, so we can simply drive to London and get
married by special license there. George can come and
stand witness."

"This ceases to be amusing," she said in a dangerous voice. "Let me go, Dominick. I am not going to
marry you."

"Why not?"

"Because—because the very idea is nonsensical!" she exclaimed. "We have nothing in common."

"It's true that men and women have little in common, but they keep getting married anyway." He smiled wickedly. "The few mutual interests they do have are usually enough."

She wasn't sure whether to laugh or blush. The sensation was familiar; Dominick had always had that effect on her. For an instant she wondered what it would be like to be his wife. She felt an ache deep inside. To go to bed with passion, and to wake up with laughter . . .

But it wouldn't be like that. Obviously he had cherished some romanticized image of her for the last ten years, and that vision was obscuring the plain, bread-and-butter reality of Miss Roxanne Elizabeth Mayfield, spinster of the parish. After taking a deep breath, she repeated, "I am not going to marry you."

"Yes, you are. You promised. Several times, in fact. Remember?" His face was amiable and ridiculously handsome. "We've been pledged to each other for ten years. It's time we marched to the altar."

"For the love of . . . !" Clamping down on her exasperation, she said, "Very well, if you want me to make it official, I will. Any engagement that was between us is *over*. Am I making myself sufficiently clear?"

"Remember the discussions we had about Mary Wollstonecraft Godwin? You liked the fact that I supported the principle of equal rights and obligations for females. I still do—if a man isn't allowed to jilt a woman, then a woman shouldn't be allowed to jilt a man." He smiled angelically. "The betrothal stands."

"It does *not*!" She glared at him, eyes smoldering.

"They say one is supposed to humor a madman. But you can't force me to marry you. No vicar will perform a ceremony when the female is gagged and that's the only way you'll be able to prevent me from protesting."

"Ah, but by the time we reach the vicar, you won't be protesting." His gaze holding hers, he stepped forward and drew her into his arms. Softly, gently, his lips met hers in a warm, thorough exploration. She gave a tiny whimper and clutched his upper arms. His embrace was as familiar as her dreams, where he had come to her a thousand times.

The kiss deepened and he drew her against him. He was so tall, so muscular. She felt desire rising and her breasts ached with longing. With a gasp she tore herself away, unconsciously wiping her mouth with the back of her hand as if that would free her of his spell.

He gave a slow, dangerous smile. "You'll not escape me so easily, Roxanne."

She turned away from him, shaking. It wasn't fair that she had to be reasonable for both of them. If it was left to Dominick, they would plunge into marriage, then make each other miserable. He would leave her, or take mistresses, and she would wish she were dead. If only she didn't love him . . .

She stopped and pressed her hands to her temples. Oh, Lord, she did love him, didn't she? Against all sense, she felt exactly as she had ten years before. Even when she had hated him for his betrayal, she had never stopped loving him. She was an utter *fool*. She must escape tonight when he was asleep, before she lost what remained of her wits.

After swallowing hard, she turned to face him. "And you'll not change my mind easily, my lord."

"It will be interesting to discover which of us is more stubborn. We're well matched, Roxanne. That's one of the reasons I fell in love with you." His caressing expression turned pragmatic. "It's too late in the day to set off for London. I don't know about you, but I'm getting hungry. There should still be some food in the pantry. Shall we see what can be made from the supplies at hand?"

Having had ample time to inventory the pantry, she said, "There are eggs and potatoes and a knob of butter, so I suppose an omelet is possible. Perhaps there might be something useful growing in the old kitchen garden."

"Excellent idea." He ushered her outside. The flowering apple trees glowed in the late afternoon sun. "A lovely day, isn't it? England at its best."

She inhaled the blossom-scented air, feeling the pulse of spring beat in in her veins. She wanted to frolic like a lamb, careen as madly as a March hare. She hadn't felt so alive since . . . since that magical season when she had fallen in love with Dominick. Hastily she examined the long-neglected garden. "There are scallions over there, and a bit of parsley. They'll liven up the eggs."

"We'll have a feast." He knelt and used his pocket knife to cut the herbs. With a mischievous smile he added, "I'll peel and fry the potatoes. I'm not sure I should trust you with a knife."

"Wise man," she said tartly. "I might use it to cut out your heart."

Scallions and parsley in one hand, he straightened to his full height. "You don't need to do that," he said simply. "You already have my heart."

His gaze held hers, his gray eyes utterly without

guile. She found that she was having trouble with her breathing. Perhaps ... perhaps it was really possible. ...

She pivoted and headed back into the cottage. "I warn you, my cooking skills are indifferent."

"No matter," he said cheerfully as he followed her inside. "I have some French wine that could make stewed boots seem ambrosial."

Dropping all references to love, lust, and marriage, he removed his coat and waistcoat, then rolled up his sleeves and built up the fire. To her surprise, they worked together as smoothly as longtime dance partners, sharing utensils and taking turns at the table and the hearth. In spite of his comment about the knife, he passed it to her without hesitation when she was ready to chop the scallions and parsley.

For a gentleman, he was surprisingly competent in the kitchen. Deftly he peeled and cut potatoes, then fired the wedges into a crispy, golden pile. Feeling naughty, she stole one from the old chipped platter. It was hot and savory and delicious.

He grinned and ate a potato wedge himself, then popped one into her mouth as if she were a baby bird. Her tongue touched his fingertips, tasting salt and sensuality. There was an odd moment of complete, mutual awareness, and she feared that he could see the accelerating beat of her heart. Nervously she turned and poured her egg mixture into the skillet.

While she cooked a fluffy, fragrant omelet, he set the table and ceremoniously poured fine French Bordeaux into a pair of thick mugs. She was folding the omelet over when he slipped up behind her and removed the pins that kept her hair in place. The whole mass tumbled down over her shoulders again.

She was about to scold him when he pressed a light kiss through the silky strands under her left ear, his tongue teasing the lobe. Her toes curled and she almost dropped the skillet. With a feeble attempt at severity, she said, "If you don't behave, your supper will end up scattered across the floor."

His lips moved down her throat. "If that happens, I'll find something else to nibble on."

Blushing, she slipped away from his embrace, then divided the omelet into unequal pieces and slid the larger onto his plate. The sun was setting as they took seats on opposite sides of the scrubbed pine table. On impulse she raised her mug of wine. "To the past."

"And the future," he added immediately.

"The past is more certain." Nonetheless, she drank the toast.

Silence reigned as they applied themselves enthusiastically to their plates. Kidnapping appeared to sharpen one's appetite.

When he had finished, Dominick pushed his plate away and leaned back in his chair with a happy sigh. "I've never had a better meal."

She eyed him askance as she neatly laid her knife and fork across her plate. "You undermine your credibility when you make remarks like that. If you say such ridiculous things about food, how can I believe the other things you say?"

Immune to setdown, he said, "I've had more elaborate meals, but plain food is just as good when it is well prepared." His warm gaze met hers. "And tonight the company is matchless."

Her gaze fell. Changing the subject, she said, "You made a very convincing savage. Were you imitating real aboriginals, or did you make everything up?"

"I blended the language and customs from different Polynesian islands. The largest part of my performance came from the Sandwich Islands, since I spent the most time there. On the other hand, the fire dance was from Samoa." He grinned. "After seeing one performed, I decided to give it a try and accidentally set my hut on fire. Everyone in the village was rolling on the ground laughing at me."

She had to laugh also as she pictured the scene. "What are the Pacific islands like?"

"Beautiful beyond imagining. The Sandwich Islanders ride giant waves on flat, narrow rafts, skimming the sea like birds. I tried that too, and almost drowned before I learned the knack. It was like flying." His gaze became distant. "The flowers and birds are so brilliantly colored that they seem the product of a painter's opium dreams. Even the sands of the beaches come in different colors, from blinding white to shimmering black. And the volcanoes—seeing one by night is a sight never forgotten. It was like looking into a rift that had opened to Hell. Where the molten stone flowed into the sea, pillars of steam billowed into the sky. It was truly awesome."

She exhaled, imagining the marvels he described.

Correctly interpreting her sigh, he asked, "Would you like to go there for our honeymoon?"

She almost said yes before she managed to stop herself. "There can't be a honeymoon if there is no marriage."

"You're a hard woman, Roxanne," he said, not seeming particularly worried. "Now that I think on it, it would be better to take you to the Caribbean. The islands are equally lovely, and a good bit closer. Turquoise seas, caressing winds—as close to paradise as one can find on this earth."

No—true paradise would be to live with a man one loved and trusted. Love alone was not enough. Trying to sound light, she said, "You should be writing travel books."

He grinned. "I considered it, but such tales should have a tone of high seriousness, and I could never manage that. It was my fate to always find the absurd instead of the sublime." He embarked on a hilarious series of stories about other misadventures in the East and the Pacific. Roxanne laughed more than she had in the last ten years combined.

As she sipped her third glass of Bordeaux, she began telling stories of her own. About the vague scholar who had visited her father with a coachful of bones, looking for help in assembling them into whole skeltons. About the gosling that had decided a dog was its mother, and the neighborhood lad who had run away to the Gypsies only to be sent back with the firm comment that they didn't need any more children, thank you very much.

Simple stories, but Dominick was amused. Mug cupped in his hands, he lounged back in his chair, dark tousled locks falling over his brow. The giddy thought passed through her mind that perhaps love was simply a matter of finding someone who would always laugh at one's jokes.

She must stop thinking of love and start thinking of escape. Yet when she looked at him, her mind filled with images of how he had appeared as a nearly naked savage. His loose shirt, open at the throat, reminded her irresistibly of the broad, muscular shoulders beneath the fabric. The way his trousers pulled across his thighs made her remember how it had felt to be pressed against him. A male body was very different in shape and texture from that of a female. . . .

Mouth dry, she rose to her feet. He'd had enough wine so that he would sleep soundly, and she should be able to slip away. "Being kidnapped is fatiguing. I think I'll retire now."

"I'll help you make up the bed." He stood and led the way into the cottage's only bedroom. It was a cozy chamber, with a broad four-poster bed, a washstand, and a pile of expensive baggage along one wall.

Dominick opened the blanket chest at the foot of the bed to reveal worn but clean bedding. After the two of them had tucked sheets and blankets and stuffed pillows into cases, he said, "I'll join you in ten minutes or so."

Her heart jerked like a terrified rabbit. "I beg your pardon?" she said in freezing accents.

"Don't worry, I'll sleep on the floor, unless you invite me to share the bed," he said mildly. "But I really can't allow you to stay in the room alone. You might decide it's your duty to try to escape."

The beastly man could read her mind. She glared at him. "So even though you claim to love me, I am your prisoner. Have you no shame?"

"I'm ashamed of many things, but not this. You aren't a prisoner—merely a bride suffering a few qualms."

To her regret, she found that she had a lamentable desire to giggle. Schooling her expression, she said, "Be sure to give me enough time to prepare. Though it shouldn't take long, since I'll have to sleep in my shift."

"If you like, I'll give you one of my nightgowns,

though you'll look like a snake about to shed its skin."
After digging out a nightgown, he bowed politely,
then left.

She undressed and washed, then donned the gar-
ment. He was right about the size; it was enormous
on her. But the fine lawn fabric was soft against her
skin, making her think wicked thoughts.

Everything made her think wicked thoughts.

She dropped a pillow on the floor, then added a
couple of blankets from the chest. The pine planks
didn't look particularly comfortable, but that was his
problem.

After braiding her hair into a long plait, she slid
into the bed and pulled the covers over her head. In
the darkness, the unreality of her situation washed
over her and her happiness leached away. The handsome, dashing man she loved wanted to marry her. It
was a romantic dream come true.

Who would have thought that fulfillment of a dream
could make one feel so wretched?

Dominick allowed Roxanne time to settle herself,
then quietly entered the bedroom. She was only a gentle mound beneath the bedcovers, with not so much
as a single auburn curl showing. He guessed that she
was only pretending to sleep, but he didn't challenge
that. After a lifetime of maidenly modesty, she was
entitled to be nervous at having him so near.

Certainly her proximity unsettled him. How much
would she protest if he joined her in the bed? His
blood quickened. Though her mind might be doubtful,
her body had welcomed his touch. It might take only
a few kisses to persuade her to give him what he had
dreamed of for a decade.

He was halfway to the bed before he managed to

stop himself. It was bad enough that he was abducting her; he could not coerce her into an intimacy for which she was not yet ready.

With a faint sigh he made up a pallet on the floor. He was unlikely to sleep much, so there was no chance she could sneak out without his knowledge.

In deference to his roommate's innocence, he donned one of his seldom-worn nightgowns. Then he blew out the candle, wrapped himself in the blankets, and tried to find a comfortable position. He would rather be in the bed . . . but it was still heaven to doze off to the sound of Roxanne's gentle breathing.

Dominick came awake with a start and lay still for a moment, wondering what had disturbed him. The moon had risen and cool, silvery light illuminated the room. But there was something wrong with the sounds. After a moment he realized that Roxanne's breathing had changed. No longer smooth, it had become a series of faint sobs.

Stricken, he got to his feet and perched on the edge of the bed. Softly he asked, "What's wrong, my darling vixen?"

"Nothing." She made a choked sound. "Everything."

He lay down on the bed and gathered her into his arms. Her small, curving body trembled as she hid her face against his shoulder. "Why did you have to come back?" she said through her tears. "My life wasn't very interesting, but I wasn't miserable. Now I feel like a child pressing my nose to the window of a candy shop, yearning for something I can never have."

"What do you yearn for?"

"F—for love, for happiness, for laughter." She swallowed convulsively. "For you."

Mary Jo Putney

"Since you already have me, why are you crying?" he murmured as he smoothed back loosened tendrils of her hair. "I love you. I want to marry you and devote the rest of my life to pleasing you. Why is that such a terrible prospect?"

She began to cry harder. "How can I trust you?" she said haltingly. "You left me once. I'm a very ordinary woman. Once you realize that, you'll leave me again."

He winced. No matter how noble his reasons, he *had* left her. And once trust was gone, how could it be regained?

Perhaps if she understood why he loved her, she might start to believe in him. "Do you remember the first time we met?"

She gave a small hiccup. "Of course. I was out riding. You were looking for the ruined Roman villa near Maybourne and got lost and wandered onto our land. On that black horse of yours, I thought you looked like a magical druid prince."

He pressed a kiss against her temples. "You never told me that."

With a touch of her usual tartness, she said, "You already had quite a good enough opinion of yourself."

He shook his head. "Not really. It's hard to have a good self-opinion when everyone is convinced that one is going to the devil. My father had gone that way, and it was universally assumed that since I resembled him, I was equally damned. In some circles I was known as the Devil's Spawn." He had meant the words to sound light, but they came out edged with regret.

By her stillness, Roxanne had noticed. "Was your father that bad?"

He shrugged. "Bad enough. He wasted most of my mother's inheritance, had the reputation of a cheat at

282

cards, and kept his word only when it suited him. When I was seven, he eloped to the Continent with a married woman. My mother never really recovered from his betrayal." Dominick took a deep breath. "I could overlook the rest but not that. She deserved better."

Roxanne's arm crept around his waist. "You never spoke of your father to me."

"Ten years ago I couldn't. Because I was young, it was very important for me to appear jaunty and unconcerned. I guess I was successful, but I felt as if there was a hole in the center of my soul. Then I met you. Riding through that clearing, your hair blazing like fire because you hated wearing hats." The image was as sharp in his mind as if it had been yesterday.

He ran one hand down her back. Under the thin fabric her flesh was warm and softly yielding. "I'd always enjoyed pretty girls. Usually I laughed and flirted a bit, then went my way without a second thought. But as soon as I saw you, I felt as if the hole in my soul had healed. I couldn't explain it then, and I can't now. Perhaps love can't be explained."

A little desperately, she said, "I can't help but fear that over the years you have built me into an impossible model of perfection. I'm no paragon, Dominick."

He laughed. "I'm well aware of that. You've a sharp tongue, a stubborn streak, and you see things perhaps a little too clearly for comfort. Yet at the same time, those are some of the qualities I love in you." He kissed her temple again. "Your intelligence." He brushed her lips lightly with his. "Your directness." He laid his hand on her heart. "Your warmth, and if you can come to trust me again, your steadfastness."

He felt the beating of her blood against his palm. "When I saw you today at the inn, I felt exactly the same sensation that I did ten years ago: that you, and only you, can fill the emptiness inside me. No one else has ever affected me that way, so I don't think you can be considered ordinary. Or if you are, perhaps ordinariness is what I need." He took an uneven breath, for honesty was painful work. "Certainly I need you."

There was a long silence before she whispered, "You make it easy to believe." Lifting her head, she touched her lips to his.

He responded with fierce sweetness, murmuring her name over and over as he kissed her. Her breath quickened and she did not object when he joined her underneath the blankets. It seemed so natural to have him beside her, to return his caresses and rejoice in his touch.

As passion claimed her, she forgot the long, empty years and pressed against him, wanting to feel the length of his body against hers. In the dark privacy of the bed, they might have been alone in the world, Adam and Even sampling the forbidden fruit of desire. The large nightgown slipped from her shoulders easily so that his mouth could simultaneously soothe and inflame the ache in her breasts.

Even so, she inhaled sharply when his hand slid beneath her gown and caressed the sensitive flesh inside her thighs. Hearing her alarm, he halted. "I have loved and wanted you so much, for so long, Roxanne," he said huskily. "I—I don't know if I can bear to wait any longer."

For a moment, fear paralyzed her. She was standing on the edge of a precipice; if she dared to leap off into the abyss, her life would change irrevocably. To accept him now was also to accept his offer of marriage and his version of the past. It would mean making herself vulnerable to the same kind of pain she had felt ten years ago, but it would be a hundred times worse if she lost him again after they became lovers.

She thought of the long, lonely years at Maybourne Towers. Since that was her life, it was high time she did change, or she would die without having lived.

And he wanted her as no one else ever had. She was not a whim to him but a necessity, just as the memory of him had been necessary to her no matter how she had tried to deny it.

Feeling a deep sense of female power, she ran her fingers tenderly through his thick, silky hair. "You don't have to wait any longer, Dominick."

He exhaled roughly. Then, curbing his urgency, he initiated her into the mysteries of passion with infinite gentleness. She expected pain, and there was some, but there was also rapture beyond anything she could have imagined.

When she fell asleep in his cradling arms, it was with the greatest peace she had ever known.

It was early when the laborer shuffled into the Black Hart Inn. "My name's Wussell," he said to the innkeeper. "Is this where the lady was stolen from?"

The innkeeper winced; he'd never live this down. On the other hand, business was booming as people came to see the premises from which the Wild Man had abducted a modest English maiden. "This is the place. For tuppence you can see the room where it took place. Some of the savage's gear is still there."

Wussell twisted his cap in his hands. "I'm not here for that. Yesterday I saw the brute and think I know where he might have taken the lady. They say her father is staying here?"

The innkeeper bustled off, and within five minutes

Sir William emerged from a private breakfast room. "Searchers have been scouring the countryside without result," he said brusquely, "yet you claim to know where my daughter is?"

"Won't swear to it, but yesterday afternoon I caught a glimpse of a shaggy, naked brute riding with a lady in front of him." Wussell pondered. "She had red hair. Right pretty she was."

"A pity you didn't come forward yesterday, when there was still time to save her virtue," the baronet snarled. "Heaven only knows what that savage might have done with her last night. She might be lying dead even as we speak."

Wussell shrugged. "Didn't know he was a savage—thought he was just a member of the gentry being odd. There's no accounting for the gentry. Wasn't till this morning that the milkmaid told me about your daughter being abducted. Came as soon as I could."

"We must collect a party and rescue her," Sir William said. "Where is she being held?" Correctly interpreting Wussell's vague expression, the baronet dug into his pocket and produced his purse. "Will five pounds help your memory?"

"Reckon it would." Wussell accepted the money. "They were riding down the lane that leads to Orchard Cottage. This morning, after I heard, I went to take a look. It's supposed to be empty, but there was smoke coming from the chimney, so I came to find you."

Sir William bellowed, "Innkeeper, find me some men! And make sure they're armed."

To go to bed with passion and wake up with laughter . . . It was even better than Roxanne had imagined. Dominick's head was pillowed on her shoulder and his arm draped over her waist. His face relaxed and peaceful, he was a bonny sight. It awed her to think that, God willing, they would be waking up like this for many years to come.

When she stretched lazily, trying not to disturb him, his gray eyes opened. There was wariness in the depths, as if he feared that she would regret what she had done. Wanting to eliminate that doubt, she said teasingly, "I had no idea that it was such fun to be ruined."

His tension disappeared and he gave her a smile that took her breath away. "You're not ruined— you're better than ever." His arm tightened around her. "I have trouble believing that this is real, not just another dream."

"In a dream, one isn't hungry, so this must be reality," she said pragmatically.

He laughed. "We'll have the rest of the eggs for breakfast. Then it's off to London for that special license."

She made a face. "My father must be half out of his mind with worry. I really can't leave without telling him."

Dominick sighed. "I suppose you're right, but there will be hell to pay when he recognizes me."

She gave him a light kiss. "I don't expect that Papa will be best pleased, but he has no power to forbid me from marrying where I choose."

He kissed her back, not at all lightly. One thing led to another, and half an hour passed most enjoyably. Making love in the daylight had a special kind of intimacy; she decided that she could grow very fond of it.

As they sprawled together in a tangle of damp, naked limbs, a shotgun blasted outside the cottage and a deep voice bellowed, "We know you're in there,

Chand-a-la. Send Miss Mayfield out right now. If she's hurt, you're a dead man."

Roxanne squeaked and sat bolt upright. More slowly, Dominick rolled from the bed and began pulling on his clothing. "Bloody hell, now we're in for it. I'm sorry, love, I didn't mean to pitch you into the middle of a scandal. We'll have to take that tropical honeymoon until the gossip dies down."

She dived from the bed and began yanking on her own garments, her heart pounding in panic. As soon as they saw her, every man out there was going to know exactly what she had been doing. Not that she was ashamed of her actions, but she would rather that all Devonshire didn't know.

Shotgun pellets rattled against the cottage wall, shattering a window. "Damnation!" Dominick swiftly pulled Roxanne to one side. "You'd better tell them you're all right, but don't stand in front of the window to do it."

Frantically she yelled, "Don't worry, I'm fine. I'll be out in a moment."

A familiar voice shouted, "Is that really you, Roxanne?"

"It's my father," she said with horror. Raising her voice, she replied, "Yes, Papa, it's really me."

Wordlessly Dominick fastened the back of her gown. His touch helped soothe her fear. She gave an unhappy thought to her hair, but if she delayed to fix it, the men outside might come in after her, and that could be disastrous.

She headed toward the front door. Before she could open it, Dominick took her hand. "We'll go out together."

She tried to disengage his clasp. "They might shoot you."

"They're looking for the Wild Man, not an Englishman, so I'll be safe enough," he said reasonably. "Besides, I don't want to let you out of my sight ever again." He accompanied his words with a quick kiss.

Certainly he looked every inch a gentleman, not a savage. She was foolish to be so concerned—yet she could not escape the fear that her newfound happiness was about to be shattered forever. Raising her chin, she led the way outside.

There was an instant of silence. Then her father roared, "Damn you to hell, Chandler! What are you doing with my daughter?"

When Roxanne flinched, Dominick murmured, "How nice to know that one hasn't been forgotten." Raising his voice, he said, "Coming to claim my bride after too long a betrothal. I hope you will wish us happy."

Face red with fury, Sir William stormed out of the shrubbery, several men behind him. "Wish you happy! You—you criminal! Did you hire that filthy savage to kidnap Roxanne?"

"Not at all," was the calm reply. "I *am* that filthy savage."

The baronet's jaw dropped as he stared at Dominick's face. When he recognized the features of Chand-a-la, he snarled, "You imposter! How dare you mock the scholarly pursuit of knowledge."

One of the searchers said with interest, "Well, I'll be, this gent here is the Wild Man." A murmur rose from the others.

Sir William snapped, "You lot get out of earshot. We have private matters to discuss."

With obvious reluctance, the other men withdrew and settled down to watch the show. Dominick waited until they were out of range, then said, "No subterfuge would have been necessary if you hadn't separated us for your own selfish reasons. But this time you will fail. My mother is dead, and there is nothing you can say to make me give Roxanne up."

Sir William appeared on the verge of explosion. Turning his attention to his daughter, he said, "Have you no shame? Allowing yourself to be seduced by this fortune hunter! Not only did he viciously extort money on the promise that he would leave you alone, but he has broken his solemn word never to see you again."

"A vow extracted under duress is not valid," Dominick pointed out.

Glaring, the baronet said, "What's your price this time? Since you've already ruined her, I won't pay as much as before, but it would be worth a couple of hundred pounds to get rid of you again."

"You never paid me a penny, Mayfield," Dominick said coldly. "I've told Roxanne the truth about how you falsified that document, so don't think you can deceive her this time."

For a moment the baronet appeared off balance. Then he said to his daughter, "You believed him? The man's a liar through and through. Having ruined God only knows how many other females in the last ten years, now he's back for another go at you."

"He loves me, Papa, and I'll not let you come between us." Though Roxanne's words were brave, Dominick saw that her fragile confidence was eroding under her father's bullying.

Sir William's contemptuous glance raked down her. "You're hardly the sort to catch the fancy of a man of the world."

"Don't speak to her that way," Dominick snapped. "Any man would be proud to have Roxanne as a wife."

THE DEVIL'S SPAWN

Despite his words, her face paled and her hand slipped out of his. Dear God, he was losing her. Even though her blazing hair still rioted around her small face, she was reverting to the meek, colorless woman who had come to the inn, and he didn't know how to prevent it from happening.

Pressing his advantage, the baronet said, "Have you no more brains than a goose? Chandler is after your fortune, for after I die, you'll be a considerable heiress. If you go with him, he'll live off your expectations. When he can't wring any more credit out of the moneylenders, he'll leave you flat. He's done it before, at least twice to my knowledge. Even if he goes through a marriage ceremony with you, it will be bigamous and illegal."

"No," she cried, horrified. "That can't be true."

"You're damned right it isn't," Dominick said sharply.

Simultaneously Sir William said, "It's all true, and more—I've followed Chandler's disgusting career for years." His lip curled. "Who are you going to believe—the father who has raised and protected you all your life, or a sly, deceitful rake?"

When her stark gaze went to him, Dominick said with anguish, "My God, Roxanne, after all that has passed between us, don't tell me that you still don't trust me!"

Her face mirroring the doubts warring within her, she said wretchedly, "I want to believe you, but—but I've never known my father to lie."

Dominick's eyes narrowed as he looked at the baronet. "On the contrary, he lies so well and so smoothly that I now wonder about the story he told me ten years ago, that my father was responsible for a young woman's suicide."

Ignoring him, Sir William said piously, "It's a sad day when a daughter doubts her father's word."

She pressed her hands to her temples, looking as if she was about to faint. She whispered, "Dominick?"

He shuddered and his hands clenched into fists. "I've told you the truth," he said tightly. "It's my word against his, and you're going to have to decide who you believe."

As she stared at him, paralyzed with indecision, her father put his arm around her shoulders and said in a gentler tone, "Come home, Roxanne. You've been a fool, but you're still my daughter. I'll pretend that this unfortunate incident never happened. We can go on the way we were."

As he tried to usher her away, she gave Dominick an agonized glance. His expression was stricken, but she saw that he would not try to stop her; he would not want a woman who did not have the courage to fight for his love as he had fought for hers.

She looked at her father, and saw the triumph in his eyes. He thought that he had won, and took more pleasure in that prospect than he had ever shown in being a parent.

Which of the men had demonstrated love by his actions? Dominick, not her father, who had systematically undermined all her friendships until her life was as narrow as that of a nun.

And which of the men did she truly love?

Again, the answer was Dominick.

Wrenching away from her father, she said, "I owe you a daughter's duty, Papa, but if you force me to choose between you, I will choose Dominick."

Unsteadily she began to walk toward her lover. In two quick strides he closed the distance between them and swept her into his arms. "Dear God, Roxanne," he said hoarsely, his hand stroking her hair over and over. "I thought I'd lost you for good this time."

"I'm sorry I doubted you," she whispered, voice trembling.

He hugged her more tightly. "Doubt is human. What matters is that you had the strength to follow your heart."

As she hid her face in his shoulder, she knew she had made the right choice.

But her father had not yet surrendered. "If you go with that man, you're no longer my daughter," he shouted furiously. "I'll leave my fortune to the British Museum. See how long he stays once you're a pauper, and don't expect me to take you back."

"I don't want or need Roxanne's inheritance, Sir William," Dominick snapped. "Frankly, I think she would be better off if she never saw you again, but I shan't forbid her to communicate with you. It's up to you whether you have a relationship with her and any future grandchildren."

Heart aching, Roxanne turned to look at her father. He had certainly not been the most affectionate of parents, but he was all the family she had, and it would hurt bitterly if he refused to ever see her again.

His face bore a desperate expression she had never seen before. After a taut silence, he barked, "Damnation, Roxanne, this man's father eloped with your mother! It would be indecent for you to marry him."

Dominick gasped, his arms going rigid around her. "If that is true, why did no one ever tell us?"

Mouth dry, she said, "It can't be true. My mother died when I was four. I scarcely remember her."

Her father growled. "The bitch didn't die, she ran

away with her lover. Haven't you ever wondered why there was no grave?"

"I never thought much about it. I assumed Mama was buried in Buckinghamshire, at her family's estate." Stunned, Roxanne searched her memory, trying to recall what had happened. Her mother had not been a frequent visitor to the nursery. After a particularly long absence, Roxanne had asked when her mama would next come.

The nursemaid had said repressively that Lady Mayfield had passed on. There had been a strong implication of death, though the word had never been used. Roxanne had been too young to question further. And because she had lived such an isolated life, she had never heard any gossip to make her wonder.

Turning to Dominick, she asked, "You didn't know either?"

"I swear to God that I had no idea." He felt numb, and sure to the bone that this time the baronet was telling the truth. "One day my mother announced that my father had left us and would not be coming back. I didn't dare ask questions, since the subject upset her terribly. She never mentioned him again, except to tell me several years later that he had died in Naples. By then I had learned from a servant that my father had run off with a married woman, but I never knew her name."

"Well, you know now," Sir William spat out. "My wife died at the same time, of the same cholera that killed your father. Yes, I lied to both of you when I forced you to leave ten years ago, but breaking up the relationship spared your mother the horror I felt when you asked for Roxanne's hand. Your mother would have been as appalled by a marriage between you two as I was." His face worked. "I've done my best to protect my daughter. I'd rather die than lose her to another Chandler."

Dominick stared at Roxanne, wondering what she was thinking. When she slipped away from him, he had the sick feeling that this time the baronet had won.

But he misjudged. Stopping in front of her father, she said quietly, "The only way you will lose me is if you refuse to accept Dominick as my husband. He is not his father any more than I am my mother, and he is just as much a victim of their selfishness as you and I. I understand now why you tried to separate us, but we are not the same as our parents. Dominick and I are both single and free to love each other."

With unexpected compassion for the older man, Dominick added, "Trying to deny our love will not change the past, Sir William. I'm sorry for what happened, for all of our sakes, but I'll be damned if I will walk away from the only woman I've ever loved to pay for my father's crime."

His breathing harsh, the baronet buried his face in his hands. Gently Roxanne said, "It can't be easy to stop feeling anger after so many years, but for my sake I hope you will try. I don't want to lose you, Papa." She gave Dominick a quick glance. "We'll be going on a long honeymoon. When we return, I hope you will receive us at Maybourne Towers."

Sir William lowered his hands. His expression was haggard, but his eyes showed a relief at having revealed his long-held secret. "Perhaps—perhaps by then I'll be able to. I—I don't want to lose you, either." With a flash of familiar belligerence, he said, "If you make my daughter miserable, Chandler, I'll make you rue the day you were born."

Dominick put his arm around Roxanne's shoulders.

"If she's unhappy, it won't be for lack of trying on my part."

After a hard look the baronet gave a small nod, then turned and left the clearing. With a sweep of his arm he collected the men, who had been watching in fascination. A few minutes later hoofbeats sounded as the would-be rescue party rode away.

Dominick gave a long, exhausted sigh. "Life is stranger even than I imagined."

She glanced up, her fox-brown eyes grave but serene. "It's not really such a coincidence. You said that you were looking for that ruined Roman villa because your father had told you about it when you were a child. That is what brought you to Maybourne Towers. Perhaps our love was meant to be."

He drew her close. "It was wickedly wrong for my father and your mother to elope. Yet ... if he loved her as much as I love you, I can understand why he did it."

"And if my mother loved him as I love you, I know why she went with him," Roxanne replied. "I do love you, you know. I don't believe that I mentioned that last night."

"You didn't, but we'll have ample time to rectify the omission." A smile in his voice, he continued, "Shall I take you to paradise for our honeymoon?"

She burrowed into his arms. "I'd like to see your islands, but there's no real need to travel that far. I've found paradise right here."

A Good Woman

❦

by Anita Mills

Texas State Penitentiary, Huntsville: July, 1881

Warden Hemphill looked over his glasses at the tall, dark-haired man across the desk from him and frowned. At thirty-one, John P. O'Neal had spent eight years of his life behind bars, and if his current manner was indicative of anything, he was going to be back, probably within the year. Rather than sit at attention in the new black serge suit the state had provided him, the obviously bored O'Neal more or less sprawled insolently, staring at a fly on the wall.

"Have you heard anything I've said, John?" the warden asked him.

"Jack."

"I beg your pardon?"

"I don't like the name John." O'Neal straightened in the hard wooden chair and leaned forward. His black eyes looked directly into Hemphill's. "Yeah, I heard it—every word. And anything else you've got to say, you'd better get it out, because the way I look at it, come noon, I'm a free man." He glanced at the clock on the office fireplace's mantel. "That gives you about two more minutes, the way I look at it."

"You won't get anywhere with that attitude, John."

"I did my time—I don't have to grovel to get out

297

of here," the younger man countered. "So why don't you just give me my belongings and I'll be going. That way you've made it easier on both of us."

Hemphill flashed him a look of dislike. "I'm not in the business of making anything easy for you," he snapped. "In fact, I hope I've made it damned hard here."

"No." A faintly derisive smile played at the corners of O'Neal's mouth. "It wasn't hard at all." He picked up the black felt hat and set it on his head, adjusted the angle, then stood, towering over the warden. "I take it this is mine," he declared, picking up the envelope.

"Have you given any thought to what you're going to do, John?"

"Yeah." An unholy light lit O'Neal's dark eyes, and his smile broadened. "I'm going to take this twenty-dollar gold piece and buy myself a real bath and a shave. Then I'm going to walk on over to the nearest whorehouse, order me up some good whiskey, and get laid until every last penny's gone."

"That's not what I meant, and you know it."

Jack shrugged. "I thought we were both pretty plain about it."

"You'll never make anything out of yourself that way, John," Hemphill persisted. "You'll be a drunken sot—you'll be no better—"

"Don't bother saying it," O'Neal cut in. "And I'm going now," he added, heading for the door.

"You think you're going to dig up that money, don't you? You think you're going to live like a king on it, but you won't. You'll be looking over your shoulder, because the Texas Rangers are going to be right behind you, just waiting to take it away from you."

The younger man turned around. "Maybe—but they haven't found it in almost nine years."

"You're already headed back here, son."

"Son?" One of O'Neal's eyebrows shot up. "I wouldn't say that too loud, if I were you—it'll make folks wonder what kind of company a fine, upstanding citizen like you keeps."

Ignoring the gibe, Hemphill tried to give one last bit of advice. "What you ought to do is go away somewhere where nobody knows you, and find yourself a good woman to help you settle down."

O'Neal's expression hardened, and his eyes went cold. "There isn't any such thing—all there are out there are a dozen different kinds of bad ones," he said harshly. "When God created Eve, the joke was on Adam." With that, he wrenched the door open. "It's past noon, Warden," he said over his shoulder.

A guard stepped forward, blocking the doorway. "You done with him, sir?" he asked Hemphill.

"Just about." The older man looked at O'Neal's back. "You're a hard case, John. And if you don't watch your step, you'll wind up getting yourself hanged." When there was no response, he sighed. "All right—take him on out," he told the guard.

As the door closed behind them, Hemphill opened a drawer and took out his Bible. God willing, the troublemaker wouldn't be coming back, but he didn't have much hope of that. Not unless the young fool got himself shot first. With that comforting thought, he opened the Good Book to Psalms, seeking respite from a thankless job.

Outside, Jack O'Neal stepped from the prison and drew his first deep breath as a free man. The air was hot and dust-filled, typical for Texas in July, he reflected, savoring it. He stood there for a moment, taking stock of the world from the outside, then he began walking toward the hotel.

The first thing he was going to need was money for clothes and a gun. Then, contrary to what he'd told Hemphill, he was going to put some distance between Huntsville and him. To pique the rangers' interest, he was going straight to San Angelo, but not after the money. Not yet. No, he was going to let it lie for a while, then when they got tired of watching him, he'd dig it up. At least he'd be near his money.

The money. All five thousand dollars of it. He closed his eyes momentarily, remembering how it had looked before he'd buried it in the lead-lined trunk, the neat rows of crisp bills staring at him, enticing him to spend it. But he hadn't, not one cent. A damned Texas Ranger had stumbled onto him soon after, and he'd never got the chance to go back for any of it. Instead, he'd done eight years for bank robbery, with only the memory of those green bills to sustain him. The way he figured it, he'd earned that money, every single penny of it.

But right now he needed the clothes, he needed the gun, and he needed a ticket to San Angelo. When he got there, he'd buy a horse, then figure out what to do while he bided his time waiting for the right moment to get his money.

"I'm done," the old man said, tossing down his cards. "Look's like m' luck's gone tonight."

"Me, too," the rough-looking cowboy decided, fanning out the worst hand Jack had ever seen. "No pairs, no runs, and no more'n two of any suit," he observed with disgust.

"Count me in for ten," decided a gentleman in a frock coat and brocade vest.

The fourth one, a sullen boy with downy peach fuzz rather than whiskers on his face, stared at his cards. Jack could almost see the wheels turn in his head as he assessed the odds. Finally, the youngster leaned forward and tossed a wad of bills into the pile.

"I'll see your ten and raise you fifty," he declared triumphantly. "Lay 'em down, and I'll take your money."

"I don't think so." Jack scooped his considerable winnings into the middle of the table, then leaned back lazily. "It'll cost you five hundred to see them."

For a moment, the boy's eyes seemed to bulge, then he found his voice. "Damn you—you can't do that!"

"I just did." Jack turned to the man in the vest. "Well?" he asked softly.

There was a pregnant pause as everyone watched the gambler. There wasn't so much as a flicker of emotion in his eyes. Finally, one corner of his mouth turned down slightly. "Not tonight, I'm afraid. I think you've got Lady Luck in your lap, friend." With that, he brushed what money he had left off the table into his hand, and stood up. "Good night."

As he left, the old man reached over and turned up his cards. "Well, I'll be—why, he had three sixes!"

The boy was looking sickly now. "I ain't got five hundred dollars, mister."

"If you can't pay, don't play," Jack murmured.

"Damn you!" Tears welled in the kid's eyes as he threw down his hand. "You cheated me out of my money!"

The old man laid a hand on his shoulder. "Them's fighting words, boy—and that's Jack O'Neal."

But he was too late. The kid had his gun out of his holster, pointed at Jack. "I'm going to kill you, mister."

O'Neal never flinched. Instead, he carefully laid down his cards, then turned them over, one by one. He had three tens and a pair of jacks. "I believe I've won, fair and square," he said quietly.

"That's a full house, son," the old man. "Can you beat that?"

Jack reached across the table to scrape in his winnings, stuffed what he could into his pockets, then tied the rest in the red-checkered tablecloth. Without so much as a look at the boy, he rose. "Maybe tomorrow night, gentlemen," he said, smiling faintly. With that, he turned his back and walked slowly toward the door.

"I think you'd better put that thing away," the cowboy told the kid. "He's gone."

But the boy was still staring at the door. "Who's Jack O'Neal?" he wanted to know.

"A hard case," the old man answered. "A real hard case."

The cowboy took the gun, then asked, "Could you have beaten a full house?"

The youth swallowed, then shook his head. "I had three aces," he whispered. "But he didn't play fair— he knew I couldn't call him—he knew I didn't have five hundred dollars."

"Way I see it, if you'd a had it, you'd a lost it," the cowboy said. "So mebbe he did you a favor, son."

Still carrying the tablecloth, Jack was picking up the key to his room when he noticed that the woman at the end of the counter looked ready to cry. She was youngish, maybe still in her twenties, and even to a man who'd been away from the world for eight years, her blue cotton dress looked outdated. His gaze moved to the two children with her, the one a boy about six or seven, the girl perhaps a year older.

As he turned to leave, he heard the woman say, "I don't have enough money, but if you need someone to clean the rooms, I can do that before I leave."

"Sorry, ma'am, but I can't do that."

"Mama, can we eat?" the little boy asked plaintively.

"Later, dear."

"But I'm hungry."

"Johnny, we don't have any money," the little girl whispered to him.

Jack didn't know whether it was the girl or the words that got to him. He turned back around to face them, taking in the child's small, delicate face, the halo of golden hair, the well-mended black stockings under the faded smock. He looked at the boy beside her, and the small, pinched face reminded him of another time. He'd seen that face in his own mirror.

"How much is it?" he asked the clerk.

"Dollar and a half apiece." Looking at the children, he relented. "But the kids are half price."

Jack pulled a thick wad of bills from the tablecloth and tossed ten dollars onto the counter. "That ought to get meals with the room," he said curtly.

The woman looked at the money in his hand for a moment, then found her voice. "It's very kind of you, sir, but we really cannot allow you to engage the room for us." As the little boy's face fell, she took his hand. "Come on, Johnny—we'll sleep on the benches," she said briskly.

"But I want to eat!" he cried.

"We'll be home tomorrow."

The little girl looked up at Jack from beneath a fringe of gold lashes. "Thank you, anyway, sir."

"Mama—please."

"Hush, Johnny—we're not charity cases. At least not yet, anyway," his mother told him.

"Look, it's been a good evening for me, and ten dollars isn't going to break me," Jack told her. "If you were any kind of a mother at all, you'd take the room, feed the kids, and get them into bed. They shouldn't be up this late, anyway," he added contemptuously. Stashing the rest of the wad back in the tablecloth, he started toward the stairs.

"Mama, we could pay him back later," the little girl ventured hopefully.

Stung by his manner, Beth Morgan stared indignantly after him. "He had no right to say that—no right at all. He doesn't know anything about us."

"If I were you, I'd take the room, ma'am," the clerk spoke up. "He left the money."

"Please, Mama," the little girl said softly.

Beth looked from Sarah to Johnny, then to the clerk. Finally, she sighed. "I don't know how we'd repay him," she reflected slowly. "We don't even know his name, and we're leaving on the stage for San Angelo in the morning."

The clerk turned the register around to read the signatures, then shook his head. "That's Jack O'Neal—from all I've heard, he ain't worth knowing. But," he added practically, "you ought to take the room. It ain't no fun trying to sleep on a stage, ma'am." He looked across the counter at the fretful boy. "It's late, but it might be I could get some bread and milk sent up to you tonight. Then you could eat breakfast and leave on a full stomach in the morning."

"Please, Mama," Sarah said wistfully. "I'm hungry, too."

Jack O'Neal was a total stranger, but obviously the money hadn't meant much to him. Beth wavered for a moment, then as Johnny laid his head against her full skirt and held on, she capitulated. They were exhausted, and in her present circumstances, there wasn't much room for pride. Right now, she couldn't afford it any more than she could afford a night in a hotel.

"All right," she decided. "I don't suppose there's much likelihood we'll ever see Mr. O'Neal again, anyway."

"Thank you, Mama," Sarah told her.

But as she led them up the stairs, Beth didn't even feel grateful to the hateful stranger. She just felt plain defeated. Now, after having humbled herself before Ben's cold, snooty sister, she was going home empty-handed. And unless she encountered a miracle, she was going to lose everything she and Ben had fought so hard to build. She was going to have to sell the sheep; then, without them, she'd have to sell the farm. If only she could somehow persuade the bank to wait a little longer for the money. If not, there'd just be the foreclosure, and there wouldn't even be a chance they'd have anything left to start over with. No, she had to last long enough to hold a sale. No matter what, she had to last that long. Ben would want her to, she told herself fiercely.

He'd almost forgotten what a real bed felt like, and now that he was in one, he couldn't sleep. He had too many plans to make, too many things to do, too much freedom to savor. He lay there, staring up in the darkness, listening to the sounds floating up from the street, thinking how good it felt to be out of prison, thinking he was never going back. He'd die before he let anyone lock him up again.

Finally, nearly overwhelmed by the flood of his thoughts, he rolled from the soft featherbed and found a match. Groping for the kerosene lamp on the dressing table, he managed to get the chimney off and light the wick. As he reset the chimney, a thin reed of black smoke climbed the glass, then the flame cast his flickering shadow over the yellowed walls.

It was then that he saw the envelope he'd picked up from Hemphill's desk. The words JOHN P. O'NEAL'S PERSONAL EFFECTS had been written in bold letters on it. The irony that one envelope had held everything of value he owned wasn't lost on him. Except for the money he'd stashed when the posse closed in on him. Money waiting near San Angelo for him.

Curious, he picked up the envelope and slit it open with his thumbnail. He shook the contents out onto the dressing table—an old pocket watch, a weathered leather wallet containing two faded dollars, and his knife. Reaching back with his fingers, he retrieved a smaller yellowed envelope marked simply "Mary O'Neal, 1875," and he considered throwing it away. Even now, six years after his mother's death, he still didn't want anything to do with her.

He felt a surge of anger as he stared at it, thinking this was all she'd left him. He'd refused to look at it at the time, and he wanted to refuse again, but there was something pathetic about it as he turned it over in his hand. All that was left of a foolish woman.

Even now he could remember the lies she'd spun, the grand dreams she'd clung to. Someday, she'd told him, his father was going to come for them. Someday, they were going to have a white clapboard house on the right side of town. But it never happened. He'd grown up in a whorehouse called Miss Hattie's in San Angelo, lying on a cot, listening to the sounds of his mother and the other girls selling their bodies to anyone who had the money. No, none of her dreams had materialized. Instead, she'd died of consumption in one of Miss Hattie's back rooms the week before she would have turned forty-two.

He'd learned early on what she did for a living. The kids at school had told him, taunting him that his mother was a whore, that he was a bastard, he recalled bitterly. At first he'd tried to defend her, but when he realized they spoke the truth, that he had no father, he'd quit going there. Instead, he learned to read by himself in the tiny, dim room he shared with her. It took his mind off what he knew she was doing down the hall.

When in the early hours of morning she finally crept past him to her bed, she smelled of whiskey, cheap perfume, and the musky odor of men. Then, bleary-eyed in the harsh light of morning, she'd tell him again how his father was a rich man, how one day when his father's wife died, he was going to come for them. "Then you won't be just my Jackie," she'd say. "Then you'll be somebody, and so will I."

At fifteen, he'd had enough. They'd quarreled, and he'd baited her, shouting that she was a fool, that if she'd been any kind of mother, she'd have gotten both of them out of there years before. Despite her tearful pleas for understanding, he'd stormed out of Miss Hattie's then, never to go back.

Not that he'd done much better for himself. At first, he'd bummed around Texas, taking ranch jobs, herding cattle up into Kansas. Then he figured out he wasn't going to amount to much that way, so he polished his card games and became a gambler. He did pretty well at that, but then one night his luck went sour, and he was too busted to get into a game. It was then he decided to rob the bank. Nearly too drunk to stand, he'd waved his gun, shooting up the place, while the frightened cashier stuffed his carpetbag with money. By the time he'd sobered, he was five thousand dollars richer, and headed back to San Angelo with a posse behind him. He'd had some dumb notion of giving his mother enough money to get out of Hattie's, but he never made it. What little bit of sentiment he had for her had cost him his freedom.

He sighed, then ripped open the smaller envelope. There wasn't much there, either. A lock of raven hair wrapped in tissue and marked "Jackie's first haircut," a pair of pearl earrings, and a worn, folded piece of paper. A pitiful showing for almost forty-two years on this earth.

Idly curious now, he unfolded the paper. She must have opened and closed it a thousand times, for it separated at the creases. Three small pieces of newspaper fell out onto the dressing table as he began to read the letter.

My dearest Mary,

Let me begin this painful letter by saying that I do love you, and I will always love you. For the past few months, you have brightened my dreary life immeasurably, giving me far more passion and joy than any man has a right to expect.

But I am a weak man, Mary, and having grown accustomed to the privileges of a wealthy wife's money, I cannot give up the comforts of my position even for you. So rather than court a disastrous scandal, I must sadly bid you farewell, and hope that you do not hate me too much. Given Susannah's precarious health, it is not too much to hope that one day we can be together, you, me, and our child. But until then all I dare offer is a measure of financial support. I pray you will accept the five hundred dollars as a small token of my eternal affection.

I think it better that you leave town before your condition is known, for society can be unkind to females in your situation, and it would be disastrous for both of us were Susannah to learn of your existence. If you will give me your direction, I will send money as I can.

The bastard had signed it simply, "Yrs, Philip Kingman."

Jack stood there for a long moment, staring at the faded paper. This pitifully inadequate letter had sustained Mary O'Neal's dream of a better life for years. In his mind he could see her as she'd once been, the pretty, soft woman who'd held a small boy close, promising him better things to come. The poor, pitifully foolish creature—she'd wanted to believe Susannah Kingman would die, that Philip Kingman would come for her.

Instead, she'd wound up at Miss Hattie's, offering

her body to any man with the money to pay for it. All because of some bastard named Philip Kingman. He looked at the worn page again, feeling an impotent anger at a man who thought five hundred dollars could pay her for the destruction of her dreams. Philip Kingman had made a whore of his mother.

He looked down, seeing the newspaper clippings. Picking them up, he held one close to the kerosene lamp. It was an obituary, announcing the death of Susannah Kingman on the 18th of October, 1865. Two months after Jack had parted company with his mother.

The second small bit of paper, dated a year and a half later, announced Philip Kingman's wedding to the daughter of a prominent banker. So much for his promise to come for Mary and the son he'd gotten on her. What a blow that must have been to her, what a bitter pill to swallow. Jack had to fight back sympathy for her, recalling instead the painful, lonely life she'd given him. His heart hardened in the flood of those memories.

But the last article was the one that intrigued him. It announced Philip Kingman's appointment as president of a bank in San Angelo, effective August 10th, 1874. Too bad Jack hadn't waited another year and robbed the bank in San Angelo instead. He might have encountered his father. If he'd known then what he knew now, he'd have put a bullet between Kingman's eyes, and the charge would have been murder.

He carefully laid the clippings on the letter and re-folded it. God, the pain she must have suffered. After wanting to believe for so long, she'd seen her first lover marry another rich woman, and she'd known he was living in the same town with her. It was hard to imagine how she could have borne it. The answer, simply enough, was that she hadn't. Within months of Kingman's arrival in San Angelo, Mary O'Neal died, coughing up blood, struggling for breath, in the back room of a whorehouse.

That was Jack's heritage—a three-dollar hooker and a dirty, lying scoundrel. The rage he felt threatened to overwhelm him. The room was too quiet, too small, and the walls were closing in on him. He had to get out of there before he broke up the damned furniture.

He dressed quickly, then made his way down the stairs and outside. The air was still hot, and as heavy as a winter blanket. He made his way across the street to a noisy cantina, where a Mexican girl danced to the music of a beat-up guitar. Her billowing skirts showed just enough leg to make his mouth go dry. Walking past her, he flipped a couple of coins onto the bar.

"Whiskey for me." He glanced at the girl, then decided. "And some tequila for the lady."

When the music ended, he leaned against the bar, sipping his drink. The barkeep, a fat fellow in a dirty apron, called out to her in Spanish. She looked up, eying Jack appraisingly. Apparently she liked what she saw. She smiled, then walked slowly, seductively toward him. Before she even got there, her eyes told him he was going to get what he wanted.

The air in the passenger compartment was close and hot. Beth Morgan idly stroked the damp hair of her sleeping son, while looking out the window. This time of year the sheep wouldn't bring much, she reflected soberly. Ben always sheared in the spring and sold mutton in the fall. There just wasn't much market for them in July.

If only Ben . . . no, she didn't want to think of that. It only made her angry with him, which in turn made her feel guilty. He hadn't meant to get himself killed, and she knew it, but she still couldn't help resenting the fact he'd let it happen. If only he'd held his tongue . . . if only he'd not drunk so much. . . .

She sighed. The world was filled with ifs and regrets. No, she had to remember happier times or she was going to be a bitter, defeated woman, the very sort of creature she despised. She had two bright, healthy children, and that had to count for something. Now all she had to do was find some way to keep a roof over their heads and food on their table.

When she got to San Angelo, she was going straight to the bank, this time to beg Mr. Kingman to give her six months' grace on Ben's loan. That would make it January though, which wasn't a good month either. No, she needed a year, and she was about as likely to get that as she was to sprout wings and fly. But he might agree to January, and with enough prayers, maybe a miracle would happen.

Having no answers, she turned her attention to the man who slept slouched in the seat across from them. At first, she'd been chagrined to discover he'd booked passage on the same stage, forcing her to offer her thanks again. But he'd just grunted, then pulled his hat down to shade his eyes.

He had no manners—or at least none she could see. As he'd swung up to take his seat, he'd almost stumbled into her lap. She'd had to push him to the other side, and when he sprawled there, his boots were resting on her skirt. She'd had to pull it out from under his feet, and whatever he'd mumbled, she was pretty sure it wasn't an apology. To make matters worse, she could smell the whiskey on him.

Realizing he was both hungover and still half-drunk, she viewed him with disgust, then turned her attention to her children. Even before the stagecoach pulled away from the station, Johnny was restless, squirming against her, asking what time they'd get to San Angelo. On her other side, Sarah had her face pressed against the window, watching the men change the horses. Always curious and inquisitive, the child was interested in everything, taking it in and storing it somewhere in that quick mind of hers.

"Mama," the child said suddenly, "Mr. Johnson says we will make just a little more than six miles in an hour."

It did no good to tell Sarah she shouldn't pester the driver. Beth sighed, wondering where this was going to lead. "Yes," she murmured cautiously.

"But did you know that in England the coaches travel faster than ten miles in the same time?"

"No."

"Well, they do—Mr. Talbot told me so, and he's English, so he ought to know."

"It's probably the roads," Beth decided. "England is more settled than we are."

The little girl nodded. "The road bed is hardened to permit speed. A man named Macadam showed them how to do it. And did you know that there really was a Mr. Mackintosh before there was a waterproof rain cape?"

"I thought Mr. Talbot was supposed to teach useful things like reading, writing, and arithmetic."

"He does, but sometimes when we ask him, he tells us all about England." Sarah cocked her head, looking up at Beth. "You know, Mama, I think he gets homesick."

"I expect he does."

"When he was my age, he lived in a grand house in Sussex—I bet you didn't know that, did you?"

"No."

"He drew us a picture of it. It looks like it ought to belong to Queen Victoria."

"Oh?" Privately, Beth thought the English-born schoolteacher was filling his pupils' minds with a great deal of nonsense, but she didn't say it. "Did he say what he did there?"

"No, but he was born last, so he didn't want to stay in England. I guess if one is a boy, he'd better be the first one. Otherwise, he has to take care of himself." When her mother said nothing, the child suddenly took a new tack. "I feel sorry for Mr. Talbot," she went on slyly. "He doesn't have anyone over here— not even a wife. Maybe we could have him over to eat with us sometime. I could show him the sheep, and you could kill one of the chickens, and—"

"I don't think so," Beth said, cutting her off. "It would look forward."

"Aunt Hetty said you could go live off a man," Sarah reminded her innocently.

"Actually, what she said was that I should get my clutches into one." Beth remembered with feeling. "It was a mistake to visit her."

"Mr. Talbot's a nice man, Mama."

"I'm sure he is, but he knows nothing about sheep."

"He says there are sheep all over Suffolk—they even have a breed named for the place."

Sarah had her there. "Well, in any event, I wouldn't wish to impose on him—and that, young lady, is that."

Reaching into her knitted purse, Beth drew out a roll left from breakfast. She unwrapped it and held it out. "Here—divide this with Johnny, will you?"

The little girl looked at her for a long moment, then ventured, "You still miss Papa, don't you?"

"Yes."

"Are we going to lose the farm?"

The last thing Beth wanted to do was air her troubles in front of the rude Mr. O'Neal. She cast a quick glance his way and was relieved to discover he'd apparently passed out. Still, rather than give her daughter something more to worry over, she wanted to deny how bad everything was, but her strict Baptist upbringing forbade lying.

"I don't know," was all she could bring herself to say. "Right now, money's rather tight."

"Maybe the bank—Papa always went to the bank, didn't he?"

"Too many times, I'm afraid."

"Mama, she's not giving me my half," Johnny complained.

"Here—if you stop whining, you can have all of it," Sarah offered. "I'm not hungry, anyway." Turning her attention back to the window, she announced, "They're finished, and Mr. Johnson's climbing up on top."

"Will we get there before noon?" her brother asked between bites.

"Of course not," Sarah retorted. "It took us days to get here, didn't it?"

"I wish I was a bird—I'd fly home."

"That makes two of us," Jack muttered. As the driver cracked the whip and the stagecoach lurched into motion, Jack sat up and fumbled for the wad of bills in his pocket. Taking the handful out, he peeled off one and tossed it onto Beth's lap. "Here's another ten for keeping your kids quiet," he muttered. As he jammed the rest of the money back into his coat, he leaned back and closed his eyes. "Damn. I haven't had a headache like this in ten years, and I'm all out of whiskey."

"For which we are thankful," Beth responded tartly. "By the looks of it, you've had more than enough to make you disagreeable." She reached over and placed the money back in his hand. "Regardless of what you must believe, I'm not yet a charity case, sir."

"No?" He opened one eye, fixing it on her. "I don't know what else you'd call it—you don't have any money, do you?"

"I didn't ask you for any. We could have managed last night."

He closed his eye again and tried to ignore the awful pain in his head. "Just keep it—it's not that much."

"I can't. Besides, you might wish for it back when you are sober."

"Papa drank too much," Sarah volunteered. "It killed him."

"He was probably driven to it," Jack murmured dryly.

"What an awful thing to tell a child." Turning to her daughter, Beth added emphatically, "And you, Sarah Jane Morgan, are never to repeat such a thing again. Your father never drank until—" She stopped, unwilling to say the painful words.

Sarah hung her head. "Yes, Mama."

"But Sheriff Hawkins *said* he was drunk," Johnny piped up. "Mama, we heard him say it."

Determined to turn the conversation away from the bitterness she still felt, his mother directed his attention to the window. "Why don't you count the birds, dearest?" she murmured encouragingly.

"That won't take long—he cannot count above twenty."

"I can too! I can get to a hunnerd!"

"Prove it," Sarah challenged him.

Beth sighed again. "In any event, he can try. As for you, young lady, you've said quite enough for now."

"Thank you," Jack muttered, pulling his hat forward again.

His grudging gratitude was short-lived. The little boy pressed his nose against the window, then jumped on his seat excitedly. "There's a bird, Mama—and it's a real big one!"

"That's just an old buzzard," his sister countered contemptuously. "Why don't you try to find a pretty one?"

"Because there aren't any."

Beth saw Jack's jaw tighten and she sought to avoid any further confrontation with him. He had, after all, paid their hotel bill, and she could see he was miserable. But if he hadn't done it to himself, she would have felt more sorry for him.

"Children, Mr. O'Neal is under the weather, and I'm sure he would appreciate it if we all tried to be quiet."

"But Mama—"

"Quiet," she repeated firmly. "Very quiet."

Johnny opened his mouth to protest, then closed it. "Yes'm," he said solemnly.

As he rested his head against the hard leather seat, Jack considered the woman's description of his condition woefully inadequate. The pulse in his temples pounded like Indian drums, nearly drowning out his thoughts, while the back of his head felt like he'd been hit there with a blacksmith's hammer, and his coated tongue tasted as if something was rotting on it. He knew he was going to be all right tomorrow; right now he was too sick to even appreciate his freedom. What he needed was a soft bed and a couple of days' sleep. Instead he was in a swaying, jolting stagecoach, cooped up with an impoverished widow and two kids bent on wrecking his peace all the way to San Angelo.

He slept sporadically during the four hours between Huntsville and the first way station. But it was his dreams rather than the children which kept waking him. Hideous nightmares of being hanged. Nightmares so real that he had to clutch at his throat to make sure there wasn't a noose there. Nightmares so real he could hear his mother calling after him.

You watch out, Jackie boy—if you keep it up, they'll hang you! You listen to me, Jackie, or you'll be swinging from a rope for your thieving ways!

He'd stolen a few dollars from her money box, and she'd caught him. And rather than give it back, he'd run, clutching it in his hand so tightly it was damp. He could still hear the laughter of the women at Miss Hattie's above the bang of the screen door slamming behind him. He'd taken that money and traded it to Greasy Joe for a rust-pocked pistol, then sat on the banks of the Concho cleaning and polishing the gun.

You ain't never going to amount to nothing, Jackie O'Neal. . . . You're going to rot in hell for them wild ways of yours. . . . One of these days, they'll be a-hanging you. . . .

Even Greasy Joe had tried to warn him. There was

a lot of irony in those words, as he recalled. The fat halfbreed had been caught stealing cattle that same year, and vigilante ranchers had strung him up on a cottonwood tree. Jack remembered his mother walking him down that dusty road on a hot summer day to see Joe's bloated, stinking body twisting in the wind on the end of that rope. The sight was to have straightened him out, but it didn't. He'd never wanted to rustle cattle, anyway.

No, he wanted to be like those rich men who spent their money so freely at Miss Hattie's. He wanted the nice clothes, the high-toned manners, the clean fingernails. And to that end, he learned to gamble. If it was a game of cards, he could win it by fair means or foul, and he'd taken great pleasure in fleecing those rich men.

Until he'd gotten drunk out of his mind and decided to go where the money was. The amazing thing about it was that he'd gotten out the door of the bank alive. He'd nearly pulled the whole thing off—would have, in fact, if it hadn't been for those damned rangers. But they were a tenacious bunch, and he hadn't been able to shake them. Still, he was going to have the last laugh. They hadn't found his money.

The coach lurched to a stop, then the driver jumped down and began unhitching the horses. The smell of smoked meat drifted out from the station.

"Mama, can I get something to eat?" Jack heard the boy ask.

"Yes—I think there's enough left for bread and butter," she murmured.

"Bread and butter!" he wailed.

"Don't be so greedy," his sister told him. "The money's got to last the whole way."

"But I'm hungry!"

Jack came grudgingly awake at that. For a moment, he regarded the boy's pinched face balefully, taking in the disappointment in his eyes, the quivering chin, then he relented. He'd been disappointed too many times himself. His gaze moved to the mother. Goaded, he demanded, "How much have you got?"

"I beg your pardon?"

"Is any of the hotel money left?"

She flushed guiltily, then dug in her knitted purse, drawing out four faded bills and some coins. "The room was a dollar and a half for me, half price for the children, which made it three dollars," she recalled, trying to account for everything. "And the bread and jam sent up from the kitchen last night was seventy-five cents for all of us. Then this morning's breakfast came to ninety cents apiece for porridge, so that leaves four dollars and fifty-five cents. But—"

"Look, I'm not asking for my change," he cut in brusquely. "You've got two mouths to feed."

"Well, if you can let the loan ride for a little while, there's enough left to get us home."

"Pride's a damned poor substitute for taking care of your kids," he snapped, tossing the other ten onto her lap. With that, he wrenched his door open and stumbled from the coach. The sudden movement sent a spear of pain through his head. Even his brain felt sore. "Damn," he muttered, catching onto the door for balance. "I think I'm going to have to get a hair of the dog that bit me," he added under his breath.

"That won't help at all," Beth said, stepping down beside him. "What you need—"

"What I need is to be left alone," he snarled at her. "If I want advice, I'll ask for it."

The boy jumped down, landing in front of Jack. He gazed up through a thick fringe of pale lashes. "You don't look good, mister."

"Johnny—"

"Well, he don't," the boy maintained stubbornly.

"I expect he needs a bromide," Sarah announced importantly. "Then he could belch it up like Papa did."

Mortified, Beth grasped both children's hands. "I'm terribly sorry, sir—I don't know where their manners have flown." Marching with a great deal of determination toward the station, she lowered her voice to scold them. "One should *never* notice the infirmity of another unless it is brought to one's attention by that person."

"What's that supposed to mean?" Johnny asked.

"It means we're supposed to keep our mouths shut except when we eat, and even then we have to close them while we chew our food," Sarah told him. "But he did say he'd been drinking, so I thought he might benefit from a bromide," she added to her mother.

"Sometimes I think you are forty rather than eight," Beth muttered. "You have an old mind in that head."

"Mr. Talbot says I'm smart."

"Mr. Talbot says too much, to my way of thinking."

"I know you'd like him, Mama. He's got eyes like Papa."

Instead of following them inside, Jack walked unsteadily toward the corral. Then when out of their sight, he grabbed a fence post. Leaning over it, he was utterly, completely sick. He retched over and over, emptying his stomach of the vilest stuff he'd ever tasted until there was nothing left. Acid and bile burned his throat. He hung on to the post as sweat poured from his body. He felt worse then he could ever remember.

"You all right, mister?" one of the station hands asked.

"What do you think?" Jack managed.

"Well, you look more'n a mite peaked."

"I am."

"Need any help?"

"No."

Sidestepping his vomit, Jack sank to sit against the lower rail, then held his head in his hands. In that moment, he felt sick enough to die. He didn't even care that the fellow left.

Beth found him like that. She'd come out to offer him what she'd been unable to eat, and one of the men had directed her to the corral. She lifted her full skirts around the mess, then bent over him.

"That must have been some pretty bad stuff you drank," she observed, taking out her handkerchief. Wadding it around her fingers, she began dabbing at his wet face. "No wonder you're so crabbed."

"Just leave me be," he croaked. "I'll get better."

But when she moved away, it was just to the pump over the horse trough, where she worked the handle until she could wring out the hanky in the rusty water. She came back and began washing his forehead, his mouth, and finally the back of his neck. It felt good, but he wasn't much for gratitude.

"I don't need a wife," he muttered.

Stung, she drew back. "Yes, well, I'd probably do the same thing for a dog." As she straightened up, she added evenly, "And I don't want another husband."

"Sorry. I just feel like hell, that's all."

"I can see. Do you do this to yourself often, Mr. O'Neal?"

"No. I haven't been drunk in over eight years." He looked up at her, meeting her sober gaze. "I've been in prison."

"Oh." She stood there, digesting what he'd just said. "Well, then I guess that explains why you're so angry, doesn't it?" she said finally.

"No." Deciding the worst had passed, he managed to pull himself up by the post. Releasing it, he passed a hand over his forehead, and he winced visibly. "God. It tasted like good whiskey going down, and rotgut coming up." Again, he glanced at her, but she didn't recoil. "Don't feel sorry for me—I had all eight years coming."

"Do you need help getting inside?"

"No. Doesn't it matter that I've been in prison? Don't you want to run?"

"Should I?"

"What the hell's wrong with you?" he demanded.

"You look too sick to hurt anyone," she pointed out reasonably. "Besides, I don't expect the acquaintance to continue beyond the ride to San Angelo, so why should I care? If you'd murdered anyone, I expect you would have been hanged, so I can only guess that you stole something."

"And that doesn't bother you?"

"Mr. O'Neal, I have nothing to steal."

"Yeah, I guess that's right." Now that the poison was out of him, he was beginning to think he'd live. "I'm all right," he lied. "You'd better get back to your kids."

"I brought you something to eat—if you got something in your stomach now, it would help. Perhaps just a crust of bread—just a little bit."

"No."

"You didn't eat anything yesterday, did you?"

"Look—"

"Well, did you?" she asked, persisting.

"No."

"Mama, Johnny threw up!" Sarah called out. "On the floor!"

"Good Lord. Here then," she said quickly, handing her purse to him. Lifting her skirts, she ran toward the station.

"What am I supposed to do with this?" he yelled.

"There's bread wrapped up inside!"

As the woman disappeared through the open doorway, the little girl hesitated, then her curiosity got the better of her. She crossed the yard to where he stood holding her mother's purse. She looked at the ground then back to his face.

"You don't travel very well either, do you?"

"Not today, anyway."

"Poor Mama. Johnny always eats too much and gets sick when he rides on the stage. But," she added, sighing, "we had to come, and at least he didn't do it while we were on the road. He's done that, too, you know, and it isn't very pleasant."

"Yeah. I can imagine."

"You ought to eat the bread. If she says it will make you better, it will. My mother's had a lot of experience with Johnny, so she knows." She turned her head toward the door, then sighed again. "She used to be pretty—really pretty—before Papa died. Now she has to work too hard."

He didn't even know how to talk to a child. "I'm sorry about your pa," was all he could think of to say.

She nodded. "It's been nearly a year. Mr. Talbot says that in England, it is proper to wait a year before finding another husband."

"I've never been to England."

"He's a nice man, but she won't even look at him. She still misses Papa."

"Don't you?"

"Of course I do—I *loved* Papa. But she can't do everything, and we're going to lose the farm. Don't you think if she married Mr. Talbot, it would solve everything?" she asked practically.

"I don't know Mr. Talbot."

"He talks real pretty. And there are lots of sheep in England—lots and lots of them. We raise sheep, you see," she added, enlightening him. "Before Papa got killed, we had hundreds of them. Now there are only about half as many as we had then."

"I see," he murmured politely. "Doesn't your mother need help in there with your brother?"

"No. I told you—she's used to it." She looked pointedly toward the purse. "Well—are you going to eat the bread or not?"

"Your mother's right," he decided. "You have an old brain in that head."

"Crust settles the stomach, Mama says. It always works for Johnny."

"Do you want it?"

She shook her head. "I had stew. It wasn't as good as Mama's, but I got it down, anyway." She cast a sly look at him, then smiled. "You aren't really a bad man, are you?"

"Yes."

"No, I don't think so. If you weren't sick, I think you'd be nice."

"Then you are a poor judge of character, Miss Morgan."

She wrinkled her nose, gathering a small band of freckles. "Nobody—not even Mr. Talbot calls me that. I'm just Sarah, sir."

"Sarah, what are you doing? I told you not to pester Mr. O'Neal, didn't I?"

The child turned innocent blue eyes on her mother. "I wasn't pestering him, Mama, I was just talking to him."

"You were wearing out his ears, you mean. Come on, it's nearly time to reboard the stage. In fact, Johnny's already on it." Beth's eyes met Jack's. "I'm sorry, truly sorry, sir."

"Actually, the conversation was pretty enlightening," he murmured, holding out her purse.

She took it, then felt the knit bag. "You didn't eat the bread, did you?"

"I never open a lady's bag."

"Do you want to try keeping the crust down?"

"I don't guess it could hurt," he allowed.

"Good."

He watched her undo the drawstring, thinking the little girl was wrong, dead wrong. Without the sadness in her eyes, Mrs. Morgan would have been a beauty.

She offered him the bread crust, and when he took it, his fingers brushed her hand. To his surprise, it was too rough and calloused to belong to a pretty woman. The kid had been right—the widow worked too hard. And, as odd as it seemed even to him, he respected her for it. With her looks, she could have just gone out and latched on to another man. Or a hundred of them like his mother had.

He hadn't expected to be welcomed, but he'd not expected the sheriff to meet the stage either. Yet, judging by the polished badge pinned onto the man in front of him, it was happening.

"Morning, Miz Morgan," the fellow said, tipping his hat.

"Sheriff Hawkins," she murmured politely.

"See you got yourself and the younguns back all right."

"Yes."

As she and the two children went around to the back to collect the worn carpetbag, he turned his attention to Jack. His smile disappeared in a frown. "You're Jack O'Neal, aren't you?" he said shortly.

"Yes."

"Hemphill wired me—warned me you might come this way."

"Oh?"

"Collect your things, and I'll ride with you out of town."

Jack's eyebrow rose for a moment, then came down. "No, I don't think so. I've waited too long to come back."

"You can't stay, O'Neal—there's no room here for your kind."

"Maybe this is my home."

"There's nothing left for you here. Your ma's dead."

"I did my time. Maybe now I'm thinking of settling down," Jack said, shrugging. With that, he turned his back on Hawkins and started down the street.

"Don't make me shoot you, Jack."

The hairs on O'Neal's neck prickled, but he had too much to lose by backing down. Instead, his hands dropped, parting his suit coat as he spun around, then came up, making play guns.

"If these were Colts, you'd have been a dead man, Sheriff," he said softly. "But I'm not armed. Shoot me, and it's murder."

Hawkins flushed as a crowd gathered, then he had to look away. "You won't get to spend a penny of that money, Jack—by tomorrow, the place will be crawling with rangers."

"My mama didn't raise no fool, Sheriff. And I'd be a fool to lead all of you to it—wouldn't I?" This time, when he started walking, Jack had no intention of stopping.

"Your ma was a whore," Hawkins said loudly.

As the surge of anger rushed through him, Jack's jaw tightened, but he kept going. Hawkins wasn't telling him anything he didn't already know.

"Do that again, mister, please."

He felt the tug on his coat sleeve and looked down, seeing Johnny Morgan trotting along beside him. "It was a fool thing to do, kid. I'm damned lucky he didn't plug me."

"But you beat him. If you'd have had a gun, you'd have beaten him to the draw. You're fast, mister—real fast," he said eagerly. "I'll bet you're faster than Wyatt Earp."

"What does your mother read to you, anyway?" Jack muttered.

"Not Mama—Sarah. She tells me all about gunfighters and everything, sir. You could beat him, couldn't you—Wyatt Earp, I mean."

"No."

Undaunted, the boy persisted. "Where'd you get so fast?"

"Playing cards."

"No, I mean the draw."

"Playing cards. If you work at it, the hand's faster than the eye."

"Huh?"

"You'd better find your mother."

"Where are you going, mister?"

"Johnny, don't pester the man," Sarah said, catching her brother's arm. She looked up. "Sorry, sir, but he gets carried away."

"I do not! Tell him—tell him he's faster than Wyatt Earp!"

"He isn't. Nobody is." This time, when her clear blue eyes met Jack's, dimples formed at the corners of her mouth. "You don't even carry a gun, do you?"

"Not today, anyway."

"Come on, Johnny," she said impatiently, "we've got to go with Mama."

The boy turned around and shaded his eyes. "Where is she?"

"The bank. Come on, I said."

"I hate it when she goes to the bank," Johnny grumbled. "Ain't never anything good comes out of it."

"There isn't any such word as ain't," his sister declared primly. "Though Mr. Talbot says Queen Victoria has been known to say it."

"If there ain't any such word, how come she uses it?" he shot back.

"I don't know." She gripped his arm tightly and started pulling him across the street. "Good-bye, Mr. O'Neal," she said over her shoulder.

Jack moved to the side of the dusty street and watched as they disappeared into the corner building. There, in an elegantly rounded script, the sign indicated the bank. But it was the name beneath it that drew his attention. PHILIP KINGMAN, PRESIDENT. As he stared at it, a shiver went down his spine.

Out of the corner of his eye, he saw the sheriff approaching, grim-faced and determined. It was all the push he needed. He started across the street. He didn't know what he was going to say to the man, but he knew he had to get a look at him. He just wanted to see the bastard who'd fathered him.

"O'Neal!" Hawkins called out.

Jack didn't even pause until he reached the single stone step. Then he hesitated ever so briefly before pressing the lever and wrenching the heavy door open. Cooler, musty air greeted him as he stepped inside. That was the thing about banks he always remembered—most of them smelled of dead paper.

As his eyes adjusted to the dimness within the limestone walls, he looked around, taking in the counter, the etched glass above it. Two men, each with garters on their shirtsleeves, stood importantly behind the barrier. One looked up as the door closed behind Jack.

"May I be of service, sir?"

"No."

"I beg your pardon?"

Ill at ease now, Jack shook his head. "I'm just waiting for someone."

"We're waiting for Mama," Johnny explained.

"Mrs. Morgan," Sarah corrected him. "We're waiting for Mrs. Morgan."

"That's what I said."

"No—you said you were waiting for Mama. Come on, we'd better sit down." Smiling at Jack, she offered, "You can sit with us, if you like."

The door opened, admitting Hawkins, who scowled at Jack. "I've seen brass in my day, but you've beat all of it."

"He's with us," Sarah said, as though that ought to make everything plain.

"What are you doing here?" the older man demanded, undeterred.

Jack shrugged. "Maybe I was thinking of opening an account."

"On twenty dollars?" the sheriff snorted. "Way I got it figured, you're planning another withdrawal."

"Not today, anyway." Again Jack brushed back his coat, exposing his pants at the waist and hips. "No gun—remember?"

A door behind the men at the counter opened, revealing a dark-paneled office. Her face pale and barely composed, Mrs. Morgan came out, followed by a portly, balding man. Jack's breath caught. Looking at Kingman was like looking at his own eyes in the mirror.

The man touched her shoulder lightly, almost like a caress, but she pulled away. "You bring the account up to date, Mrs. Morgan, and maybe we can arrange something," he told her. "That's about all I can offer. I've got the board to satisfy, you understand."

"I understand completely, sir," she managed between clenched teeth.

"If you get the money, come back, and we'll talk some more."

She passed them almost as if she couldn't see. Johnny started to rise from his seat, but his sister held him back. "Leave her alone," she whispered. "He's not going to help us."

"Are we going to lose the farm?" he asked, not quite believing it.

"Yes. The sheep, the house—all of it. I heard Mama talking to Aunt Hetty about everything."

"I don't want to live with Aunt Hetty, Sarah," he said, his voice suddenly small.

"Don't worry. She won't have us—after all, we're half Mama's. And most of the Allisons are dead, so I don't know what we're going to do." She sighed. "I guess Mama's just going to have to think of something." They rose to follow their mother.

"Wait here," Jack ordered.

He'd meant to confront Kingman then, and he didn't know why he didn't. Instead, he found himself running after the Morgan woman. He didn't have to go far. She'd just made it around the corner before she went to pieces. When he found her, she was facing the outside wall of the bank, her head resting against the cool limestone blocks, her hands clenched in tight little balls, her body racked with great, wrenching sobs.

"How much do you owe him?" Jack heard himself ask her. When she didn't answer, he reached out to touch her shoulder gently. "How much is it?"

"T-too m-much. Please—just g-go away!"

He could feel her shoulder shake beneath his hand. "How much is too much? Give me a figure, and maybe I can help."

"You c-couldn't. Besides, why w-would you w-want to?"

"I don't know," he answered honestly. "So—how much is it?"

"B-Ben b-borrowed over five th-thousand dollars—and he n-never told me about it!" she wailed. "I—I didn't know until he was d-dead!" Trying to regain her composure, she sucked in her breath and held it. It was a losing proposition. She hiccoughed, and the tears began again. "I w-wouldn't mind so m-much, but what am I going to d-do about the k-kids?"

It was hell for a woman alone. He'd learned that much from living in a whorehouse. He grasped her arm and pulled her into an alleyway. "Get a hold on yourself," he said, shaking her. As her eyes widened, he thrust her away. "Now—quit bawling and tell me what you need. He said something about bringing the loan current, didn't he?"

For a moment, she stared at him, then she nodded. "I don't have three hundred dollars, either," she said almost too low for him to hear. "It might as well be the whole five thousand." She sniffed, trying to stop her runny nose. "And even if I had the three hundred, I'd have to sell off at a loss. I can't last the winter, and I can't work the place alone."

He'd never done anything he could be proud of, but there was something in her reddened eyes that made him want to try. He reached into his pocket and took out the wad of bills. Peeling from the outside in, he counted it. Three hundred and four dollars. It was going to take almost everything he had to make him feel good.

"I've got it. Here." As he said it, he pressed the money into her hands. "Now you go back there and stuff it in that rich bastard's craw—you hear me?" He closed her fingers over the bills.

She looked down at her hands, then back to his face. Her chin quivered as though she would cry again.

"But, Mr. O'Neal, you don't even know me," she whispered.

"Just take it, and don't try to talk me out of giving it."

"But—"

"Look, you've got two kids, and I don't have anybody. Besides, all I need is a good game of poker, and I'm in business again." His hand tightened around hers. "That's where I got this, anyway."

"Really?" She caught herself guiltily. "But I can't take a stranger's money. It might be years before I could pay you back—it might be never." She forced a smile as she met his gaze. "As Mr. Kingman was quick to point out, I'm not a very good risk, I'm afraid."

"Yeah—well, I've never bought into a business before, so I don't know much about risks, I guess." Feeling suddenly awkward, he tried to keep his voice light. "Well, then," he said, exhaling, "now that we're partners of sorts, I guess I ought to ask you your name."

"Partners of sorts," she repeated, looking down at the money. "Yes, I guess I could accept that easier than just taking three hundred dollars in exchange for nothing." She lifted her eyes to his, and this time, her smile came easily. She held out her other hand. "Morgan—Elizabeth Morgan—but most people call me Beth."

Despite the calluses on her fingers and palm, her hand was small and delicately made. His hand closed around it briefly, clasping it warmly, then he let go and stepped back.

"Well, that about does it, I guess. Now you go back in there and tell that fancy, highfallutin' banker you've got the money."

"Since this quarterly was late, I'll have to make another payment at the end of next month. "I—uh—I think you ought to know that."

"It doesn't matter."

"Mr. O'Neal, I'm telling you it might be like pouring your money down a prairie dog hole."

"The name's John P. O'Neal, but my friends call me Jack," he said softly. "Speaking as the lesser partner in the operation, I'd think it wouldn't be improper for you to say it."

She held out her hand again, and as he took it, she nodded. "Jack, then."

"Beth."

It was almost as if they'd signed a compact between them. He backed away from her uncertainly, then took a deep breath. Exhaling, he settled his shoulders.

"You'd better take care of business and get those kids home, Beth." Even as he said it, it seemed right to him.

"You aren't coming with me? Aren't you afraid I might take the money and run away with it?"

"No. Just remember to get a receipt."

He leaned against the building and watched her disappear around the corner. For a man who'd just parted with his money, he felt pretty good about it. Besides, he reminded himself, he still had five thousand dollars buried in a lead-lined trunk, just waiting for him less than five miles out of town. All he had to do was wait long enough to throw Hawkins and the rangers off, and then he was going to claim it.

"I don't like to see you around a bank, O'Neal. Where'd you get the money you gave her?"

It was Hawkins. Jack straightened, then shrugged his shoulders insolently. "I won it in a game."

"You dug it up, didn't you?"

"They make anybody a sheriff these days, don't they?" Jack murmured. "If you don't believe your own eyes, you can ask the stage driver or the Morgans, and they'll tell you I came all the way from Huntsville."

Hawkins stared hard for a long moment. "How much have you got on you now?" he asked finally.

"Not much."

"I didn't ask that—I asked how much."

"Four dollars, and I'm just about ready to spend it on a bath and a meal."

"It's not enough." A slow smile curved Hawkins' mouth. "I'm afraid you're under arrest."

"For what?"

"Public vagrancy. Maybe resisting a peace officer, if you don't come quietly."

"Mr. O'Neal! Mr. O'Neal!" With a total lack of decorum, Sarah Morgan came running at Jack and threw her arms around his waist, hugging him. "God sent you—I know it! I prayed and he sent you!"

"Sarah Jane Morgan, you will unhand Mr. O'Neal immediately! Honestly, I don't know what gets into you sometimes," Beth said, catching up to her daughter. Flushing with embarrassment, she turned to Hawkins. "Is something the matter, Sheriff?" she asked innocently.

"He's arresting me," Jack said.

"*What*?" Her voice rose incredulously. "For what?"

"Vagrancy."

"But you just got here!"

"He thinks I'm going to rob the bank."

"Oh, now that's too much! Is this true, sir?" she demanded of Hawkins.

"I'm just asking him to leave town quietly or spend the night in jail."

Her jaw dropped, and she stared. "But he hasn't done anything."

"He will. He's always been a troublemaker."

"I guess I forgot to tell him I've developed an interest in sheep," Jack murmured, adding significantly, "partner."

"Oh—yes, of course. You can release Mr. O'Neal, Sheriff—he—" She glanced apprehensively at Jack, then made up her mind. Her chin came up, daring Hawkins to say anything. "Jack has bought a share of the farm, and he will be coming home with us," she declared defiantly.

"Jack, is it?" The older man's eyes narrowed, then he muttered, "Ben Morgan'd be rolling over in his grave before he'd let the likes of Jack O'Neal on his place."

"Ben's dead," she reminded him coldly. "Mr. O'Neal is kind enough to help us survive, which is a great deal more than can be said of Philip Kingman," she added bitterly. "He cannot wait to foreclose on us." Opening her purse, she drew out a paper and handed it to Jack. "Here's the receipt." She took a deep breath, then said, "Shall we go—or did you have business in town?"

"I was going to get some clothes, but I guess that'll have to wait."

"I left the wagon over at the livery."

Jack nodded. "I'll get it for you."

"Mrs. Morgan—" As she turned back to him, Hawkins demanded, "Did he get on the stage at Huntsville?"

"Yes."

"And he didn't leave it anywhere between there and here?"

"He went into the way stations, but other than that, he rode the entire distance with us." She looked up at him. "Why?"

"Just wondering," he muttered. "I hope you know what you're doing, ma'am."

"I think so. In any event, it isn't really your business, is it?"

"The man's been in the penitentiary."

"So he told me. But I understand also that he has served the sentence for whatever he did."

"He robbed a bank and shot up the place. The man's bad. Why, his ma was nothing but a—"

"Sheriff," she cut in impatiently, "I have no interest in his pedigree or lack of it. He is a business partner, and nothing more, I assure you." Before he could say anything further, she added, "Good day, sir," then reached to take her son's hand. "Come on, Johnny— we've got to get home and make sure everything's as we left it."

"People are going to talk," Hawkins said to her back.

"Let them."

Leaving him, she walked purposefully toward the livery stable. Sarah trotted alongside, keeping up with her. "Well, I don't care what Mr. Hawkins said, Mama," she declared. "God sent Mr. O'Neal—I know he did. We're going to keep the farm."

It was hard to fly in the face of a child's faith, but Beth knew that all Jack O'Neal had bought with his three hundred dollars was a few weeks' time. And when the next payment came due, she knew that she probably couldn't make it. Indeed, she felt as though by taking his money, she was swindling him.

"Mama, I thought you didn't like Mr. O'Neal," Johnny said.

"Whether I like him or not is immaterial. Without his money, we would be packing up tomorrow. Now we can at least wait until September."

"Are you going to marry Mr. O'Neal?" Sarah wanted to know.

"Of course not. I scarcely know the man."

"Then can we invite Mr. Talbot to dinner? He's a real nice man, Mama."

"I don't know."

"He never has anywhere to go."

"Maybe."

"He'll tell you all about England."

Beth didn't respond. Given the harshness of the life she faced, England might as well be on another planet. When she got home, she'd have to muck out the sheep house and the pens and try to catch up on all the work she'd missed during the abortive trip to Huntsville. And she had no illusions that Jack O'Neal would want to do any of it. No, it was more than likely that once he saw the place, he'd wish for his money back. Even a blind man could see that it would take more than either of them had to make it profitable.

He had the team hitched and waiting for her. "Ready?" he asked.

"Yes."

There was an awkward moment when he steadied her elbow as she climbed into the wagon, then he turned his attention to her children. As he swung the boy up and onto the ancient wooden seat, he still felt good about what he was doing. And it wasn't lost on him that now he had a place to outwait the sheriff and the rangers, who were certain to be watching him.

The white clapboard house was surrounded by a neat, whitewashed picket fence that separated it from the barn and pens behind it. While it was small, it was the sort of place his mother had longed for. He could almost hear her describe it for the hundredth time in his mind.

Beth took a deep breath, then exhaled. "Ben put nine years of work into this, and it's still not much, is it?"

"After Huntsville, it's a palace," he assured her. "No, actually, it's better than what I was used to before then."

She straightened her shoulders and nodded. "In any event, it's mine for a little longer."

"Where's he going to sleep, Mama?" Johnny wondered.

"I can make a place in the barn."

"No—not after what you did for us today. You can either share a bed with Johnny, or Sarah can sleep with me, and you can have her room."

"It doesn't matter."

"Stay with me—please," the boy begged him.

"All right."

"Then it's settled, isn't it? You can put your things—" Beth caught herself. "You don't have anything with you, do you?"

"Not much. I'm wearing most of it."

"Yes—well, Johnny, why don't you show him your room? Sarah can bring up some fresh water for the washbasin, so the both of you can wash the dust off."

"Suits me fine," Jack murmured.

As they went inside, Beth watched them, wondering if she was doing the right thing. Here she was, a widow with two children, living in the middle of nowhere, and she'd just brought home a convicted bank robber. But then she recalled the way he'd looked when he'd given her his money, and despite what the sheriff had said about him, she couldn't bring herself to believe he was a bad man.

"Sarah, take in the bag, please, then fetch them the pitcher of water. I'm going out to count the sheep."

Inside, Jack looked around, taking in the lace-trimmed runners, the starched white doilies that covered the timeworn furniture. In his mind, he could still see the ornate parlor, the thick carpets, the fancy chandeliers at Miss Hattie's. It didn't seem right that those who preyed on a man's weakness should have so much.

"Come on, I'll show you my bed," Johnny said eagerly, tugging at Jack's arm. Pulling him inside the small room off the faded parlor, he pointed proudly to a carved poster bed. "It used to be Mama's, but she didn't want to sleep in it anymore, so I got it. It came with Mama's family all the way from Ohio."

"It's pretty grand," Jack admitted.

"Grand! Wait until you see Mama's piano. It's in her room, 'cause there wasn't room for it out front." Recapturing Jack's arm, the boy pushed him to the other side of the parlor. Opening the door, he announced, "There it is—right there. My grandpa made it out of beechwood, then somebody else put the insides in it."

But it wasn't the piano that drew Jack. Aside from it, the furnishings were almost Spartan, and yet there was a decided femininity to the room. A bedskirt of crocheted roses hung below the faded quilt, while lace-edged pillows rested against the plain headboard. At the side, a handpainted kerosene lamp the stood on a doily which matched the skirt. And the sunlight cast the same pattern on the wall where it came through the crocheted curtains. A painted dresser held a tarnished silver mirror, a hairbrush, some hairpins on a small tray, and a pretty glass perfume bottle. A woman's things. He drew back, feeling as though he was trespassing.

Coming back through the parlor, he found something he'd missed before. A couple stared at him from an oval silver frame. He stopped to stare at it, seeing a lovely, smiling woman standing beside a fair-haired young man.

"That's your mother, isn't it?"

"And Papa."

"That's Mama's wedding picture," Sarah said, coming up behind him. "They were in Grandma Crawford's parlor, back in Ohio." She cocked her head to study it for a moment. "Mama was awfully young then."

"How young?" Jack found himself asking.

"Eighteen. She's eight and twenty now."

"Oh."

"She used to be real pretty," Sarah offered.

"She still is."

"Not like that, though. I don't think when she married him, she knew they were going to raise sheep. She came from Cleveland," she added, as though that ought to explain everything. "Cleveland's a big town—nothing like Texas."

"I've never been there."

"Well, we went once, and I didn't like it," she con-

fided. "My grandma was sick, and the whole house
smelled like camphor. But I was little then, so I might
like it better now."

"My grandpa died last year," Johnny told him. "We
didn't get to go, 'cause it was time to shear the sheep,
and Papa couldn't spare Mama's help."

"It was year before last," Sarah corrected her
brother. "And by the time Mama found out about it,
it was too late to go to the funeral, anyway."

"What happened to your grandma?"

"She lives with my Uncle James, 'cause she couldn't
keep up the house."

He wondered why Beth Morgan hadn't gone back,
but even as he thought it, Johnny volunteered the answer. "Uncle James hated Papa."

"He didn't *hate* him," Sarah countered judiciously.
"He said he ran through all of Mama's money."

"Where's your mother now? Didn't she come in?"

"She went to look after the sheep." She looked up
at him. "Do you want the water now?"

"No. I think I'll just go outside and walk around."

As Jack started for the door, Johnny blurted out,
"Were you really in jail, Mr. O'Neal?"

Jack paused. "Yes—yes, I was."

"Did you shoot somebody?"

"No."

"Oh." Clearly disappointed, Johnny turned his attention to his sister. "Did we lose a lot of sheep?"

"I don't know. Mama's counting them now."

Nearly blinded by the afternoon sun, Jack stood in
the doorway for a moment, shading his eyes. If there
was anything that could be said of Texas in July, it
was hell on earth. Too damned hot for anything.

There was no sign of Beth Morgan. He walked

around the corner of the house and looked toward the pens. Beyond them, the flock was crowded together in a stand of trees, seeking shade. The ground around them was bare where they'd eaten whatever grass there'd been.

The barn was open and so were the pen gates. As he crossed the yard toward them, the dust he stirred up clung to his shoes and his pantlegs. The heat intensified the odors of musty straw and sheep manure, nearly overwhelming him. And flies were everywhere—on the walls of the barn, on the fences, swarming around what looked to be empty feed pans. He ducked inside the door and stood there, letting his eyes adjust to the dimness. The air was close, hot, and rank. Then he saw her.

She had the sleeves of her dress rolled up above her elbows, and her wide, full skirt was hitched up and tied with a cord around her waist, exposing the ugliest pair of shoes he'd ever seen. She was shoveling straw and sheep waste—bending, scraping, and turning it over into a cart. She worked rhythmically, keeping a pace, despite the awful heat.

"You shouldn't be doing that," he said, coming up behind her.

She straightened up and turned around. Pushing damp golden hair from her sweaty face with the back of her hand, she favored him with a look of exasperation. "It has to be done, and there's no one else to do it," she declared flatly. "If I don't get it cleaned out and washed down with limewater, the place won't even be fit for the animals. And since the wolves and coyotes got almost twenty of them while we were gone, I can't afford to lose any more." With that, she went back to shoveling. "I shouldn't have wasted my time going to Huntsville," she muttered. "There's more than a week's work to catch up."

He'd never seen a woman work like that. "Here— let me," he offered, reaching for the shovel.

"No, it's not your problem," she said shortly.

"Oh, I don't know about that. I've got a three hundred dollar investment in it." Seeing that she wasn't relinquishing the shovel, he pried it from her hands. "Good God, are those blisters?" he asked incredulously.

She looked down at her raw palms. "The gloves are worn out, so I've quit wearing them. I'll put some Dr. Nathan's salve on when I'm done."

"I thought that was for horses."

"It is, but it works on almost everything, so I don't have to buy anything else."

"Well, go do it now, and I'll finish up."

"You don't know how."

"What is there to know? I get the stuff up and throw it over here—that's it, isn't it?"

She met his eyes for a moment, then looked away. "You'll ruin your suit," she muttered.

"I wasn't planning on keeping it, anyway. It reminds me of Huntsville," he countered. "Go on, take care of those hands."

"Mr. O'Neal—"

"Jack. Look—I'm not going to be here very long, so you might as well take advantage of it while you've got me. This is a man's work, Beth."

She still hesitated. "I'll have to mix the limewater."

"When I'm finished."

It had been so long since she'd had any help. She searched his face to make sure he meant it, then she capitulated. "All right. I'll gather eggs and start supper."

"That's more like it," he murmured approvingly. Taking off his coat, he hung it on a peg, then he unbuttoned his cuffs and rolled up his shirtsleeves. "Well, what are you waiting for? Afraid I can't lift a shovel?" he asked when she didn't move.

"No."

He began shoveling then, digging up the muck and tossing it onto the cart. The barn was so hot and airless that his shirt was soaked almost immediately. Beth watched his shoulders ripple as he hit a stride. Down, across, up, and over. He looked up, catching her watching him.

"Still don't think I can do it?" he gibed.

"You're surprising me," she admitted.

"I didn't exactly play cards during eight years in prison. They call it hard labor for a reason."

"Oh." Feeling almost free for the first time in a year, she tried to pay him back. "Would you rather have the chicken fried or stewed with dumplings?"

"It's too hot to chase a chicken around the yard."

"I didn't ask that—I asked which way you prefer it."

"I don't care. I guess you could say I'm easy to please."

"All right. When you're done, you'll want to wash up. There's a pump out back where you can get the worst of it off, and I'll set out Ben's shaving things for you in Johnny's room."

"Fine."

After she left, he regretted his offer. The more muck he dug up, the more there seemed to be. His shoulders ached, his hands smarted from splinters, and he was drowning in his own sweat, but he'd committed himself to finishing the job. With each thrust of the shovel, his admiration for Beth Morgan grew. He didn't know how one lone female could have kept things up like she did. With her looks, there were other ways she could have survived, but she'd chosen to stick it out, trying to keep her dead husband's dream alive.

The cart was full. He looked around to see what she did with the manure, then came back. Rather than try to hitch the horse up, he dragged the cart out into the pen himself. And out of the corner of his eye, he caught Beth killing a chicken.

"I thought I told you to take care of those hands!" he called out.

"I will, but I have to clean this first!" she shouted back. "You don't want Dr. Nathan's Salve in your dumplings, do you?"

"Where do you want this stuff?"

"Throw it over the fence. Come fall, I'll work it into the garden." Carrying the dead chicken in one hand, she filled a bucket at the pump, then started back to the house. "When I bang on a pan, it's time to start washing up!" she yelled over her shoulder.

When he finished the job, he hunted for the lime rather than call for her help. He was reading the faded print on the sack when Sarah came out. She looked around, wrinkling her nose. "Well, it's *almost* as clean as when Mama does it," she decided.

"It'd better be. I've worked damned hard at it."

She climbed up onto a wooden stall gate to watch him. "Papa never cussed. He said Mama wouldn't let him."

"Yeah—well, I didn't come from Ohio," Jack murmured. "Where I come from, people say a lot worse things than damn."

"Where's that?" she wanted to know.

"Here."

"Did you have a house in San Angelo?"

"Yeah," he lied.

"Did you have a yard full of flowers?"

"No."

"That's a pity. You should see Mama's yard in the spring. She's got lilacs and all sorts of pretty things. And when they are dead, then there are the roses. Do you like roses, Mr. O'Neal?"

"Very much."

"Then you will have to stay until next spring."

By next spring, he was going to be across the Mexican border, living like a king on his five thousand dollars. With that kind of money there, he'd be set for life.

"Shouldn't you be helping your mother?"

"I plucked the chicken. *And* I set the table with Grandma Crawford's dishes."

"Do you know how much lime your mother uses in here?" he asked impatiently.

"One cup to a bucket," the child answered promptly. "Then she just sort of throws it around, and when it sinks into the ground, it kills the maggots. Flies make maggots, you know."

"They ought to be everywhere, then."

"Well—" She stopped to listen as her mother pounded on a tin pan. "I'd better go," she decided quickly. "I want to wear my best dress for dinner. I was going to wear it when Mr. Talbot came, but you're going to be eating his chicken."

"I saw more than one chicken out there," he pointed out.

"Yes, but those are layers, not fryers."

"Tell her I'll be in as soon as I get this stuff on the ground."

"Sarah, Mama said—" Johnny stopped when he saw Jack. "You're supposed to be at the pump," he said accusingly. "The dumplings is boiling."

"*Are*, Johnny. The dumplings *are* boiling," his sister corrected him.

"I don't care—they're cooking, anyways."

The little girl jumped down from her perch. "Come on—you aren't going to get it right ever." Looking back at Jack, she advised him, "You'll have to pump real hard, sir, because the well's low."

"I'll keep that in mind," he promised.

Rather than be late to eat, Jack headed for the pump. Later, he'd throw out the limewater, but right now he was hot, tired, and damned hungry. He soon discovered Sarah was right—the pump yielded water grudgingly. Finally, when he was just about to give up, the trickle turned into a full flow.

He ducked his head under it, first drinking his fill, then washing his sweaty head with the cold water. He let it splash over his face, his hair, his neck, and his shoulders, soaking his shirt and spotting the black trousers. But he didn't care—it felt good.

Beth met him at the door with a towel, then stood aside as he dripped his way through the small kitchen and the parlor to Johnny's bedroom. To his surprise, she'd not only laid out a straight razor and a strop by the washbasin, but she'd also left a pair of boots and some folded clothes on the bed.

"They're Papa's," Johnny said behind him. "She said you was to wear 'em."

"Tell her thanks."

"If they don't fit, she'll let 'em out for you."

"Fine."

He shaved quickly, rinsed his face, and toweled it dry. Pulling on the soft lawn shirt, he buttoned the collarless neck. It wasn't a bad fit at all. The pants were a little short, but wearable. He sat on the side of the bed and tried Ben Morgan's boots. He could wear them.

When he emerged, they were standing by the table, waiting for him. As they sat down, Beth bowed her head. Sarah nudged him, whispering, "Say grace."

He was at a loss. Nobody he knew bothered praying over food. Finally, he just struck out on his own. Lowering his head, he said, "Lord, fill our stomachs with this chicken, and make us worthy of it."

"Amen," Beth murmured.

"Is that all?" Sarah asked incredulously.

"Hush. The important thing is to say what is in your heart," her mother told her. "Words don't mean anything unless you believe in them."

"You aren't a Baptist, are you?" the little girl asked him.

"Why do you say that?"

"Because our preacher prays for hours. He would *never* just talk about the chicken," Johnny answered for her. "He'd talk about Jesus and the Holy Ghost, too. Dinner's always cold by the time he gets done."

"I'll have to remember that."

"The food starts with you," Sarah announced. "Papa always went first."

Clean, fresh-shaven, and sitting in front of a plate of chicken and dumplings with boiled potatoes, beans, and biscuits, he knew he ought to feel like a king in Ben Morgan's chair. But as he looked around the table, seeing Beth and her well-scrubbed children, Jack was acutely aware that he didn't belong there.

The wind blew, rattling the windowpanes, but the boy slept soundly. Jack lay beside him, staring into the darkness. His body ached, and his mind wouldn't let go. He turned over, facing the wall, listening to the howl of wind and coyotes, wondering how Beth Morgan kept going with so many cards stacked against her.

At the other end of the house, a door blew shut, telling him that someone went out. And then he heard the shots. He rolled from the bed and pulled on Ben Morgan's pants. Moving to the window, he could see a woman silhouetted by the moonlight. She took aim and fired again. There was a yelp, followed by high-pitched yips.

Groping his way through the house, he let himself outside. As he came up behind her, she swung around. "Whoa—it's just me," he told her.

"You startled me."

"What in the world are you doing out here?" he wanted to know.

"Shooting coyotes before they kill more of my sheep."

"You need a dog."

"I had one, but a rattlesnake got it."

"Is there anything that hasn't happened to you?"

"If there is, I can't think of it," she responded tiredly. Handing him the rifle, she started toward the pasture. "I'm going to try getting them in."

"You can't do that alone."

"I always do."

As she walked away from him, her nightgown

flapped about her legs. He watched for a moment, then started after her. "Here—let me do it."

"They don't know you."

"What the hell difference does that make?"

"Sheep are cowardly creatures." She stopped to look up at him, and her hair whipped across her face. "If you want to help, keep the coyotes away."

About fifteen yards away from him, she cried out, then went down. By the time he got to her, she'd struggled to her feet, and was hobbling toward the flock.

"What happened?" he asked her.

"I stepped in a hole and twisted my ankle," she managed through clenched teeth.

It was obvious that she'd hurt herself, but she refused to stop. Limping badly, she kept going. Finally, when it became obvious that she couldn't walk that far, she leaned her head against a dead tree and closed her eyes. The moonlight caught the tears on her lashes.

"I can't," she whispered. "I just can't."

"Hold the gun, and I'll come back for you," he promised.

Striking out across the pasture, he circled behind the sheep, then began shouting, trying to drive them toward the house. At first they milled, bawling, until he began whooping like an Indian. Then several began to run, and most of the rest followed. By the time he caught up to them, they'd crowded into the pens, packing themselves together. He closed the gates, then went after Beth.

"Do you need carrying?" he asked.

"No." But as she took a step on the injured ankle, she nearly went down again. "I don't need this—not now," she choked out. "I can't get hurt. I have to keep going."

He took the gun and used his free hand to steady her. "Just put an arm around me and hang on." As he spoke, he reached around her. "All right, lean on me, and we'll try to keep the weight off that foot. Yeah, that's the way. Now just take it real easy."

As he walked her back, he was all too aware that there was nothing but thin lawn between his hand and her body. And when she stumbled against him, and her breast brushed his arm, he could tell by the sharp intake of her breath that she felt it also.

"I'm all right," she said, pulling away.

"No, you aren't." His grip on her waist tightened. "Look—before you think I've got any ideas, I want you to know that I know the difference between a good woman and a fast one."

He was just too close, too warm, too alive. She'd thought that when Ben died, that part of her had died also, but it hadn't. There was still within her a yearning to be held, to know a man's strength, to feel his passion.

"No, I'm all right, I tell you," she said almost desperately. "I can walk by myself."

Reluctantly, he let her go. As she struggled beside him, favoring her ankle to the point where it looked like she might fall again, he realized that she just didn't want him touching her. And he couldn't really blame her. No good woman in her right mind would look twice at Jack O'Neal.

Finally, the pain was more than she could bear. "I was wrong," she whispered. "I can't stand it."

He dropped the gun then and swung her up in his arms. Carrying her, he managed to get her back into the house. "Do you want me to put you in your bed?" he asked.

She knew better than to dare it. "No. I'd just like to sit a minute."

He laid her on the settee, then looked around for the lamp. "Matches?"

"In the tin box."

He took one out and struck it on his fingernail. The sulfur flared. Taking off the chimney, he lit the wick, then trimmed it down to a steady flame. His shadow climbed the orange wall. When he turned back to her, Beth was leaning over, feeling her ankle.

"How bad is it?"

"Well, it's not good."

"Do you think it's broken?"

"No."

He knelt down and lifted the hem of her nightgown. He didn't have to see much to know that it was a bad sprain. He could feel the swelling. "Yeah—well, I'd say your barn-mucking days are over for a while," he said lightly.

Her chin quivered, then her face crumpled. "This can't happen to me—it just can't!"

Without thinking, he leaned forward, pulling her head against his shoulder. His arms closed around her. "Go ahead, cry," he said softly. "You've earned it."

"I can't cry!" she wailed. "If I do, I'll never stop! Don't you understand? I'm going to lose the farm! I'm going to lose the farm! If I can't take care of everything, I can't keep it!"

"Shhhhhh." His hand stroked her soft hair, smoothing it against her shaking shoulders. "Just tell me what you want done, and I'll try to do it."

"You can't! Nobody can! It was foolish of me to

think I could hold on—just foolish of me. And now I've wasted your three hundred dollars just to stay here a few more weeks!" she sobbed.

"Three hundred dollars isn't much," he murmured.

"It is to me—I can't pay it back."

He set her back gently, then stood up. "I'm going out to get the gun. Otherwise, it'll rust from the dew. Then I'm going to make you some coffee, and we'll talk about it, all right?"

"There's nothing to talk about," she said dully. "Nothing. Besides, there's no coffee. I haven't kept coffee since Ben died."

"What do you usually drink?"

"Tea. It's a habit I got from my mother."

"I don't think I've ever had a cup of tea in my life," he muttered. "But I've drunk damned near everything else, so I guess I can try it."

"You don't have to."

"I don't suppose you've got any whiskey? We both could probably use a belt."

"No. When Ben died, I poured it out."

"Will you be all right until I get back in?"

"Yes."

She sat there for a moment after he left. She was useless, and the situation was hopeless, she reflected wearily. Her eyes strayed to the picture taken in her parents' parlor. Her wedding day more than ten years ago. If anybody had told her then she'd be living in Texas, eking out the barest existence, she'd have laughed. But she was. And the place was defeating her just as surely as it had defeated Ben.

It was time to give up and move on. She hadn't wanted to admit it, but that was what was going to happen, anyway. Now that she had made up her mind, there was a certain peace to it, a certain resolution.

She rose from the settee and held on to the table, then carefully hopped her way into the kitchen, where the coals still glowed in the old iron stove. Gathering wood chips she'd cut herself, she threw a handful in, then blew until they caught. In the semidarkness, she found her kettle and dipped water from the bucket into it. Setting it on the stove, she sank into one of the kitchen chairs and waited.

He found her there. He emptied the rifle and stood it up against the door frame. Then he went into the parlor and got the kerosene lamp. As he placed it on the table, he sat down across from her.

"All right, now, let's figure out how you can keep this place."

"I've decided to let it go."

There were no tears, no anger—just resignation in her voice. He regarded her soberly for a moment. "You know, I haven't known you very long, but I could have sworn you're not a quitter."

"I have to think of Sarah and Johnny, Jack. It's wrong of me to sacrifice them to my selfishness. The sooner I let go of Ben—and of this place—the sooner we can start over."

"What do you think you'll do?" he asked quietly.

"I don't know. I guess I'll go back to Ohio. I have a brother in Cleveland, and although we're not very close, I know if I showed up on his doorstep, he wouldn't turn me away."

"And then?"

"Well, I'm a pretty fair seamstress. I could probably become a dressmaker." She looked around her. "There's not many sheep in Cleveland."

"What about this woman you went to see in Huntsville? Maybe if she knew how bad things really are, she'd do something for the kids at least."

"Hetty?" Her voice rose incredulously, then she shook her head. "She'd rather see me lose everything. If she could, she'd see me in my grave, I'm afraid." She looked across the table at him. "She's Ben's sister—his only sister—no, actually, his only relative. When their parents died, she raised him, and she felt almost like she owned him. I was the interloper who took him away from her."

"She doesn't care about Sarah or Johnny?"

"No—not if it means helping me. She blames me for Ben's death." She took a deep breath and let it out slowly. "When things began to get bad, when we lost nearly half the flock, Ben went to the bank, and he wasn't entirely honest with them. He listed loan collateral we didn't have in order to persuade Mr. Kingman to lend us enough money to get through the winter. He wasn't thinking clearly, Jack."

"He couldn't pay it back."

"No." She stared at the lamp for a moment, then said carefully, "Ben Morgan was a good man with bad luck. Once things started going bad, he got caught up in more lies, borrowing more rather than defaulting, until we owed more than we could ever even reasonably expect to make. As long as he was borrowing more money, as long as he could make them think he could back it up, they didn't press him. They didn't know he was borrowing to make the payments on what he already owed them."

He just shook his head. "God."

"Oh, I even tried that, too. I prayed and prayed,

but God didn't listen—or if He did, He decided I didn't need to raise sheep."

"What do you do with this?" he asked, gesturing to the kettle.

"There's tea in that container by the stove. Just put a couple of spoons of it in the kettle with the water, then wait a few minutes before straining it out. If you want it sweet, there's honey in a jar over there."

"All right. I'll take care of it. Go on, finish your story."

"There's not much else. Ben started to drink. Then, when things were really bad, when we had nothing left to eat on after he made the payment, he decided he was going to win food money playing cards. He got drunk, he lost, and then he got belligerent. He and a cowboy exchanged insults, then shots. When it was over, Ben was dead."

"How can his sister blame you for that? You weren't even there."

She looked up at him. "Don't you see? The fact that he died in a saloon brawl means to her that I drove him to drink," she answered bitterly.

"What do I strain this in?"

"That cloth. Just pour it through."

"All right." He finished the task and swung around to face her. "How much money would it take to get you out of this mess?"

"More than you would want to know—more than this place is even worth."

"Which is?"

"Almost five thousand dollars."

"How much are the sheep worth?"

"Right now—or next spring after lambing and shearing?"

"Right now."

"Well, for mutton, I might get seven hundred dollars—which could get me through the winter, but then there wouldn't be any spring lambing or shearing. But there's still the mortgage to pay. After expenses, I'd be lucky to clear two or three hundred." She shook her head. "And Johnny needs shoes, not to mention that Sarah needs nearly everything. She's growing like a weed right now."

"And next spring? If you could wait for spring?"

"Maybe a thousand."

He found the honey and put a spoonful in each cup. Carrying both cups back to the table, he sat down again. "Why didn't you just throw in your chips earlier and cut your losses?"

"I don't know. I was just trying to hang on—I was just praying for a miracle."

"Miracles don't happen anymore."

"So I've discovered."

"All right—so you're going to Cleveland to live with your brother and become a seamstress. Will that make you happy?"

"No, of course it won't. I guess what I hate giving up the most is my freedom," she mused slowly. "My brother is the sort of man who will wish to control everything. He'll think Sarah too forward, and he won't like Johnny because he gets sick a lot. But," she added, sighing, "we'll survive." She stirred the tea, then took a sip. "I'm tired of talking about it tonight. I'd rather discover how you came to be a bank robber. I'd rather hear about anything rather than the pickle I'm in. So ... how *did* you decide to rob a bank?"

"One thing just led to another, I guess. I was earning my living playing cards, and one day I decided it was taking too long to get rich. So I went where the money was, which seemed logical to me at the time. I was drunk enough to think that they wouldn't miss a few thousand dollars."

"You had to be really drunk if you believed that."

"Yeah. I robbed it about nine o'clock in the morning, and by nightfall, there was a whole posse after me. I doubled back and lost them, only to find out the Texas Rangers weren't quite as stupid as the sheriff. They tracked me down, and the rest is history. They never got the money, though."

"Why don't you give back the money, Jack?" she asked suddenly. "Then it wouldn't be hanging over your head. Then you could start over."

It was obvious that she was serious. "Not on your life. I paid for that money—for eight years I paid for that money. It's mine now."

"No. It'll never be yours. You'll be like Ben—you'll have to lie and cheat to keep it." She caught his hands and said earnestly. "You'll be diminished by what you have to do to keep it."

He looked at the slender fingers covering his, then exhaled. "Yeah, well, I wasn't very much to start with, Beth. If I left this world, nobody'd shed a tear over it."

"Your mother would."

"My mother?" He snorted. "I was the bane of her existence, the reminder of her sin. She couldn't care about me—hell, she couldn't even care about herself." He pulled his hands from beneath hers. "My mother was a common whore." As her eyes widened in shock, he nodded. "Yeah. I didn't grow up very far from here. Beth—I grew up at Miss Hattie's."

"Miss Hattie's?"

"Don't tell me you never heard of it? Well, let me tell you all about it. A lot of so-called respectable men go there, and for a few dollars they can get whatever they want. They can even get two girls at the same time—does that shock you?"

"No."

"I can remember my mother coming up to sleep smelling like whiskey and men. I guess she had to drink to keep doing it."

"You don't have to tell me this, Jack."

"I've got to tell somebody. She was always promising me things would get better—she was always telling me we were going to leave the place. But you know what? *We* never did. *I* got out, but she died there. So don't tell me that I'm going to be diminished if I keep some bank's money, Beth. There's nothing in me to diminish."

"I'm sorry," she said simply. "I guess life doesn't have to give us what we want, does it?"

"No." Suddenly ashamed of himself for telling her more than he wanted her to know, he pushed away from the table. "Do you need help getting up to bed?"

"No." She started to rise, but the ankle wouldn't hold her. "Yes." As she said it, she flushed. "It's been a long time since I was this helpless."

He came around the table and reached to help her up. As she stood, she was but inches from him. He could actually feel the heat of her body. For a long moment, time seemed to stand still as he looked into her blue eyes. She stared back, saying nothing.

"What would you do if I kissed you?" he heard himself ask.

"I don't know," she whispered.

His arms closed around her, holding her close. "You

deserve better than this," he murmured, bending his head to hers. Her lips parted slightly, possibly to protest, then went soft beneath his. His arms tightened as he explored her mouth, searching, lingering, taking his time. Just as she began responding wholeheartedly to his kiss, he knew he didn't want it like that. He didn't want to make her into a woman he'd despise. He released her abruptly and stepped back.

"I guess I'm no better than those women, am I?"

"Don't say that—you're not selling it," he answered harshly. "You're just lonely, that's all."

"Maybe she was, too."

"You don't belong in the same sentence with her. She didn't have the guts to try it alone."

"She had you." Her blue eyes were like dark pools in the dim light. "I think I can get there by myself," she decided.

"Yes."

She managed to hold on to things as she hobbled along the walls. At the doorway, she turned back to him. "I wish we could have met years ago. I would have liked knowing you before you were so bitter."

"You'd have had to get there real early—I knew what she was by the time I was five."

"Good night, Jack."

Long after he heard her close her door, he lay awake. Dawn came, and he was still awake. Beside him, Johnny Morgan lay curled up, almost in a ball. He remembered that—it was a defensive sort of thing. He knew, because he used to sleep like that. And why wouldn't the boy feel defensive? Everything around him was falling apart.

Ever since he'd come back to bed, he'd thought of little beyond the feel of Beth Morgan's body, of her soft lips beneath his. And instead of blind lust, he felt an almost aching tenderness for her. He just wanted to hold her and caress her and make only good things happen for the both of them. But he was too far gone for that.

The irony wasn't lost on him. By the time he'd actually found a good woman, he was already a hopelessly bad man. And there was no way he could dig up his money and stay anywhere near San Angelo. No, he either had to take it and run or leave it where he'd buried it. Either way he couldn't have her. And somehow he knew she wouldn't take his money, even if it meant paying off Kingman.

No, he was going to have to do that. The thought came crystal clear and utterly unbidden to his mind. He could wipe out her debt, and she could keep her independence. He looked over at the sleeping boy, wondering how different things might have been for himself if Mary O'Neal had had Beth Morgan's courage. Then he might have grown up right. He might have stayed out of trouble.

She had until the end of September, she said. That ought to give him time to throw off Hawkins and the rangers. No, he was kidding himself. If he stuck around that long, it'd be because he didn't want to leave her. Maybe, for a little while at least, he wanted to pretend he had a family.

A rooster crowed nearby. And then Jack heard a steady thudding. Curious, he rolled from the bed and looked out the window. He had to pass a hand over his disbelieving eyes. The sun wasn't even fully up yet, but Beth Morgan was out there swinging an axe. He raised the window.

"What the hell are you doing?" he demanded.

"Getting wood. I need it for the fire," she said loudly. "Otherwise, there won't be breakfast."

"I thought you couldn't walk! What about your ankle?"

She lifted the hem of her skirt just enough to show him where she'd tied rags around it. "It doesn't hurt as much when it's bound up."

"Damn." He let the window down and dressed hastily. Then he marched outside and took the axe out of her hands. "Quit trying to prove you're an Amazon, will you?" he muttered. He took a swing, and a piece of wood went flying.

"You haven't split many logs, have you?" she murmured.

"Why?"

"Because you pound the splitter in, then separate the pieces."

"I'm a bank robber—remember? Just go on inside and put Dr. Nathan's Salve on those hands."

"I've got to get the eggs first. There weren't many last night, probably because the snakes eat them if they're left very long." She wiped the offending hands on her skirt, then limped off toward the barn.

Goaded, he went after her. "Let somebody else do that. Send one of the kids out."

"They have their own chores."

"Well, maybe it wouldn't hurt to give them some more."

"Sarah fixes the table, does the dishes, and helps with the ironing. Since she's only eight, I think that's probably enough. As for Johnny, ever since Ben died, he's gone out and fed and watered the sheep. And since the water bucket's pretty heavy, and he has to make up to twenty trips, I think he does plenty for a child of six, don't you? He's not really strong enough to do all that he does."

"I didn't see any hens' nests when I was out here," he grumbled.

"They're up in the loft," she told him, pointing to a ladder.

"You think you're going up there on one foot, do you?"

"Yes."

"Well, you're not." He tossed the axe down and climbed into the barn's loft. A hen, unsettled by his sudden appearance, flew at him. "Get out of my way, or you'll be dinner," he warned it. Dust seemed to float in the air, and it was already hot, even though the sun was still resting on the horizon. He thrust his hand into the nest and felt around the straw. It moved, then uncoiled and slithered off. Jack knew then he wasn't made to be a farmer. "I found your snake!" he called out.

"There won't be anything left in that nest, then. You'll have to try the others."

In the end, he managed to get eight warm eggs. Two apiece ought to just about do it, he decided. Cradling them in his shirt, he gingerly descended the ladder.

"You would have killed yourself going up there," he told her.

His hair was mussed from sleep, his shirttail was hanging out of the too-short trousers, and he was barefoot. "You don't look very dangerous right now," she said, suppressing a giggle.

"No?"

"No."

"Well, I am—and you ought to remember it."

Her smile warmed her blue eyes. "Are you trying to warn me, Mr. O'Neal?"

"Maybe. Yeah, I guess I am."

She cocked her head to one side, studying him. "You know what I think?" Before he could say anything, she answered herself. "I think you underrate yourself. I think you could become anything you wanted, if you put your mind to it."

"Save that for your Sunday school class, will you?" he muttered, moving away.

"Wait—" She ran her tongue across her lips as he swung around to face her again. She could feel the blood rise in her cheeks. "You are welcome to stay here as long as you like—or at least until we have to move. That is, if you want to."

In that moment, it was as though the world stood still while he looked at her. With that golden hair, and in a blue-checked dress which matched her eyes, she was without doubt the prettiest woman of his memory. He wondered how he could have missed that before.

"Yeah," he said finally. "Yeah, for now."

Her gaze dropped. "Johnny needs a man around. He misses Ben so."

"And you?" he dared to ask.

She was slow to answer. "I don't know," she said, her voice almost too low to be heard. "A lot of me died with Ben."

"You've still got a lot to offer."

"Sometimes I wonder." She collected herself then and reached for the eggs. "I'll take these if you'll bring in the wood."

Her hand, where she brushed his arm, almost burned him. It was his mind that did it—it was racing too far ahead, letting him think more than he had a right to. He waited until she put a safe distance between them, then he said softly, "You're still alive, Beth. You're full of life."

He'd been there nearly eight weeks, and in that time, he'd worked harder than he'd ever worked in his life. Hard, almost brutal physical labor that punished his body, sent him to bed every night exhausted. And still he dreamed of her—hot, torrid dreams that left him sweating. Then by light of day he'd force himself to forget them. He knew she wasn't that kind of woman.

He'd cleaned up the place the way it needed to be. He and Johnny had mended the fences around the pens and built several small adobe enclosures to keep the coyotes and wolves away from the weaker sheep. They weren't beautiful, by any means, but they were adequate.

He was learning a lot more about sheep than he'd ever wanted to know. He'd always sort of thought of them as just sheep. But Sarah set him straight on that. At the Morgan farm, they raised Rambouillets rather than Merino, because Ben Morgan had been convinced that the French breed gave better wool. Jack didn't know about that, but he did know that every time he handled one of them, he almost needed a bath. There was a lot of grease in wool.

On a hot day in mid-September, he and the kids were sprawled beneath a cluster of trees, sharing a jug of tepid mint tea, waiting for the freshly whitewashed picket fence to dry. Beth was behind the house, boiling clothes over an open fire. The strong smells of mesquite smoke and lye soap hung in the sweltering air.

"Somebody's coming!" Johnny shouted, jumping up.

Sarah shaded her eyes, then squinted. "Uh-oh," she said, "it's the sheriff."

There was momentary panic in the boy's eyes, then

he ran to the back of the house. "The last time Sheriff Hawkins came here, it was because Papa was dead," Sarah confided. "This time, he's got somebody with him—and they're dirty," she added, sniffing.

The two men on either side of Hawkins looked pretty rough. Both were unshaven and wearing clothes that looked as though they'd not been changed in a month. The one with the drooping mustache lifted a hand in greeting.

"They're rangers," Jack decided. "Texas Rangers."

"I wonder what they're doing here?"

"I reckon I've got a notion."

"Well, they're still dirty," she declared.

"There aren't too many places to bathe on the trail." Jack heaved himself up and waited for them. "Yeah—they're rangers, all right. The big one is Hank Johnson."

"O'Neal," Johnson acknowledged as he rode up. "It's been a while—eight or nine years, I guess."

"Eight years and ten months."

"You keep better track of it than I have."

Jack shrugged. "There wasn't much else to do."

Johnson surveyed the place from beneath heavy brows, then leaned forward in his saddle, resting a shotgun across the pommel. "Real homey place," he observed.

"Yeah."

"Funny—I never figured you for a farmer."

"Oh, I sort of fell into it. I guess you could say I made a little investment here."

"You going to come up with the money next week?" Hawkins wanted to know.

"Maybe."

Johnson's eyes narrowed. "Got tipped off about something that might interest you."

"Oh?"

"There's a Mex up on the North Concho who says you buried the bank money there."

"He's a liar."

"Yeah, I kinda figured that. Way I look at it, if he knew, he'd have dug it up himself. But we got to look at these rumors, Jack."

"You been prospecting, Hank?"

"You could say that."

"Borrowed soldiers from the fort, but it didn't help none," the other ranger added.

"I don't like wasting my time, Jack," Johnson said quietly.

"You should have asked me—I could have told you you wouldn't find anything there."

"I'm asking you now."

"It's not on the Concho—North or Middle," Jack answered easily.

This time when Hank Johnson leaned forward, his eyes were cold, emotionless. Sarah backed behind Jack and put her hand in his. His fingers closed reassuringly around her small ones.

"If you think you're going to pay off Ben Morgan's note with that money, you'd better think again. Way I look at it, you only got a week, and I'm going to be right behind you."

"Yeah—well, I'm not going anywhere. The money's gone."

He had the satisfaction of seeing the ranger's eyes widen slightly, then narrow again. "You're lying. You're a lying son of a—"

"That's enough," Jack cut in curtly. "There's a kid here."

"The truth's the truth." With that, the big ranger

yanked his reins, turning his horse's head. "Come on, boys—all we got to do is wait."

Beth had come from behind the house to watch, but she'd kept her silence until they left. "Why didn't you just tell them?" she asked.

"I didn't want to."

"You aren't going to try to get it? I won't take it if you do."

"No."

"Then why—?"

"Maybe I like the notion of insurance. Maybe I'll never be broke as long as I know where it is."

"It's stolen."

He'd just heard Johnson warn him, and now she was trying to play him the same tune, and that angered him. "I don't know why you're so hellfire concerned about a damned bank!" he snapped. "Do you think Kingman cares whether you live or starve? Hell, he'll be out here next week evicting you—and—and I'll have done all the damned work for nothing! For nothing—you hear that? Tell me he didn't steal your money, Beth! Tell me he didn't swindle Ben! He had to have a fair notion what this place was worth before he let you get in over your head!" When she said nothing, he shouted, "Dammit—answer me!"

Instead, she turned on her heel and walked toward the house. He watched until she disappeared inside, then he looked down at her children. Both were white faced.

"Don't quarrel with Mama—please," Sarah whispered. "It was bad enough with Papa."

Goaded, he went after Beth. He hit the door with such force that it banged on its hinges. "All right, where the devil are you?" he called out.

"There's no need to shout."

She was in the parlor, sitting in her rocking chair, rocking slowly back and forth. The anger went out of him.

"Look, I blame myself for this. I should have just got the money and paid off the note without telling you. Now I'm too damned late."

"It's all right," she said woodenly.

"No, it's not."

"I couldn't live here on stolen money."

"Oh, for—didn't you hear anything I said outside?" he demanded. "Didn't you?"

"That doesn't make it right."

"What about your precious Ben? Don't you think the reason he lied and cheated was to keep a roof over your head?"

She rocked silently.

"You know, woman, you make it damned hard on a man."

Still nothing.

He cast about the room for something to get her attention, and he was about to pull the cloth off the table when he saw it. There, neatly folded, was a snowy white shirt with the initials JPO embroidered on it.

"You did this for me?" he asked quietly.

"Yes."

"Why?"

"Because I wanted to." She looked up, and a smile twisted her mouth. "Because I've come to love you."

"Oh, God."

"That surprises you, doesn't it? That anybody could love Jack O'Neal, I mean."

"You don't know what you're saying," he said harshly. "You don't know what you'd be getting."

"I have an idea."

"No."

It took every iota of his resolve to turn around and walk out, leaving her sitting there. He strode unseeing toward the barn. Perplexed, Johnny trotted alongside.

"Where are you going, Mr. O'Neal?" he asked anxiously.

"To town."

The boy's lower lip quivered, then he burst out crying. "You're like my father—you're leaving us!"

"Leave him alone, Johnny—he's not a bird in a cage," Sarah told her brother. She looked up at Jack. "What are you going to do in town?" she wanted to know.

"I'm going to see my father," he answered tersely.

"Thought you didn't have one!"

"Hush, Johnny—you're not supposed to say it."

The bank was so empty it seemed almost cavernous when Jack stalked in. As he started around the counter, the same clerk he'd seen before confronted him.

"May I be of service, sir?"

"No," Jack growled, pushing him aside.

"I—no, you can't go in there!" he protested.

Kingman was seated at his desk, frowning as he studied some papers. When he looked up and saw Jack, he paled visibly.

"Hello, Papa."

The older man gave a start, then recovered. "Anybody teach you any manners, boy?"

"I'm afraid I didn't have anyone for that." Jack moved closer, towering over the banker. "You son of a bitch. You didn't even wonder what happened to Mary O'Neal, did you?"

"Mary!"

"Well, let me tell you all about it, Mr. Kingman." Even the name sounded like a sneer. "She was good enough that you got me on her, but she wasn't good enough to marry."

"It wasn't like that at all. I already had a wife."

"You did the cruelest thing you could, Kingman—you fed her a pack of lies. She built a life of hope on those lies. She wanted to believe so bad, she kept that damned letter you wrote her until it fell apart. You were going to come for us, she told me. You were going to take us away from that godawful place when your wife died." Jack leaned across the desk and took hold of the banker's tie. "She wasn't anything but your leavings, Kingman. She wound up selling herself to anybody who walked through Miss Hattie's door, because she had to live. Because she had a son to feed." He pulled the ends, tightening the tie. "I ought to kill you for what you did to us."

"I didn't know she was going to wind up in that place. Believe me, I didn't know."

"Where did you think she'd go? Home? A nice Catholic girl doesn't take a bastard home, Kingman."

"I sent money—when I found out she was at Hattie's, I sent money."

"Liar! She never got one dime she didn't earn there."

"I sent a thousand dollars, Jack. I told Hattie I wanted you to go to school somewhere where nobody'd have to know."

"My mother died waiting for you to take her away from there! If she'd had a thousand dollars, we'd have left on our own!"

"I couldn't come for you." Despite the tightness of his necktie, Philip Kingman turned his head away. "I couldn't live with what she became."

"Damn you! Damn you! *You* couldn't live with it? Well, what about her? Did you ever think of that?"

"Yes. Whether you want to believe it or not, I did. And whether you want to believe it or not, I've spent a lifetime of being sorry for what happened to you."

"You never gave me a thought!"

"You're the only son I had, Jack. That's rich, isn't it? A man wants sons, Jack, and all my heirs are girls. I guess the Lord made me pay for what happened."

"Not nearly enough."

"I'm sorry. If I could make it up to you I would."

"Would you, now?" Jack asked softly. "Well, I'm going to give you that chance, Papa. I'm going to let you pay Mary O'Neal back for everything."

"What do you want? Money?"

"No. I want—" Jack sucked in his breath, and let it out slowly. "I want the mortgage Ben Morgan signed."

Kingman looked at him for a long moment. "His widow owes a lot of money on it, Jack."

"I know."

"What about the five thousand you stole? Why don't you give her that?"

"She won't take it."

"I see. Well, she's a good woman, Jack. A fine woman with fine children. It was too bad about Ben."

"I could lay that at your door, too."

"I didn't make him falsify his application." Kingman sat up in his chair and pulled his tie loose. "I was sorry for what it did to her."

"Yeah, I'll just bet you were."

"Is she fool enough to have you?"

"What?"

"Can you learn to raise sheep?"

"I don't think I get this."

The older man leaned forward, folding his hands together. "I suppose I owe you a stake, don't I? All right." Pushing his chair back, he rose and went to a mahogany cabinet, where he pulled out a drawer. "What do you want me to do with this?" he asked, handing the paper to Jack.

It was the mortgage. Ben Morgan's bold script seemed to leap off the page at Jack. He held it, staring at that signature until he mastered the elation he felt.

"I'd like it marked 'Paid.' "

"All right." Taking the paper back, Kingman leaned over his desk and wrote the words PAID IN FULL with a flourish. Underneath them, he added his initials and the date, September 16, 1881. "There," he said, handing it back. "Now what do you want for yourself?"

"Nothing. I wouldn't take a dime off you."

"No, I suppose not."

"All right—what's going on here?" Hawkins demanded, bursting through the door with his gun drawn. "You can't stay out of trouble, can you, O'Neal?"

"You've been misinformed, Sheriff," Kingman said coldly. "Mr. O'Neal and I were merely sharing news of an old acquaintance."

"Are you armed?" Hawkins demanded of Jack.

"No."

The banker held out his hand. "It has been a pleasure meeting you, Mr. O'Neal. Perhaps we shall share a conversation again sometime."

It took just about everything Jack had, but he managed to shake the older man's hand. "Maybe, but I doubt it." As the chagrined sheriff turned to leave,

Jack spoke up. "Wait a minute, Hawkins—I'll walk back with you."

It was nearly dark by the time he got home. Home. He savored the sound of the word in his mind. He reined in and dismounted, then checked his pockets to make sure he hadn't forgotten anything. It was all there.

"You're back!" Johnny shouted, running toward him.

He caught the boy, swinging him up onto his shoulders. "Of course I'm back—you couldn't get rid of me. Where's your mother?"

"She's not feeling good. She's been in bed all day." As they approached the house, Johnny wanted down. "Sarah's in the barn feeding the chickens. She's going to want to know you're home."

"Well, you go tell her, then. Oh, and give her this." Reaching into his pocket, he took out a small bag of candy. "It's horehound, and you'll have to share it."

"Yes, sir!"

"Beth?" he asked as he walked into her room. "Are you all right?"

"I just have a headache, that's all. It must have been all the excitement. Jack, you'll never guess what happened."

"I've got the bigger news," he told her, smiling. The room was so dim he could scarce see her. "Where's the lamp?"

"Over here. The matches are beside it." She sat up and found them. Striking the match, she removed the chimney and lit the wick. "Is that better?"

"Much." He was so eager, he almost couldn't contain himself. "Did you mean what you said today?"

"About what?" she asked cautiously.

"Loving me."

"Yes."

"If I asked you, would you marry me?"

"Are you asking?"

"I haven't had any experience at this, but—" He sat on the bed beside her and possessed her hand. "Elizabeth Morgan, I love you more than my life, but I'll understand if you don't feel like you want to invest the rest of yours reforming me."

"Oh, Jack!" Her face puckered up, then she threw herself against his chest. "I was afraid I'd lost you— so afraid I'd lost you," she whispered.

He sat there, holding her, savoring her softness, her warmth. "Hey," he said softly, "you aren't going to cry, are you?"

"No." Her eyes brimming with tears, she lifted her face to his. "Kiss me, Jack."

It was the longest, most thorough kiss of his life. When he drew away, his heart was pounding in his ears. "I'll tell you one thing, Beth Morgan—it's going to be a damned short engagement."

"Yes." She remembered what she'd been about to tell him. "You'll never guess what happened this afternoon—never in your life."

"In a minute. I've brought you something." Reaching into his coat, he drew out the paper and handed it to her. "You're all paid up, Beth."

"What?" She stared incredulously at Kingman's signature, then she turned away. "No, it's not right, Jack."

For a moment, he didn't follow her, then it dawned on him that she thought he'd paid it with his stolen money. "Now wait a minute—here." He thrust the other piece of paper into her hand. "Read this before you jump to any conclusion."

"It's a receipt," she said slowly. "From the sheriff."

"For five thousand dollars. I'd have been here sooner, but I was helping him dig up the money."

"Then how—?"

"I had one ace left to play. Let's just say I had help from a long-lost relative."

"What?"

"You heard me."

"It's almost too much to believe." She turned to the bedside table and picked up a slender piece of paper. "But I was trying to tell you—the oddest thing happened today. Mr. Kingman came out, and well, you're never going to believe this, but—" She held the paper under his nose. "It's a bank draft for three hundred dollars, Jack—three hundred dollars. He said I should count it as a wedding present. I don't know how he knew I would be getting married again, but he did."

"I told you he was back!" Johnny said, pulling Sarah into the room.

She looked from her mother to Jack, then back again. "I'm glad," she said. "I don't think Mr. Talbot knows how to get dirty, anyway, and I can't see him cleaning the barn."

But Jack didn't even hear her. He was looking at Beth, thinking he had it all—a farm, money to last through the winter, a ready-made family—and the love of a good woman. As the Bible said, his cup truly runneth over.

🔷 TOPAZ

PASSION'S PROMISES

☐ **THE TOPAZ MAN FAVORITES: SECRETS OF THE HEART Five Stories by Madeline Baker, Jennifer Blake, Georgina Gentry, Shirl Henke, and Patricia Rice.** In this collection of romances, the Topaz Man has gathered together stories from five of his favorite authors—tales which he truly believes capture all the passion and promise of love.
(405528—$4.99)

☐ **DASHING AND DANGEROUS Five Sinfully Seductive Heroes by Mary Balogh, Edith Layton, Melinda McRae, Anita Mills, Mary Jo Putney.** They're shameless, seductive, and steal your heart with a smile. Now these irresistible rogues, rakes, rebels, and renegades are captured in five all new, deliciously sexy stories by America's favorite authors of romantic fiction.
(405315—$4.99)

☐ **BLOSSOMS Five Stories Mary Balogh, Patricia Rice, Margaret Evans Porter, Karen Harper, Patricia Oliver.** Celebrate the arrival of spring with a bouquet of exquisite stories by five acclaimed authors of romantic fiction. Full of passion and promise, scandal and heartache, and rekindled desire, these heartfelt tales prove that spring is a time for new beginnings as well as second chances.
(182499—$4.99)

☐ **THE TOPAZ MAN PRESENTS: A DREAM COME TRUE** Here is a collection of love stories from such authors as Jennifer Blake, Georgina Gentry, Shirl Henke, Anita Mills, and Becky Lee Weyrich. Each story is unique, and each author has a special way of making dreams come true.
(404513—$4.99)

*Prices slightly higher in Canada

Buy them at your local bookstore or use this convenient coupon for ordering.

PENGUIN USA
P.O. Box 999 — Dept. #17109
Bergenfield, New Jersey 07621

Please send me the books I have checked above.
I am enclosing $_____ (please add $2.00 to cover postage and handling). Send check or money order (no cash or C.O.D.'s) or charge by Mastercard or VISA (with a $15.00 minimum). Prices and numbers are subject to change without notice.

Card #_____ Exp. Date _____
Signature_____
Name_____
Address_____
City _____ State _____ Zip Code _____

For faster service when ordering by credit card call **1-800-253-6476**

Allow a minimum of 4-6 weeks for delivery. This offer is subject to change without notice.

T TOPAZ

WONDERFUL LOVE STORIES

☐ **SECRET NIGHTS by Anita Mills.** Elise Rand had once been humiliated by her father's attempt to arrange a marriage for her with London's most brilliant and ambitious criminal lawyer, Patrick Hamilton. Hamilton wanted her, but as a mistress, not a wife. Now she was committed to a desperate act—giving her body to Hamilton if he would defend her father in a scandalous case of murder.
(404815—$4.99)

☐ **A LIGHT FOR MY LOVE by Alexis Harrington.** Determined to make the beautiful China Sullivan forget the lonely hellion he'd once been, Jake Chastaine must make her see the new man he'd become. But even as love begins to heal the wounds of the past, Jake must battle a new obstacle—a danger that threatens to destroy all they hold dear.
(405013—$4.99)

☐ **THE WARFIELD BRIDE by Bronwyn Williams.** None of the Warfield brothers expected Hannah Ballinger to change their lives; none of them expected the joy she and her new baby would bring to their household. But most of all, Penn never expected to lose his heart to the woman he wanted his brother to marry—a mail order bride. "Delightful, heartwarming, a winner!—Amanda Quick (404556—$4.99)

☐ **GATEWAY TO THE HEART by Barbara Cockrell.** A lyrical and deeply moving novel of an indomitable woman who will win your heart and admiration—and make your spirit soar with the triumph of love in frontier St. Louis. (404998—$4.99)

*Prices slightly higher in Canada

Buy them at your local bookstore or use this convenient coupon for ordering.

PENGUIN USA
P.O. Box 999 — Dept. #17109
Bergenfield, New Jersey 07621

Please send me the books I have checked above.
I am enclosing $_____ (please add $2.00 to cover postage and handling). Send check or money order (no cash or C.O.D.'s) or charge by Mastercard or VISA (with a $15.00 minimum). Prices and numbers are subject to change without notice.

Card #_____ Exp. Date _____
Signature_____
Name_____
Address_____
City _____ State _____ Zip Code _____

For faster service when ordering by credit card call **1-800-253-6476**

Allow a minimum of 4-6 weeks for delivery. This offer is subject to change without notice.

☖ TOPAZ

SIMMERING DESIRES

☐ **HARVEST OF DREAMS by Jaroldeen Edwards.** A magnificent saga of family threatened both from within and without—and of the love and pride, strength and honor, that would make the difference between tragedy and triumph.
(404742—$4.99)

☐ **BEDEVILED by Bronwyn Williams.** Flame-haired Annie O'Neal and fiercely proud T'maho Hamilton, who chose the path of his Indian forebears rather than his white father, were as different as night and day. T'maho taught Annie the power of desire, and she showed him the meaning of love. But their fire was doused by the wealthy and iron-willed Jackson Snell, who demanded Annie be his bride. Now Annie was torn between the man she loved and the man it was folly to fight.
(404564—$4.99)

☐ **WIND SONG by Margaret Brownley.** When a feisty, red-haired schoolmarm arrives in Colton, Kansas and finds the town burned to the ground, she is forced to live with widower Luke Taylor and his young son, Matthew. Not only is she stealing Matthew's heart, but she is also igniting a desire as dangerous as love in his father's heart.
(405269—$4.99)

☐ **BECAUSE YOU'RE MINE by Nan Ryan.** Golden-haired Sabella Rios vowed she would seduce the handsome Burt Burnett into marrying her and become mistress of the Lindo Vista ranch, which was rightfully hers. Sabella succeeded beyond her dreams, but there was one thing she had not counted on. In Burt's caressing arms, in his bed, her cold calculations turned into flames of passion as she fell deeply in love with this man, this enemy of her family.
(405951—$5.50)

*Prices slightly higher in Canada

Buy them at your local bookstore or use this convenient coupon for ordering.

PENGUIN USA
P.O. Box 999 — Dept. #17109
Bergenfield, New Jersey 07621

Please send me the books I have checked above.
I am enclosing $_____ (please add $2.00 to cover postage and handling). Send check or money order (no cash or C.O.D.'s) or charge by Mastercard or VISA (with a $15.00 minimum). Prices and numbers are subject to change without notice.

Card #_____ Exp. Date _____
Signature_____
Name_____
Address_____
City _____ State _____ Zip Code _____

For faster service when ordering by credit card call **1-800-253-6476**

Allow a minimum of 4-6 weeks for delivery. This offer is subject to change without notice.

◀T▶ TOPAZ

EXPERIENCE A NEW WORLD
OF ROMANCE

☐ **DANGEROUS ANGEL by Deborah Martin.** When the upright Sebastian Kent, Duke of Waverley, and Cordelia Shaleston, the daughter of a country vicar, set off for London to launch her musical career, the Duke's resolve to hold his lust in check is overruled by Cordelia's refusal to deny her own ardent yearnings.
(405285—$4.99)

☐ **PRINCE OF THIEVES by Melinda McRae.** "Gentleman Jack" and Honoria are playing a hazardous game of deception, but together they are discovering the desire between them is no game.
(404890—$4.99)

☐ **DARLING ANNIE by Raine Cantrell.** When the likes of Kell York, leanly built, lazily handsome with a dangerous streak, meets up with the beautiful barefoot girl Annie Muldoon, she is not what he expected. Neither was the gun she pointed between his eyes when he insisted he and his "soiled doves" be allowed to move into Annie's boarding house. But both of them soon learn that true love changes everything.
(405145—$4.99)

☐ **DAWN SHADOWS by Susannah Leigh.** Maria McClintock is a beautiful and free-spirited as the windswept Hawaiian island of Maui where she was born and raised. And soon she catches the eye and wakes the lust of powerful planter Royall Perralt, who traps her in a web of lies and manipulations to get what he wants.
(405102—$4.99)

*Prices slightly higher in Canada

Buy them at your local bookstore or use this convenient coupon for ordering.

PENGUIN USA
P.O. Box 999 — Dept. #17109
Bergenfield, New Jersey 07621

Please send me the books I have checked above.
I am enclosing $_____ (please add $2.00 to cover postage and handling). Send check or money order (no cash or C.O.D.'s) or charge by Mastercard or VISA (with a $15.00 minimum). Prices and numbers are subject to change without notice.

Card #_____ Exp. Date _____
Signature_____
Name_____
Address_____
City _____ State _____ Zip Code _____

For faster service when ordering by credit card call **1-800-253-6476**

Allow a minimum of 4-6 weeks for delivery. This offer is subject to change without notice.

⬥ TOPAZ

SEARING ROMANCES

☐ **TEMPTING FATE by Jaclyn Reding.** Beautiful, flame-haired Mara Despenser hated the English under Oliver Cromwell, and she vowed to avenge Ireland and become mistress of Kulhaven Castle again. She would lure the castle's new master, the infamous Hadrian Ross, the bastard Earl of St. Aubyn, into marriage. But even with her lies and lust, Mara was not prepared to find herself wed to a man whose iron will was matched by his irresistible good looks.   (405587—$4.99)

☐ **SPRING'S FURY by Denise Domning.** Nicola of Ashby swore to kill Gilliam Fitz-Henry—murderer of her father, destroyer of her home—the man who would wed her in a forced match. Amid treachery and tragedy, rival knights and the pain of past wounds, Gilliam knew he must win Nicola's respect. Then, with kisses and hot caresses, he intended to win her heart.   (405218—$4.99)

☐ **PIRATE'S ROSE by Janet Lynnford.** The Rozalinde Cavendish, independent daughter of England's richest merchant, was taking an impetuous moonlit walk along the turbulent shore when she encountered Lord Christopher Howard, a legendary pirate. Carried aboard his ship, she entered his storm-tossed world and became intimate with his troubled soul. Could their passion burn away the veil shrouding Christopher's secret past and hidden agenda?   (405978—$4.99)

☐ **DIAMOND IN DISGUISE by Elizabeth Hewitt.** Isobel Leyland knew better than to fall in love with the handsome stranger from America, Adrian Renville. Despite his rugged good looks and his powerful animal magnetism, he was socially inept compared to the polished dandies of English aristocratic society—and a citizen of England's enemy in the War of 1812. How could she trust this man whom she suspected of playing the boor in a mocking masquerade?   (405641—$4.99)

*Prices slightly higher in Canada

Buy them at your local bookstore or use this convenient coupon for ordering.

PENGUIN USA
P.O. Box 999 — Dept. #17109
Bergenfield, New Jersey 07621

Please send me the books I have checked above.
I am enclosing $_____ (please add $2.00 to cover postage and handling). Send check or money order (no cash or C.O.D.'s) or charge by Mastercard or VISA (with a $15.00 minimum). Prices and numbers are subject to change without notice.

Card #_____ Exp. Date _____
Signature_____
Name_____
Address_____
City _____ State _____ Zip Code _____

For faster service when ordering by credit card call **1-800-253-6476**

Allow a minimum of 4-6 weeks for delivery. This offer is subject to change without notice.

Don't go to bed without Romance...

Romantic Times MAGAZINE

Suddenly, romance has a whole new face!

Introducing TOPAZ
The Gem of Historical Romance

♥ 150 BOOK REVIEWS AND RATINGS
  ♣ CONTEMPORARY
  ♣ HISTORICAL
  ♣ TIME - TRAVEL
♥ AUTHOR PROFILES
♥ PUBLISHERS PREVIEWS
♥ MARKET NEWS
♥ TIPS ON WRITING BESTSELLING ROMANCES

Read *Romantic Times* Magazine
122 page Monthly Magazine • 6 issues $21
Sample Issue $4.00   (718) 237-1097
Send Order To: Romantic Times
55 Bergen St., Brooklyn, NY 11201

I enclose $_____in ☐ check ☐ money order

Credit Card#_____Exp. Date_____

Tel_____

Name_____

Address_____

City_____State_____Zip_____